D1149991

The House
on
Silver Street

Waterford City & County Libraries
WITHDRAWN

Also by Geraldine O'Neill

Tara Flynn

Aisling Gayle

Tara's Fortune

The Grace Girls

The Flowers of Ballygrace

Tara's Destiny

Leaving Clare

Sarah Love

Summer's End

Music from Home

A Letter from America

Published by Poolbeg

The House
on
Silver Street

Waterford City and County
Libraries WITHDRAWN

Geraldine
O'NEILL

POOLBEG

This novel is entirely a work of fiction. The names, characters and incidents portrayed in it are the work of the author's imagination. Any resemblance to actual persons, living or dead, events or localities is entirely coincidental.

Published 2016
by Poolbeg Press Ltd
123 Grange Hill, Baldoyle
Dublin 13, Ireland
E-mail: poolbeg@poolbeg.com
www.poolbeg.com

© Geraldine O'Neill 2016

Copyright for editing, typesetting, layout, design, ebook
© Poolbeg Press Ltd

The moral right of the author has been asserted.

A catalogue record for this book is available from the British Library.

ISBN 978-1-78199-890-8

All rights reserved. No part of this publication may be reproduced or transmitted in any form or by any means, electronic or mechanical, including photography, recording, or any information storage or retrieval system, without permission in writing from the publisher. The book is sold subject to the condition that it shall not, by way of trade or otherwise, be lent, resold or otherwise circulated without the publisher's prior consent in any form of binding or cover other than that in which it is published and without a similar condition, including this condition, being imposed on the subsequent purchaser.

Typeset by Poolbeg in Sabon 11/14.5

www.poolbeg.com

About the Author

Geraldine O'Neill grew up in Lanarkshire, Scotland. She has lived in County Offaly, Ireland, since 1991.

She is married to Michael Brosnahan and has two adult children, Christopher and Clare. She became a grandmother in 2015.

In addition to her writing career, Geraldine also taught for over thirty years as a Primary School teacher in Scotland, England and Ireland.

The House on Silver Street is Geraldine O'Neill's twelfth book.

Acknowledgements

My heartfelt thanks to Paula Campbell and Kieran Devlin at Poolbeg Press for believing in my writing from my very first book. Thanks as always to my editor Gaye Shortland for her perfectionist eye working on my long manuscripts, and her excellent suggestions which have always improved them. Thanks also to David Prendergast and the staff who have worked on my lovely book covers. It has been a pleasure working with you all on this book and the previous ones.

Thanks to my literary agents for many years, at Watson Little in London.

Many thanks to John McGlynn (of Anúna and original male lead singer with *Riverdance*) for allowing me to use the beautiful lyrics from one of his songs in a scene in this book.

I'd also like to mention the Tyrone Guthrie Centre in Annaghmakerrig, County Monaghan, for once again giving me the peace and solitude to pull this book together.

Thanks to my old Scottish friend, Dr Tom Lafferty, for sharing details of his medical training during my characters' time.

I must also acknowledge the constant support given to me by the people of County Offaly, which has featured in all my twelve books. Thanks especially to Offaly Libraries and their staff, who have always been a wonderful support. Also, Offaly Arts for recognising my work in many different ways, and for the members of Offaly County Council who have supported my work and book launches.

Thanks to all the people who constantly support my writing – my parents, Teddy and Be-Be O'Neill, my brother and sisters, Mike's family and our dear friends from Stockport, my teaching colleagues, especially Kate and Brid, my writing group in Offaly, the Irish Post-Polio Support Group, the ladies in our business support group and my old Rehab colleagues.

Much appreciation to three ladies who have helped with my book launches: my sister Berni Doherty, Pat Slamman and Bernie O'Sullivan.

This past year has been momentous for people dear to me. Congratulations to Martin and Berni Doherty on their wedding, and 40th Anniversary wishes to dear friends John and Helen Fahy and Ann and Phil Read.

Thanks as always to Chris and Kate, Clare + Mark.

My biggest debt of gratitude and love is to my husband, Mike Brosnahan. As I've said before, I could not begin to count the ways in which he supports me.

A final thanks to all my lovely readers worldwide, who help me through the long night hours writing!

The House on Silver Street is dedicated to
our darling boy, Leo Feely

It takes a wise man
To learn from his mistakes,
but an even wiser man
to learn from others'.
Zen proverb

Chapter 1

Tullamore, Co Offaly

1973

The summer rain trickled down the large square windows on either side of the shop door. Connie Devine stood with her back against the counter, breathing in the comforting scent of the flowers. Slimly built, her dark curly hair tied back, her dark-green waxed apron covering her T-shirt and jeans, she was staring out into the grey street, thinking about the two very different paths her life might take in the next few weeks. She was weighing up her options. Either direction, she knew, would work out somehow. What would be would be. Either direction would make her happy in the long run. And if she was happy, her father would be happy. But it wasn't her father she was concerned about. It wasn't even herself. It was her mother.

If things went in the wrong direction her mother would be devastated. And Connie wasn't just imagining the worst. It was fact. Her mother had made no bones about her feelings. Connie closed her eyes now, imagining both scenarios. Dublin or England. She could see it all quite plainly. She had gone over and over it, and she knew exactly what either option entailed.

Then, footsteps sounded. Her eyes flew open and she took in the customer outside the door, the middle-aged lady shaking her umbrella before entering the shop. Connie quickly brought herself back to the here and now: working at her summer job in the

1

unimaginatively named Eileen's Flower Shop.

She moved to stand behind the counter.

The customer came in, taking her plastic Rainmate off her head and giving it a good shake, sending little droplets of water onto the floor.

Connie watched her, smiling and thinking that customers were more casual in a flower shop, as there were no carpets or fancy furnishings to worry about. They brought in dogs of all sizes, they came in wearing shoes caked in mud, and they dropped wet umbrellas on the floor.

"Terrible day for the month of August, isn't it?" Connie said. When she started working in the shop two years ago, at the age of sixteen, she discovered that the weather was the easiest and most general thing to talk about to a new customer.

"We've had nothing but shocking weather this year so far," the woman replied. Then her eyes flitted to the containers on the shelves and then down to the buckets of flowers on the floor. "I'm looking for a nice bunch. Nothing too fancy ... I'm not much good with flowers ..."

Connie went over to a bucket with pink carnations. "Anything like this?" Then she lifted a potted azalea and held it up. "Or maybe this?"

"I was thinking more along the line of roses ... not too expensive though."

Connie paused. "We might have something in the back. I won't be a minute."

She went into the much cooler area at the back of the shop, where all the bouquets and the wreaths for funerals were made up. Eileen, the shop proprietor, was standing at a small desk, checking the list of flowers that had arrived that morning. When she saw Connie, she lifted her glasses up onto her head.

"You go on home for your lunch now," she said. "You must be anxious, waiting to hear."

Connie smiled at her boss. She was being let go half an hour earlier than usual. "Oh thanks, Mrs Sheridan, that's good of you! I'll just finish serving the lady out front first."

"*Eileen* – I keep telling you! Mrs Sheridan makes me feel ancient. I know I might seem like an old lady to you, but I haven't even hit forty yet."

Connie bit her lip and smiled awkwardly. "Sorry, I keep forgetting ... I'm just so used to calling you Mrs Sheridan."

She went over to a large galvanised bucket and lifted out a bunch of creamy white roses with pink tips.

"I think these will be just fine," she said.

Then, she went back out to the front of the shop where her customer was waiting. Holding the roses away from her, she wiped the wet stems with a dry cloth, and then showed them to her. "Are these okay?"

The woman nodded. "They're more like it. I'll take them."

Connie took them over to the counter to wrap. "Gorgeous, aren't they?"

"They are." The woman smiled. "But, to be honest, I don't know one flower from another. They're for an elderly neighbour who's in hospital. She's a diabetic, so I couldn't get her chocolates or anything like that."

"She'll love them." Connie began cutting the stems so they were all even. She then laid a sheet of gold wrapping paper on the counter and picked up the roll of white ribbon. When she had finished wrapping the flowers, her heart gave a little lift as she looked at the beautiful, delicate blooms.

She held the tidy bouquet out to the woman. "Is that okay for you?"

"Lovely," the woman said, handing over the money. "Although I'd prefer a nice box of biscuits any day!"

The rain had eased off by the time Connie had got her anorak on and left the shop. As she walked down Convent View towards the house, she felt her heart begin to race, and she suddenly wondered which streets in which town she would be walking down in just two months' time.

She turned the corner and then she saw her mother, rushing down their garden path waving an envelope. Her heart rate suddenly doubled as she realised what it was. She ran to meet her at the gate.

"I've been watching at the window for you this half an hour," her mother panted, handing her the large brown envelope. "They've come! Your results are here."

Chapter 2

Connie looked down at the envelope, while her mother stood with her arms folded and her face anxious, waiting.

"I'm not opening it out here," Connie said. She could just imagine their neighbours watching from behind their curtains. Anybody who was interested knew that the Leaving Certificate results were due out today. News travelled fast in the small town, and how she and her classmates had done would soon be common knowledge.

Her heart pounding, Connie followed her mother into the house, down the small dark hallway and into the kitchen.

"Is Daddy in?"

Both her father and mother had taken the day off work – Seán Devine worked as a foreman in the local textile factory while the petite, blonde Kate was a Staff Nurse in Tullamore Hospital.

"He's in the back garden as usual," her mother said. She went towards the back door. "I suppose he should be here. I'll go and call him."

Connie felt her chest tighten as she waited, and wondered if it would have been better or worse if her two brothers had been home. Ollie, who was three years older than her, was a clerk in the local railway station and was on the early shift today, while Terry,

4

who was just a year older than her, was training as a mechanic in a garage at the edge of the town.

She had just opened the envelope and slipped the top of the certificate out when her parents appeared at the door. She glanced up at them and could see the strained look on her mother's face. The weeks of waiting had told on Kate Devine, as she was now thin as opposed to nicely slim. Her father's face was blank as usual. It gave nothing away.

She looked down at the certificate now and studied the grades. She had done much better than she had expected. What her mother hoped for was a different matter.

"Well?" Kate said. "Tell us."

"The results are good overall ..." her voice faltered, "but I think I've just missed the entrance qualification for medicine at UCD."

She looked over and saw her mother's shoulders slump. She had also closed her eyes as she did when she got any sort of bad news. Connie knew without a word being spoken that she had failed her.

"But you'll get into the English university?" her father checked, his eyes flitting from one to the other. "You'll still be able to study to be a doctor?"

Connie nodded. "Yes, I've higher grades than they asked for." She paused. "I'm sorry, Mammy. I know you're probably disappointed ... you'd have preferred me to go to Dublin."

Her mother lifted her head and looked at her now. "I was half expecting it. I'm well used to being disappointed ..."

"Ah Kate!" Seán Devine put his arm around his wife's shoulders. "Don't be saying things like that. She's done well to get into university. She'll be the first in either of our families."

Kate lifted her eyes and looked at her daughter. "Are you absolutely sure UCD won't take you?"

Connie slowly nodded. "They told me at the interview the exact results I needed to get in. I've only missed it by a few marks but they said they couldn't lower it, and there would be no exceptions made."

"Well, that's it then. It's England for you." Kate shrugged out of her husband's hold, and turned towards the cooker. As she lifted the recently boiled kettle back onto the hob there was an obvious tremor to her hand.

"Well, I think we should all be delighted," Seán said. He looked at Connie now and held his hands up. "*I'm* proud and delighted to have a daughter of mine who is clever enough to go to university to study to be a doctor."

Connie noticed the slight twitch that came to her father's mouth when he was anxious and she felt a wave of pity for him. "Thanks, Daddy." He was always the peacemaker, the one trying to find the good in things. But she also felt pity for her mother. She would have liked to make this particular dream come true for her, instead of feeling she had let her down.

There was a silence, then her mother eventually turned around. "It's not that I'm not proud of you, Connie – of course I am. You've done well. I'm just upset that for the sake of a few marks you're going to have to go to Manchester."

"I'll be grand," Connie said. "There are lots of Irish people studying at English universities. And a lot of them come back home when they get their degrees. Our geography teacher went to university in London."

Her mother shook her head and sighed. "It's so far away from home – and it's across the sea. Manchester is not a place I would have chosen for you. It's too big and too full of different kinds of people ... we'll be worried about you." She looked directly at her daughter now. "And I don't think Emmet Ferguson is going to be too happy when he hears the news."

Connie's eyebrows shot up in surprise. "I'm sure he won't mind – it's not like we've been going out for very long."

It was the first time her mother had shown any great interest in Emmet Ferguson. He was the son of the local furniture-shop owner, and worked with his father. When she'd told her mother that he had asked her to go to the pictures with him, she had said that in her opinion he was a bit loud and too full of himself, and that he drove too fast, showing off his car.

"Emmet asked you to his sister's twenty-first birthday party," her mother said now. "He must think a lot of you to invite you to a family occasion."

"Well, I made it quite clear to him that I would be moving away either to Dublin or England, so he knew I wasn't going to be around here as often." Connie shrugged. "He's popular enough and he's the type that will easily meet someone else."

6

"If you had got into UCD, you could have been home every weekend and you could have kept your job on at Eileen's as well."

"That's not going to happen now, Mam," Connie said quietly. "So there's no point in us going over it all again. It's not as if you'll be left on your own – Ollie and Frank will still be here."

"I know that," her mother said, "but it's not the same as having a girl at home."

Seán moved over to his wife's side. "She'll come back home at the holidays, and she has relations over there – people who will look out for her."

Kate's eyes widened and she put her hand up to halt her husband. "I don't want to hear any more about the relations. They're the very people I wouldn't want her to have anything to do with."

"Ah, Mam!" Connie said. "I don't want you and Daddy arguing about who I'll be seeing in Manchester before I've even gone. I'm nearly nineteen years old, and I've got to make my own way in the world whether I'm in Dublin or Manchester. You need to have a bit of faith in me."

"There's no need for backchat," her mother said, but her voice was lower and less argumentative. "It would be a bad day if I didn't try to look after my own daughter." She took a deep breath. "And, thankfully, we won't need to go looking for loans to pay for your university fees or asking help from anyone else. The money I got from Uncle Arthur's farm will cover it all."

"That's great, Mam," Connie said. "Although I will look for a weekend job to help out. All the students do that."

"Just work hard and pass your exams. Your father and I will help you with everything else." Kate turned back to the kettle. "You need to have a bite to eat now before going back to the shop. I have some nice fresh-cut ham and tomatoes. Will I make you a sandwich?"

"That would be fine," Connie said, although her stomach was churning so much she doubted that she could eat anything.

Seán and Kate Devine stood at the window, watching as Connie went out the gate and headed down the street in the direction of the flower shop.

"How is it things never turn out the way I want them?" Kate said, her eyes filling with tears. "All the prayers I've said, the Novenas ... all the candles I've lit. My really important prayers never get answered."

"That's not true," Seán said quietly. "A lot of our prayers have been answered. It's only a few months since we were all praying about the test results on your stomach and it all came back clear. And what about the candles we all lit for Ollie to get his job and Frank to get his apprenticeship? All those prayers were answered, weren't they?"

There was a pause and then she gave a slight nod.

"It will be all right," Seán said, squeezing his wife's arm. "She's a sensible girl. She'll come home often, and we can go over to visit her. We could even take the car on the boat."

"I know Connie is sensible, but it's who she'll meet that worries me. There are all kinds over in England." She paused. "I'm worried enough about the strangers she'll meet, but my biggest worry is the people we already know. I don't want to think of her over beside Tara Flynn – or Tara Kennedy or whatever she's called now. Her and that Bridget one from Ballygrace are not the sort I want her to see regularly."

Seán gave a deep, weary sigh. Tara was his stepsister, his mother having married Tara's father, Shay Flynn, when he was a young boy. "I don't want us to start rowing about Tara again. I don't know what you have against her. She's been nothing but kind to this family and all her other relations. She has never missed a Christmas or birthday with any of us."

"Anyone can throw money around when they have plenty of it," Kate said bitterly. "The rest of us have to work hard for it, and we're made to feel we've achieved nothing because she's always the big 'I-am', ahead of everyone else with her hotels and fancy cars."

"I'm going back out to the garden if you keep going on like this about Tara," Seán said. "It gives me a pain in my chest to hear it."

"Okay," Kate said. "I'll just keep quiet about it."

There was a silence and when Seán looked over at his wife he saw tears streaming down her face.

"I can't help it," she said, her voice choking. "It's everything I hoped wouldn't happen. Connie is never going to come back home to live. She's going to meet an Englishman and she'll end up getting married and staying over in England."

"You don't know that," Seán said. "She could just as easily meet a nice Irish fellow. She might even keep in touch with Emmet Ferguson. He seems very keen on her."

"I'm not sure what to make of him," Kate said, "but, even so, I'd sooner she married someone local like him than an English stranger."

"Now it's far too early to be talking about weddings and the like," Seán said. He came back to her and drew her close to him. "We'll both miss her, but we just have to accept the way things are and make the best of it – for Connie's sake."

Kate leaned into her husband. "I'll do my best. But give me a bit of time to get used to it." She looked across the kitchen to the picture of the Sacred Heart – the image she had prayed to every day these last few weeks.

She stared at it now, tears flooding her eyes. *Why couldn't you have let her get those few extra marks? It would have made all the difference in the world if she could have got into the university in Dublin. All the candles I lit and all the Novenas I said, and you couldn't answer my most important prayer!*

Chapter 3

The flower shop was busier than usual that afternoon, although Connie was aware that half the people who came in didn't actually buy any flowers. Since the shop was in one of the streets just off the town centre, several of her friends called in and so did some other girls from school who were keen to know how she had got on. She was the only one in her class who had ambitions to become a doctor and they all knew she needed the highest grades to study medicine. A few of the other girls were hoping to go into teaching, some to secretarial college, and others just happy to get any sort of reasonable job locally.

Everyone congratulated her on her Honours results, but almost every single girl – like her mother – commented on the fact that it was a shame she had to go to England to study. Connie told them she was happy to go to Manchester and that it was a really exciting place, but only a few of the girls agreed with her. Most said they would rather stay in Ireland.

As the afternoon wore on, each time the shop-bell rang Connie felt her heart sinking as she dreaded yet another person asking her how she had got on in her Leaving Cert.

While Connie looked after the main shop, Eileen was busy in the back area making wreaths for a funeral the following morning. At one point in the afternoon Eileen went out to the bank and when she came back she made them both a cup of tea. Then she produced a plate with half a dozen fresh cream cakes she had bought at the local baker's shop. It was rare they both sat down at the same time in the privacy of the back shop, on the two old kitchen chairs brought from Eileen's house on the Arden Road.

"A little treat for us to celebrate your exam results. I think you've done brilliantly! Imagine you being a doctor in a few years' time!" Eileen gestured to the cakes. "Pick whatever you like, and any that we don't eat you can take home. With my sweet tooth, I couldn't trust myself not to eat them all if they were left here."

"Thanks. That's very good of you." Connie picked a chocolate éclair, took a bite out of it, chewed it slowly and then took a sip of her tea.

They sat together in silence for a few minutes, then Eileen said, "Are you okay, Connie? You've been very quiet in yourself. I suppose you're fed up with everybody asking you about your results?"

Connie's face flushed red. "Oh, I don't mean to be in any way awkward ... I'm really grateful to you for getting the cakes ..."

"No, no, it's nothing to do with me or the cakes. I'm just concerned that you don't seem as delighted about your results as you should be. You've done great, and you should be proud of yourself. You're a very clever girl."

Connie suddenly felt a big lump come into her throat. She put her éclair down on the plate and took a sip of her tea. Then she felt her eyes filling up, and she knew she couldn't hide her feelings from her boss any longer.

"It's my mother," she blurted out. "She's really disappointed that I didn't get accepted by UCD."

"So that's what it is!" Eileen's face was serious. "It must be hard for your mother, knowing you'll be so far away. It must be hard for any mother, losing her daughter. But, it's the way life goes and she'll get over it. One way or another, families all have to grow up and leave home. We all have to do it. And she'll still have your father and brothers to keep her busy, and she has her work in the hospital." She looked at Connie and shrugged. "Don't feel guilty about living your own life. Your mother will be fine when she gets used to the idea."

When they had finished their tea and cakes, Eileen went back to the wreaths while Connie tidied up the shop. She started with the flower-containers on the floor, checking for any wilting flowers or leaves that were turning yellow. As always, she got a great lift just looking at the variety of blooms – the colours, the different sizes and shapes and the different scents.

Afterwards, she went around with a brush, sweeping between the containers, and when she was finished she gave the counter and the shelves a general tidy-up. Then she went around, moving containers into different-sized groups and colours that she thought made an eye-catching display.

At one point, when she stopped to admire her handiwork, she realised she felt happier than she had all day. She had been so engrossed in the customers who had come in and sorting out the flowers that she hadn't thought of her mother or Manchester for over an hour.

The shop perfect, she went into the back to clear up there, and found Eileen nursing a bleeding finger.

"Oh, what happened?"

Eileen rolled her eyes to the ceiling. "A bit of wire," she said. "I was rushing and didn't notice it sticking out at the back of the cross I was working on. This is all I need with a big funeral on in the morning." She went over to a cupboard, took out a box of tissues and wrapped one around her finger.

"Is it bad?"

"No," she said, "it's only a bit of a scratch, but it's at the corner of my nail which is a nuisance." She took a packet of sticking plasters out of the drawer.

"Can I help?" Connie offered.

Eileen held her finger out while Connie carefully put the plaster over the cut.

"The shop is quiet at the minute," Connie said, "and I've given it a good clean – so, if you like, I could give you a hand in here with the flowers. There's nothing much to be done unless a customer comes in."

Eileen looked down at the half-constructed floral cross consisting of a background of small green leaves overlaid with white chrysanthemums. "Do you think you could manage to finish this one off? That would let me concentrate on the floral arrangements which are a bit trickier."

"No problem," Connie said. "I'll just follow the pattern you've already started, and if I get stuck, I'll ask you for help."

Eileen gestured to the pile of white flowers, which had a smaller pile of wire cuttings alongside. "The crysanths are already cut to the right size, so you just have to put a small piece of wire in each one and stick them in the oasis." She held her finger up, and rolled her eyes. "And don't do what I did – be careful with that feckin' wire!"

Connie got to work. Then the doorbell went twice and she went out to serve two ladies, one with a bunch of roses and the other with lilies. When she came back to the cross, she saw Eileen examining it.

"Is it okay?" she asked.

"It's perfect. You have a good eye – you've made a better job of decorating that than I could have!" She smiled. "I could easily have trained you into being a good florist. I hope the medical profession appreciates you."

Connie smiled back at her, delighted with the compliment. "It will be a long time before I'm qualified. I have years of studying ahead of me." She went back to sticking the wire into the remaining flowers.

"Have you always wanted to be a doctor?"

"No, not really. It was only when I did well in my Junior Certificate that I started to think about what course I might be accepted for. I'd always thought I might be a nurse like Mam …" She shrugged. "I suppose growing up with her working in the hospital and hearing her talking about it, it seemed the obvious thing to do, but then some of my teachers said they thought I would be fit enough to study medicine …" She looked back down at the flowers, suddenly self-conscious as though she was praising herself.

"So it's what you really want to do now?"

She nodded. "I think it would be great to be able to help make people better."

"It certainly would."

A few minutes later the cross was finished and Eileen let Connie take over the arrangement she was working on while she started on the last, which was a display which would be placed on top of the coffin.

"Aren't flowers very soothing?" Connie said. "They make lovely gifts, they cheer people up when they're sick, and they're the only colourful and beautiful things at a funeral."

"You're right – I never thought about them like that before," Eileen said.

"Do you mind me asking how you got into the florist business?" She had never asked her boss anything so personal but, with the two of them working so closely together this afternoon and talking about her own plans, she felt it was okay to ask.

The older woman paused, thinking. "I suppose I was looking for something to do when the youngest one went to Secondary School. I found the day at home long with Jimmy being away so much with the building business. He could be in Dublin one week and down in Cork the next, and he often works away from a Monday to a Friday. Anyway, Jimmy saw the shop was for sale and he suggested it to me." She laughed. "I loved gardening, but when it came to putting bouquets together, I didn't know one flower from another at the time. But the previous owners were a great help. They advised me where I could do a course in Dublin, and then the wife stayed on with me for the first few weeks to help me get started. And after a while I took on Frances, and she's been with me since. And of course I have you or other girls to fill in when she's off."

"And do you enjoy it now?" Connie asked.

"I love it," Eileen said. Then she laughed. "Well, most days I do – when I'm not rushed off my feet or cutting my finger. It was doing the course that got me more involved in it. I really enjoyed learning how to do bouquets and flower arrangements."

"I can understand," Connie said. "I love doing it too."

"You're a natural at it," Eileen said, "although it's still best to do a course and learn all the basics – then you know exactly what you're doing." She paused, then raised her eyebrows. "And it's definitely necessary to do a course if you're going to be a doctor!"

Connie pushed a piece of the florists' wire into a stem. "I've a long road ahead of me. Years and years of it."

"It's one of the best jobs you could do. Think of all the thousands of people you will be able to help."

14

Connie nodded. "That's the reason I'm going into medicine."

A short while later the final piece was finished and, while Eileen carefully watered them all to keep them fresh for the funeral in the morning, Connie got busy brushing again and clearing and washing the work tables.

The doorbell rang and Eileen looked up at the clock on the wall and then over at Connie. It was near closing time and too late to start making up bunches of flowers for people.

She went out into the shop and then a few seconds later she called, "Connie, it's for you!"

When Connie went through she was surprised to see Emmet Ferguson standing there. He was smartly dressed in his work suit, and he looked as though he had just had a fresh haircut. She felt awkward as he had never come into the shop before, and he had never seen her wearing the dark-green waxed apron. Eileen asked him how his father and mother were and they had a few words together, and then she went back to watering her flowers.

"I just thought I'd catch you before you closed," he said. "I heard your news and wanted to say well done."

"Thanks," she said. "It's definite now that I'll be going to Manchester. I just missed getting into UCD."

"It's still a fantastic result," he said. "To get in anywhere to study medicine is a huge achievement. Especially for a girl."

His last comment irked her a little. "I think a lot of women don't push themselves enough," she said, smiling at him, "and some don't get the same encouragement at school or at home as lads do."

"Are your parents delighted for you?"

Connie's heart sank. "Yes," she said, "but I suppose they wish I was nearer to home."

Emmet shrugged and looked bemused. "You're going to be a doctor! They can't *not* be happy. Any girl's family would be proud of that."

She vaguely smiled and nodded as though she agreed. She didn't know Emmet Ferguson well enough to confide the full truth about her mother.

"Anyway, you'll be back and forth from England every few months, won't you? And you'll be home once your training is finished."

"I haven't really had any time to think things through," she told him honestly. "I suppose I'll just have to take one step at a time."

There was a pause and then he said, "Are you doing anything tonight?" When she didn't answer immediately, a tinge of red came over his face. "It's just that one of my friends – Jim Fay – he lives out towards Athlone – is having a party tonight. He has the house to himself as his parents are in Spain, and he's invited a few of us over. It's a lovely big old house, and they even have a swimming pool."

"A swimming pool?" Connie repeated incredulously.

He nodded, then laughed. "It's outdoors, and I doubt if anyone is going to be swimming in it tonight. But you never know."

She thought for a few moments. She had more or less decided to let things drift between herself and Emmet. She knew he wasn't the sort she could get really serious with. He was nice enough, reasonably good-looking and very well dressed, and she knew lots of other girls in the town fancied him. He was generous, had nice manners and paid her compliments, but there was something about him that told her they were not a good match. She guessed that they would soon start clashing over the loud, juvenile jokes he made and the comments about other people that he thought were funny.

She also thought he was old-fashioned in his opinions about the difference between men and women – about things like driving or being paid the same wages. *Old-fashioned* was maybe the wrong word because that gave the impression of a naïve sort of fellow, which she didn't think Emmet was. Perhaps a new term she had heard recently was more suited to him: *chauvinistic*.

She could tell that he liked her a lot and going out with him tonight might just encourage him further. Every night she prolonged their relationship might make it harder to get the courage up to break off with him later. Then she pictured spending the whole evening at home with her disappointed mother and the party suddenly seemed a lot more appealing. She would go, she decided. But, before she did, it was only fair to make things plain to him about their relationship.

"It sounds as if could be a good night."

"Oh, it will be," he assured her. "There'll be a nice crowd there, and that girl who was in your class – the little blocky one that's going out with Patrick Kelly – will be there."

Connie's eyes widened and then she laughed in amazement. "That's Martina O'Leary you're talking about, and you better not let her hear you describing her as 'blocky'. She would absolutely kill you."

Emmet started to laugh. "I'm hardly going to say it to her face, am I? But there's no denying that she's a bit on the square side. I'd better be careful she doesn't hear me. I'd say she packs a good punch!"

"You are terrible," she said, rolling her eyes. "I wouldn't like to hear what you say about me behind my back."

"Nothing but good." Then his face became serious. "In all seriousness, you're gorgeous, Connie. Everything about you – your lovely figure, your lovely long hair. Sure, you must know that."

"Get away with you," she said, but inside she was flattered. It was nice to get a compliment from someone outside the family. While her mother had a sharp tongue a lot of the time, she often told her how nice she looked when she was going out, and how she should be proud of such a thick head of hair. She also told her that she should be more confident about herself, given that she was always near the top of the class – but Connie didn't take it too seriously, as she guessed most mothers did that to build up their daughters' confidence.

"There are a few cars going from Tullamore, so we can pick you up," Emmet said now. "I might even take my own car. The lads are all bringing something to drink and Jim's family have a woman who helps around the house, and she's going to make a bit of food as well." He took Connie's hand. "You'll come, won't you?"

She took a deep breath. "You might want to take somebody else …" She moved a few steps out of his grasp, and folded her arms.

"Why would I do that?" There was an uncertain note in his voice now. "We're still going out together, aren't we?"

Connie glanced over her shoulder, feeling awkward with Eileen so close by. "With me going away soon, you might feel you're wasting your time when you could meet another girl who'll be staying around Tullamore."

"Well, you're not gone yet and, as we said, you'll be home regularly."

"But nothing like as often as I would be if I was in Dublin," she pointed out. "And you don't know what might happen for either of us in the future."

"That's very true." He looked very serious for a few moments, and then he smiled back at her. "So we might as well make the most of the time you have left."

Connie heard Eileen's footsteps and then her employer came through, carrying one of the wreaths.

"Will I call to the house for you around eight?" Emmet said in a low voice.

Connie thought of her mother again and pictured a long night sitting in the depressing atmosphere at home.

She had been straight with Emmet Ferguson, so no one could say she was leading him on.

"Yes," she said, "that should be fine."

Chapter 4

Kate Devine looked out of the kitchen window. "I've decided I'm not going in to work tomorrow or Sunday," she said. "I couldn't face them all asking how Connie got on. They'll all be thinking, *'That's what she gets for blabbing on about her daughter going to UCD'*. And that Ward Sister I can't stand is on for the rest of the week. She'll be only too delighted to rub it in." She looked up at her husband with red-rimmed eyes. "If you would just phone the hospital for me and leave a message on the ward."

"But you'll still have to face them next week." His voice was gentle. He knew the situation had knocked her for six, and was trying not to make it worse.

"By the time I get back they'll all have heard and it won't be the same big news. They will have moved on to something else."

"If you're sure that's what you want …"

She ran a hand over her forehead. "It's the truth anyway, I'm not feeling well. I've got a splitting headache and my stomach is not right."

"Will I get you a couple of aspirin?"

She nodded. "I was just going to look for some."

He went over to the old pine dresser. "I'm sure I saw a packet in the drawer here." He opened the drawer and rummaged around for

19

a few seconds, then found the box of aspirin. He opened a cupboard and lifted out a glass etched with small colourful birds, went over to the sink and filled it with water. Then he handed it with the aspirins to her. "Why don't you have a lie-down? You hardly slept last night and you'll feel the better of a rest."

She washed two aspirins down with a few mouthfuls of water. "I've the dinner to get ready before they all come in."

Seán looked over at the dish on top of the cooker. "The meat is all done, and I can easily do the potatoes and whatever vegetables you want." He waited for her to make some comment about how he only half-did the potatoes and left the little black eyes in them or peeled the skins too thickly.

This time Kate just shrugged. "Okay," she said. "I'm going to lie down."

When she came home after work, Connie found her father and brother down at the bottom of the garden. Ollie congratulated her on her great results, and she could tell he genuinely meant it. Seán explained about her mother not feeling the best and then said that he was just going back in to check on the potatoes.

"Fair play to you," Ollie said. "You did great getting the marks you needed to go in for medicine." He shook his head and laughed. "Jeez, I can't imagine somebody in our family being a doctor! Isn't it gas?"

"Mammy would have preferred me to go to Dublin," she said quietly.

Ollie pulled an incredulous face. "Never mind Mammy," he said. "You know what she's like. She'll soon get over that when she hears the reaction from other people about you studying medicine. How many other girls in your class are going to be doing that?"

Connie shrugged. "None," she said. "I'm the only one."

"Well, there you are," he said, nodding. "And you're a lucky devil going over to Manchester. It's a brilliant place. I absolutely love it there." A broad grin broke out on his face. "God, when I think of all the places we went with Tara and Frank – Blackpool, Belle Vue, and the football and the wrestling matches that Bridget's husband took me and Fran to. We had some great times, didn't we?"

"We did," Connie said. "I've always loved it too, and I was delighted when I saw there was a medical school over there."

For the very first time that day, she felt herself beginning to perk up. Like Ollie, she had only good memories of the family holidays they had when they went over to stay with Tara and Frank and the children, in their lovely big house just outside of Stockport.

"I don't know why we haven't been these last few years," Ollie said, wrinkling his brow. "I suppose it was when we started working and then it was hard for everybody to get the same holidays." Then he remembered. "And didn't Mammy decide about five years ago that it was time we saw a bit more of Ireland?"

Connie nodded. "That's when they started booking holidays down in places like Waterford and Kerry."

"That's it." He grinned again and rubbed his hands together. "It'll be Manchester for me every year from now on!" He winked at her. "I'll be over hoping to be introduced to all your lovely student friends."

Connie pushed him playfully. "Get away, you!" she said, laughing. "I don't know who's the worst, you or Terry."

When her younger brother came in a short while later, the four of them sat at the table eating the dinner that Seán had prepared. She was relieved that Terry had the same attitude as Ollie and he recounted similar memories about their visits to Stockport and Manchester, and said he would be over to visit her for a weekend as soon as she got settled in.

"It's easy enough to get the coach from Tullamore up to Dublin and then the boat and the coach straight to Manchester."

"You have it all worked out," Connie laughed, "and I haven't even got time to think about it myself."

At one point Seán got up from the table and went down to the bedroom to check if his wife was still asleep, and when he came back he closed the kitchen door.

"Now, lads," he said, looking his two sons, "your mother isn't taking this too well about Connie going to Manchester. She'll get over it after a while but, until she does, if the subject comes up I'd like you to tell her about how easy it is to travel over there and that kind of thing." He gestured with his hands. "Just the sort of things you've been genuinely saying while we were eating. It will make her realise that Connie isn't going to the ends of the earth."

"Thanks, Daddy," Connie said, touching his hand. As always, he was the peacemaker. She felt guilty about her mother being in bed, but glad the atmosphere was much cheerier. On the rare occasions her mother did this, Connie knew it was usually because she was upset as opposed to being ill.

The four of them chatted and then Connie looked at her watch. "If any of you want to use the bathroom before I go in, I'm having a bath."

"Is it that time of the year already?" Ollie remarked, as he did every time anyone in the house had a bath.

"Change the record," Connie said. She made a face at him, but her eyes were laughing.

"Are you off out celebrating tonight?" Terry asked.

She nodded and then felt herself blushing. "I'm going to a party with Emmet Ferguson."

"Oh ... so you're still hobnobbing with the businessmen in the town?" Ollie said.

"That's a great car he's got," Terry said. "He comes to the garage to get it serviced."

"I won't be seeing much of him after tonight," Connie said, taking her plate over to the sink. "There's no point when I'll be going away and, even if I was staying, I doubt if we're really that suited."

Chapter 5

Connie came out of the bathroom with one towel around her hair and a bigger one wrapped completely around her, then went padding barefoot across the hallway to her small bedroom.

She had realised when she was having her bath that she hadn't checked with Emmet whether it was a dressy sort of party. Normally, she wouldn't even think about it, and would happily just wear whatever was her newest or favourite outfit – but she had never gone to a party in a house with a swimming pool before. She presumed that since it was people her own age it would be fairly casual. At the moment all her friends were wearing long peasant-style dresses or bell-bottom jeans and colourful tops or shirts.

She opened her wardrobe and looked at the colourful mixture which her mother had ironed and hung up for her. She was lucky that her mother was interested in fashion too, and her parents were always generous with her and made sure she had everything she needed. They made jokes about some of the fashions she and her friends wore like hot pants and what her father called 'flower-power' things, but for the last few years they had left her to pick her own clothes.

She towel-dried her long dark curly hair and left it loose to dry. Then, she stood in front of the wardrobe deciding. She lifted out a long sparkly halter-neck dress and after a few seconds put it back in again. If all the other girls were dressed in jeans and T-shirts she would feel ridiculously overdressed. Then, she reached in for a pair of purple velvet bell-bottoms and a close-fitting, stretchy black-lace shirt. With a few strands of beads and some bangles and earrings it would be perfect along with her black suede blazer and her platform sandals.

Her mother got up just as she was putting her make-up on and, although there was a distance about her, Connie thought she seemed easier than she had earlier in the day.

When she told her she was going to a party with Emmet Ferguson and Martina O'Leary she just nodded and said, "You might as well enjoy yourself while you can – the summer will be gone before we know it. Just be careful now and don't drink anything stronger than a shandy."

Connie was ready and waiting when Emmet Ferguson's blue Ford Capri pulled up outside the house just after eight o'clock. Martina and Patrick Kelly were in the back seat together.

Connie opened the front passenger door and leaned into the back to say hello to them. She immediately noticed the blue sparkling lurex dress that Martina was wearing with a diamante choker, which was more formal than her own outfit, and it made her wonder if she had underestimated the occasion. She was relieved then to see that Emmet was wearing a casual, open-necked shirt and jeans. She told them how well they both looked and then she got into the car.

"I heard you did great in the Leaving Cert," Martina said. "So you'll be going over to England to train to be a doctor?"

Connie turned back in her seat to look at her. "That's the plan. How did you get on yourself?" she said quickly, hoping Martina wouldn't go on about her not getting the qualifications for UCD. She was fed up with discussing it with everyone.

"Two Honours, thank God – so I'm hoping to start work in the Bank of Ireland next month."

"I'm delighted for you." Connie then went on to ask her all about the job and Martina was happy to give her every little detail.

"It's great to have the pressure of the exams all lifted and to know what you're doing, isn't it?" Martina said.

Patrick leaned forward. "And great to be able to relax and enjoy the rest of the summer."

"Absolutely!" Connie said, turning to smile at him.

As they drove out of Tullamore and headed out towards Athlone, Emmet and Patrick got into a conversation about sport, while Martina filled Connie in on the other girls' results and what she thought certain girls were going to do after the summer. Then she said that she was going on holiday with her family down to her auntie's caravan park in Kerry the following week.

At one point Martina leaned over the back of Connie's seat so the boys couldn't hear. "I'm hoping Patrick will come down to Kerry for a few days too," she whispered to Connie, "but my mother's not keen on him coming and says it's a holiday just for our own family. I was talking to my auntie on the phone, and she said Patrick can stay in the house with them, and she'll talk my mother round. I hope she can as a fortnight away with all the family will drive me mad – and God knows who might make a play for him while I'm away."

Connie was glad that Martina could not see her face, because she couldn't help smiling at the thought of anyone making a play for Patrick Kelly. He was a nice fellow, a good worker and a good laugh, but – God help him – he didn't have much going for him in the looks department and was hardly likely to be the target of many women in Tullamore.

The car turned off a road between Moate and Athlone and then a few minutes later they drove down a laneway bordered on one side by a high wall.

"I think the gates are down here," Emmet said. "I've only been out to it a couple of times and I wasn't the driver so I wasn't paying attention."

He drove a bit further and then the car slowed down as they came to an impressive walled gateway with a lamp on either side.

"Yep – I recognise the lamps!" he said triumphantly. "This is definitely it."

"It's some place, isn't it?" Patrick said as they drove in through the gates and up a long driveway. "Jim's granny left it to them a few years ago."

"The Fays had a nice big house in Tullamore out near Charleville

Castle," Martina said, "but it was nothing compared to this."

The ground suddenly became bumpy.

"Hold onto your hats, lads!" Emmet said, laughing. "I think we have some nice big potholes here."

"Jim said the place is eating money with the work that needs doing on the house and the grounds," Patrick commented, "and I can see what he means. It will cost them a fortune for the upkeep of this drive alone."

They laughed as Emmet deliberately drove into some of the holes, so they bumped their way up the driveway.

Connie caught her breath when they came to the front of a huge rambling grey house with walled gardens. The house was much bigger than anything she had imagined, and a world away from the Devine's plain three-bedroom house in Tullamore. She suddenly felt intimidated by it and the sort of people who she might meet inside.

"I think they park around the back," Emmet said. He drove through a big archway at the side of the house to a courtyard where around a dozen other cars were already parked.

Connie was relieved when she heard Martina gasping at the size of the house.

"God, it's huge! It's much bigger than anything I imagined. I think I'm a bit nervous going in." She leaned forward and gripped the back of Connie's seat. "What about you, Connie?"

Before she had a chance to reply, Patrick put a hand on the girls' shoulders. "Ah, you'll be grand," he said laughing. "Nobody's going to take a bite out of you! Weren't we all invited?"

"And Jim's an easy-going fella," Emmet said. "He was at school with us in Tullamore and was no different to any of the other lads. None of us knew his grandparents had a place like this until they died and his father inherited it."

"And where's the swimming pool?" Martina asked.

"Out the back, beside the tennis court," Emmet said, laughing. "Where else would you expect it to be? Were you not brought up with a swimming pool, Martina?"

"Yeah," she said. "The same as everyone else I know in Tullamore – the public swimming pool."

They all laughed and then got out of the car.

Martina started pulling at the hem of her lurex dress. She looked at Connie and shook her head. "I wish I'd worn trousers, this damn thing is full of static and it keeps creeping up over my knees."

The back door of the house opened and a group of lads spilled onto the flagstone area outside, all talking and laughing – then the sound of Elton John singing 'Crocodile Rock' suddenly blared across the courtyard. The music made Connie smile and she immediately felt herself relax. The lively, modern music somehow made everything seem more normal and ordinary.

Emmet came over and threw his arm around her shoulder. "C'mon," he said to the others. "Let's go and find Jim and then we can come back out to the car and get the beer and the LPs I brought."

The two couples made their way across the old uneven flagstones side by side, Martina complaining all the way about the heels of her stilettos catching in the gaps.

"I wish I'd worn platforms," she told Connie in a low voice. "I'm terrified I'll break my feckin' ankle before we even get in. I never imagined we would have to walk across a mucky old yard. I thought when Patrick said it was in a big fancy house it would be paved at least."

Connie tucked her arm through Martina's. "You'll be grand. I'll catch you if you go over."

The door opened again and a tall dark-haired lad, wearing jeans and a black T-shirt with a big red star on the front, came out. He came towards them, grinning broadly.

"You made it!"

"Hi, Jim!" said Emmet.

Connie felt even happier now, seeing the host dressed so casually, and she could tell from his manner that he was an easy, friendly sort of lad.

"Of course we made it," Emmet said, clapping him on the shoulder. He nodded towards the house. "Are there many here yet?"

Jim shrugged "Ah, around thirty or forty, I'd say. A nice crowd. If you come into the house we'll get you sorted with drinks, and there's a table laid out with sandwiches and that kind of thing."

"We have a couple of boxes of beer in the car and some drinks for the girls."

"You can get them later," Jim said. "We have plenty inside to be going on with."

They all moved towards the back door of the house now, where the group of lads were still laughing and messing around.

Jim turned back to Emmet.

"Aren't you going to introduce these two lovely girls?"

"This is Martina," Patrick said, pulling her close to him. "We've been courting for over a year now."

Jim shook Martina's hand and said he was delighted to meet her and then he turned to Connie. "I take it you're the young lady that Emmet has been going on about for months?"

"She is indeed," Emmet laughed. "This is Connie, and I somehow managed to talk her into coming out with me tonight. She just got her Leaving Cert results today and she's going to study medicine."

"*Medicine?*" Jim said, his voice high with surprise. He looked at Connie and winked. "Emmet didn't say you were that clever."

Connie shrugged and rolled her eyes. "I haven't even got my acceptance letter yet."

"Connie Devine," Emmet said, squeezing her around the waist, "your place is guaranteed and, as always, you're just being modest."

Everyone was looking at her now and smiling and she suddenly felt self-conscious again. Thankfully, Jim opened the door and Patrick and Martina followed him inside.

Emmet stepped inside and then held the door open for Connie but, just as she started to go in, she felt a hand on her shoulder. She turned quickly and saw that it was one of the lads who had been standing on the steps. He looked to be a few years older than her, and he had dark hair which curled down over the collar of his blue-velvet jacket, under which he was wearing a casual shirt and jeans.

"I hope you don't mind me interrupting," he said in a well-spoken English voice, "but did I hear someone say your name was Connie Devine?"

Connie's eyes narrowed as she looked at him, taking in his tanned handsome face and his dark-brown eyes. Boys often used chat-up lines like that to get to know girls. In fact, it was the sort of thing that Emmet or Patrick would do. But this particular fellow didn't look or sound like the sort that had to resort to those sorts of tactics.

28

"Yes," she said. "I am Connie Devine."

She glanced at Emmet who was still holding the door open. He was staring at the lad and had straightened up to his full height, his chest pushed out as though he was ready to square up to him.

"Connie from Tullamore? Your father is Seán – Tara's brother?"

She looked back at the boy.

He smiled at her. "You don't recognise me, do you?" He put his hand up to his forehead now, embarrassed.

There was a small silence during which Elton John stopped singing and 'Sylvia's Mother' started up.

Connie shook her head. "How would I know you?" Then, as she looked at him, she saw something familiar about him. But yet, how could she know him? He was a friend of Jim Fay, who she didn't know either, and from the sound of his accent he was English.

"We used to know each other when we were younger," he told her. "We're sort of related. It's a few years now, and you probably don't even remember my name – it's William Fitzgerald."

Chapter 6

"William Fitzgerald?" Connie was staring at him now, her mind racing as she tried to put things into place.

And then it clicked. He was the younger brother of Gabriel Fitzgerald – Tara's first husband. Her face suddenly lit up. "My God! Of course I remember you. We met up with you a few times out at Ballygrace House when we were young and then during that summer visit over to Stockport, when you were staying with Tara!"

A look of relief washed over his face. "I'm really sorry for catching you unawares like that – both of you." He smiled apologetically, first at Connie and then at Emmet who had come back to stand beside her. "I got such a surprise when I saw you because I knew I recognised you from somewhere, and when I heard your name I just automatically came over. Thank goodness it actually *was* you." He shrugged and laughed. "I'm not usually so impulsive."

"I'm glad you did speak to me." Connie smiled warmly at him now. "It's really lovely to see you again, William."

"And you too," he said.

"God, when I think of all the times we spent playing hide and seek in the gardens in Ballygrace," Connie said, "and that summer in England, when we had the trips out to Blackpool and ..." she halted, trying to remember, "the place with the zoo and the funfair …" She shook her head. "I can't think of the name, and we were only talking about it at home recently."

There was a moment's silence then William clicked his fingers together. "Belle Vue! I loved it – Frank and Tara used to take me there every time I visited them."

Connie nodded her head vigorously, her eyes bright. "And Tara's hotel," she said. "We could pick anything we wanted off the menu, and we used to run mad out in the garden. It's amazing now when I think back."

"Sorry now," Emmet said, putting an arm around Connie's shoulders and guiding her playfully towards the door. "Patrick and Martina will be waiting on us, and Jim will be thinking we've disappeared on him. He went to get us a drink."

William stepped back now, clearly embarrassed. "Apologies, it's my fault for interrupting you."

Connie caught his eye and said, "I've got to go and see my friend but I'll probably see you later."

He smiled again and she noticed how bright his eyes were. She could still hardly believe who it was, and was disappointed she couldn't stand and chat to him for longer.

They went inside and into a large kitchen full of young people. It took her a few moments to get her bearings as the room was very dimly lit with just a few lamps in the corners – though it was relieved a little more by rows of flickering candles on the deep windowsills which were stuck into a variety of empty jars and wine bottles.

She heard Martina call, "Connie!"

She looked around but couldn't see her.

"They're over there," Emmet said, pointing to the doorway at the opposite side of the room.

He took her hand and they wound their way through groups of chatting, laughing people that she had never met before, to the sound of Roxy Music blaring out 'Virginia Plain'.

"Where did you go to?" Martina asked, her forehead wrinkled. "We've been standing here waiting for you for ages."

Connie could tell Martina was annoyed and she felt awkward. "I'm sorry, but I met somebody I know that I haven't seen for a long time."

"Well, I hardly know a soul here apart from you and the two lads." Martina rolled her eyes. "That Jim fella went to get us a drink ages ago and he's not come back either."

"Ah, sure, he probably got caught up talking to somebody too," Emmet said. "Patrick, we'll go out and get the bottles from the car, and then we can help ourselves." He tipped Connie's elbow. "I won't be long."

The girls' eyes followed the two boys as they made their way back through the crowd.

Martina leaned in towards Connie and said in a low voice, "You wouldn't imagine that you would be in a huge house like this, and be left waiting on a drink." She shook her head. "And the state of the place too – it's not what you expect when you see the outside. Did you ever see the like of it? It's cluttered everywhere." She indicated an old pine dresser beside them. "There are books and empty boxes and bits of cardboard and papers piled on top of it. And if you look over at the windows, there are oul' candles stuck in jars and bottles. You'd think that his mother would have organised things in the house before letting Jim invite anybody back. My mother would have a heart attack if anybody came in and she had a few dishes in the sink or if the beds weren't made." She pulled a face now and gave a little shudder. "Can you imagine what the bedrooms and bathroom are like?"

Connie shrugged. "Maybe they don't bother about that kind of thing. Jim seems a nice lad and his family are probably nice too. Not everyone is the same."

"True …" Martina said, but her tone did not sound convinced.

Connie looked around the room again and, although she couldn't disagree with her schoolmate that things were on the ramshackle side, there was something about the informality of the big kitchen that she really liked. Even though she didn't know anyone there, something about it felt warm, relaxing and welcoming. In a way it reminded her of the kitchen in Ballygrace House, the house her step-aunt – Tara Flynn – had lived in for years. It was now a small hotel, owned by another of her father's sisters, Angela.

When they were children her granda, Shay Flynn, had often brought Connie and her brothers out to the house for the afternoon when he was cutting the grass or doing some sort of handiwork around the grounds for Tara. Connie had always loved going to the big old rambling house, and had very fond memories of it. Something about this old place she was in now made her feel the same way, although Ballygrace House had been more elegant, with beautiful furniture and a piano. The kitchen, although comfortable and warm like this one – had been perfectly clean and very well organised. It was probably the size or the age of the house, or something she couldn't really explain. And it was something that people like Martina would not understand anyway.

As she remembered Ballygrace House, her thoughts shifted back to William Fitzgerald. What a coincidence it had been, them meeting up again after all those years! It was a pity they had lost contact, because he seemed a really nice lad – just as he had been a very nice young boy. And when they met up in Stockport as young teenagers they had got on very well there too. For a time, she had presumed that they always would see each other, but then Ballygrace House was sold to Angela and her husband, and Tara didn't come back to Offaly quite so often or stay for as long as she used to. And then, regular contact between the families just fizzled out. Connie didn't have to think too hard to work out why that had happened. It had been purely down to her mother.

She had noticed over the years that her mother had increasingly become critical of Tara, constantly referring to her having married a man who was divorced and how it wasn't right in the eyes of the Church. She also talked about Tara's friend Bridget who she disliked even more. She told Connie that Bridget had had a baby when she was young and unmarried, and had it adopted, before heading over to England where she no doubt continued with her wanton behaviour.

And Angela – half-sister to her father and Tara – wasn't exactly popular with her mother either. Angela had offered Connie and her brothers summer jobs out at the Ballygrace House Hotel, but her mother had refused to let them work there saying it was too far to cycle out to, and their father hadn't time to be driving them there and back. When Connie argued with her, Kate had said that she didn't want any of her family working as skivvies for the Flynns.

All the women were lovely to any members of the Devine or

Flynn family, and always had been. Tara made everyone welcome wherever she lived, and both her husbands had always been friendly too. Bridget was equally as kind, and her husband Fred was great with Ollie and Terry, taking them to wrestling and boxing matches.

Tara had even put the family up in the hotel she was part-owner of, and made sure the staff had treated them all like special guests. Angela had invited everyone out to the hotel for a meal each time Tara came back home or for special occasions like Christmas or Easter, but her mother was never keen on going. Nothing any of them ever did was right and, although Connie hated to admit it about her own mother, the logical reason was that her mother was jealous of them – and jealous of Tara in particular.

"You're very quiet this evening, Connie," Martina said. "Are you all right?"

"Oh, sorry," she said, smiling. "I'm grand. Don't mind me, I was just thinking …"

"I suppose you have a lot on your mind with going away soon?"

Connie nodded. "I suppose I have."

There was a little silence.

"Emmet is very obliging, isn't he?" Martina said now. "Patrick is the same. We're very lucky."

Connie felt a small stab of alarm. "Emmet and I are not serious," she said in a low voice. "It's not like you and Patrick. Even if we wanted it to be serious, it wouldn't work with me going over to England soon."

Martina's brow wrinkled. "But I thought you would keep in touch …"

"Only as *friends*," Connie said. "It wouldn't be fair to either of us to keep it going."

"But you didn't mind coming here with him tonight?"

Connie shrugged. "Emmet really wanted me to come and I didn't want to hurt his feelings … But, I have been honest with him. He knows where we stand."

Martina pursed her mouth together, thinking. "Well, he told Patrick he was really keen on you and that if you went to England that he'd go back and forth to visit you."

Connie took a deep breath. "I really don't think it's a good idea."

There was a small silence then Martina crossed her arms over her ample chest. "Who was it that you met earlier on? Somebody from Tullamore?"

Connie could tell she was trying to change the subject and was grateful. "No," she said. "It was a lad I used to know when I was younger. I haven't seen him for years."

Martina's eyebrows lifted in interest. "A neighbour?"

"No," Connie said. "He's actually related to me in a way."

Martina turned to face her now, full of interest as she always was with local gossip. "Is he a Flynn or a Devine?"

"Neither, he's related by marriage ..." Connie didn't know which was worse, being quizzed by Martina over her relationship with Emmet Ferguson or having to relate every little detail about someone her classmate didn't even know.

Just at that point, the door from the yard opened and the group of lads who were standing outside came in. Connie watched and her stomach tightened as she saw the subject of their conversation in the middle of them. From a distance, where she could observe him now, she could see that he stood out as taller than most of the others. But, even if he hadn't been tall, Connie guessed that he would still have stood out as different. The velvet jacket really suited his dark hair and she liked the way he wore such a normally formal item with a casual shirt and jeans – and a fashionable pair of pale blue desert boots. She supposed it was because he was English, and had lots of different men's shops to choose from. Even his hairstyle was more modern – it looked as though it had actually been layered into a shape and then allowed to grow longer, as opposed to some of the others whose hair was in an old-fashioned style that had just been let grow whatever way it went.

The door opened again and Patrick and Emmet came in, each carrying a box with cans and bottles. Some of the other guests commented on their load, and the two boys chatted and laughed to them as they passed through. Connie watched as William caught Emmet's eye and held his can up in a friendly greeting and Emmet in turn made some light-hearted comment and then they both laughed. Then, she felt a little wave of disappointment as William turned his back to her as he moved in to join his group of friends.

"Who is that fella, I wonder?" Martina said.

Connie looked at her but, before she had time to answer, the boys were coming towards them.

"Supplies are here!" Patrick said. He had a box with eight cans of beer and two packs of Babycham.

"Thank God!" Martina said, rolling her eyes. "I've never waited so long for a drink in my life." She looked at the cans and bottles. "How are we going to drink the Babycham without any glasses?"

"We just have to find some for you, ladies!" Emmet said, laughing.

He put the cans of beer down on the floor. "Guard them with your life," he told Patrick, "and I'll just go and see where the glasses are. They will probably be set out in one of the other rooms."

"I'll come with you," Patrick said. "We need a bottle-opener too."

Martina grabbed his shirt sleeve. "See if there's any food out yet," she said in a low voice. "He mentioned something about sandwiches when we arrived, and I don't see any in here."

Patrick winked at her. "I'll do my best."

As the lads moved off Martina turned to Connie. "What are you having to drink, Connie?"

Connie shrugged. "A shandy or something like that. I don't really drink."

Martina lifted two of the little bottles out of the box. "You can have one of these Babychams if you like. They're lovely and light. You'd hardly know there was any alcohol in them. Patrick bought eight bottles for me and I won't drink them all."

"Thanks," Connie said, smiling at her. "I've had Babycham at Christmas and it's lovely." She also thought it was something that her mother wouldn't complain about her drinking, so she was safe enough.

"Imagine thinking I'd drink *eight* of them!" Martina gave a sidelong grin. "I hope he's not trying to get me drunk so he can chance his luck with me." She nudged Connie. "After you've been going out with them a while, it's all they can think of. Do you not find that?"

Connie felt herself stiffen. She didn't feel she was a close enough friend to get into such a personal conversation. But they had a long night ahead and she didn't want to create an atmosphere. She managed a smile and rolled her eyes as though in agreement.

Martina put her hand up to her mouth. "Sorry, Connie, I wasn't thinking. You've never really gone out with anyone for very long, have you? You've never been really serious with a lad?"

Connie shrugged. "Not really. I've been out with quite a few lads but there was no one I ever felt that serious about."

Martina looked at her sympathetically. "You'll meet the right lad one of these days. I mean, it's not as if you're not good-looking and you've got that lovely long hair."

"It's more than looks though – you've got to have things in common – things that you both enjoy and can talk about together. Things like music and books."

"I can't imagine Patrick ever talking about books. All he talks about is work."

The sound of James Tayler singing 'You've Got a Friend' could be heard now.

"Oh, I love this," Connie said, glad of the diversion. "Do you like it?"

Martina raised her eyebrows, thinking. "It's nice enough, but I like cheery singers like Neil Diamond or Joe Dolan. I absolutely love 'Sweet Caroline'."

"That's definitely a cheery song." Connie's mother was a big fan of both singers, but she said nothing as it might sound like she was suggesting that Martina was old-fashioned.

Martina started laughing. "Patrick always says that when he hears Joe singing 'You're Such a Good-Looking Woman' it reminds him of me! Isn't he some eejit, talking rubbish like that?"

"Well, it's nice of him to say it. It's very romantic."

"I don't know about that – I think he just says it to get on my good side."

They stopped talking as the boys came back through the crowd, carrying glasses and followed by Jim.

"Sorry for disappearing!" Jim said, smiling good-naturedly at them. "I got caught with a fellow I haven't seen for a while. But I see you've got sorted out with drinks, so that's a good start." He held out two Babycham glasses decorated with the little deer emblem. "These are for the ladies." He handed one to Martina and the other to Connie. "And the food is out on the table in the dining-room just down the hallway – and there are some chairs in there or in the sitting-room further down. There are a few people in there already, although nobody has touched the buffet yet." He grinned at them. "Just follow the music – the record player is in the dining-room."

Martina leaned in to Connie. "Thank God," she whispered, "although God knows what the buffet will be like with the haphazard way the house is run."

Patrick opened a bottle of the sparkling drink for each of the girls and poured them, and the boys then opened the cans of beer. Emmet had a few mouthfuls before he put the box with the remainder of the drink in a cupboard to come back to later. Then they set out to get some food.

As they all walked down the dimly lit hall, Martina caught Connie by the elbow. "Look at that pair," she said, indicating a couple further down the hallway who were in a passionate clinch. The girl was wearing a short tan waistcoat with fringes and the boy had his hands up inside the back of it. "They don't care who's looking at them. Good job Jim Fay's parents aren't here or we'd all be put out."

Connie didn't want the couple to think she was watching them so instead she looked at the lovely dark old furniture and the rows of paintings and photos on the wall. Her eyes then moved to the decorative border of flowers above a picture rail, and the crystal chandelier which she thought beautiful even though it had a few cobwebs and half the lightbulbs were missing.

Patrick was just leading them into the dining-room when Martina turned back to Emmet. "When you came back into the kitchen earlier," she said, in a low voice, "who was the lad you were talking to?"

Emmet looked at her quizzically.

"The one with the fancy blue-velvet jacket," she said. "He had longish dark hair."

"Oh, do you mean the English lad?"

Connie held her breath. It confirmed what she thought about her schoolmate, that she was nosey and never missed a thing.

"Oh, I didn't know he was English. He was too far away to hear him speaking. How do you know him?"

"I don't know him at all," Emmet said. "It's Connie who knows him. He came over to speak to her when we arrived."

Martina turned back to Connie. "You never said anything about knowing him to me."

Connie looked at her. "Who?" she said, deliberately vaguely.

Then, before Martina had time to grill her any more, Patrick came back to the door. "What's keeping you all?" he said, laughing. "I went on ahead like an eejit and found I was talking to myself."

The dining-room had a more flamboyant chandelier which was also bedecked with cobwebs, and the largest marble fireplace Connie had ever seen. On top of the mantelpiece stood an old black clock and a conglomeration of candles in all sizes. There was a miscellaneous collection of furniture, some antique mixed with modern. The scuffed red flocked wallpaper, the pink velvet curtains and pelmet, and the Oriental rugs on the bare wooden floor added to the faded grandeur.

Connie had never been in a house so imposing and yet so casual before. The shabby style took away any feelings she might have had about it being intimidating, and made her warm to Jim Fay and his obviously easy-going family.

"Food at last, thanks be to God!" Martina whispered as she spotted a table over by the window which had an assortment of plates on it. "I hope it's not too fancy or weird. Let's get over there before everyone comes in and it's all gone."

The two lads didn't seem so interested in the food and were standing drinking and talking. Connie had to stop herself from smiling as she watched Martina first make a quick round of the table to check what there was, then lift a paper plate and start filling it with sandwiches and the various savouries on offer.

"It all seems quite nice," she told Connie, although there was a note of reservation in her tone. Then she stopped and ate a sandwich in three quick mouthfuls. She moved on again, reaching across the table for a vol-au-vent. "I don't know what's inside this, but I'll chance it." She put it on her plate then she moved towards another platter. "The sausage rolls look lovely," she said, putting three on her plate. "And they look home-made."

Connie went around the table, picking up a few sandwiches and a sausage roll. "It's a lovely spread," she said, adding an egg mayonnaise sandwich.

"They've got a woman who helps out," Martina told her, taking a bite out of a sausage roll. "I heard one of the lads saying that. Well, she's definitely a good cook. She's used all the best of ingredients. You can tell the pastry is home-made and she's used a good butter on the sandwiches." She pointed across the table at a plate with cream cakes. "God, don't they look lovely?"

"They do," Connie said, trying not to sound bored with the mundane comments – the sort of comments an older woman like her mother would make. Martina was always going on about her weight, and yet she didn't seem to see the connection between her obsession with food and her waistline.

Plates in hand, the two girls wandered out into the hallway and down to the sitting-room. Further along the corridor Connie could see a dark-wood winding staircase, and halfway up she noticed another couple wrapped around each other. Martina didn't seem to have noticed them as she said nothing.

The room was empty apart from an older couple who looked to be in their thirties, and were sitting on a sofa in the bay window, deep in conversation. It was a long room painted a deep red which should have made it darker, but the tall bay windows with their flowing golden-velvet curtains trimmed with red-and-silver tassels brought streams of late-evening light into the room. One wall was fully lined with bookshelves, packed full of books of every shape and size, and stacked at all angles. There were also piles of books on the floor which had obviously been taken out and not replaced. Most of the other walls were covered with paintings or wood-carvings which Connie thought were possibly African. An old upright piano with brass candlesticks stood against the back wall, its top scattered with music books and miscellaneous objects. A white marble fireplace faced the door – the grate empty for summer – above which was an elaborate, mirrored over-mantel glittering with candles.

"What a gorgeous room!" Connie said, her eyes moving around. "I love all the books and the art. There's so much to look at."

"Do you think so?" Martina said, wrinkling her nose. "Would the untidiness and the dust not drive you mad?

"Not a bit." Connie smiled at her. "I think it's nice and real friendly and relaxed." She motioned her to a low table, which was covered with a purple-velvet cloth decorated with colourful embroidery and tiny mirrors. Two well-worn tapestry armchairs stood on either side. "We might as well sit down while we're eating."

They sat down, putting their glasses and plates on the table.

"About that English lad ..." Martina suddenly said, "was it he kept you back when you were coming in?"

Connie nodded. "Yes," she said, then lifted a sausage roll and took a small bite of it.

"I'm surprised you didn't mention him," Martina said. "He's really good-looking. He's like a pop star or a male model or something like that."

"Do you think so?" Connie found what Martina had just said interesting. She too had thought William Fitzgerald surprisingly good-looking. He had turned out to be a much better-looking young man than she had ever imagined he would when they were youngsters. Back then he had seemed very formal to her, always dressed in smart clothes and with a very tidy haircut. He was so different now – so casual and modern that she would never have recognised him if he hadn't introduced himself.

"How did you say you are related to him?"

Connie shrugged. "It's by marriage. He's the young brother-in-law of one of Daddy's sisters."

"The one that has Ballygrace House Hotel?"

"No, not Angela. I don't think you know Tara."

Martina was in the process of raising a sausage roll when her hand halted halfway to her mouth. "Tara Flynn from Ballygrace? The one that married into the Fitzgeralds?"

Connie's heart sank. She might have guessed that Martina would know any gossip about her family. "Yes, Tara is my dad's stepsister. And the lad you saw me talking to is William Fitzgerald. We used to play together out at Ballygrace House when we were young."

"Ah ... it all makes sense now."

"And before you ask me, I don't know how he knows James Fay or anything like that. I hadn't seen him for years until tonight, and I've told you everything I know."

Martina's head jerked up now at Connie's sharp tone, and then a flush came on her face. "I was just curious. He kind of stands out from the other lads, and it's only natural to wonder about him."

"Well, he's a very private sort of chap." Connie lifted her glass now and drained it. Just as she set it back down on the table, Emmet appeared with another two opened little green bottles in one hand and Simon and Garfunkel's *Bridge Over Troubled Water* LP in the other.

"How are you doing, girls?" he said, crouching down beside them. "Are you enjoying yourselves?"

"I love it," Connie said. "It's a beautiful old house."

Martina nodded. "It's very different ..."

"We're having great craic out in the kitchen, and it's still only early. Have another little Babycham each and then we might have you up dancing." He laughed as he filled their glasses, then waved a hand around the room. "This really is some place, isn't it?"

"It's a lovely room," said Connie.

"Another crowd has just arrived in a mini-bus from Athlone," he told them. "Must be around fifteen or sixteen of them. A fairly lively crowd anyway. They're all out in the kitchen. It's packed there now."

"It looks like it's going to be a great party," Martina said, "but the only thing is that Patrick and I hardly know anyone here."

"Well, he was chatting to a group of lads there a few minutes ago. I don't know that many myself," Emmet said. "But, sure, wouldn't it be boring if you met the same people all the time? And all the ones I've spoken to so far are very friendly. Once you've been here for a while you'll get chatting to some of the others." He straightened up and then held out his Simon and Garfunkel LP. "I'm going back to the record player to put this on before somebody else beats me to it."

More people drifted into the sitting-room and Connie did her best to catch people's eyes and nod in greeting to them or say hello. Emmet came back with Patrick, delighted he had got his album playing. They brought more Babychams for the girls and then, as the room filled up, two girls came to stand next to where Connie and Martina were sitting. They were very similar looking: both tall, thin and plain-looking with short curly hair and glasses – and not a scrap of make-up. It was immediately obvious they were sisters just looking at their narrow sloping shoulders and their out-ofproportion wide hips. They were both dressed in jeans and boyish-looking checked shirts – one in blue and the other in green. It was also obvious from their self-conscious manner that they, too, didn't know anyone. Connie felt sorry for them and, as soon as she got a chance, she said hello and then introduced them to Martina and the boys.

They all got chatting and the sisters said that although they only lived down the lane from the Fays they didn't really know that many local people because they went to a boarding school up in Dublin. They were a year younger than the girls and doing their Leaving Certificate the following year. Martina told them about Connie's and her good results, and about her job in the bank and Connie going to England to study medicine. The girls were very impressed and asked them details about the exams and the questions that had come up in Irish and English Literature.

Connie noticed that Martina had brightened up and was obviously enjoying the girls' company. She listened as her classmate elaborated about the exam papers and then quizzed them about their boarding school, as she had a second cousin who went to the same one – until it was ascertained that the cousin was a few years older and the girls definitely did not know her. Martina then went on to ask them who they knew in Tullamore, and it eventually emerged – as it usually did in small Irish towns – that there were people they all knew.

After a while Connie found herself tuning out of the girls' talk and she turned to join in with the more interesting discussion the boys were having about the lyrics on the *Bridge Over Troubled Waters* album. They had the LP cover on the table in front of them and were going down the songs one by one. She told them her favourite was the title song and they chatted about it for a few minutes.

"Connie, I think I'll be listening to this a lot when you go over to England." Emmet pointed at 'Bye Bye Love', then gave a sad smile and crossed his hands across his heart.

Connie shrugged and smiled back at him. "We knew it was probably going to happen. That, as they say, is life."

"You're right. I suppose we'll just have to wait and see what happens." He pulled her closer to him. "Hopefully I won't be thinking about the track above it." He moved his finger to 'Why Don't You Write Me?'

Patrick clapped an encouraging hand on his friend's shoulder. "Ah, you're not the first couple to have to spend a bit of time apart, and you won't be the last. Plenty of romances last the course, and you can always go over to Manchester every now and again to keep the flames alive. And Connie will be home regularly. Don't forget one of the most famous Simon and Garfunkel songs is 'Homeward Bound'!"

"Good man, Patrick!" Emmet said, clapping his hands together.

Connie felt very uneasy at this exchange but she said nothing.

Two girls who had been in the kitchen came in carrying a tray with tumblers filled with a red-coloured drink.

"Fruit punch," one of them said, beginning to offer the tray around the room. "We made a huge bowl of it earlier and forgot about it."

When they got to their little group, Martina took a glass and put her nose to its rim. She wrinkled her nose. "Do you mind me asking what's in it?"

"Take a sip and guess!" the girl said.

Cautiously, she took a sip. "Oh, it's lovely! It has a peach flavour, doesn't it?"

The girl nodded. "There's Peach Schnapps in it amongst other things …"

"I'd say there's a drop of brandy in it too," Emmet said.

"Oh, that sounds dangerous!" Patrick joked.

Connie took a drink of hers and thought it was lovely, and then sat back in her chair half-listening to the conversations going on and half-looking around at the interesting things on the walls and shelves surrounding her. The house, she felt, induced a sort of lazy relaxed feeling, unlike their own small house at home. Her mother seemed to be involved in a constant war against dust and muddy footprints from Seán's gardening, clothes that needed to be laundered or ironed, vegetables that needed peeling and a never-ending stream of cups and dishes to be washed and put back in place. There was rarely a time when the family just sat and actually enjoyed the peace around them.

Connie wondered what it would be like to live in a rambling

place like this. A place so big you could roam around it without bumping into anyone. She had only seen some of the downstairs rooms, but she had a feeling that there was a lot more to see upstairs.

They were all relaxed and chatting when Jim stuck his head into the room, announcing, "One of my friends from Galway has just arrived outside on an absolutely amazing, brand-new Harley Davidson. It's like the one in *Easy Rider*. He's outside on it now if anyone is interested in having a look."

"Brilliant!" Emmet said.

He and Patrick moved immediately to follow Jim.

Connie glanced at Martina, but she was deep in conversation with the two girls. She thought for a few moments then she stood up too. She wasn't overly interested in the motorbike but she was even less interested in the conversation that the girls were having. She thought she might just go and find the bathroom, and while she was there she could touch up her lipstick and check her hair.

She took another drink of her punch and then leaned across and tapped Martina on the shoulder. "I'm just going outside for a few minutes."

"Grand," Martina said, making a little waving gesture without looking around.

She went out of the sitting-room and down the hallway. There was only one other door which she tried only to discover a serious-looking room with a big, leather-topped desk and more bookshelves, which she presumed might be Jim's father's study.

She glanced at the staircase when she came back along the hallway and, seeing no sign of the couple who were there previously, she decided to try upstairs. She had just reached the top of the stairs when she heard a door opening and a toilet flushing. She stopped in her tracks, not wanting to embarrass anyone by looking as if she had been waiting outside. A girl came out of the bathroom, smiled at her as she passed by and went downstairs.

Connie went in to find a big echoing room which had pink painted walls, old wooden shutters at the dusty windows instead of curtains, and a log basket piled with toilet rolls. There was a shower over the green, claw-footed bath, and towels of varying sizes hung from half a dozen hooks on the back of the door. There was also a stack of magazines and books on the floor by the side of the toilet, and even a crossword-puzzle book, which amused her.

The sink was big, square and plain, and twice the size of the one they had at home. The thing that caught Connie's eye more than anything else was the oval mirror above the sink, as it was the most striking, feminine item in the bathroom. The glass was framed with a gilt garland, and decorated with colourful flowers and vines. The bottom part was adorned with a small nymph-like creature, her modesty covered by her long golden hair and a coloured robe which flowed downwards into the edge of the frame. Connie thought it the most beautiful piece of art she had ever seen.

Standing to the side of the sink was a small table, dressed in what looked like an antique wedding veil, which held an assortment of soaps, hand-creams and jars of bath salts. Some had handwritten labels on them, and when she examined a round jar, she saw it was inscribed in French. Using one of the bars of soap, she washed her hands, imagining what her mother and her friends at work would think of the mirror, the books and the foreign toiletries on the table.

She dried her hands and then, as she bent to lift her handbag from the floor, she felt herself slightly swaying and it occurred to her that there was more to the glass of sweet punch than she had realised. The Babychams, she was sure, were harmless enough, but she reckoned she would have to be careful – she didn't want to get on her mother's wrong side for drinking too much. As she brushed her long hair in the mirror and then re-applied her eye make-up and lipstick, she wondered why she had taken such a liking to this house, and then she wondered about the new life that lay before her in England. It had only been this afternoon she realised that she was going to university in Manchester – but already she felt things were changing.

Already she felt that *she* was changing.

Chapter 7

A short while later, as she came out of the bathroom, she could hear 'The Boxer' playing downstairs, mingled with loud voices and laughter and the revving of the motorbike outside. It had all the sounds of a good party, and she guessed it would get livelier in the next few hours as people drank and mixed more. She looked right and then left along the empty hallway. She was filled with curiosity as to how the bedrooms might be furnished. She hesitated for a few moments, and then gave a small sigh. She could just imagine how she would feel if someone caught her nosing around where she had no business being.

She turned back towards the stairs and her heart almost stopped when she saw a figure standing there watching her.

"Oh, my God!" she gasped, clutching her handbag to her chest.

William Fitzgerald was leaning against the staircase, his arms folded casually. He started to laugh.

"You gave me the fright of my life!" she said.

"Oh, I'm so sorry," he said. "I thought you would have heard me coming up the stairs as they're fairly creaky."

She shook her head. "The noise from downstairs would drown anything else out."

As she walked towards him now she felt herself blush, realising that he had been watching her as she stood considering whether to look in the rooms. Or, even more embarrassing, he had probably been waiting outside to use the bathroom, speculating as to why anyone would take so long, while she had dawdled doing her make-up.

"I was actually looking for you," he said, as though he had guessed what she was thinking. "I was wondering where you had got to. I saw your friends outside at the motorbike and then I came back into the house and couldn't see you anywhere. Your girlfriend was downstairs with another group. This was the obvious place you might have gone to." He grinned at her. "Sorry I cornered you earlier as soon as you arrived, but I was so delighted to see you again after all this time."

He was so friendly and nice that she found herself relaxing and smiling back at him. "It's lovely to see you again too," she said.

There was a pause as they both stood looking at each other, then, just as the silence became slightly awkward, William started to laugh. Connie found herself joining in with him, although she wasn't quite sure what they were actually laughing at.

"This is an amazing house," she eventually said.

"I love it too," he told her. "And I've been invited to stay the night. Jim has offered me a pull-down bed in the studio."

"An art studio?"

"Yes, they're all very arty. Jim is at art college in Dublin and his mother paints and does sculpting." He gestured down the hallway. "It's the last room at the bottom. It overlooks the front of the house.

Connie was curious again but felt a little out of her depth. Nobody she knew had an artist's studio in their house.

"You're obviously good friends with him then?"

"Yes," he said, "although we only see each other every six months or so, if he comes over to London or Manchester or when I come over here in the summer."

"I didn't know you still came over to Ireland regularly?"

He shrugged. "It's never for long."

"When we were all younger," she said, "we used to have those big get-togethers when you and Tara and everyone came over, but they don't happen so often now. It's a pity – we really enjoyed them."

"Me too." He nodded slowly. "How are the two boys? The last time I heard Ollie was working at the railway station."

"He's still there," she said, "and Terry is training to be a mechanic."

"I'm not surprised – he was always car mad." He smiled at her. "And what about yourself? What are you up to?"

She took a deep breath and then, although she wanted to appear casual, as though it were no big deal, she could feel her heart racing. "I'm actually preparing to head over to Manchester University to study medicine."

His eyes widened. "Wow – medicine! That is absolutely amazing. Congratulations!"

He looked so truly delighted that Connie couldn't stop herself from smiling. "I can hardly believe it myself," she said. "I only found out this morning. It was either going to be Dublin or Manchester and it's turned out to be Manchester."

"And are you happy about moving over to England?"

"Yes, I am." Connie's eyes were now sparkling as she envisaged the big step she was about to make. The party and the lovely old house, and meeting up with William again had lent a distance to her mother's reaction earlier in the day. "I'm really happy about it. I'm ready for a change."

"Well ..." He shook his head. "I had no idea that you were on the verge of such a big change in your life. And I am hugely impressed about your future career plans. Medicine is a tough one but you've obviously done brilliantly in your exams to get the grades to study it – so you're on the right path."

"Thank you, that's very nice of you." She could tell that his praise was genuine and it made her feel almost emotional hearing it. "What about you?"

"I've just finished my law degree," he said, "and I'm about to start my LPC."

Connie looked blankly at him.

"Sorry, I didn't mean to talk in jargon. I'm so used to it in class. It just means the year's Legal Practice Course we have to do after the Law Degree."

"It sounds very high-flying, whatever it is. You've done very, very well. Are you enjoying it?"

"Yes," he said, smiling at her. "I am, actually. I find it really interesting." He looked back down the stairs and then he turned to look down the hallway. "Would you like to see the studio?"

"I'd love to see it – but what if anyone comes up and wonders what we're doing?"

William shrugged. "I'm sure Jim won't mind, since I'm going to be sleeping in it tonight." Then, he suddenly stopped. "I didn't think about your boyfriend. He might not be too happy with you being up here with me."

"Emmet?" Connie shook her head. "He's not really my boyfriend."

"Really?"

Connie suddenly remembered William meeting them as they arrived and how it must have looked. "We've been out a few times, but it was never anything serious. He's a lovely lad –" She paused. "But we're different in a lot of ways." She could see he was listening intently, and she wondered why she was explaining all this to him. "Earlier today I told him there was no point in us continuing to see each other – especially with me going to England."

He nodded. "It's never easy when you're moving away. I've moved between places a number of times, so I understand."

"I suppose it would be different if I had deep feelings for him ..."

"What about Emmet's feelings?"

"He seems keener." Her voice was quiet, aware that Emmet or someone else might suddenly appear at the top of the stairs. "He says he wants us to keep in touch."

He shrugged. "Some relationships do last even though people are apart ... but sometimes it's better to make a fresh start. Especially if you have any doubts."

"That's what I think."

There was a pause, then he said. "The studio?"

"Are you sure it's okay?"

"Of course." He grinned and stretched his hand out to her. It was the friendly, reassuring sort of gesture that might be made to a child. "I've told you – it will be absolutely fine."

As he caught her hand, she suddenly felt something like a little jolt deep inside her. And it was that moment – with that single touch – that Connie realised she was attracted to him. But it was more than that. It was not the usual feelings of meeting a boy at a dance or that sort of thing. She had felt that friendly, light-hearted thing with all the lads she knew who had liked her. But now, after talking to William on their own, she knew she was experiencing something different.

When his hand tightened on hers, her head automatically turned towards him – she saw him looking at her and she began to blush. And then she blushed some more as she wondered if he guessed what she had felt. She looked straight ahead, but she did not take her hand away and let him lead her down the hallway.

William opened the door to the studio, switched on the light and they went inside.

"Oh, this is amazing!" she said, looking around her.

He led her into the middle of the room and then let go of her hand. "I thought you would like it. I don't know about you, but I'm not very knowledgeable about art myself – I find all this fascinating, though."

"I'm exactly the same," she told him. "I'm more interested in it now than when I was younger. I went up to the National Art Gallery at Easter with a friend who was taking it in the Leaving Cert and I just loved it. I wandered about for ages, just looking at everything and wishing I knew more about the artists." She smiled at him. "And wishing I had picked art as a subject at school. It's really enjoyable and so different from any other subject."

"True," William said, "but I suppose art wouldn't have been so useful to you for studying medicine!"

Her eyes moved over to the large bay window, to the sofa draped with heavy red velvet, which at a closer look she thought might actually be an old curtain. It had a variety of Indian cushions on it in bright pinks and purples and turquoise, adorned with beads. A few of them of them depicted elephants on their own or in groups and the large cushion in the middle featured a bright-eyed owl.

William must have followed her gaze. "That," he informed her, "is my bed for the night. It's a pull-down sofa affair."

"Well, it's certainly a great room to wake up in," she said, smiling at him.

She turned slowly around, looking from wall to wall at the colourful paintings, and then her eyes moved to the tables dotted around the room which had a variety of objects and curios on them, which she guessed were used for still-life compositions. There was a long trestle table covered with newspapers which held a series of sculptures in various stages of completion. There were also several large pieces on the floor – one, still in progress, which looked like the outline of a swan made from coat-hangers. Over in a corner there was a pile of dried branches, painted silver and black. She dropped her handbag onto the sofa then moved around the room, her eyes taking in everything – her mind trying to digest it and wonder what some of it was about.

"It must be wonderful having a room like this in your own house," she said. "The freedom of just coming up here to create something when you feel like it."

"I think Jim's mother has had an exhibition of her work in Dublin," he told her, "so she must be fairly successful."

Connie paused now to examine a sculpture made from metal and painted wood which depicted three large golden sunflowers. "Amazing …" Then she moved over to a table which held small sculptures of thin, almost stick-like human figures cast in bronze. They were caught in a variety of poses, some just sitting, some dancing, some standing. There was even one of two children on a swing. She paused to study it closer and then her gaze gradually shifted to the sculpture next to it and she suddenly realised she was staring at one of a naked couple, kneeling closely together and embracing.

"Beautiful, aren't they?" William said.

Connie looked up, embarrassed at being caught examining the naked piece, and as she did so she felt herself sway a little. She put her hand on the edge of the table to steady herself. The punch had certainly affected her. Then, as William's hand came out to catch her, she gave a gasp as she immediately felt the same little electric shock at his touch.

"Are you okay?" he checked, his hand still on her upper arm. "You have to watch out in this room – there are obstacles everywhere."

"I'm fine, thanks. But I think I'd better go back downstairs before I knock something over!" She moved away from him now, feeling awkward again.

"Of course," he said. "I don't want to keep you from the fun

52

downstairs, and your friends will probably be back now and wondering where you are."

"There's plenty going on downstairs," she said, "so they probably haven't even missed me. But your friends will probably wonder where you are. I've really enjoyed looking around the studio. Thanks for taking the time." She looked up at him and saw his expressive brown eyes smiling at her. She went to say something more about the art pieces she liked, but the words seemed to get stuck.

"It's been lovely spending time with you again, Connie." He was still looking at her. "And I hope it won't be as long next time ..." He put his hand out as though to shake hers and then he started to laugh. "I suppose shaking hands is a bit formal at our age, and when I think of how easy we were when we were younger!"

She started to laugh too. Then, before she had a chance to think about it, he had leaned forward and kissed her gently on the cheek. Afterwards, he just stood there, so close to her that she could feel his breath on her cheek and neck. Again, she felt something suddenly stir inside and she began to feel flustered. She fleetingly thought of Emmet who, she guessed, would not be happy to see her like this with William Fitzgerald.

A moment, then several more moments passed. Connie knew she should move away and break whatever this thing was between them. Jim Fay or Emmet or anyone else could walk in and wonder what she was doing in a room on her own with this lad whom no one else seemed to know. But fear of this new, lovely feeling coming to end kept her rooted to the same spot. In the silence of the studio she became aware of all the noise downstairs again – everyone singing and cheering out loud to the chorus of Alice Cooper's 'School's Out'.

Then, as William's hand reached to touch her hair, a feeling of anticipation rushed through her. And, as his arm wound around her neck she felt her body curving naturally towards his, and still she did not move. And then, as easily as if he had done it a hundred times, he bent his head to kiss her fully on the lips.

Connie felt herself melting completely into him as she kissed him back.

After a few seconds, he gently pulled away to look at her. "You have grown into the most beautiful girl," he said, his deep brown eyes looking straight into hers. "And I am so, so glad we met up again."

She smiled at him. "And I am glad too."

And then, slowly, his head bent towards her again.

Connie's heart raced as his mouth came down on hers and, as he kissed her harder, she wondered at how completely natural and familiar it felt, as though they had been together for a long time. As she felt their bodies moving tightly together, she at last understood all the things she had heard and read about regarding romance and passion. All the things she had never experienced up until this moment, she now knew did exist. In this very short time with William Fitzgerald she had discovered something about herself. The passionless feeling she'd had with every other boy had been because she had not been truly attracted to them. There may have been passion on their side – but not on hers. She now knew from the way her heart was beating, from the sensation low down in her stomach, that this was a very different thing.

The long kiss ended but they stood there with his arms around her, and her head resting on his chest. Then he moved, and held her back far enough so he could look into her eyes.

"I'd love to see you again," he said. "I'm here for another four or five days. I'm staying out at the hotel in Ballygrace with Angela. We could do something. I have a car with me – we could go to Galway or Dublin for the day."

Connie looked up at him and nodded. The only thing she wanted was to see him again. There was no point in pretending otherwise.

"Have you a phone?" he asked. "I just need to check if there is anything arranged for me. They are so good and Angela often invites friends over when I'm there." Then, he suddenly thought. "Or I could call out to your house and catch up with your parents and the boys. I was planning to visit Shay and Tessie as well."

Her mind worked quickly now. How would her mother react to this renewed friendship with Tara's brother-in-law? After all that had gone on today, not very well she suspected. She couldn't handle any more difficulties at home. She decided to be straight with him.

"My mother is not great at the moment. She's upset about me going to university in Manchester, because I'll be much farther away and everything. I might have to pick the right time to tell her I'm meeting you. In fact, it might be best if you rang me at the shop tomorrow to make arrangements for us to meet up."

"Really?" He sounded surprised now. "Would she mind me ringing the house?"

She could not launch into the whole thing about Tara and how her mother was so unfathomably awkward about her. But, there was another reason she could mention. "It's about Emmet." She made a little face. "She probably won't be too pleased if another boy is ringing me when I've been seeing him."

"Maybe if you remind her that we already know each other?" he suggested. "We all got on so well when we met up in Stockport at Tara's."

Connie nodded but didn't say anything.

"I know it's a few years since I met your mother," he said. "Do you think she would remember me?"

"Oh, I'm sure she would," Connie said quickly, "and I'm sure she thought you were very nice."

His brow furrowed. "Is she very keen on Emmet?"

"I don't think it's that. I've a suspicion she feels that if I keep in touch with him it will be a reason for me to come home more often."

"Believe me, I understand that only too well," he said. "I know how very difficult family situations can be at times. My own mother is not the easiest person to deal with."

"Really?" Connie was surprised. He struck her as the sort of person who would find life easier than most. His family were well off and, from what she had heard about them, they didn't seem the sort of people who would worry about what others thought of them.

He smiled and rolled his eyes. "She is a kind and lovely person most of the time but she has some values that are very different from mine, and she tends on occasions to get a bit too wound up about things we clash over like politics and that sort of thing." He laughed. "Most families I know are like that – I suppose it's what's described as the 'generation gap'."

Connie felt a wave of relief wash over her. He understood without her having to explain any further, and he wasn't just being nice – he had told her that his own mother was difficult. Having this kind of discussion about her mother was something new for Connie as she had always been very private when it came to her family.

"So, is it okay with you to phone me at the shop tomorrow?" she checked. She didn't want anything to come between them now.

"Yes, of course."

She had a sudden thought. "If you're in Tullamore, you could even call into the shop. It's very near to Grandad and Granny's house." She then went on to give him directions.

"That's a good idea," he said, smiling. "That's exactly what I will do. I would like to see where you work – see you amongst all the flowers."

It crossed her mind that her boss might think it strange for two different lads to call in at the shop in such quick succession but, as quickly as she thought about it, she decided she would not worry over it. Like the situation with her mother and Emmet, it would all eventually work out. She wasn't going to lose whatever time she had over the next few days with William because of worrying about them.

He caught her eye again and they both smiled. Then, they sort of fell towards each other and his arms tightened around her and he began kissing her again. This time there was no shyness or awkwardness and she wondered at how totally relaxed she was with him.

After a while, they leaned apart to catch their breath and look at one another.

"I really don't want to," he said, "but I suppose we're going to have to go back downstairs to our separate groups." He sighed. "It would have been far easier if we had met in a bar in London or somewhere like that, where we could just go off on our own now, without thinking about anyone else."

"I know," she said, "but things don't work like that in small places in rural Ireland." She wondered if Emmet and Patrick were still outside admiring the motorbike, and then she thought of Martina downstairs and wondered if she had missed her yet, or whether she was still engaged in chat with the two sisters. She looked at her watch but, not having checked it earlier, she had no real idea how long she had been with William. She guessed it was long enough to have been missed.

She picked her handbag up and took her brush and compact with the mirror out, and quickly sorted her hair. Then she looked at him, with a glint in her eyes. "I think I might need to re-do my lipstick."

He laughed. "You look beautiful, but it might be just a little smudged."

She turned to the side, quickly powdered her face then reapplied her lipstick. Then, she straightened her shirt and jacket. "Am I okay?"

He studied her, his face quite serious now. "You're more than okay – you're perfect, Connie. Absolutely perfect."

"I don't think I'm ever that!" She rolled her eyes, being funny, then saw the serious way he was staring at her. Her smile faded and she became serious as well. "But I wouldn't like Emmet to see me and guess we had been ... you know ... I wouldn't like to hurt his feelings."

"And neither would I," he said. "It's the last thing I expected to happen." He shrugged. "I almost didn't come. I was just going to spend the evening in the hotel and then Jim rang me, and he sounded so keen that I couldn't say no, so I thought I'd drive over for an hour and then head back." He caught her hand. "But I can't tell you how glad I am that I decided to come."

"I'm glad too," Connie said in a soft voice. Then she looked towards the door. "I'd better go ..."

A small silence fell between them and they both started to move across the floor, still holding hands. William went first to open the door, glancing cautiously out, then he leaned back towards her smiling and whispered. "I think we're okay – the coast is clear ..."

As they walked down the corridor together, they could hear heavy, thumping music accompanied by singing and shouting.

William laughed. "Sounds like Led Zep, and I think we've got some head-banging going on downstairs."

They stopped at the top of the stairs and he looked down, checking if anyone was around. Seeing no one, he turned back to her, his arms circling her waist. "One last kiss?"

She looked up at him, her eyes wide and laughing. She was going to make some joke but instead she just shook her head. Then, just as his lips touched hers, the bathroom door opened and Emmet came out, doing up the zip on his jeans. They sprang apart, Connie's face flushing.

Emmet stopped in his tracks, his gaze moving from one to the other. "I wondered where you'd gone ..."

"Hi ..." she said, her heart thumping now. "We were just heading back downstairs." She couldn't tell whether he had seen them, and she felt awful in case he had. Whilst she had no great feelings for him and hoped he understood that, she would not deliberately hurt him.

"I looked for you when we came back in," he said. "Martina said you had gone off a while ago." He paused. "I was beginning to get worried that you had disappeared on me."

There was something about his face that reminded Connie of her brother, Ollie. Then she suddenly realised that Emmet looked like Ollie looked and sounded when he came home from the pub after a late night. Whatever Emmet had been drinking had now begun to have an effect on him.

"We bumped into each other," she said. "And then William was just showing me around. We were just in the studio with all the art."

Emmet raised his eyebrows and then smiled at her. "That could be taken the wrong way. I hope your old friend wasn't showing you his etchings?"

Connie put her head to one side. "Very funny."

"Look, I'll leave you to it," William said, starting down the stairs. He looked back at Connie. "It was lovely catching up with you again – give my regards to your family."

"I will," she replied, her eyes meeting his. Then, as she turned back to Emmet she felt her heart sinking. He was looking very closely at her – almost studying her.

"Will we go back downstairs?" she said. "It sounds like things have got very lively there with all the rock music."

He slowly nodded. "So what was so interesting in the studio?"

She started walking down the stairs now, Emmet following behind.

"There were lots of things," she said. "Jim's mother has some lovely sculptures."

"She might not be too pleased with people wandering about looking at her stuff."

"William has known the family since they were all young, and he's staying the night in the studio."

"He seems fairly confident, but I suppose that's the way of those English types."

"His family are from Offaly," she said, "but, like a lot of families, some of them moved to England."

"He doesn't sound like any Irish lad I know," Emmet said, a sulky note in his voice. "Is he living in Manchester too?"

"No, he lives in London," Connie said.

His eyes narrowed. "There's a fair distance between London and Manchester," he said. "So you won't be seeing him when you move over there?"

"I doubt it."

"And I won't be bumping into him again when I come to see you?"

Connie suddenly had a sinking feeling in her stomach. He had not taken any of the hints she had given him earlier in the day, and was still hoping that they would continue seeing each other. She had hoped it would gradually dawn on him, but obviously it hadn't happened yet. She knew that she could not spend another evening in his company pretending to be his girlfriend, and it would be unfair to string him along.

She had only come to the party to save his feelings, but she now felt it had not been the right thing to do. But, she thought, it had turned out to be right in another way, for if she hadn't come she would not have met up with William again.

They were halfway down when she heard Martina's voice drifting up towards them, then she appeared at the foot of the stairs.

"Here she is!" Martina said. "Connie, we thought you'd been kidnapped!"

"No," Connie said, her voice deliberately light, "I just got chatting and then I was looking at some art stuff."

"Poor Emmet thought somebody had run off with you. I guessed you'd met up with the lad with the velvet jacket again." She thumbed in the direction of the hallway. "I saw him just now."

59

They joined her in the hallway.

"Well, your guess was right," Connie told her. "I bumped into him when I was waiting to go into the bathroom."

Martina nodded at Emmet. "Lucky they're related," she said, laughing, "or you'd be getting worried."

"Very funny," Connie said, before he could answer. She could see where the conversation would lead to if she didn't stop Martina. "Where are the two nice girls you were chatting to?"

"They're around somewhere," Martina said, raising her voice to be heard. "Some eejit decided to jump into the swimming pool so they all went down to have a look. I wouldn't be a bit surprised if more of them followed him in."

"It's a lot livelier now," Connie said, as they walked along the hallway. She hoped she wouldn't meet William again as it would be very awkward, and was trying to check where he was so they didn't come face to face.

Then she suddenly felt Emmet's arm draping around her.

"Why don't we get another drink and then go for a walk down to the pool?" he suggested.

She thought now, after the close call upstairs, that she really had to do the decent thing for the rest of the night as far as Emmet was concerned. There was no escaping being with him for a while now, although hopefully there were still some of Jim Fay's other friends outside.

"Okay," she said.

When he went back to where they had left the drinks, Connie turned to Martina. "Are you coming outside?"

"No chance," Martina said. "I'm not walking around that yard again with these heels. They nearly got ruined just walking in."

Connie looked at her watch. "To be honest, I'm tired now, and feel ready to go home."

"We can't go home yet!" Martina's voice was high with surprise. "Sure, it's not even eleven o'clock yet." Her brow creased. "Are you all right? That lad didn't upset you, did he?"

"Who?"

"That William fella. You've been very quiet since you came back downstairs. He didn't try anything on with you or that kind of thing?"

60

"No, of course not," she said. "He's a lovely lad – we were only chatting."

"Even the lovely lads can have wandering hands."

A group came out of the kitchen and along the hallway, and Connie was relieved to see the two sisters making a beeline for Martina again. They started telling her and Connie all about the exploits of the lads who had been jumping in and out of the pool.

Emmet came back with Patrick and the drinks. He came and put his arm around Connie.

"Are we going outside for a while? It's a lovely night."

"We might as well." It would be easier if she went with him rather than have Martina grill her over William Fitzgerald again. It would also help pass the time until she could press them to start thinking of getting home.

Drinks in hand, they went through the kitchen out into the yard. It was a clear night with a full moon, so their way down through the garden path was lit well enough. Emmet stopped every so often to take a drink from his can of beer.

"It's turned into a great party," he said, slipping his arm around her again. "A bigger crowd than I imagined, great music and a good bit of craic." He motioned with his can. "There's a high hedge and we take the path just to the side of it – and they have the tennis court and the pool down here. There are lights around the tennis court – as Jim was saying, they often play late in the summer nights."

Connie suddenly noticed that it was very quiet. "There doesn't seem to be anyone else here," she said. "They must have all gone back inside."

"Well, there was a crowd of them here earlier, when you were off touring around the house."

Then, before she had a chance to think of a reply, he drew her to a standstill. "No harm in us having a bit of time on our own, is there?" he said. "Sure, we've hardly had any time together since we arrived."

Connie caught her breath. There was the same sulky note in his voice, which made her feel uncomfortable. He then turned to face her and aimed a kiss in the direction of her mouth, but Connie managed to move her head in time and his wet mouth slipped down onto her cheek.

"Sorry," she said, "but I nearly spilled my drink."

As she moved out of his reach, she felt a small wave of panic rising inside her. Compared to William Fitzgerald, the thought of kissing Emmet suddenly repelled her. The effect of all the beers was now showing on him, in both his speech and his movements. She glanced at his face, guessing he must feel rejected.

He suddenly moved on ahead of her. As she followed him, it crossed her mind that coming down to this darkened part of the garden alone with him was not the most sensible of ideas. It was the obvious place for couples to go who wanted to be alone. She had presumed that there would still be others around, and they would join up and chat and have a bit of a laugh – but she had obviously been mistaken.

As they walked along, the further they went from the house the quieter everything became as the music and the sound of voices faded behind them. Then, without a word, Emmet reached his hand back to take hers and guide her down six wide steps to the garden level where the pool was. Further ahead, Connie could see there were two tall lights which lit up the tennis court. As soon as they reached the bottom step, she slid her hand out of his.

"This is amazing," she said, walking over to the narrow wrought-iron ladder that led into the water. She stopped for a few moments to take a drink of her Babycham, then looked along the edge of the pool and the white trellised railing which went all the way around it. "Imagine having your own swimming pool! Wouldn't it be great to have this to come out to any time you wanted in the fine weather?"

Emmet nodded his head, looking deep in thought. He looked across at her. "We could take a walk down to the tennis court," he said, "before heading back up to the house."

This time, she walked ahead of him, chatting all the way, passing comments on the flowerbeds and the high hedge with the archway which led into the court and anything else that came into her head. Anything to pass the time until they were safely back in the house, where Martina and Patrick and all the other young people were noisily enjoying themselves. She did not let her thoughts drift back to William Fitzgerald. He was for tomorrow and hopefully the other days he had left before returning to England. And if they got on as well as they had tonight, she hoped he might even be part of the coming weeks and months when she moved to England. But, she could not think of that until she was alone in her bed later. Tonight was still about Emmet and keeping things on an even keel.

When they came through the arched hedge and into the area of the tennis court, Emmet made straight for the side of the court where there was a white wrought-iron bench placed between two large plant pots filled with red, trailing geraniums. While Connie wandered about, sipping from her glass and making comments about the court, he quietly sat down in the middle of the bench, his arm thrown along the back while he finished drinking his can of beer. When he finished the last mouthful, he squashed the can between both his hands and then dropped it down at the side of one of the plant pots.

"Why don't you come and sit down for a few minutes?" he called to her.

Connie's chest tightened because she knew exactly why he wanted her to sit beside him.

"Do you not think it's getting a bit cold now?" she hedged. "Wouldn't we be better going back inside to sit down?"

"Five minutes," he said, patting the space on the bench beside him. "It's nice to have the peace outside."

She took another drink from the glass, hoping that it would make her feel more relaxed. And then – because there was nothing she could say that would not be construed as another rejection – she walked towards the bench. She felt a sense of relief when he moved to one end of the bench to leave room for her. But as soon as she sat down at the opposite end of the bench, her elbow resting on the arm of it, he slid alongside her and put his arm around her.

She sat still, holding her glass tightly.

"It really is a lovely house and a lovely garden, isn't it?" she said, looking around.

Without saying a word, he leaned across her, took the glass from her hand and put it down on the ground. Then he turned back towards her and went to take her in his arms.

Connie felt her body instantly stiffen at his touch. "Don't!" she said.

He moved his face closer to hers. "What's the problem, Connie?

We're supposed to be going out together."

She closed her eyes for a few moments, wishing she was home – wishing she was anywhere else but here.

"I've got a bit of a headache," she told him. "I think it might have been the punch earlier."

"The fresh air will help clear your head," he said. "Why don't you lean it on my shoulder for a few minutes?"

"No, honestly," she said. "I'm better just sitting like this."

He went to kiss her neck now and she pulled away.

"I'm sorry, Emmet … but I think we should go back up to the house."

"You didn't say that to the English fella earlier, did you? You didn't seem to mind when he was kissing you."

Connie's heart was thudding now. He *had* seen them together after all when he came out of the bathroom. And whilst she didn't want to hurt him, she knew it would only make fools out of both of them if she tried to deny it.

"Did you know he was coming here tonight?" he asked. "Did you just come here with me in the hope you might see him?"

She turned towards him. "Emmet, I'm really sorry about all this. It certainly was not planned – I wouldn't do that." She sucked her breath in. "It just happened. I haven't seen William Fitzgerald for years and I had no idea I was going to meet up with him again. I'm sure you could tell, by the way he came over to me and introduced himself when we arrived, that it was a surprise for both of us."

"Well, it was a bigger surprise for me when I came out of the bathroom and the two of you were all over each other on the landing!"

"I didn't mean that to happen … we were just so delighted to meet up again …"

"A blind man on a galloping horse could see that! If I'd thought for a minute you would carry on with another fella like that, I'd never have dreamed of asking you to come here with me tonight."

His voice sounded so full of disappointment that Connie felt sick.

"Emmet, I am really sorry about the way this has happened," she said, "but the truth is, when you asked me to come to the party, I had already realised you and I weren't going to last. I tried to tell you this afternoon that it would be better if we break it off before I go to England, but you didn't want to. I came tonight because I didn't want to hurt you by suddenly breaking off with you."

"So you thought it might be better if you just make a feckin' fool out of me?" He sat up straight on the bench now. "Do you know there are loads of girls around Offaly who would like to go out with me? Any night I'm out in the town with the lads, girls always come over to chat and ask me if I want to dance with them or go to a party or whatever. Even just the other week there was a girl asking if I fancied going on a holiday out to Spain with a group of them. Of course, I was so stupid I told her I had a serious girlfriend and it wouldn't be right to do anything like that."

"Oh, Emmet!" She felt swamped with a mixture of pity and guilt, and was desperately searching for something to say to make them both feel better.

He shook his head. "Haven't I been the feckin' eejit? Thinking that you had the same feelings for me that I had for you, and you can't even stand me touching you."

"It's not like that … it's not like that at all … it's just the way things have worked out. You're a really nice lad and I like you a lot." She sighed and shrugged, at a loss to find anything better to say.

He suddenly became still and turned to look her straight in the face. "Be honest with me now. If you weren't going to England, do you think we might have had a chance? If we'd got to know each other better?"

"I don't know …" Her voice was almost a whisper now. She closed her eyes, trying to gather her thoughts. Trying to think of the right thing to say to let them both walk away without feeling really bad. "I think sometimes you know when it's going to work and when it's not –"

Before she had a chance to say anything more, she suddenly felt herself being pulled roughly against him, and when she tried to jerk away from him she felt his hand clamping down on her thigh. As she struggled to get out of his grasp, she could feel panic rising inside her.

"Don't push me away again, Connie." His voice was trembling and emotional now, almost as if he was close to breaking down.

His damp face was so close to hers that she was overpowered by the strong smell of beer and whatever other alcohol he had been drinking.

"We just haven't had enough time on our own," he said. "It would all be different if we could have had some time getting to know each other a bit more."

Connie tried to twist away – his fingers were now so tight over the top of her leg that it was really painful.

"Emmet," she said, "I'm sure you don't mean it, but you're hurting me now!"

She became still, realising that he had drunk too much and that arguing with him was not the best thing to do.

"Let go of me, Emmet," she said in a quiet voice. "You know this isn't right."

"I'm only trying to get close to you ... the same way you let the English fella ..."

"I never let him do anything like this!" she said, her voice rising.

Then he lurched forward, pushing her back, his arms now pinning her down on the bench and his mouth coming down on hers so hard she could feel his teeth biting into her lips. His legs and body moved on top of hers, and then his hands quickly moved to find her breasts.

"*Get off me!*" she said, her voice louder and echoing around them. She dashed his hands away from her, trying to break free. "*Let me go!*"

"Ah, don't be like that!" he said, lifting his head to look at her. "If you would just give us a chance to get to know each other ..."

"*No! Not like this, not like this!*" she cried, her head moving from side to side to avoid him kissing her again.

A claustrophobic feeling came over her and she pushed with all her might against him, but he was too large and strong for her. Then, when he started to grind his pelvis into hers and she could feel his hard erection against her, a monumental wave of fear washed over her. She had never been so physically close to a male before and had no sexual experience, but instinct warned her what was likely to happen next. And her panic increased further when she felt his hand move down over the waistband of her trousers, and before she could attempt to stop him his hand moved further down between her legs.

She twisted away from him and took a gulp of air. Then she screamed, "*Emmet, get off me!*"

He suddenly stopped and then moved his body back from hers so he was sitting up. "I don't know what the big deal is," he said, sounding confused and angry. "All I wanted was a kiss and a cuddle. What's the harm in that?"

As soon as she was physically free from him, Connie moved from the bench and on to her feet.

"*You know what you did!*" she shouted at him as she straightened out her lace shirt. She started to slowly walk backwards away from him. "You had no right to touch me." She stabbed an angry finger in his direction. "You know *exactly* what you did!"

"Calm down, Connie, for God's sake," he said. "I hardly laid a hand on you!"

"I told you I didn't want you to kiss me or touch me!" Her voice was trembling now and hot tears came into her eyes.

She turned away from him, starting to run back out of the tennis court. She needed to get as far away from him as she could, and back to the safety of the house where there were other people.

Chapter 8

Connie suddenly became aware of the sound of running feet, and then a breathless voice calling stopped her in her tracks.

A couple a little older than herself came into view – a long-haired boy who she had seen in the house earlier and a tall girl with short blonde hair. Relief flooded through her.

"Are you okay?" The boy looked at her with concern. "We thought we heard some screaming ..." He looked over to the white bench where Emmet was sitting with his head in his hands. "We were over the other side of the garden when we heard you and thought we'd better check. You sounded as if you were in trouble."

Connie nodded. "I'm okay now." She wiped her damp face with the back of her hand.

"Did something happen?" the girl asked, her eyes darting back and forth to the bench. "Did he hurt you or anything?"

Connie closed her eyes for a moment and thought back to the way he had been with her. Had he actually hurt her? He had gripped her thigh which had been sore, and he had held her by the wrists – but the worst thing had been the way he had put his whole body weight on top of her. Pinning her down so he could touch her wherever he wanted without her being able to stop him. Just thinking about it again made her feel sick to her stomach.

"He was forcing himself on me," she said, "but I stopped him and managed to get away before he could do anything really serious."

"She's completely exaggerating." Emmet came walking towards them. He addressed the other lad. "I hardly touched her," he said. "It was only a bit of a kiss and cuddle."

"You know you did more than that!" Connie said. "You're lying through your teeth!"

"Why did you come down here with me in the first place?" he said, raising his eyebrows. "Didn't we come down to have a bit of privacy on our own?"

"You know perfectly well there was a lot more than kissing involved," Connie said. "I wouldn't have been screaming at you if there wasn't."

He made a dismissive gesture with his hand towards the lad. "She's making a drama out of nothing. We've been going out for months now, and she's looking for an excuse to blame me because I caught her earlier on with another lad. She's had too much to drink."

Connie's mouth fell open in shock and then before she had a chance to reply, the boy held his thumb up to Emmet.

"If it's only a private row between the two of you, that puts a different light on things," he said, and then he turned and put his arm around the girl's waist. "There's no need for us to get involved. They can sort this out on their own."

They turned away and, with their arms wrapped around each other, they started walking back towards the house.

Connie suddenly felt sick, as though she had just been punched hard in the stomach. They didn't believe her! They had heard her screaming and then seen how upset she was, but now they didn't think it was genuine. They thought she was a cheap sort – drunk and hysterical – and making a big drama out of an ordinary argument. And, for whatever reason, they chose to believe what Emmet had told them instead of believing her.

She turned to look at Emmet now and he was staring straight at her, his white face made whiter still by the lighting in the court.

"Connie, I'm sorry this all got out of hand," he said. "I didn't mean to get so carried away. I promise you it won't happen again."

"Too true it won't!" she said, her voice as cold as ice. "You will never get the chance to come near me ever again." She shook her head. "You know what you are, don't you? An absolute liar."

Then, she turned and half-walked and half-ran out of the tennis court after the couple. She didn't know them and probably wouldn't ever see them again, but she couldn't let them go without putting her side to them.

She caught up with them at the pool area.

"I'm grateful to you for checking that I was okay," she told them in a shaky tone, "and I'm not trying to involve you in any way, but I just want you to know that I was telling the truth about what happened. He did see me earlier with an old friend in the house," her voice cracked, "but, whatever he felt about that, he should not have tried to force himself on me – and then try to make it sound to you as if it was only a light-hearted thing. He really had me pinned down and was hurting me."

"God, that's terrible!" the girl said. "I wish we'd been there a few minutes' earlier and stopped him."

Connie closed her eyes and swallowed hard. "And we're not a serious or close couple in any kind of way. We have only been out a few times to the pictures, and I would never have gone down there in the dark on my own with him – I thought there were more people around." She shook her head. "I never let him put a hand on me before, and I never would have."

The girl reached out and touched her arm. "I believe you," she said. "I can tell by the way you're talking that you're telling the truth. I'm really sorry to hear what has happened to you."

"I didn't want to let you go away thinking I was the cheap sort of girl that he was making me out to be," Connie said.

"Are you going to be okay?" the boy asked.

Connie nodded. "I'll be fine. I don't want to make a big thing out of this and ruin the party. I'll be fine as long as I'm back in the house with everyone else." She moved on a few steps ahead of them now. "Thanks again."

Then she rushed as quickly as she could in the direction of the house. It was only as she was going back up the six wide steps that led back to the garden and the yard where all the cars were parked, that it dawned on her about travelling back home. They had all come in Emmet's car and the plan was to travel back the same way. The thought of it now filled her with anxiety. She didn't want to sit anywhere near him in his car, but maybe she could sit in the back with the other two? She'd have to explain to them what had happened or at least that she and Emmet had quarrelled. Would he even agree to take her if she did that? Apart from that, she also knew that after all the drink he had taken, he was in no fit state to be driving. The main road to Tullamore should be quiet enough at that time, but from what she remembered of the inward journey, there were a few winding small roads – possibly with deep ditches – that needed careful negotiation, and she wasn't sure that he was up to it. But, she would have to get home somehow. Buses were out. Even if there were buses at this time of night that went to Tullamore, it was a very long walk down small country lanes to get out onto a main road and she didn't really have a clue where she was.

She thought then that she could ask Jim Fay if she could use the house phone to phone home and ask her father to come and pick her up in his Morris Minor. But, just as quickly as she thought of it, she dismissed the idea. It would cause a commotion at home if she rang at this hour of the night as everyone would be in bed. Her mother didn't like her father driving to strange places in the dark, and she would end up coming out with him. Connie could imagine it all now – how she would have to explain why she hadn't stuck to her original travel plans, and she certainly didn't want to tell them about what had happened.

She didn't have many options, she knew. Another which flitted into her mind was to ask Jim Fay if she could stay overnight in the house and then ring her father early in the morning to collect her. But she hardly knew Jim, and, since he was Emmet's friend, it would be putting him in a very awkward situation.

As she came into the yard, she slowed down to catch her breath and to work things out before she went inside. The only other option she could think of now was to ask William Fitzgerald if he would run her home. Like most of the other lads here tonight, she knew he'd had a few drinks, but he had seemed perfectly capable of driving. She really didn't want to have to ask him, but she could not think of anything else – of any other way of getting home. She was dreading it, because they had such a lovely time together earlier, and now she would be telling him something serious which might put him off her. There was no other way to explain why she was not going home with her friends, and she did not want him to think she was the sort of girl who had taken a fancy to him and was making up some sort of dramatic story to be with him.

The door of the house opened and a group of three came out and headed over to one of the cars near where Emmet had parked when they arrived. Connie suddenly thought about Emmet again and glanced over her shoulder, checking if he was coming back up to the house. He could appear any minute, and she knew she would have to move fast to be gone before he turned up.

She ran up to the kitchen door and, after taking a few seconds to straighten her clothes and then smooth her hair down, she opened the door and slipped inside. Things seemed generally quieter now. The talk wasn't quite so loud and the Leonard Cohen album on the record player was more subdued than the music from earlier on. The smell of cigarette smoke and beer hit her as she eased her way through the small groups, looking to see if William was there. It was darker inside now as some of the candles had died out, and it made it more difficult to see. In a way, Connie was glad as she guessed her eyes and make-up would be smudged after rubbing them earlier.

She went back down the hallway to the dining-room, cautiously glancing inside from the doorway as she did not want to meet Martina and Patrick before she had organised her way home. There was no sign of them or William. She moved on to the sitting-room and had barely stuck her head around the door when she heard Martina calling out, "Here she is now!"

She looked over by the fireplace and her heart sank when she saw Patrick and Martina in a group, and her throat tightened when she saw who was standing next to them – William. He was smiling warmly at her and Martina was waving one hand, beckoning her to come and join them. She had a glass of beer in her other hand, an indicator that she had drunk the remainder of the Babychams. Connie had imagined catching William quietly on his own, where she could ask him if he would help her to get home. Seeing them all together now, she realised it wasn't going to be easy. She would have to try to get him on his own and, if he could drive her, she would then have to give Martina and Patrick some sort of excuse. After that she would get out of the house as quickly as she could and hope she didn't run into Emmet.

"Where is Emmet?" Martina asked.

For a moment, no words would come, then eventually she said, "I'm not sure ... I think he's still outside."

Martina touched William's arm and then winked over at Connie. "We've had a great oul' chat here," she said, a slight slur in her voice. "William has been telling me all about how you knew each other when you were young, and all the great times you had together." She gestured with her glass to William first and then back to Connie. "Isn't it just amazing you both meeting up here together after all this time?"

Connie nodded. "It is, isn't it?" She looked over at William and when he caught her eye he smiled. She tried to smile back but, after everything that had just happened, her face just could not form the correct positon. When she tried to smile a second time, she felt tears pricking at the back of her eyes. She blinked the tears back, and then she turned her head to look towards the door, dreading what would happen if Emmet walked in.

"Well, while you've been gone," Martina said, her eyes sparkling, "I got an invitation. You know the two sisters we met earlier – Tricia and Úna? They've asked me and Patrick to Úna's twenty-first party in two weeks' time. It's in a hotel in Athlone. Can you believe it? And me only meeting them tonight for the first time!"

"That's great," Connie said. "You must have made a great impression on them."

"I doubt it," Martina laughed, obviously delighted with herself. "I think the poor souls were just grateful to have somebody take a bit of notice of them and, you know me, I can talk the hind legs off a donkey!"

"You can say that again!" Patrick said. "More like a dozen donkeys!" He grabbed her around the waist, pulling her affectionately towards him, and they both fell against other laughing.

Martina then went on to talk more about the girls and where they lived and Connie nodded at all the right times and tried to look interested in everything her classmate had to say. It was only a minute or two, but it all felt like a long, drawn-out nightmare. Eventually, she got an opening to ask, "Can I just check where you put my handbag?"

"Over there, behind the sofa," Martina said. "Mine is next to it."

Connie thanked her and as she turned her head she saw William looking at her with narrowed, concerned eyes.

Then he mouthed to her, "Are you okay?"

She closed her eyes and shook her head, then she said, "I won't be a minute, I must go and find that bag."

She went across the room to the empty sofa in the corner, and leaned over it to retrieve her handbag. She had just straightened up when she saw William coming towards her.

"What's wrong?" His voice was low and serious.

"I need to ask you a big favour," she said. There was no time to waste. "Could you drive me back to Tullamore right now?"

"What's happened?"

"I need to get out of here. I've had a really serious problem with Emmet, and I cannot travel back in the car with him." She closed her eyes and took a deep shuddering breath. "I feel mortified landing this on you, but there's no one else I can ask."

"Don't even think about it," he said. "I'm glad to help you in any way." He felt in the pocket of his jacket and pulled out his car keys.

"Are you sure it's okay?" she said. "I know it's not fair to ask you to drive in the dark if you think you've had too much to drink ..."

"It's not a problem," he said, taking her elbow and guiding her towards the door. "I've only had three or four beers over the night, so I'm absolutely fine. Believe it or not, the last drink I had was a mug of tea that one of the girls made."

She slowed to a stop. "What about Jim? I don't want to put you in an awkward situation with him – after he invited you to stay – I suppose you won't drive back here again tonight?"

"No, I won't. If I see him on the way out I'll tell him, and if I don't I'll ask one of the other guys to let him know. To be honest, there are so many people staying, he'll hardly miss me."

"I wish things were as easy for me ..." Connie glanced over towards Martina and saw she was engrossed in conversation now with another girl. Then she saw Patrick grinning over at her and William and she beckoned him over.

"I'm not coming back with you and Martina in Emmet's car," she said. "I don't want to go into details, but Emmet and I have had a serious row and William is going to drive me home now." When she saw the look of confusion on Patrick's face, she said, "It's not how it looks. I'm not using the row to go off with somebody else. I'll just say that Emmet has behaved so badly tonight that I can't be anywhere near him ever again."

Patrick nodded. "Grand," he said. "It's your own business. Whatever suits you."

"Will you let Martina know? I don't want to have to explain it again."

"I'll go and tell her now," Patrick said.

They went into the kitchen and could see Jim standing by the window, chatting to the two sisters. William went over to him and, after only a brief few words, they shook hands and he came straight back over to her.

"No problem," he said, as they went towards the door. "Jim was fine. I'll catch up with him again over the next few days."

He held the door open for her and they went out into the cool night air.

"I'm really sorry for dragging you away from the party," she said as they went down the steps. "It's not even twelve o'clock yet."

"I don't mind in the slightest," he said. "I'd rather be with you than be in there with anyone else. I'm just sorry about the circumstances, and I think it's best if we get off now before your friend Emmet comes back." They were heading down to the parking area when William caught her hand and squeezed it. "You don't need to feel so bad – look, we're not the only ones leaving." He gestured towards a car which had the interior light on.

Connie looked to where he was pointing and, just as her gaze fixed on the car, the car engine roared up and headlights came on full, blinding them.

Connie's heart lurched. "It's Emmet!" she said, trying to shield her eyes with her hand. "I'm positive that's his car."

The car suddenly reversed with a screech and then it quickly turned and sped off out of the courtyard and through the entrance to the front of the house. They stood listening as it rattled off down the gravelled driveway towards the tall gates.

"Are you sure it was him?" William asked.

"Yes," Connie said. "That's exactly where we parked."

"Well, at least you don't need to worry about seeing him again tonight." He tucked her arm through his. "I'm parked around at the front of the house."

They had just gone a few steps when Connie halted. When he looked at her, she said, "I don't believe it ... I forgot ..." She put her hand up to her mouth and then gave a deep sigh. "Patrick and Martina – they won't have a lift home."

William looked at her. "Do you want me to go back in and offer them a lift?"

It was the very last thing she wanted: to have to sit in the car while Martina interrogated her as to what had happened between herself and Emmet. She didn't want to have to relive the awful scenario down at the tennis court again. And she knew that no matter what she told Martina, she would be convinced that he had gone off in a huff because Connie had dumped him for William Fitzgerald.

William was standing, waiting for an answer.

She knew that no matter how awkward it was for her, the decent thing had to be done. She couldn't leave them stranded there, as she nearly had been herself.

"Yes," she sighed. "I'd be really grateful if you did."

Chapter 9

Kate Devine brought the plate of toast to the table. "You're very quiet – did you not have a good night at the party?"

"It was fine," Connie said, reaching for a piece of toast. "I'm just a bit tired."

Kate was determined to be brighter today and make it up to Connie for reacting so badly about the results. She had promised Seán she would accept the situation, and would do all she could to help Connie. "I suppose you're wishing you'd left the party an hour earlier and had a better sleep, what with going into the shop this morning?" Her tone was light-hearted and casual now.

Connie took a sip of her tea. "I'll be grand," she said. "I can have an early night tonight." Then, she looked directly at her mother. "I didn't expect you to be going into work, with you not being well last night. Daddy said you were going to take a few days off work."

"I changed my mind. I had a good rest and I'm feeling a bit better now. I rang into the ward early this morning and said I would be in around ten o'clock and they were fine with that." She looked at Connie, and then she said in a quiet tone, "I had a heavy period last night, so I think that didn't help yesterday morning ... you know, when you got your results. I wasn't feeling the best – it's

77

always the same the day before it's due." Her voice faltered. "I'm sorry about the way I was. I should have said how well you've done in your exams. When I look at all the doctors in the hospital doing their rounds, and everyone so respectful of them – to think that one day you will be the same as them ... I should have said I was really proud of you, because I am."

As Connie looked at her mother, her eyes suddenly filled with tears. "Thanks, Mam, that's nice to hear."

Kate put her cup down and moved to put her arms around her daughter. She kissed her on the forehead. "I'm very sorry, Connie. It's just that I'll miss you so much, but I know we'll manage. We'll get used to it, and then we'll all be so proud and celebrating when you've qualified." She just stopped herself from adding, 'and come back home to Ireland'.

"And I will miss everyone too," Connie said. "But I'll be back home often and the time will go by quicker than we think."

As she walked to Eileen's Flower Shop, Connie was glad to be working and out of the house so she could think things over. She felt guilty about not telling her mother about what had happened at the party, and how she had not travelled home with Emmet. It was just the wrong time when they were getting ready for work, and she didn't want to upset her mother any further.

After William had dropped her off at the end of the road the previous night, she had hurried to bed but had lain awake until it was practically daylight. Never before had so much happened to her in twenty-four hours. From the excitement of meeting up again with William Fitzgerald to the dreadful ending of the night with Emmet.

And then all the awkwardness with Martina and Patrick on the way home. Patrick had sat in the front with William while Martina tried to unravel the reason for Emmet's quick disappearance.

"It doesn't make sense," Martina said in a low voice, so the boys couldn't hear. "Why would he drive off without telling us? If William hadn't been there, we would all have been stranded in that old house all night."

"We had a row – didn't Patrick tell you?" Connie said, feeling her stomach churn at the memory of it.

"Yes, he did – but what did you row about?"

"He behaved really badly."

"What do you mean?"

"He had drunk too much and then he turned very awkward with me when we were down at the pool."

Martina had leaned in closer to her. "Well, I don't mean to speak out of turn, but we all know he was annoyed at you for going off with William at the party. He was looking everywhere for you."

"We didn't go off anywhere," Connie whispered back. "I was just talking to him at the top of the stairs. And that's not the reason we argued – there was a lot more to it than that." She shook her head. "I really don't want to talk about it now."

Martina folded her arms over her chest. "Please yourself!" she snapped. "But if we hadn't got a lift home, my mother would have killed me."

Lying in bed later, Connie had gone over the events of the night again and again, trying to make sense of the way things had turned out. Trying to see what her part in it all was – whether she had been responsible for triggering Emmet's terrifying behaviour. Had seeing her kissing another lad made him feel so humiliated that he couldn't control himself – or had he been trying to punish her?

Next morning, as she got washed and dressed and ready for work, she still didn't know.

After they had dropped Patrick and then Martina off, she had spent an hour in the car alone with William, going over what had happened. He was adamant that nothing she did had given Emmet the excuse or the right to hurt and sexually assault her in retaliation.

"That's exactly what it is," William had said. "There is no other way of looking at it. If you decided to prosecute him, legally you would have a case."

The thought of something as serious as a court case terrified her. "I really don't want to do anything like that," Connie had said. "I did manage to stop him – and he did apologise in a way ..."

"Maybe you were lucky, because he had been drinking. What if he had done that to another girl who wasn't able to fight him off?"

That unsettling thought had stayed in Connie's head. But, every so often, she had managed to stop dwelling on the incident, and let her mind focus back on the lovely parts of the evening with William

– and look forward to spending time together over the next few days.

The shop had an order in for wedding flowers for the following day, so the morning flew by with Eileen making up trailing bouquets of pink roses, gypsophila and freesias, while Connie served in the shop. When it was quiet, she went into the back of the shop to help make dozens of pink and white buttonholes for the guests.

When she went home for her lunch break, although she felt more tired than usual, she felt easier than she had earlier. Her father was out at work, so she had the house to herself. The night before had faded in her mind and, as she made herself a ham sandwich and poured a glass of milk, she wondered when she would hear from William again. She had told him he could ring the shop or call in, as Eileen was easy-going about it as long as she didn't take too long off work. She didn't give him her home phone number as she didn't want her mother finding out about them. Although her mother had put a brave face on things this morning, Connie did not want to risk upsetting her any further. And, if by any remote possibility the friendship between her and William developed into anything more serious when she moved to England, she could tell her mother down the line when things were all settled down.

She was just finishing the last quarter of her sandwich when she heard the front door opening, and her mother's voice calling out to check if Connie was home.

Connie called back, wondering at her mother's serious tone, and she felt a small stab of alarm as she listened to the sound of her mother's heels until she entered the kitchen.

Kate Devine came in and, without saying a word, took her navy nurse's coat off and hung it on the back of the chair opposite Connie's chair.

Then she sat down to face her.

"What happened last night?"

"What do you mean?"

"I want the whole truth, Connie," her mother said. "I have no time to play guessing-games. I have to be back at the ward at two o'clock." She clasped her hands together on the table. "As soon as I went into work this morning, I heard that Emmet Ferguson was brought into the Accident and Emergency department last night."

Connie's hands flew to cover her mouth. "Oh, my God!"

"One of the nurses in A&E said she was told that he crashed into a tractor on the road between Clara and Tullamore and, from what she heard, he was full of drink."

"And is he all right?"

"As far as I know he's broken some ribs and he's had to have an operation on his leg. It's bad enough, but it doesn't sound as though anything is going to kill him."

"Was anyone else hurt?"

"No, thank God. The tractor was parked at the side of the road and he drove into it. There was no one else in his car." Kate prodded her finger on the Formica table top. "Now, Connie, what I want to know is where were *you* when all this happened? You left here to go to a party with him, and you were supposed to have come back with him. Isn't that right?"

Her mother was angry and Connie knew she had every right to be. She went to speak, to explain, but her voice seemed to have disappeared. She cleared her throat.

"We had a falling-out at the party. He drove off on his own, and I had to get a lift home from someone else, along with Martina and Patrick." She looked up at her mother. "I didn't want to start telling you all about it this morning when we were getting ready for work. I had no idea about the crash."

Her mother slowly nodded her head. "What was the row about?"

Connie took a deep breath. "He's annoyed that I don't want to keep things going with him when I go to university." She shrugged. "I just don't have the same feelings for him as he has for me."

Kate's eyes narrowed. "And he took the huff and left you all stranded in Athlone over that?" She shook her head. "I have a feeling there is more to this than you're telling me, Connie."

"I didn't want to worry you ... but the row *was* about more than just that."

Kate waited in silence.

"We went a walk out in the garden, and he ..." Connie suddenly found it hard to breathe as she remembered it all again. "We were sitting chatting and he suddenly grabbed me and wouldn't let me go ..." She started to cry now. "He pinned me down on the bench and

81

... he really frightened me."

"Mother of God!" Kate put her hand out to cover her daughter's. "Did he do anything really serious? You can tell me. He didn't rape you or anything?"

She shook her head. "No ... he was trying to touch me, but I managed to get him off me before he could do anything else."

"And where was everybody else? Martina and the other lad?"

"They were back up in the house ..."

"And there were just the two of you in the garden – in the dark and late at night?"

"Loads of people were down in the garden all evening, but most of them had gone back into the house. There was another couple, who came running over when they heard me shouting."

"You went down to a garden in the dark with a lad on your own!" Kate made a noise of exasperation. "What were you thinking of, Connie? That was a ridiculous risk you took."

"Mam!" Connie said, her eyes wide and hurt. "Everyone was out in the garden at different times because it was a nice night, and some of them were messing about at the swimming pool. It was all good-natured and harmless. There was no-one around, apart from that couple, at that point, but I never thought for a minute that anything would happen."

"Were they all drinking at the party?" Kate asked.

Connie caught her breath. "Well, there was drink there. There's no party these days where people don't drink."

Her mother raised her eyes to the ceiling. "Don't tell me you had been drinking too? Were you drunk?"

"No, I wasn't drunk. I had a couple of Babychams, that's all." She felt guilty thinking of the punch but she daren't tell Kate about that.

"When you're not used to drink it can go to your head very easily. That's why I'm always warning you about it. Anything can happen when there's drink involved."

"Mam, I can't believe you're blaming me for what happened!"

"Now, I didn't say that, but it's perfectly obvious that Emmet had drunk too much when he crashed the car into a tractor." Her mother gave a huge sigh. "Well, thanks be to God he didn't hurt you and thank God you weren't in that car with him."

"I just want to forget all about it," Connie told her.

"It might not be that easy. I'll have to talk to your father about it." Kate rubbed her fingers over her chin, thinking. "I wonder if his parents know what happened. They're bound to have known you went with him to the party and they'll be asking questions about why he was on his own in the car."

Connie suddenly felt overwhelmed. She hadn't thought that other people might become involved. Up until she heard of the crash, she presumed that Emmet would have gone home to bed. In the morning, when he remembered what he had done, she was sure he would feel ashamed. She had been sure that he would not have spoken to anyone about what had happened between them at the party, and why he had driven away on his own. She realised now that him crashing the car and then being taken to hospital changed everything.

"I wonder if the Guards were involved in the accident," her mother said. "They are often called when there is a crash, and especially if the driver is drunk."

Connie stared out of the window into the garden.

There was silence for a few moments, and then the front doorbell suddenly rang, startling them both.

Kate got up to answer it and, as she did so, Connie felt grateful for the diversion. It was probably a neighbour who would hopefully keep her mother chatting, and then it would be time for them both to go back to work.

Although she could not make out what her mother was saying, she could hear her talking in a more formal tone than normal. The sort of voice she used when she was talking to the priest or the teachers in school. Connie's heart quickened.

After a while, her mother came back into the kitchen. "It's for you," she said, in a strained tone. "You have two visitors in the front room."

Connie moved her chair back and got to her feet. "Who is it?" she asked. Whoever it was, she could tell by her mother's face it was serious.

Her mother turned away, not making eye contact. "It's Martina and her mother. They called to the shop to see you and Mrs Sheridan told her you were here at the house. They came to let us know about Emmet in case you hadn't heard."

"That was good of them ..."

"Martina is in a state about it all," her mother said. "They're worried that the Guards will want to speak to you all."

Connie felt her legs suddenly weak. "I'll go and see them now. You need to get a cup of tea before going back to the hospital."

Her mother went over to stand by the sink, her back pressed against the cold white enamel and her arms folded. "I put them in the front room because I want to ask you something while we're on our own ... I don't want to look a fool in front of them."

Connie looked at her mother.

"Martina said the English lad who brought you home was called William Fitzgerald." She closed her eyes for a few seconds, as though steeling herself. "Is that the young lad from Ballygrace? Gabriel Fitzgerald's brother?"

There was a silence then Connie said, "Yes, I was going to tell you ..."

"Martina's mother said the reason that Emmet went off in a rage was because he caught you and the Fitzgerald lad canoodling together. Is that true?"

"I told you exactly why Emmet went off ... I told you what he did to me."

"Is it true about the Fitzgerald lad?"

"I was only chatting to him," Connie said.

She couldn't tell her mother any more details. If she confessed that they had kissed, the mood her mother was now in, she would take it as an indication that she had been making herself available to all and sundry. That her cheap behaviour was the cause of Emmet thinking he was entitled to a bit more than a lad she had only met that night.

"William recognised me at the party and came over to talk to me. He's a friend of the boy who had the party – their families have known each other for years. I didn't get a chance to tell you this morning and I was going to tell you about it tonight."

"It seems you were going to tell me a lot, Connie," her mother said. "But you didn't." She gave a long weary sigh. "The Fitzgeralds – Tara's in-laws. Of all people! You couldn't wait until you got over to England to get in with them. You had to do it before you even left ..."

Chapter 10

As Kate Devine walked from the hospital down towards the Kilbeggan Bridge she thought she could not remember a worse day. The only good thing was that it was almost over.

In the morning all the talk amongst the nurses and auxiliary staff on her ward had been about the Leaving Certificate results of their own children, nieces and nephews, friends and neighbours' children. Kate had been asked about Connie's results and then been showered with congratulations over Connie having got the grades to study medicine. Then, when they heard she was going to Manchester University, she had been asked how Connie felt about going to England – and then about how she and Seán felt about Connie going to England. It had, she thought, been a morning of interrogation.

And then the talk had shifted to Emmet Ferguson and the crash, as most of the staff knew his family because of their furniture business in the town. The operation on his leg had gone fine, and his ribs had been strapped up. All going well, he would be back to full health in the next month or so. And Kate had been grateful to get through her shift without anything being said about Connie having gone to the party with him.

As she walked towards the house, Kate wondered how she and

85

Connie were going to get through the next few weeks until she left home. It was her own fault, of course, for not being able to hide her disappointment about Connie going to Manchester. But, she had listened to Seán and then she had talked herself around into accepting it. To have this situation with Emmet Ferguson and William Fitzgerald within twenty-four hours was just too, too much. And it wasn't going to just fizzle out, because she or Connie would have to explain it all to Seán tonight, because he would no doubt hear it from someone else in the town.

Where she would find the strength and the trust again in Connie to get over this, she just did not know. Then, just as she should have taken the turn down their road, she decided to keep walking. She walked over the bridge and across the road and then she kept walking until she came to the junction for Harbour Street.

She turned down and found herself walking straight towards the church. Although she felt her recent Novenas had been ignored, she could not let it get in the way of her deep faith. She told herself that often prayers are unanswered for a reason, and that she would just have to wait and see what God had in store for them all.

The church was empty apart from two other people who were kneeling in prayer, one at the back of the church and one at the small side altar. Not wanting to get into conversation with anyone, Kate went halfway up the main aisle, genuflected and then went into one of the varnished pews. She put her handbag down on the floor in front of the kneeler, and then she knelt down. She felt in her coat pocket for her pearl rosary beads and then she held the cross in her right hand and entwined the beads around her the fingers of her left hand. She closed her eyes, and then moved the cross to bless herself – touching her forehead then the middle of her chest and either side of her breast bone. Then, unsure exactly how to communicate her silent prayers about Connie, she started off with three silent decades of the Rosary to put her in the right frame of mind. The frame of mind that would make her feel that God would lift – or at least lighten – the burden of worry on her shoulders.

When she had finished, she felt lighter and easier. She felt she had cleared her mind enough now to be able to talk to God and state clearly in her mind what she was praying for. She took a deep, restorative breath, opened her eyes to look up to the altar and then let her gaze move around to the other statues. She then whispered in a barely audible voice the 'Memorare' prayer to Our Lady. She felt, as a mother who had suffered herself, the Blessed Virgin would understand her worries more than any man.

Each line she whispered slowly, emphasising certain phrases that she felt were more important – the way she would talk to someone who she trusted and who understood how she felt.

Remember, O most gracious Virgin Mary, that never was it known that anyone who fled to thy protection, implored thy help, or sought thy intercession was left unaided. Inspired with this confidence, I fly to thee, O Virgin of Virgins, my Mother; to thee do I come; before thee I stand, sinful and sorrowful. O Mother of the Word Incarnate, despise not my petitions, but in thy mercy hear and answer me. Amen.

She finished her prayer and, as she lifted her eyes once again to the altar, she felt a wave of sadness envelop her. If only she actually had someone who understood. Seán was good at listening – as good as any man could be, and he tried to advise her. But he often ended up confused and frustrated because he did not understand all the things, big and small, that mattered so deeply to her. She needed another woman who understood those things, someone who she could trust not to gossip behind her back. It had been so different when she was younger – then she hadn't needed anyone outside the family. Her mother and her elder sister Maeve had been her closest confidantes and the keepers of all her secrets and worries. They all thought about things the exact same way, they understood things without even speaking. If they were out and in a crowd and something happened or someone said something, they only had to catch each other's eye and they all knew what the others were thinking. Then, in two short years, all the supports she relied on had suddenly been taken from under her. Maeve got a new job in a travel agent's in Dublin, and within a year she had met and married an American, and then moved out to Boston with him. The following year Kate married Seán and, when she was expecting Ollie, her mother had a sudden heart attack and died.

Her father had lived another ten years and, although she loved him and helped look after him, life was never the same again without her mother and sister. She had friends she saw at church and other nurses she went on staff nights out with, but she never had the same female closeness again.

When she began seeing Seán, she had thought that she might become friends with his sisters and half-sisters, but they turned out to be very different from him. He was quiet and easy-going while his sisters were much more ambitious and opinionated – the sort Kate felt she had nothing at all in common with.

She moved from her kneeling position now to sit on the wooden bench and, as she did so, she became conscious of a figure coming towards her from the front of the church. She bent back down to retrieve her handbag, and let whoever it was go past.

"Mrs Devine – Connie's mother?"

Kate looked up. She saw a woman, of a similar age – and vaguely familiar – standing at the end of the pew in front, smiling at her. It suddenly hit her who it was, and she felt her heart speed up.

"Mrs Foley," she said, smiling back. "How are you?"

Mrs Foley put her hand on the pew as though to steady herself. "Ah, well ..." She gave a little sigh. "You know how it is ... these things don't get easier."

Kate desperately tried to think of something to say. "I'm sure it's still very hard on you all."

"Life, as they say, has to go on ... especially when you have younger ones. I heard Connie did very well in her Leaving Certificate. And did I hear that she's going to study medicine?"

"Yes," Kate said. "Over in England."

"Isn't that great news? You must all be very proud of her. She was always a great girl for studying and a lovely friend to Noreen. She visited her regularly when she was in hospital – and even went up to the hospital in Dublin when she got very sick." She looked towards the altar for a few moments then turned back to Kate, her eyes moist. "I'd say you're in here saying your prayer of thanks for your great news?"

Kate nodded without saying anything.

"Of course you'll miss her," Mrs Foley said. "But travelling abroad for university or for work is common enough nowadays." She smiled again. "It always was. I remember when your sister Maeve went to America. I was in Maeve's class in school."

"You were, of course."

"Well, at least Connie will only be in England. It's an awful lot closer than America. You'll get to see her often. I have a brother in Liverpool and we go over to him every year." She paused. "I'd give anything to have Noreen alive and well over in England or even America or anywhere else. Just to know she was out there living the life she was meant to have." She suddenly stopped and then closed her eyes, blinking back tears. "Don't mind me now ..."

Kate reached out and gently squeezed Mrs Foley's hand. "I wish there was something I could say ..."

"I know," she said, nodding. "It's difficult for people to say anything, but I appreciate the kind intentions ..." She pushed her handbag up to the crook of her arm. "Pass on my congratulations to Connie and say I wish her all the very best for her studies at university."

"I will, of course. She'll be delighted to hear I was speaking to you."

Kate listened to the sound of Mrs Foley's heels going back down the church aisle, and then she knelt back down and put her elbows on the ledge of the pew in front. She covered her face with her hands and let the tears she had been holding back trickle down through her fingers.

When her tears eventually dried up, she stayed there in the silence of the church, thinking and praying and then thinking again.

Chapter 11

Kate arrived back home half an hour later, more at peace with herself. As soon as she opened the front door she heard the laughter and the loud familiar voices. She gave a small inward sigh as she had hoped to catch her husband and daughter on their own.

The visitors were Seán's mother Tessie and her husband, Shay Flynn – Seán's stepfather. They lived only a few streets away and often called in when they were shopping in the town or just out for a stroll in the fine weather. They were both doing well considering their age, although Shay had problems with his knee and arthritis in other areas, and Tessie had recently been diagnosed with diabetes.

Kate had always been fond of them both, although recently Shay was irritating her more and more by constantly going on about Tara as though she was the lady of the manor. He kept everyone up to date with every little detail of Tara's family and work life over in England, as though she was the heart and soul of all the Flynn and Devine families. And when Shay had no great news to report about Stockport, he kept them up to date on Seán's younger sister Angela and her husband Aiden out at the Ballygrace House Hotel.

As Kate walked along the hallway, Shay called good-naturedly from the kitchen. "Here she comes now – the woman of the house!"

Kate took a deep breath and willed herself to smile. When she went into the kitchen, Seán, Tessie and Shay were seated at the table drinking mugs of tea and eating slices of apple tart. Seán immediately got up to get the china cup and saucer she used, so she could join them.

Kate pulled the chair out at the bottom of the table. "And how are you both?" she asked, taking her coat off. She put it on the back of the chair. "It's lovely outside now, isn't it?"

"Lovely, lovely, thank God," Shay said. "We've heard all the great news about Connie." He looked around at everyone with a proud, beaming smile. "Imagine us having a doctor in the family. Talk about brains. Isn't that something now?"

"Ah, we're delighted," Seán said, lifting the teapot to pour Kate's tea. "She did better than we could have hoped for." Then he put a slice of the apple tart on a plate and slid it across to her, saying, "My mother brought it."

"I baked it just before we came out," Tessie said. "It's still warm inside."

Kate smiled over at her mother-in-law. "Thanks," she said. "That was good of you."

"So," Shay said, "we'll have another excuse to go over to Manchester more often now, with Connie going to university there. Seán says he'll take the car over on the boat and we can go over with you."

Kate nodded and took a sip of her tea.

Tessie caught the tight look on her daughter-in-law's face. "We don't mean straight away, of course. Once she's had a chance to settle in."

"We haven't had time to think about it," Seán said, "but when Connie gets all the details from the university, we'll know better."

"And where will she be staying?" Shay asked. "I was just thinking that she can't be too far from Stockport, and the train goes in and out to Manchester every quarter of an hour or so during the day. Sure, she might be able to stay with Tara and Frank. They have plenty of room there and they're always delighted to help out."

Kate shook her head. "She won't need to stay with anybody. There should be student accommodation at the university."

Shay looked disappointed. "Well, no doubt she'll go out to them at the weekends. You won't need to worry about her being homesick anyway, when she has family so close."

Kate turned to Seán. "I've just remembered," she said. "I had a phone call I was supposed to make." She stood up, taking her teacup with her. "Don't mind me now, you just chat amongst yourselves."

She closed the door and went down the hallway to where the phone sat on a small low wooden table which had a gold-velvet-covered seat attached.

She took out the phone book and leafed through it until she found the page with the number she needed. She wasn't looking forward to the conversation, but it had to be done. She took a deep breath and then she put her finger in the dial.

Two minutes into her mother's phone call, Connie arrived home from the shop. She came in quietly and as she passed her mother, who was sitting at the phone table, she put a hand of greeting on her shoulder.

She was grateful when her mother put her hand on top of hers and squeezed it. Then, Kate covered the receiver and whispered, "Your granny and grandad are inside in the kitchen with your father."

Connie smiled at her, relieved that things seemed a bit easier. She could not bear another evening of arguments and feeling as if she were the source of all her mother's disappointments. The incident with Emmet and the news about his accident had hung over her today like a dark, heavy cloud. She kept waiting for someone to come into the shop or for the Guards to ring. Or even for someone to tell her that he was dead. She had felt slightly better after the visit from Martina and her mother, but when she went back to the shop she felt fragile and vulnerable – and guilty about it all. And yet she knew logically she was not to blame for what had happened. She had not poured drink down him, nor had she led him on in any way to make him think that she would have allowed him to do all the things he had tried to do to her.

In between working with the flowers and serving customers and sweeping up, her mind had constantly swung from the awful situation with Emmet to reliving each minute she had spent with

William Fitzgerald. He had been so different to any boy she had ever known – or imagined ever knowing. If she had written a list with all the things she wanted in a boyfriend, he would have ticked every single item on it. He had listened carefully as she spoke as though every word she said was important. He was interesting, funny and intelligent. He was also very physically attractive, and each time she remembered how he had kissed her, she found herself blushing. She had gone over it in her head a hundred times. Wondering if there was the remotest possibility that something might come of their meeting last night. He had given the impression that he felt the same way, but today she hardly dared to imagine that he would remember and act upon it.

But he had.

He had called to the flower shop that afternoon and asked her to go to the cinema that night. When he suggested that he pick her up at the house, her mother's tight, disapproving face had flown into her mind, and she had quickly said it would be easier to meet him in town. She did not like making up excuses why he couldn't come to the house, but the thought of her mother being rude or awkward with him was even worse.

Connie knew that when her mother found out she was planning to see William again it would exacerbate all the unreasonable feelings she had about Tara and everyone connected to her. Her mother might not speak to her at all when she knew she had arranged to go to the cinema with him, but Connie instinctively felt it would be wrong to give in to her. If she agreed not to see him, she knew it would set a precedent about not seeing him or anyone else her mother took against when she went over to England.

She had a reprieve at the moment with her mother on the phone. If her grandparents had got to know she had seen William last night, and brought the subject up, hopefully she could brush it aside before her mother came back to join them.

When she went into the kitchen, she immediately felt herself relax when she saw the happy smiles on her father's and grandparents' faces.

Shay and Tessie got to their feet to hug and congratulate her.

"A doctor in the family – who would believe it?" Shay's voice was so high with delight, it sounded as though he was singing.

"And you couldn't be going to a better university. Manchester has got to be one of the top ones in England if not in the whole world."

Connie knew that Shay didn't know one university from another – and was just glad she was going to Manchester because he was so familiar with all that area.

Tessie patted Connie's hand. "We must make sure and let Tara know. She'll be delighted to hear that you'll be living so close. Your mother said you would be booking into the student accommodation."

"Yes," Connie confirmed, "For my first year anyway."

Her father looked over at Shay. "Any news in the family?"

"We saw Assumpta and the children yesterday," Shay said, "and they were all in good form. And when Tara rang last week they were all fine in England too, but I'll be on to her about Connie's news tonight or tomorrow." He suddenly thought. "And I believe young William Fitzgerald is out at the hotel with Angela."

Connie's heart lurched. She looked across the table at her grandfather, waiting on him to say something to her now.

"They never knew he was coming until the day before," Shay went on. "He must have taken a figary and decided to come over on the spur of the moment."

"He usually calls out to the house," Tessie said. "So no doubt we'll see him."

It dawned on Connie how bad it would look if she said nothing and William told them about last night. She looked back at the door to check her mother wasn't around.

"I actually met William last night," she said. "I was at a party just outside Moate with some of my friends, and he was there."

Shay's eyebrows shot up in surprise. "Begod!" he said. "You and young Fitzgerald meeting up in Moate of all places!" He shook his head. "Who would believe it?"

Kate suddenly appeared at the door.

"Who would believe what?" she said, looking from one to the other.

Seán looked at his wife. "Shay was just saying about William Fitzgerald being over in Offaly, and then Connie said she met him last night. Isn't that a coincidence now?"

"It is," Kate said, her voice even. "She told me all about it this morning. And he was good enough to drive her and some of her

94

friends back home to Tullamore."

"Ah, he's a decent lad altogether," Shay said. "None of the uppity ways you get with some of the English types."

Connie wondered now at the change in her mother. Her whole attitude seemed somehow calmer and softer, and her voice sounded genuine.

"Isn't it a small world?" Tessie said.

Connie's mind flitted back to the party and she felt herself stiffen as she recalled the scenario with Emmet.

Shay looked over at Connie now. "And was he in good form? Young Master Fitzgerald?"

She felt herself colour up again. "He was grand ... although it was so long since I had last seen him it took me a few minutes to recognise him."

"He has got older-looking in the last few years," Tessie said. "I noticed that myself the last time he was over."

"Ah sure, it's the way they dress up in the smart clothes and everything, especially with him being a lawyer now. Tara was saying he's not up in Stockport as often. Seemingly he has to put in hours with different lawyers' offices in London, to get experience in the job before he can set up for himself."

"That's probably why he's not been over here recently," Tessie said.

Connie nodded. "He said he would be calling out to see you before he goes back home."

"Ah, he's a lovely young lad," Tessie said. "He's always so cheery and easy-going, you'd never think he came from an uppity family like the Fitzgeralds."

"The ould lady was always on her dignity," Shay commented, "although Gabriel, God rest his soul, was a nice, quiet chap who would always do you a good turn."

"Any other news in the town?" Kate asked.

"No," Shay said, leaning his folded arms on the table, "not a ha'porth. All quiet as far as we know."

"I hear we might have a new factory coming to Tullamore," Seán said.

Connie was relieved as the talk switched from William Fitzgerald to the safer subject of the factory and what hundreds of new jobs would do for the town.

Later, after she and her mother had seen her grandparents off at the door, Connie took a deep breath and said, "I need your advice."

Her mother's eyebrows lifted in question.

"I've been wondering what to do about Emmet ... I don't know whether I should go up to the hospital. In one way I feel I should, but I'm not sure ... after what happened."

Her mother guided her into the front sitting-room where they were less likely to be disturbed. "I was just waiting until we were on our own to tell you," Kate said quietly. "I rang his mother this afternoon."

Connie held her breath.

"He's doing okay," she said, "and he's probably getting out in the morning. They've strapped his ribs up and sorted out his leg, so he's not going to be doing much for the next few weeks. But his mother said he's lucky that it wasn't a lot more serious."

"What else did she say?" Connie asked.

"Just that he was stupid for drinking so much and that he's sorry he went off and left you all."

"Nothing about what happened between us?"

Her mother shook her head. "He's hardly likely to tell his mother that now, is he?"

There was a small silence.

"I don't know what to do ..."

"He mentioned something to his mother about driving off after you had a row."

"Oh, God!" Connie's stomach turned again at the thought of it all. "Did she seem annoyed with me?"

"No, no, she didn't say anything like that. She said it was very nice of me to phone, but she actually said very little about Emmet crashing the car because it's obvious he was drunk. I think the woman was embarrassed and didn't want to make any more of it."

"Is he in trouble with the Guards or anything like that?"

"They called out at the hospital, but when there was nobody else involved they let it go. His father is well known in the town and he's never been in any kind of trouble before, so the Guards probably went easy on him. His mother did say they were calling out to see the old farmer that owns the tractor Emmet hit. It seems he's been warned about abandoning it wherever he likes, and it was ridiculous to have it sitting at the side of the road with no lights to warn anyone driving."

"True ..." Connie said. There was silence for a few moments, and then she looked over at her mother. "I'm really sorry about all this ... the whole thing about the party."

Kate looked back at her. "Well, I'm sorry too. I know I was annoyed at you when I first heard about it all, and I jumped the gun a bit. Now I've had time to think it through, I know what happened wasn't your fault."

"I really didn't lead Emmet on about us, Mam," she said, a sob in her voice now. "I've known from the beginning that he's not right for me long-term. And when he called to the shop yesterday afternoon, I told him about me going to Manchester and when he said we would keep in touch and he would come over to visit me, I tried to be straight with him. I told him I wouldn't be home very often and that we couldn't predict what might happen for either of us in the future." She gave a shuddering breath. "The big mistake I made was agreeing to go to the party with him. I thought that if I saw him just a few more times it might be easier than suddenly breaking up with him."

"It's called 'letting him down gently' and it never works," her mother said, rolling her eyes. "Especially where lads are concerned. They just don't get it. I know that from when I was young myself."

Connie glanced at her mother, wondering if she was talking generally or talking about her own personal experiences with boyfriends. They had rarely talked about her as a young woman going out with her father, and it had never crossed her mind that her mother had gone out with anyone else before that.

"Were you ever in that situation yourself?" she asked.

"Yes," Kate said. "There was somebody I worked with in the hospital before I met your father. He was nice enough, and I went out with him a few times but he wasn't my type. Any time he asked me out I just said I was too busy, but he never took the hint, and eventually I just had to tell him straight. Even then he haunted me for a few months but thankfully he met someone else."

Since she seemed to be so understanding, Connie decided to take a chance. "I know you have your own reasons for not being happy about it," she said, "and I don't want to annoy or upset you, but William Fitzgerald called into the shop –"

"And no doubt asked you out," Kate interrupted.

Connie looked at her in trepidation. "He asked me to go to the cinema with him tonight ..." There was an awkward pause and, feeling that the response was going to be negative, she added, "He's only here for a couple of days." She watched as her mother slowly nodded her head. She couldn't tell if she was agreeing or still digesting the information. "Is it okay if I go?" she asked, her heart thumping now. "I half arranged to meet him outside the cinema, but I said I would ring him at the hotel if there was a problem and couldn't make it. As I said, he's going back to London in a few days ..."

"It has to be your decision, Connie." Kate's voice was a resigned sigh. "I don't want us falling out again. In a few weeks you're going to be living your own life in England and all the decisions will have to be your own."

"But, Mam, I just don't understand what the problem is. He's a lovely, polite fellow and you heard all the nice things Granny and Grandad said about him. Daddy likes him too ..."

Kate turned to look at her now with narrowed, worried eyes. "You don't get it about the Fitzgeralds, Connie. Do you?"

"Get what?"

"That he's only using you to pass the time while he's here. The truth is – lovely-looking though you are – William Fitzgerald is not looking for a girl like you."

"But we're only friends ... I don't know what you mean." Connie knew she had to play things carefully or they would be back to warring again – whether it was openly arguing or a cold, distant war. And, as her mother had pointed out, she was going away in a matter of weeks. She wanted to leave on good terms.

"You only have to listen to your grandad to know that the whole Flynn family are obsessed with Tara Flynn and how she married into the Fitzgeralds. They think that everyone from that class is the same as Gabriel, but they're not. He got to know Tara well because she was friends with his sister from when they were at school."

"Well, that's reasonable enough," Connie said. "That happens to a lot of people. Martina O'Leary's older brother is friends with Patrick."

"Sure, that's different altogether. They're from the same kind of background."

"But if Tara and Gabriel's sister were friends ..."

"It wasn't like that." Her mother shook her head. "I never knew her myself, but it seems that Madeleine Fitzgerald wasn't right ... she was in and out of hospital. She was mentally sick – obsessed with religion and that sort of thing. It was well known around the town. Tara was good with her, and she spent a lot of time up in Ballygrace House with the family and that's how she and Gabriel got together. He was grateful to her, no doubt, as a lot of the other local girls would have been nervous around someone who was having holy visions and hearing voices and all that sort of stuff." She gave a deep sigh. "It's all very sad when you think that Madeleine and the father were killed in a car accident, and of course that kind of double tragedy would have brought Tara and Gabriel even closer." She held her hands out. "So you can see that Tara didn't just meet him at a dance or anything – it wasn't just an ordinary boy meets girl story for them."

Connie nodded as though she agreed. She had heard parts of this story before, and although it hadn't been said outright, she knew her mother thought that Tara had conveniently inveigled her way into the Fitzgerald family and their upper-class world. She wanted to point out to her mother that if all went to plan, she, Connie, was going to be in the professional classes herself. William might be working as a lawyer, but she was going to be a fully qualified doctor. That, Connie thought, surely put them on the same social scale? But, for the time being, she knew it was wiser to keep those views to herself.

Instead she said, "It seemed to have been the right thing for Tara and Gabriel."

"It wasn't an easy ride for them," Kate went on. "From what I hear it took his mother a long time to accept Tara – if the old lady ever did accept her deep down. William was only a young boy at the time, and he grew very attached to Tara and was over here all the time when she lived in Ballygrace House. But he has been in London for years and lives a very different life now."

Connie shrugged. "I can see what you're saying, but me going to the pictures with William is nothing serious, Mam. And don't forget, I'm going to be mixing with all kinds when I go to Manchester University – and it would have been the same if I'd gone to Dublin. There are students from different places and backgrounds studying in all the universities."

"And that's fine," Kate said. "And you are going to be every bit as good as anyone else."

"William and I just got on well as friends ..." Her mind flitted back to the previous night, and she pictured again how relaxed and easy they were as they walked around the studio and how they had talked later in the car that night. "We just chatted and laughed about the things we all used to do when we were younger. It was completely harmless."

Her mother's hand reached out to tap the back of hers. "You can't fool me, Connie," she said quietly. "I can tell by the way your face just lit up when you were thinking about him that you feel more for him than just a friend."

There was a noise in the kitchen and then the sound of a chair being scraped back from the table.

"That will be your father in from the garden," Kate said in a low voice. "We don't need him to hear any of this. All I'm going to say is that it's up to you if you want to go out with William Fitzgerald tonight. But when he goes home, I'd advise you to leave it at that."

Connie stifled the wave of euphoria that rose inside her. This response was better than anything she could have hoped for. After all that had been said earlier, her mother – for some unfathomable reason – had done a complete turnaround. She was free to see William tonight and possibly the next few nights if he asked her.

Chapter 12

As Connie walked up the short incline towards the cinema, she saw William's car parked across from the entrance. He got out as soon as he saw her, waving a confident hand to catch her attention. He was wearing the same blue-velvet jacket from the night before, but with wine-coloured jeans and a T-shirt. She waved back, feeling slightly self-conscious as she negotiated the rough pavement in her high wedge shoes. She watched him as he locked the car and put the keys in his jacket pocket then strode towards her. When she saw the warm, familiar smile on his face, a feeling of relief flooded through her.

"You're looking very lovely," he said, taking in her long dark hair, pale grey embroidered smock and white jeans. When he reached her, he put a casual arm around her shoulders, drew her towards him and kissed her on the side of the head.

"You're looking very nice yourself," she said, grinning back at him. She knew by his manner that, despite her mother's misgivings and the drama of the night before, it was going to be okay.

"I checked what film is on tonight and it's *The Godfather*," he told her. "Is that okay with you?"

"Grand," she said, shrugging. "I've heard it's good."

They crossed the street over to the picture house, then William slowed to a halt.

"Before we go in and have to be quiet," he said, "I just want to check how things were for you at home."

"Do you mean about Emmet?"

"And how your mother is about you going to Manchester."

She quickly filled him in on both situations and told him about Shay and Tessie as well.

"I'll call out to see them tomorrow," he said. "I meant to go today, but something came up that I had to deal with, and I didn't manage to get into town."

Connie noticed that his face had suddenly become serious and she wondered what kind of problems could come up when he was on holiday in Ireland.

"I think you took Grandad by surprise on this occasion," she said, smiling.

William nodded. "I usually plan my trips over in advance and Shay is often at the hotel when I arrive. This time I did it on impulse to clear my head."

"I suppose your work can be stressful at times?"

He smiled at her, but something made her feel that he was distracted and somehow not as connected with her as he had been at the party. It struck her now that maybe he was seeing her in a different light than he had at the Fays' house.

If that was the case they now had to get through tonight as painlessly as possible. And Connie was determined that she would do it without any loss to her pride.

She looked at her watch now. "We'd better get a move on," she said, moving towards the cinema entrance, "or we might not get decent seats."

They got to the door and she turned back to him. "I'm paying for the tickets tonight. You did me a big favour last night. We would have been stranded without you."

"No – I invited you to come here tonight and I was only too delighted to take you home last night." He touched her hand. "I really enjoyed being with you at the party and I meant everything that I said to you."

As he looked into her eyes, Connie felt her heart lift again.

William guided her inside the door, then he went to the till and got the tickets while she stood to the side of the small shop.

When he came back, he asked, "Would you like a box of sweets or a mineral to take into the film?"

"Not just now, thanks," Connie said

"We could have an ice cream at the interval," he said.

"I'm buying," she said.

"We'll see," he said, smiling.

People started moving across the foyer, and then, with his hand on the small of her back, William led her inside the dimly lit auditorium. When her eyes adjusted to it, she could see it was around two-thirds full. He whispered that there were empty seats up towards the back, and she motioned to him to go ahead and she would follow. He stopped four rows from the back. When she nodded, he stood back to allow her to move in before him.

There was another couple at the far end of the row near the wall, and she went in only half a dozen or so seats so that they were not too close to them.

As the film credits came up, his arm moved around her shoulders and pulled her closer to him.

The film was much better than she had imagined. It had never appealed to her before, as she thought it was more a man's type of film, being all about the Mafia and gangsters and shooting.

But, at various points, Connie found her attention drifting off. And it was then that she wondered what it would be like if she was going out with William Fitzgerald, and seeing him every night like a real boyfriend. Doing ordinary things together like going to the cinema or going to dances.

Connie had been in this cinema many times with her friends. She had also been there on a number of occasions with different boys, including Emmet Ferguson. Each time, with each boy, she had at some point during the film begun to feel uncomfortable sitting so close to him. And on almost every occasion she knew it would probably be the last time she would see the boy

Most of her friends seemed happy enough to go out with a local lad on a few dates, and then continue seeing him.

There were always occasional romances that fizzled out, ones that broke up when one side of the couple let the other down or 'did the dirty' on them. There were also the quiet 'shotgun weddings' that caught people by surprise. But most of the couples took the traditional route. The route, Connie guessed, that would soon be taken by her brother Ollie and his girlfriend, Brid, and in a year or two she wouldn't be surprised to hear news about Martina and Patrick.

But, Connie already knew that it wasn't going to happen to her. So far she had not met the right person locally – or anyone who had come close to being the right person.

She was still only eighteen and had plenty of time to meet someone when she was at university or afterwards. She hadn't thought she might be looking for someone different until last night when William Fitzgerald had suddenly come back into her life. It would only be for the few days, she knew, but it was still lovely and being with him made her feel good about herself, and all the exciting things that might happen in the future.

Then, as if he had read her thoughts, he turned towards her and bent his head to kiss her as he had done the night before. At first the kiss was slow, but as it went on it became more passionate. When Connie felt his tongue in her mouth, an excitement started to build up in the pit of her stomach and became so intense she had to stop herself from pulling him closer to her.

Eventually, the kisses slowed down and after a while they parted. She settled back into the chair, William holding her hand tightly between his. And as the film flickered on the screen she began to wonder what would have happened if they were alone and not in public view in the cinema.

She knew she would be too terrified to get involved sexually with someone so soon – and she guessed he was the same.

But still, she could not help imagining how things would be if they continued to see each other when she moved over to England. It was not beyond the realms of possibility.

If, by some amazing miracle, he did want to keep on seeing her, Connie knew that they would just have to talk and work these things out. She was not naïve. She knew perfectly well what could happen if she did not have her mother and the Parish Priest and the people back home watching her. If she and William – or some other boy she felt like this about – suddenly let things go beyond their control. She had never had to consider this before but, since meeting William and feeling all the physical things she was now experiencing, she now knew how easily things could happen.

At the interval, William turned to her and said in a low voice, "I'm awfully sorry, Connie, but I've just remembered something, and I'm going to have to go out to the phone box to make a quick call back to London. Will you be all right until I come back?"

"Of course I will," she said. "The nearest one is in O'Connor Square. Do you know where it is?"

"Yes," he said, nodding and reaching for his jacket. "I promise I'll only be five minutes."

She waited five minutes and then she went to join the queue for the ice-cream vendor, who was standing in front of the stage. A short while later she came back to her seat with two large cones. William couldn't argue with her about paying, when she had already bought them.

Ten minutes came and went as people moved in and out of the auditorium, going to the toilets or shop. Two lads Connie knew spoke to her on their way back to their seats. One commented on what a good film it was and then the other made a joke about her eating two ice creams. She was relieved that neither knew her well enough to mention Emmet or ask her about William Fitzgerald.

Connie noticed the ice-creams were beginning to melt, so she ate one of them quickly. Then, shortly afterwards, William's cone began to drip ice cream and raspberry sauce down her hand and onto the sleeve of her grey smock-top. She dabbed at it with the damp serviettes around the cones and then with her free hand went into her bag for the small packet of tissues she always carried.

She checked her watch and wondered what on earth could be keeping William on the phone so long. Then she saw the usherette coming up the steps and she moved out of her seat to catch her. As she did so, some of the ice cream dripped down her hand and ran onto her jeans. She explained about the ice cream, feeling very embarrassed, and the girl kindly took the sodden cone and tissues from her.

She sat back down, her hands damp and sticky, and tried to discreetly clean herself up. She wondered if anyone had noticed, and felt both self-conscious and foolish.

The cinema lights dimmed and the film came back on. She sat staring at Al Pacino on the screen, wondering if it were possible that William Fitzgerald had left her on her own and was not coming back.

Then, just as she was deciding what she should do, she saw a figure coming up the steps towards her. Relief flooded her but was quickly replaced by a feeling of confusion and annoyance.

"I am so, so sorry," he whispered, sliding into the seat beside her. "The first phone box wasn't working and then when I found another one down in Church Street it wouldn't take the coins."

"Was it that important?" she whispered back. "Couldn't you have waited until later?"

He leaned closer to her now, so she could feel his sweet breath on her cheek. It was a smell of mint mixed with something else.

"I'm really sorry," he said again, "but it was a work thing and it couldn't wait until tomorrow."

She knew she should leave it alone, and that he had apologised and given a reasonable explanation but she couldn't help herself.

"*Work*?" she repeated in an incredulous tone. "At this time of night?"

To her own ears she suddenly sounded like her mother when she was quizzing her or the boys. She knew she had to stop and give him the benefit of the doubt. Things sometimes happened like that, where one thing goes wrong and then another. And maybe William had to deal with work things at night. But, something just didn't feel quite right about it all.

"I'll explain later," he said.

And then it suddenly dawned on her why she felt so uneasy. She had smelled alcohol on his breath. Brandy or whiskey or something sweetish like that. Had he lied to her about making the phone call and gone into a bar for a drink? Why on earth would he do such a thing?

"William," she whispered, "why did I ..." But she didn't know how to put her question.

"Why did you what?" he said softly.

Then, she heard someone from behind telling them to "Shush and let us watch the feckin' film!" and they both went silent. But this time there were no knowing glances at each other or silent laughter at the incident, as there would have been before he had gone out to make the phone call.

They went back to watching the film and after a while Connie felt William's hand reaching for hers again. When she looked at him, he was staring at her with great seriousness.

"I'm very sorry," he whispered quietly to her. "I'll explain about it later."

She suddenly felt everything was going to be okay. She smiled reassuringly at him and whispered back, "It's okay."

When the film ended people started to move out.

"If you don't mind, we'll let them out first," William said. He indicated towards the couple who had been seated further along the row and were moving towards them.

They stood and let them pass, and then they sat down again.

"What on earth happened?" she asked. "I thought you had run out on me."

He looked back at her. "I'd never do that to you," he said. "It was just one of those awful situations where everything goes wrong. All the time I was racing from one duff phone box to another I was thinking of you back in the cinema."

She raised her eyes to the black cinema ceiling. "Holding the two, melting ice creams …"

"Oh, no!" he said. "Tell me you're joking!"

"I'm not."

He closed his eyes and shook his head. "Those phones! Eventually, I had to ask someone if they knew where a third phone box was likely to be, and they told me to go into one of the bars." He shrugged. "There was someone on it, and while I was waiting, the barman came over and said to me that it wasn't a public phone, it was only for customers." He shook his head. "So of course, then I had to buy a drink. More time wasted."

Connie felt her shoulders suddenly relax, and she was grateful that she hadn't made the remark that was on the tip of her tongue about smelling alcohol when he returned.

"All I can say again is that I'm really sorry I spoiled the night for you," William said. "And I know I need to make it up to you."

"Forget about it," Connie said. "These things happen." She didn't want to make him feel any worse after all the running around he had to do, plus she could tell he was embarrassed. She herself felt much better about it all now, and had been reassured with his explanations.

Most people had gone now, so they gathered their belongings and headed out.

"The days are flying by now," he said as they walked towards his car. "I don't know if you have any plans for tomorrow night? If you're free, I wondered if you and maybe Ollie and Terry would like to come out to the hotel for a meal? It would be nice to catch up with the two lads again."

Connie suddenly felt flustered at his suggestion – and a little out of her depth. "I'm not sure," she said. "I think Ollie will be out with his girlfriend and Terry usually goes out with the lads on a Saturday night ..."

She could just imagine her mother's reaction if she said she was going out for a meal to the hotel. It just wasn't the sort of thing that their family did unless it was a special occasion. She just couldn't really imagine her mother and father sitting over a candle-lit meal on their own, and her two brothers never went for meals unless it was a sports dinner or a Christmas night out.

Her mother would be annoyed at the fact she was seeing William again, without rubbing salt into the wound by going out to the hotel. It also crossed her mind that it would be more public being with him in a restaurant, and she might run into people who knew Emmet. No, she decided, she wouldn't go. She had taken a chance with the cinema tonight, but there was no point in pushing her luck.

"No problem," he said, seeing her hesitation. "It was just an idea. Is there anywhere else you'd like to go?"

Connie tried to think. There was the usual Saturday-night dancing in Tullamore Rugby Club – or even Portlaoise or Kildare – but people usually went to those in groups and she worried that they might stand out if they went on their own. Plus – there was the usual problem of bumping into people who knew Emmet.

She shrugged. "I don't really fancy anywhere local to be honest."

"Okay," he said. "What time do you finish in the shop tomorrow?"

"I'm finished around four," she told him. "We finish early on a Saturday."

"How about Dublin? We could just drive up in the car and have a walk around and have something to eat. We could find a bar with music or something like that. There are always things going on in Dublin."

She thought for a few moments. She would love to go to Dublin. She rarely got the chance to go there and she had never been for a night out in the city.

"Okay," she said. "That sounds really good."

"If you don't mind," he said, "I have a university friend, Malcolm McKenzie, who lives near Stephen's Green, and I haven't had the chance to see him in the last couple of years. He was away travelling for a while and I'd love to hear how he got on. Maybe we could call in?"

"That's fine by me," Connie said.

"I'll ring beforehand," William said, "and make sure he's there."

Chapter 13

Stockport

Tara, still in her dressing-gown, brought the two plates of poached eggs to the table, placing one in front of Frank and the other at her own chair.

"Thanks, darling," Frank said, touching her hand.

"You are welcome, Mr Kennedy." She wound her arm around his neck and then leaned forward to kiss him on the lips. As she did so her long, curly red hair fell like a curtain over her shoulder. Then, as Frank's grip tightened around her waist, she had to pull away. "The toast will burn," she said, "and the eggs will get cold."

"Excuses, excuses," he laughed.

"We don't often have breakfast together in the middle of the week," she said, "and if we don't get started, your youngest son, who is in the next room in his playpen with a pile of building bricks, might decide to join us at any minute." She glanced around to look through the open door where fifteen-month-old Leo was gurgling happily away to himself. Frank had already dropped Noel down to his morning playgroup in a local church hall.

"True," Frank said, raising his eyebrows. "Let's just say we're on a promise for later today."

While Tara was at the worktop, Frank went over to the record player and put on an easy-listening jazz record that they both liked.

Tara came back to the table a minute later carrying the silver rack filled with slices of toast made from one of Bridget's soda-bread loaves, and a pot of coffee. Frank filled the two mugs and then they both took toast and buttered it and started on the eggs.

"It's the loveliest morning," Tara said, looking out of the window overlooking the side garden, which was filled with roses and a variety of flowering bushes.

"And even lovelier not rushing into work for a change," he said. "I wish I could start the day like this every morning. Good coffee, a home-cooked breakfast and a beautiful woman sitting across from me."

"God bless your ageing eyes," she sighed. "Because I'm certainly not the young girl you first met all those years ago."

"You are to me, Tara," Frank said, "and you always will be. Your lovely red hair and your amazing eyes have never changed."

"Oh, there are a few silver threads among the gold if you look closely. My hairdresser has been pointing them out recently. She says I'll have to start colouring them soon."

Frank ran his hands through his hair and sighed. "I don't think there would be any point in colouring mine, do you? The grey is definitely winning the race here."

"The trials of marrying an older man," she laughed. Then she covered his hand with hers. "Aren't we lucky that's all we have to worry about? When we think of all the young people we have lost, who never had a chance to find a silver hair."

"I count my blessings every day – when I look at that little fellow over there, and think of Noel running around at the playgroup. You and the boys are the things I could only have dreamed of, and I often think that as I'm moving around between the office and the building sites."

"Well, I certainly appreciate being here every single morning," Tara said. "It's amazing how things change, isn't it? I never imagined that I would ever consider giving up fulltime work, and yet, here I am, a contented stay-at-home mother now. Well, apart from dropping into the Cale Green Hotel every other day to see that things are running okay and to check the books, but that's hardly hard work."

Tara had owned the small Cale Green Hotel for a few years now, but with an excellent manager in place and good staff, it almost ran itself. They had a regular clientele of commercial travellers and businessmen who travelled up and down the country, along with conferences and regular local functions such as weddings and christenings.

Both she and Frank were also part of a group who owned the much bigger, grander Grosvenor Hotel in a busier part of Stockport. Tara had taken on the position of manager for the first few years, when the group was extending and refurbishing the hotel. Again, on her decision to stay at home with four-year-old Noel and fifteen-month-old Leo, a new manager had been found to take her place.

"I'm delighted you're home too," Frank said. "It makes much more sense than you killing yourself to be out of the house every morning for the Grosvenor, and then worrying about the two boys all day. Plus, you were exhausted trying to make up the time with them every night." He squeezed her hand. "I love knowing you're at home with them and being here when I arrive home every day. We would never have managed when we moved in here last year if both of us had been working. Can you imagine what it would have been like with the workmen in, putting in new bathrooms and kitchen and fitted wardrobes? Painting and decorating the boys' rooms?"

"It worked out well," Tara said. "Although we had no idea when we were doing this up that the sale of your house in Alderley Edge would fall through."

"I'm glad that particular nightmare is over. Paying mortgages on two houses for nearly a year! I am just so grateful that it's all gone through this time." He checked his watch. "I should be signing the deeds over to Mr Pickford in two hours' time."

Tara joined her hands as though in prayer. "Thank God," she said. "That will be a big weight off both our minds." She took a sip of her coffee. "I still feel bad about it. We could have pulled out of this house and stayed in Alderley Edge. There wasn't a single thing wrong with it."

"Forget about it, Tara. This is the house we both wanted for us and the boys. It's the one we chose together for our little family. It's exactly right for us at this stage in our lives."

Whilst this new house was probably as big as Frank's house, the layout of it seemed cosier and more family-orientated. Similar in that it was a Mock-Tudor style which they both liked – white with black beams both inside and out. It had five bedrooms and three bathrooms – some upstairs, some downstairs – and it had a big, traditional farmhouse-style kitchen with an L-shaped area at the bottom which held the big old pine table in front of a cosy fireplace that guests seemed to naturally gravitate towards.

"Sometimes I feel guilty because it was me who saw it advertised," she said. "And when I called into Pickfords to look at a brochure, I had no notion of us buying it and moving to Bramhall. I was really only being nosey because I knew the house and had always admired it."

Frank laughed. "Well, look where being nosey got you!"

"Ah, don't, Frank, I'm not laughing. In all seriousness, I wasn't thinking for a minute of moving. Your house was amazing and I was really content in it."

"Well, I wasn't," he said. "Alderley Edge was great, but it was too far out from Stockport and Bridget and Fred and the Cale Green, and we didn't need a garden so big we could lose the boys in it. To be honest, I bought it because it made me feel successful at a point in my life where nothing was going right. I had money but I wasn't content in myself. But you know all that …"

"It wasn't a great time for either of us," she said quietly, "but thank God that time has passed."

"We're much handier here in Bramhall, and we don't need that huge garden when we have Bramall Park within a few minutes' walk."

Tara nodded, but the money they had lost with the sale falling through had preyed on her mind. And in that year, a sudden slump in house prices had made the house worth even less, and she knew that Frank had actually dropped the asking price to rock bottom to make sure it sold this time around and to get rid of the mortgage on it. He wasn't saying much, but she knew he had lost a substantial amount of money.

He leaned across the table now and took her hand, entwining his fingers through hers. "I wanted us to have a place that was completely our own – a place that had no history of other people. After all these years, I think we deserve a fresh start, whatever it costs. Don't you?"

Tara looked at him and then she closed her eyes and nodded. "You're right."

Today was a day to be happy about the house sale going through, and to be grateful for all the good things in their lives. They had both been through so much loss and pain in different ways, and they had both worked hard for years for every penny they had earned. She knew it behoved them both to enjoy and share this beautiful new family house.

He waved his hand around the large, airy kitchen. "This house feels just right for us, and we have plenty of room for people coming over from Ireland or when young William comes up from London. I honestly could not be happier."

"The house sale will make things easier with financing the new estate as well," she said. "The profit from the house will sort out any shortage there."

"Stop worrying about it," he told her. "Everything has worked out fine. Having the new investor who has come on board has made all the difference there." He reached over for another piece of toast, which he then spread with marmalade.

They heard a noise and then an insistent voice calling, "*Ma-ma-ma!*" then "*Da-Da-Da!*" Then "*Na-na-na!*"

They looked at each other and then started to laugh. The 'Na-na-na' part was his newest word and meant he was ready for his porridge with banana. So far, he was in a good routine with both eating and sleeping, and Tara was grateful that he still had a late-morning nap and then one in the afternoon before they went to pick up Noel from his playgroup.

Frank took a quick bite of his toast then stood up. "I'll get him, I've still got half an hour, so I've time to feed him if you want to go and have your shower."

Tara finished her coffee. "That would be great," she said. "We have an important meeting this afternoon, so we have to look our best."

Frank raised his eyebrows in query. "You didn't mention any meeting ..."

She laughed. "The mother and toddler group."

Tara ran out to the hallway to catch the phone before the ringing

114

woke Leo from his morning nap.

She smiled when she heard the voice on the other end. "Angela! I was just thinking about you this morning and was going to give you a ring later, after check-out time."

Although she found it comforting to know that Ballygrace House was still in the hands of her own family, Tara still found it strange to picture it now as a small hotel. Apart from one very dark incident when she was a naïve, unsuspecting young woman, she had mainly happy memories of the house.

She had first entered the old house as a school friend of Madeleine Fitzgerald when the family owned it, and then years later she had lived there very happily with the son, Gabriel Fitzgerald, when she was a young bride. Tragically, her marriage was cut short when Gabriel suddenly died. A lot of water had passed under the bridge since then – some of it very troubled, like when her brother Joe the priest was killed in an accident – but on the whole Tara knew her life was very good compared to others'. Work had always been her salvation through all the difficult times, and she was well known in Stockport as a successful businesswoman. She still had close ties with her family in Offaly and had a solid network of friends and colleagues in Stockport that she could rely on, especially her closest and dearest friend, Bridget Roberts. But, more importantly, Tara knew she had been especially lucky to have found love and marriage again with Irish businessman Frank Kennedy. And she counted her blessings every day when she looked at their two boys.

They'd had more than their share of ups and downs in the beginning with Frank being older than her and having been married before — but her faith in Frank was now unshakeable. The longer they were together, the more she realised how alike they were in all the things that mattered in life.

"We have a quiet spell," Angela told her. "We had a coachload on their way to Kerry and they all checked out before eleven, so I thought they could manage the desk without me."

"Lovely to hear from you," Tara said. "Any news out in Ballygrace?"

"Yes," Angela said. "For a change I do have some news, unless you've already heard? It's about Connie."

"No, I haven't heard a thing," Tara said. "I haven't been speaking to Seán or Daddy. Is it about her Leaving Cert? I was just thinking that the results would be due out soon."

"It is," Angela said, "and it's really good news. She's got enough A's to study medicine at Manchester University."

Tara caught her breath. "Manchester University? Really?"

"Yes! Hasn't she done well?"

"My God! What a clever girl! Her marks must have been really high to study medicine. I am so delighted for her. Seán and Kate must be over the moon. When did you hear?"

"Well, I only heard this morning when Daddy cycled out to tell me. Seemingly, they've all been very quiet about it, because the results came out a few days ago. I knew of course they were due out, because it's all you hear about. I didn't want to phone to ask how she got on, just in case she hadn't got the results she was hoping for. You know what it's like ..."

"Of course," Tara said. "It can be awkward asking about exam results – you never know if someone has just missed getting the grades they need for a job or university – or even failed. But this is great news about Connie – the Devine family will be celebrating."

"Well, you would think so." Angela lowered her voice. "According to Daddy, Seán is delighted, but Kate has been very quiet about it. She's not happy about Connie going over to England – she had hoped she'd get into UCD but she didn't make the grade for that."

"Oh gosh, that's a pity! And how does Connie feel?"

"I think she's happy about it, and she told Daddy she picked Manchester so she would have you and Frank and the children nearby. From what he said, she's really excited about going over."

"That's great," Tara said. "And she knows she'll be welcome here anytime. We would be delighted to have her here when she's free. And Seán and Kate can come over and stay here any time they want to visit her. It's ages since they've been over."

"I'm sure they will," Angela said. "They're bound to miss her. Seán is always the one way, pleasant and easy-going, but you know Kate can be a bit odd. She rarely comes out to the hotel unless it's a function she's been invited to. She always says she's working shifts at the hospital and then has to catch up with things at home. But, to be honest, Tara, I've often seen her in Tullamore, and I'd swear she does her best to avoid me."

"Do you really think so?"

"I do," Angela said. "She's nice enough when you're talking to her, but you can just tell she's looking for an excuse to get away. She's always looking over your shoulder to catch someone else's eye so she doesn't have to spend any time with you." She sighed. "I don't know what any of us have ever done to make her act like that but, whatever it is, she's decided to keep her distance from us."

"It might be nothing to do with anyone – maybe she's just busy with work," Tara said. "Nursing isn't an easy job and Kate does shifts as well, which takes up your time and takes more out of you."

"True," Angela said. "Or she could even be starting the change of life. My mother wasn't herself for a while with that."

"Whatever it is, hopefully she will come around. And we will certainly be looking forward to seeing more of Connie. She's always been a lovely, friendly girl." She paused. "And talking of seeing more of people – how is my young brother-in-law getting on with you all in Offaly?"

"Oh, he's grand!" Angela's voice lifted now. "He's always the same cheery and polite young fellow. I was chatting to him while he was having his breakfast earlier on. He's gone out now to meet up with some friends and he said he might call out to Mammy and Daddy later."

"Sounds like he's keeping himself busy!" Tara laughed.

"And you're never going to believe it – he ran into Connie at a party out in Moate the other night – they got on great by all accounts. And he was out at the cinema with her and the lads last night."

"I'm delighted to hear that he went over for a break," Tara said, "because it's a while since he was in Offaly. I would hate him to lose his Irish links, and it's easy to get caught up in work and everything and before you know it time has flown by." There was a little pause. "Did he mention anything about Pamela when he was over?"

"God, I'd forgotten all about her," Angela said. "He hasn't mentioned her at all, at least not when I've been around. Of course I asked after his mother and everyone else generally, but I've been rushing around as usual. But, to be honest, he's been quieter than usual, and said it's because he's tired and needed a break because he's been so busy at work himself. He's been great with the children, playing games and reading to them and that kind of thing. He seems to be enjoying his time back in Ireland."

"Good," Tara said. "Life in London is a lot more stressful."

"And how is Frank? "

"Oh, he's working non-stop as usual," Tara said. "Up early in the morning and working in his office upstairs until late at night. Although he's good in that he always makes sure to be home most evenings to have his meals with us and put the boys to bed."

"Any more news on the new houses in Bramhall?"

"It all seems to be moving ahead but it's never as quick as Frank would like. You know what he's like. It's all talk now about architects and surveyors. I think I told you one of the investors had to pull out as the bank wouldn't fund him for the venture and they were looking for another one?"

"You did – how did they get on?"

"A new fellow from Birmingham has joined them and seems to have no trouble with finances, so it all seems to be moving again. Frank says they're hoping to have the foundations in by the end of the month. It's going to be one of the most modern estates in the North-West."

"That sound amazing," Angela said. "I wish we had the spare money to buy one of the houses."

"What would you want with a house in Bramhall? Sure you're all settled where you are with the house and hotel."

"I know," Angela laughed. "And we're only starting to break even with the hotel now. Aiden would have a heart attack if he heard me saying it. I suppose I feel that Stockport is my second home and I would love to have a place there as well."

"You're doing great as you are," Tara told her. "And you have a place here with us any time you want, without getting yourself up to your eyes in debt for a house you would only use now and again."

"True, true."

They chatted on for a while about Angela's children, how well Clare was doing at school and the various escapades that the lively four-year-old David had got up to.

"Thank God Noel is a bit quieter," Tara laughed. "Although I don't know what they will be like together. Any thoughts on coming over soon?"

"I'm not sure," Angela said. "It's hard for us to get away together. Maybe I'll take a flight over some weekend when Connie's in Manchester. I'd love to see her university and where she's living."

"Well, sort it out," Tara said. "And we'll make a weekend out of it. We'll take Connie out for a meal and a night out in Manchester. Bridget would love it too."

"It's a date," Angela said. "I'll try and sort it before Christmas."

Chapter 14

Connie was standing ironing a pair of white jeans when her father came in from the garden.

"So you're heading up to Dublin this evening with William Fitzgerald?" Seán Devine said, as he washed his hands under the tap in the kitchen sink. "Your mother just mentioned it to me in the garden."

"Yes," she said. "I think he must be at a bit of a loose end and in need of company."

"It's well for some," he said. "It's a lovely evening for a stroll around O'Connell Street or Grafton Street. Are you sure he can't squeeze another two into the car?" Then, when he saw the hesitant look on her face he laughed.

Connie laughed too.

Earlier, her mother's reaction had not been as favourable. She had sighed and raised her eyes to the ceiling and asked when William was going back to England.

The back door opened and Kate came in, carrying the basket of laundry. "It's been a great day for drying." Her voice sounded like a weary sigh. She put the basket down on the table. "And you can leave that iron on, Connie, because I'll do these sheets and pillowcases while they're still slightly damp.

"Do you want me to do them for you?"

"Not at all," her mother said, without looking directly at her. "Sure, aren't you going out soon? You'll be too busy putting the make-up on and doing the hair to have time to iron bedding."

"And when does Master Fitzgerald go back to England?" her father asked.

Connie felt her face start to flush. "I'm not sure, but he has only a few more days."

"Where are you meeting him?" he asked.

Connie's eyes flitted over to her mother, who was straightening out a damp towel. "He said he would beep the horn for me outside around half past five."

"I must go out and have a few words with him," Seán said. Her father's statement hung in the air for a few seconds, then he asked, "Have you enough money for tonight?"

"I'm grand," she told him. "I got paid yesterday." She had given her mother half and kept a half for herself, as they had agreed when she started working in the flower shop.

"That's what I like to hear," he joked, "a woman of independent means."

"Sure, you've been used to having an independent woman in the house for years," Connie said light-heartedly. "Didn't my mother have her own career and everything long before it became fashionable?"

Seán went over to put his arm around his wife and pull her in close to him. "I have, of course," he said, kissing her on the side of the head. "Miss Florence Nightingale here. And I wouldn't change her for all the tea in China."

Kate Devine shook her head and ducked out of his embrace. "Go away with all that nonsense, will you? Nursing is hardly a big career." She glanced over at the stove. "Will you turn those potatoes down for me, before they boil over?"

Connie noticed that there was a lighter tone in her mother's voice as though she had been pleased with the idea that she was a career woman.

She finished her jeans and went down to her bedroom and put the radio on to listen to a pop channel while she got ready. She heard the front door open and then heard her brothers' voices laughing and chatting. She would miss them, she thought, when she went to Manchester. She brushed her long brown hair out, then put on her white jeans and a white cheesecloth-and-lace top, which had bell sleeves and a lace panel at the bottom. She tried on a pair of sandals with high wooden heels, then thought that they might be uncomfortable if they walked around Dublin, and changed them for a pair of navy-and-white embroidered espadrilles.

When she went down to the kitchen all the men made a great fuss of her white outfit, whistling and teasing her, saying that she looked like a model from the television.

"Leave her alone now," Kate said, handing out the plates with the chops and vegetables, "and get on with your dinners."

"I'll just have a small amount," Connie said. "I'll be eating later."

Kate went back to the cooker to pour the gravy into a jug. "That's one of the nicest outfits I've ever seen you in, Connie. The white really suits you. What jacket are you wearing with it?"

"I thought I would bring the denim one," she said.

Her mother nodded in approval. She went over to a drawer and brought out a clean dish-towel which she handed to Connie. "Put that over your lap just in case you spill anything on the white trousers."

"Good idea, thanks." Connie looked up and caught her mother's eye and they both smiled.

It was some kind of truce, she thought.

Chapter 15

As they pulled up outside the old Georgian terraced building in Pearse Square where Malcolm McKenzie lived, Connie felt her confidence beginning to seep away. Whilst some of the houses were a bit rundown, it was a world of difference from their street of small houses in Tullamore. And no doubt meeting this old university friend was going to make her see the real difference in her and William's backgrounds.

While they were driving along and chatting about music they both liked and William was telling her about bands he had seen in Dublin and England, she had felt they had a lot of things in common – though she knew he was a few years older than her, had been to university and was obviously now more independent and experienced in life than she was. He was also a lot more travelled than her, since she had only been as far as Manchester and the surrounding areas in Cheshire and Derbyshire. It was further than most of her school friends but she was very aware that, compared to him, her life had been pretty limited. He recounted funny stories about his university days and his travels to Spain and Italy, and made her laugh until she was in tears about a teenage exchange visit he did through school with a family in a rural part of France.

"My mother would have liked to keep me wrapped up in cotton

wool," he told her as they drove through Lucan, "and I had to plead with her to let me go. I said I would fail my French oral exam if I didn't get a chance to spend time among the natives and learn to speak it fluently. Thankfully, Harry, my stepfather, backed me up. When she finally agreed, it was organised that I would go to a family with a farm in Provence in August for two weeks and their son Florian would come back to London with me for his two weeks. My mother felt that they would have a simple family life where I would be well looked after, and less likely to be led astray than I might be if I went to Paris or one of the other cities."

"How did it go?" Connie asked, intrigued.

William shook his head and smiled. "Not at all as either of us expected! Florian's family were lovely people, but they were not the strict sort that my mother imagined. The first day I arrived I was shown around the farm and offered wine by his father and cigarettes by Florian's older brother Pierre."

"How old were you?" Connie asked.

"Thirteen or fourteen. I was so delighted that I gulped two glasses of red wine down and later on I had to lie down as my head was spinning so much. Later that evening when Florian's parents were working on the farm, I asked if I could use the phone to let my mother know I had arrived safely, and Pierre said the children weren't allowed to use the phone. Florian tried to argue with him, but he said he was in charge when their parents were out. He offered me a bicycle to ride to the nearest town five miles away so I could use the public phone. Florian wanted to come with me, but there was a problem with the tyre on his bicycle, so I had to go on my own."

Connie's hands flew to her mouth. "Oh, my God! It sounds like something you would hear in remote, backward parts of Ireland. What happened?"

He could hardly tell her for laughing. "Naturally, after a few miles I got lost! I then had to go into a local pub and try and explain my situation in broken French. The barman drew me a map and I had to follow that until I eventually came to this small town and found the phone box."

"What did your mother say when you told her?"

"Well, at first I tried to pretend I was in their house so as not to worry her, but then the pips went and I had to put more money in and she realised."

They both dissolved into peals of laughter.

"She nearly had a heart attack when she found out I had cycled miles on my own to the phone box in a strange town and wanted me to come home straight away."

"What happened when you got back to the farm?"

"Florian and his father met me halfway in the car – they had come looking for me." William closed his eyes at the memory. "His father actually lifted me off the ground and hugged me because he was so relieved I was okay. And when I got back to the house they were plying me with cakes and biscuits and sweets to make up for it. They then insisted on phoning my mother to reassure her that all was well and that I was being looked after. It all settled down after that and my mother phoned me twice a week to check on me."

Connie was laughing so hard she couldn't speak.

"The best bit came later," he told her. "The weekend I was due home the family took me up to Paris, where we all stayed in an uncle's small hotel in Montmartre. After my mother making sure that I was in a safe, quiet village environment with no threats or temptations, I was let loose with Florian's older brother who was supposed to take me on a cultural trip around places like Notre Dame, the Sacré-Cœur and an art gallery. He rushed me around the two churches and then paid for me to go into the Louvre and told me he would collect me three hours later."

"Where did he go?"

William shrugged and rolled his eyes. "He said he was going to see an afternoon show in the Moulin Rouge or somewhere like that and that he would kill me if I told his parents. God knows if he did – he was an odd fellow and you never knew whether to believe him or not. He was the sort who would say anything to shock you. For all I know he could have gone and sat in a café for hours ..." He suddenly laughed again. "Looking back on it, I might have been even more naïve than I ever thought. He was always alluding to sex, so he might have gone to visit a prostitute or something like that."

"Oh, my God!" Connie gasped. "Do you really think so?"

He nodded, grinning. "Who knows? I can't remember the last

time I told anyone the story about that holiday," he said. "I just felt so absolutely stupid and gauche."

"Ah, but did you learn any French?"

"Yes, believe it or not I did, although a lot of the vocabulary was based around French farming. I became an expert on the names of French cattle."

They had chatted and laughed all the way into Dublin, and Connie had felt that same great connection with him as she had from the start. Now, as William moved to get out of the car, she suddenly began to feel out of her depth again.

"Just to warn you," he said, as they moved towards the steps at the front of the house, "Malcolm is a bit older than us. He was one of my law lecturers."

"Oh! I thought he was just a student the same age as you."

"No," he said, grinning, "but you don't need to worry, I think you'll get on with him. He's a really interesting guy."

"Is he married?" She wondered if he had a wife or children who she might meet as well. "Or is he on his own?"

"He's single," William replied. "I'll tell you about it later."

He guided her towards the wide stone steps, with wrought-iron railings, which led up to the doors of two, side-by-side, identical houses. As they drew nearer she noticed that there was a short flight of wrought-iron stairs to the side of each house going downwards, which led to basement floors or flats underneath. One of the houses had a smartly painted red door with a white-painted surround and fanlight. The windows of that house were also painted white and had identical Venetian blinds on each one. The colourful window boxes of pansies caught her eye, as did the display of matching plant pots surrounding the front door. It was exactly the sort of house that a law lecturer at Trinity would live in.

She was quite taken aback at the house attached to it and thought it let the whole terrace, if not the whole square, down. The side of the steps belonging to the house were ingrained with years of dirt and covered extensively in moss. It had a shabby, black-painted door and the grey window frames looked as if they had not been painted for many years. The paint on all of the window frames had worn away or been chipped, and several panes of glass in the windows were obviously cracked. There was one upstairs window which was actually broken and the missing glass was boarded up with plywood.

On some of the windows the curtains were closed over completely, even though it was still daylight, whilst on other windows, pieces of greying lace hung at odd angles. They walked up the stairs, William leading the way. Just as they got near the top step, an upstairs window on the shabby house opened and a man wearing a red-checked shirt with wild-looking red hair and a beard called down.

"William! How lovely to see you!"

Connie tried not to show the shock she felt, as she realised that the run-down, dilapidated house was Malcolm McKenzie's and not the smart, well-maintained one next door. She registered that his accent was Irish, but he spoke in such a refined manner it was hard to tell whether he was from Dublin or somewhere else. He was certainly older than William, she thought, but not as old as her parents. Possibly around his late thirties or perhaps even forty.

"Great to see you too!" William called back. He touched her arm. "This is Connie, the friend from Offaly I was telling you about."

Malcolm gave a small salute. "A pleasure to meet you, Connie." A beaming smile lit up his entire face. "Apologies for the window greeting. I'll be downstairs in two ticks."

Connie stood still for a moment, trying to register the fact that the academic they had come to see was actually the owner of this shambolic, neglected house.

"I should warn you," William said, "that he is a bit of an unusual character. Extremely clever, but not your average university lecturer."

"I can see that already," Connie said.

"He doesn't put value on the same things as most people," he said. "He has his own way of looking at things. To be honest, I find it quite refreshing."

"It certainly sounds interesting."

"I promise we won't stay long," he said, putting his arm around her. "I wouldn't have dragged you out here, but he's not been too well recently and I wouldn't like to go home without seeing him."

"I don't mind at all," Connie said.

She wondered now if the house inside would be like the Fays', faded grandeur but still lovely. Yet she couldn't help but imagine what Malcolm's neighbours must make of having him as a neighbour. Admittedly, the next-door house was probably the best in the row of houses, as the others she could see were plain. Having the worst and the best-looking houses side by side, she imagined, probably made it even worse.

When the door was finally opened, Malcolm held it back with a great flourish to allow them to walk in. He was wearing jeans and she observed that, in the few minutes since he had spoken to them, he had changed into a plain blue shirt with a sort of cravat tucked in at the neck and had brushed his hair down and made an attempt to tame it with some sort of lotion.

"Welcome, welcome!" he said, giving a sort of bow then formally shaking their hands.

After closing the door behind them, he moved quickly in front to lead them down a dim, narrow hallway, where they had to pick their way past boxes and piles of books and magazines.

"We'll go into the front room, William. Thankfully the house is quiet today, no noise to disturb us."

Connie wondered what noise he was referring to, if he lived alone. And, as they walked along behind him, she could tell that this house bore no comparison to Fays' lovely old house and wondered what William thought of it. It smelled damp and musty and, so far, she had seen nothing that looked interesting or vaguely artistic.

Malcolm led them into the sitting-room which was brighter than the hall, and had a modern-looking sofa covered with what looked like a worn bedspread and two odd, wooden-framed fireside chairs that were so old-fashioned looking Connie thought even her granny and grandad wouldn't give them house-room. There was a glass-topped coffee-table in the middle, littered with two grubby teacups and an empty tumbler, newspapers and books and an overflowing ashtray. When she glanced around she saw a big old desk over by the wall, and again there were piles of books and papers around the sides of the room.

"Make yourself comfortable," Malcolm told them, gesturing to them to sit down on the sofa. "Now," he said, smiling and rubbing his hands together. "I have tea, coffee, home-brewed beer and a bottle of very nice dry sherry." He looked at Connie. "Well? Would you like a small sherry? It's that time of the evening when it goes down very well, isn't it?"

She had been going to say she would have a cup of tea, but looking around she wondered if the cups mightn't be clean. The sherry she thought might actually be safer. "That would be lovely," she heard herself say.

"William – a beer? Home-brewed by one of my student guests, and I can highly recommend it. It has a bit of a kick to it."

"Fantastic," William said.

"Okay, I won't be two ticks," Malcolm said. "I'll see if I can rustle us up some cake or the like."

William made a little gesture with his hands. "Don't go to any trouble," he said. "We're going to eat somewhere around Stephen's Green – something fairly casual – and you're very welcome to join us if you're free. I owe you at least a meal for the advice you gave me on that case a few weeks ago."

"That's very kind of you, but let me think about that one."

When he left the room William turned to Connie and said in a low voice, "Are you all right?" He waved his hand around the room. "I know this isn't probably what you expected. To be honest it's gone really downhill since I was last here …"

"It's fine," Connie said. "And he seems a very nice man."

"He is but …" William looked cautiously towards the door, then he leaned in closer, whispering, "he's rather fond of a drink and I think it's caused him more than a few problems over the years. Apparently he lost his post in Trinity the summer after I left because of it."

Connie bit her lip. "Oh, God, that must have been terrible for him."

"Well, he does bits and pieces for other universities and colleges, but he told me when I last spoke to him on the phone that he's had to take in a couple of students to help pay the mortgage on the house."

She wondered if that's what he had been referring to when he said about the noise in the house. "And are they living with him now?"

William shrugged. "Apparently … they must be out this evening."

Connie moved her head up and down. The description of Malcolm's lifestyle just did not fit in with the picture she had in her mind of his old lecturer. And he did not seem to be the sort of person that she would have imagined William being friendly with. Everything about the situation was alien to her, but yet it made William seem more intriguing and engaging to her. Made her admire him for being more open-minded than she thought.

When Malcolm came back he was carrying a glass of the home-brewed beer for William which had a thick, beige-coloured froth on top. He gave a half-filled wineglass to Connie, saying, "I'm sorry I don't have a more appropriate glass for the sherry, but unfortunately the shelf they were on decided to part company with the wall."

"It's grand, thanks," Connie assured him, and was grateful to see the glass looked clean.

"I won't be a tick," he said, going out of the room again.

When he left, William turned towards the window and held his glass up to the light. "God knows what's in this beer," he said. "It's the weirdest colour I've ever seen." He sniffed it and shrugged. "It's smells okay, but I'm sure it shouldn't have a head on it like that …"

"Taste it and see what it's like …"

He took a sip, grimaced and then looked at Connie and started to laugh. He took another few sips and then said, "It's a bit yeasty but it kind of grows on you."

Connie started to silently giggle, her shoulders shaking. She put her hand up and shook her head. Then, she turned away so he could not catch her eye and lifted her own glass and took a mouthful of the sherry. "This tastes quite nice," she said, trying not to start laughing again.

Malcolm came back in carrying a tumbler of sherry for himself and a plate with half a dozen Jaffa Cakes. He put the plate down on the coffee table on top of the newspapers. "Apologies for the meagre offerings," he said, "but the cakes et cetera have all disappeared. I've rummaged around and these are all that are to be had. It appears that no one seems to have done any shopping this weekend. I'm afraid the two chaps I have staying are rather lax on the housekeeping front." He looked over at William and smiled.

"And I would be very happy to take you up on your kind offer of dining out." He then lifted his sherry glass, first to William and then to Connie. "To your good health!"

Malcolm asked William and Connie how they knew each other and was delighted to hear they had been childhood friends. "The best basis for a romance, no nasty surprises," he said, taking another drink of his sherry.

Connie glanced over at William, wondering at how he had described their relationship. She thought he might have just said they were friends, but she could see how Malcolm would be an easy person to confide in.

"Love at first sight and then rushing into matrimony too quickly is a common mistake that many couples make. That was the rock that Sandra and I perished on. And in Holy Ireland, as we know to our sorrow, it's all about making your bed and lying in it regardless." He looked over at Connie and sadly shook his head. "That's the problem when you marry a Catholic."

Connie smiled back at him, hoping her face did not reveal her shock at realising that Malcolm was not only a Protestant but a married man who was separated from his wife.

"As you can imagine, very difficult indeed." He took two mouthfuls of his sherry then continued his story. "In the beginning, of course, it was all music, champagne and poetry as one would hope for. Sandra was an English and Latin teacher and well-read in the Classics which was most unusual in a female, and we had both read many of the same books which we took to be a great sign that we were compatible. We took a year out of our various teachings, and spent the time travelling around the warm countries in Europe, eating like the locals and not minding whether we slept in the most basic youth hostels or in the grandest hotels." He looked over at William, his eyebrows raised, and then gave a great sigh. "Paris, Provence, Florence, Lucca, the Italian Lakes, Malaga, Ronda, Seville, visiting the vineyards in the Moselle Valley and the fairy-tale castles on the Rhine. And those are only the places I can instantly recall. A month in one place and a week in another, exactly as we fancied. It was all paradise, and over and above what one could dream of in a first year of marriage."

Listening to the names of the places and Malcolm's descriptions of them made Connie suddenly wish she was not so ignorant. She wished she knew something about the countries so she could add even the smallest comment. Malcolm's experiences in travelling seemed like a great achievement to her. It came to her that one day she would want to tell people she had been to such a list of countries.

She felt self-conscious because she had no travel experiences of her own to talk about and, since she was so young, he might not be interested in her opinions, but something made her push herself. "You are so lucky to have travelled to all those places," she said. "I think it sounds really, really exciting."

His face lit up. "And that, Connie, is exactly what it was." Looking at her, he nodded. "We came back to Ireland filled with all the wonderful experiences we had been through together, and reliving it as we went about the day-to-day life in Dublin. As time went on and the pressures of work and living in a house together grew, we discovered we had much less in common than we'd had as strangers abroad. She suddenly began to prefer the company of her six sisters and two brothers and all their families, scattered around the various parts of Dublin." He shook his head. "Something I just could not get to grips with, coming from a family of two siblings, which was quite enough. We stumbled along for five years and then she went to a nephew's wedding in London and met a Galway chap who was living there and she decided she would prefer to be with him."

"That must have been difficult for you," William said quietly.

The way he spoke made Connie guess that he had heard it all before.

"In the final analysis, I would say we hardly knew each other. And, by the time we split up, we were like two enemies firing across the trenches at each other." He held his glass up again, and smiled at them both. "But, unbelievable as it sounds, the wonderful experiences we had at the beginning were worth it all. I wouldn't have missed them for anything. Therefore, my advice to any young couple – for what it is worth – is to enjoy every moment of passion while it lasts, and to look at life through rose-tinted spectacles for as long as possible." He drained the last of the sherry, then he held out his glass. "Anyone for a refill yet?"

"Not for me, thanks," Connie said, "I've still some left." She took another sip, not sure whether she was drinking too slowly or whether Malcolm had been drinking too quickly.

"Actually, if you don't mind," William said, checking his watch, "we could set off now and find somewhere to eat? We can have a few drinks in town if that suits you."

"Of course," Malcolm said. "I'll just collect my jacket. Won't be two ticks."

When he went out of the room, William turned to Connie. "I'm afraid he's gone to have another quick sherry before we leave." He took her hand. "He told me he had stopped drinking at one point, and then recently he said he had cut down. So I knew he was drinking to some extent. But, seeing him now, it looks as though he's back drinking as heavily as ever. If I'd known, I wouldn't have brought you here." He ran his hand through his hair. "And I didn't get a chance to ask you if you minded him joining us. It's just that I think it might do him good to get out of here for a few hours."

"It's fine," she said, touching his hand so he knew she was genuine. "He's a nice man and very interesting, and I think it's the right thing to do."

"Are you sure?" he checked. "I'm worried that this is not what you expected of a trip to Dublin, that it might all be very boring for you."

"It's not," she said. "It's absolutely fine." She held up her sherry glass which was almost empty. "I've enjoyed hearing all Malcolm's stories and I've enjoyed my drink too." Then she drank the last mouthful of it.

"You're great," he said. "I don't know any other girl I would have brought here. I knew you would understand."

"There's nothing to understand," she said. "It's just one of your friends."

Then they both went silent as the front door opened and footsteps came along the hallway and stopped just outside the door.

"Malcolm?" a male voice called.

Then, a small, slim boy around Connie's age, with hair tied back in a pony-tail and wearing a denim shirt with appliqued stars and moons on it, looked into the room where they were.

"Oh, hi ..." he said, his accent unmistakably Dublin. "I didn't realise Malcolm had visitors."

He came in and over to greet them, his hand stretched out to William.

"Paul Murphy," he said. "I'm staying in one of the rooms here."

William introduced himself then shook his hand, and then he introduced Connie and Paul shook her hand too.

"Nice to meet you," William said, smiling at him, "I know Malcolm from Trinity a few years back. We're all actually just heading out now."

"I've just called in for my guitar," Paul said, "There's a session down in the International tonight and there are quite a few well-known people expected. They said Luke Kelly and some of the Dubliners might even be there." He grinned. "But sure, they say that nearly every weekend and I've yet to see them there. But it's always a good night whoever turns up."

The boy's gaze shifted to Connie and lingered on her for a few moments and then it moved to the table to William's three-quarters drunk pint of beer. He slapped his hand to his forehead.

"Oh, Jayz!" he said. "That's not Jimmy's home brew, is it? Don't tell me Malcolm's been at it?"

William looked at the glass. "He did say it was home-brewed."

"I don't think it's ready for drinking yet. I'm sure Jimmy said it would be another while. He said he was going to hide it somewhere so Malcolm wouldn't touch it." He pulled a face. "I hope it doesn't upset your stomach or anything!"

Connie looked over at William. "Are you okay? Do you feel sick or anything?"

"I'm fine," he told her. "It wasn't that bad."

Malcolm came into the room then, wearing a pin-striped jacket. "Ah, you're back, Paul!"

Paul pointed to the pint glass. "If that's Jimmy's stuff, I don't know if it's ready for drinking yet."

Malcolm put his hand on his shoulder. "He told me if I wanted to sample it, to go ahead. I had a drop from one of the containers and it tasted fine to me." He looked over at William. "How did you find it?"

William nodded. "Okay – a slight taste of yeast from it."

"Oh, you have a good palate," Malcolm said. "Freshly brewed beer is bound to have a hint of yeast in it."

Connie did not dare to catch William's eye. Instead, she looked over at the beer glass and as she saw the dried-in layer of beige froth around the rim, she had to put her hand up to her mouth in case a bubble of laughter escaped

William clapped his hands together. "I think we should move now – it might get busy if we waste any more time."

"Good session on in the International, Malcolm," Paul said as they went out into the hallway. "There's talk that Christy Moore or some of the Dubliners could show up."

"Sounds interesting," Malcolm said. "I might drop in later. It all depends on how the night turns out."

"If you meet up with that Tony fella," Paul said, "don't bring him with you. I don't think they will let him in anyway after the trouble he caused."

Malcolm raised his eyebrows, and then ran his hands over his bushy red hair.

Paul looked at Connie. "He thinks he's an opera singer, and after he had a few drinks he started singing over everybody else and then he was abusive to a table of girls who told him to shut up."

"Tony is actually a trained baritone," Malcolm said. "And he's sung in Covent Garden."

"I'm not saying he can't sing," Paul said, "and I'm not speaking for myself – it's just that some people feel he's a bit of a troublemaker and a drunk. The bar manager said they had another night where he came in staggering all over the place, then went to tip a table full of glasses over because they told him they wouldn't serve him."

"He's a talented man, but sadly misunderstood. I certainly won't ask or encourage him to come again." Malcolm went to open the front door. "But, like all of us, he has the freedom to go wherever he chooses and say what he likes."

Connie glanced at William, who she thought looked more serious than usual. It struck her that he felt uncomfortable that Malcolm was in a position to be advised by someone as young as Paul and less educated than he was. She guessed William was also saddened to hear that Malcolm was mixing with people who also had drink problems and behaved badly.

They drove into the city and William found a parking place at the Grafton Street entrance to the Stephen's Green park. "It's still open," he said as they all got out of the car. He glanced at Connie. "I know you haven't been around the park before, so if Malcolm doesn't mind, we could have a bit of a walk before we eat."

"That sounds an excellent idea," Malcolm said. He looked at his watch. "My suggestion is that you two young people go and enjoy an amble around it."

"We can all go," Connie said, thinking that he might feel left out. "It would be nice for the three of us."

"Not at all – I can walk around it anytime, and I have a couple of old university friends who live in Leeson St who I'd like to catch up with for a quick chat. What shall we say – half an hour? An hour?"

William looked at the sky and then at his watch. "It's nearly quarter to eight. Shall we say half past eight? I don't think the park will be open much longer than that."

"Excellent," Malcolm said. "I'll see you at the main gates at approximately eight thirty." He saluted them and then went off.

They started walking towards the gates, and William reached for her hand. "It's good that we have some time on our own."

At first Connie thought it might feel strange to walk along in Dublin hand in hand with a boy, and that people's eyes would be drawn to them. She had never walked hand in hand with any other boy for long. Emmet and the other boys back home usually only did that when they were drunk or when they were guiding a girl through a crowd. The few couples in Tullamore who did that were quietly jeered at by others. Connie loved the feel of his warm hand around hers and, as they passed groups of people and other couples and walked in through the gates, she was surprised that she didn't feel at all self-conscious.

They walked along for a while, stopping to look at the flowerbeds and the ducks and the fountains.

"I can't believe I've never been here before," Connie said, as they strolled along. "I'd heard how lovely Stephen's Green was but it never occurred to me or my friends to take the train or coach up here and have a day wandering around this part of Dublin."

"Well, I'm sure you'll come up more often now," William said. "I've been here numerous times over the years, and somebody even bought me a book with the history of the park. It might even be around Ballygrace House somewhere, in one of the bookcases. I must give it to you – you'd find it interesting." He paused. "But, it's funny, just now a memory flashed into my mind. Something I've not thought about for years." He smiled and shook his head. "I feel embarrassed now when I think of it ..."

Connie looked at him. "What happened?"

"It was during one of our visits back to Ballygrace House after Gabriel died, when I was a teenager, and Tara had brought me up to Dublin for the day. We'd had lunch and everything, and we were walking around here, probably with ice creams, when I suddenly noticed Angela walking arm-in-arm with Aiden. Naturally, I wanted to run over and chat to them, but Tara stopped me. She said something along the lines of them obviously wanting to have a private day out, and it wasn't fair to spoil it. I didn't understand it at the time, but, looking back on it now, I realise that Angela hadn't told Tara anything about her romance."

Connie raised her eyebrows then shrugged and smiled. "I really like Angela, but I've heard Daddy and Granny and Grandad talking about her when she was young, and saying how determined she could be to get her own way. Grandad can be quite funny telling stories about things like that."

"Well, you can imagine how Angela must have felt when I piped up at the wrong time later, saying that Tara and I had seen them. I must remind her of that some time, as I bet she would find it funny now. She has a good sense of humour." He put his hand over his face, laughing. "Oh, God, I hadn't a clue back then. I must have been the most awful pain to poor Tara. When I think back on some of the stupid things I've said and done."

"We've all done that," Connie said. "It's part and parcel of growing up, I suppose. There are times I'm sure, when Ollie and Terry could have killed me for putting my foot in it with Mam and Dad or a new girlfriend."

As they walked, she asked William what he knew about the park and the surrounding area. He told her what he could remember about the history of the park and how in the last century a group of wealthy householders who lived nearby had set up a Commission to restore it. Later, when broken rails and walls were fixed and new trees and flowerbeds were planted, and the park was looking better than it ever had, the Commissioners rented keys to the privileged neighbours to keep the park private for their sole use. And then he explained how Arthur Guinness had bought it years later and handed it back to the Government on the condition that it was open to all the public who wanted to use it.

On the way back they stopped for a few minutes to sit on a bridge.

Connie looked at William. "I feel a bit guilty that Malcolm went off on his own. Do you think he really is meeting up with friends?"

"He was being genuine when he says he can walk around the park any time, and he's happy to go off on his own or meet up with friends." He shrugged. "But, on this occasion – at a guess – I'd say the names of the friends he is meeting are Mr Powers and Mr Jameson."

"Oh God," Connie said, "is his drink problem really that bad?"

William nodded. "There are times when he has got on top of it, but at the moment he seems pretty bad. Going by previous form, he will drink for the rest of the night and possibly tomorrow. It's almost an illness with him and he just doesn't seem to have the willpower to beat it. It has cost him his marriage, several jobs and he almost lost his house because he has re-mortgaged it on a number of occasions to finance his lifestyle when he is out of work. That's why he has students living in the house with him. Their rent helps to keep his head above water."

"That's very sad."

"It is," William said. "Because he's one of the cleverest men I've ever met and I'm very fond of him."

When they reached the gates of the park at half past eight, there was no sign of Malcolm. They stood for another ten minutes and were just about to go when Connie recognised his unruly, faded-red hair coming across the road. He was walking quite smartly and she felt relieved for William that he did not look obviously drunk.

He gave a quick apology for being late, without giving any real reason, and then he and William had a discussion about where was suitable to eat without being too pricey.

While they chatted, Connie walked to the edge of the pavement to look around her, and to observe all the people coming and going on a Saturday night in Grafton Street. It was summer, so of course there were foreign tourists around who would be staying in the city hotels and bed and breakfasts, as well as people who lived in Dublin. She noticed there were people of all ages and backgrounds and, as a large group of foreigners passed them by, she wondered whether they were Chinese or Japanese. She had no way of knowing, because she had never seen any around Tullamore and did not know how to tell the difference. She listened as couples and groups passed her, trying to hear their accents and guess where they were from. Further in the background she could hear music floating out from some of the restaurants and the bars and she suddenly felt a little surge of excitement run through her, knowing that she was actually part of it all.

She wouldn't make too much of it with her mother, but she couldn't wait to tell her friends about her night in Dublin when they met up at Mass tomorrow morning. And when she was back in the shop, Eileen, she knew, would be interested in hearing about it too, because she often went to Dublin and would know all the places Connie was talking about.

William and Malcolm came walking towards her.

"Malcolm has suggested a bar off Grafton Street which serves all different kinds of food. It's relaxed and casual, but we'd be best to go now as he isn't sure what time the meals finish. Does that sound okay to you?"

"Anything will be fine for me," she said, smiling at him and then at Malcolm.

And as Malcolm smiled warmly back at her, showing a row of unexpectedly even and white teeth, she could see what William liked about him. And now that she was getting used to him herself, she thought that she actually liked him too.

The bar was busy but they were lucky to get a table through the back, and then within minutes a waiter came and gave them a menu which had a long list of foods on it. There were dishes with spaghetti and rice which Connie had never tried before, so she decided to be careful and ordered a steak with chips and mushrooms and onion rings in batter. Malcolm decided he would have the same, while William decided on salmon with sauté potatoes.

"We must have a bottle of red wine to go with our steaks," Malcolm said to Connie.

She looked back at him and smiled. She knew absolutely nothing about wines, so she thought it better to keep quiet rather than pretend.

He must have taken her silence for agreement because he looked at William now. "You will probably prefer white with the fish? We could order half a bottle for you?"

William shrugged. "I can just as easily have a glass of red wine. I won't drink any more as I have to drive back to Tullamore."

"In that case," Malcolm said, "we will order a carafe, and I would like to pay for it."

"We've already agreed the food and drink is my treat," William said, a friendly but firm note in his voice.

Malcolm held his hands up. "I won't argue if you insist."

They talked while they were drinking wine and waiting for their food, William about his work since qualifying and the different law firms he had gained experience with and then he told Malcolm about Connie's impending move to Manchester and how she was going to study medicine. Malcolm congratulated her and said how a number of years ago – before he met Sandra – he had lectured in the university there for a year and then moved to Liverpool for two years.

"It's easy to settle over in the North-West of England," he told her. "There are so many Irish there, it's almost a home from home. But don't be sucked into it – the Irish clubs, the Irish dances, Mass every Sunday." He shook his head. "If you are going to broaden your experiences in life you need to mix with the whole community and not just one small section of it." He looked at William. "Don't you agree?"

William raised his eyes and shook his head from side to side as though weighing the question up. "It's something to bear in mind," he said, "but I think the main thing is to find like-minded people whatever their background."

"I'll certainly concede on that one," Malcolm said, holding his glass up.

William laughed. "I must get that in writing," he said. "A concession from you must be a first?"

"I admit I do like to stir things up now and then," he said.

William put his arm around Connie and left it there for a few moments. "I think Connie is looking forward to the big change in her life, aren't you?"

"Absolutely," she said.

After they had eaten, William sorted the bill and then they made their way back out onto Grafton Street.

William said he thought it was time he and Connie headed back home. "It will be late by the time we get back to Tullamore," he told Malcolm, "and I don't want Connie's parents wondering where she has got to."

"One drink in the International," Malcolm said. "It's only a couple of streets away."

William looked at Connie and held his hands out, leaving the decision with her.

Connie knew he had made the excuse about time to give her the choice. "That's fine by me," she said. "It sounds as though it's a great place."

"Excellent!" Malcolm said and started moving smartly across the street. "It's not too late, so we should get a table. It doesn't usually liven up until well after ten."

"Half an hour," William said, "then we need to head home."

As they walked along Wicklow Street, they could hear music playing from the bar. Connie was more than happy to go there, as this, she felt, was a special night she would remember. From the way Paul had described it, the bar sounded good and she didn't want to feel she had missed a thing. She had loved walking around Stephen's Green and she'd had a nice meal and wine in the previous bar, and now she was heading to another bar where someone famous could walk in at any minute. She had never done anything like this before and it was all because she was with William Fitzgerald.

As they came up to the bar, it suddenly became clear to her that anything she did with William seemed enjoyable and interesting. And she did not mind being with Malcolm at all, because she knew that in a short time she and William would be on their own in the car for the long journey home.

The International was packed with no hope of seats. Four women, who were positioned at a table just inside the door, pulled their chairs in a bit to allow them to stand more easily in beside the wall, and out of the main thoroughfare of the bar where people were passing, coming in and out.

Malcolm went to stand at the end of the busy bar and, even though William said he didn't want any alcohol, when he caught the eye of one of the barmen, he ordered three more glasses of wine.

"He's unbelievable where drink is concerned," William said, when he saw the barman pouring the glasses, "but in his own way, he means well." He raised his eyebrows and smiled. "At least it's not the home-brewed beer!"

Malcolm brought the drinks back and then they stood listening to the band and chatting when it wasn't too loud. The band was lively and played quickly, moving from one song to the next, playing a mixture of folk and popular music. When they started playing 'Bridge Over Troubled Water' Connie immediately thought back to the party in Jim Fay's house, when she and William met up again, and when she had all the trouble with Emmet. It was only a few days ago, but she had done so much in that time it seemed much longer. Long enough to have changed her, and, she thought, if she could change that much in such a short time – how much more would she change when she left home altogether?

"What are we going to do?" William asked as they walked back towards the car. He had his arm around her shoulder and she had her arm around his waist.

Connie looked up at him quizzically. "What do you mean?"

"After this, when I go back to London. I know it's not practical and possibly not fair on you when you are starting your new student life ... but, at this moment, I just can't imagine not seeing you again, or not seeing you for a long time."

Connie felt her heart beginning to race, as she wasn't sure exactly what he was suggesting. "I feel the same," she said. Whether it was the second glass of wine making her brave she wasn't sure, but she knew there was no point in being coy. "I know it might be difficult with one being in Manchester and one in London, but I would really like to see you again."

"Well, that's a good start," he said. "We just have to work things out."

Then, just as they came towards the top of Grafton Street, a drunk who was walking past them suddenly seemed to lose his momentum and veered over in Connie's direction. Instinctively, William moved his arm to guide Connie quickly to the inside, so the drunk's shoulder glanced off his own.

"Sorry ... sorry now ..." the drunk muttered. "Are you okay?" He halted, then he turned in a circle to face them and said in a demanding tone, "I said, are you okay?"

"I'm fine, thanks," William called over his shoulder, but kept them both walking quickly.

The drunk kept talking, but they could not make out what he was saying. When they were out of earshot, William's pace slowed down and then he looked at Connie. "There is absolutely no point in engaging with anyone as drunk as that at this hour of the night. You don't know where it could end up."

As she waited for him to open the car, she thought how easily he had dealt with the situation and how safe she felt with him.

They were driving out past the Spa Hotel at Lucan when William took his left hand off the steering-wheel and squeezed hers. "We didn't get a chance to finish our conversation about seeing each other again."

She looked at him and, as she went to smile and say something light-hearted, she saw his face was very serious. He looked the way he had looked in the cinema the night before and she wondered again what he was thinking.

"You decide," she said. "Because it might be you who has to travel to Manchester, because I won't have a clue how to get to London."

He squeezed her hand gently again and then let go and put his hand back on the wheel. "We'll manage something," he said. "It's not going to be easy, but we'll just have to work something out. When I think I have time to come up, I can always use the excuse that I'm coming to see family."

Connie was surprised he had to make excuses to anyone. She wondered if his mother had a similar problem with Tara to hers. "Do you mean you have to make excuses to your mother?"

"No, not at all." He didn't turn to her, and instead kept his gaze on the dark, tree-lined road ahead of them. "I suppose I was thinking of work … taking time off from the new firm I have just started with."

"Will you be working weekends?"

"At the beginning until I've found my feet. Reading up on court reports and that sort of thing."

The world of law was something Connie could not pretend to know anything about. "Well, it will be lovely to see you if you do manage to come up to Manchester, but don't worry about it," she said, "because it will probably take me a few weeks to find my feet at university."

"Of course," he said. "It's a whole new, exciting chapter of your life starting. You will be meeting new people, learning new things."

He turned his head towards her now.

"I'll definitely come up to Manchester to see you, Connie," he said. "Whatever happens, I want us to keep in touch."

Chapter 16

Tara took the *Congratulations* card out of her bag and went over to her desk. She then slid open a drawer and took out a writing set which Bridget had given her at Christmas.

She had thought about what Angela had said about Connie's results and her mother's reaction to her coming to Manchester. Initially, she had planned to phone and congratulate Connie on her results, and say how delighted she would be to see her more often, but something had made her hold back.

After some thought she decided that if Connie's moving away had caused upset at home, it might be best to write instead. It would give them more time to get used to it, and by the time her letter arrived things might be easier.

She wrote the card to Connie first, which was quick and easy, then she started on the letter to her parents. She took more time over the letter to ensure that she worded it carefully.

Dear Seán and Kate,

I hope you and all the family are well. I just wanted to write a note to say how delighted we were to hear that Connie has done so well in her Leaving Certificate. No surprise there as we've always known what a clever girl she is! We are all so proud to hear that she is going to study medicine and that we are going to soon have a doctor in the family!

She had paused then, thinking of Ollie and Terry. She didn't want it to seem as though she was suggesting that the boys hadn't done as well as Connie. She thought for a few minutes then continued to write.

Of course, Kate, you are well used to the medical world with your own work, so no doubt you will be a great help to her with her studies – and it is fantastic that Connie has succeeded in getting the results to study in her chosen field. Enjoying your work – whatever it is –- is the best thing anyone can do, because we spend so many hours of our life at it.

It must be heartening for you both to see all three of your children doing what they enjoy in life, as the two boys always seem content and happy in their work too. We hope our two little ones do as well when they grow up – we are only at the start of things with them and have a long way to go!

We are all well here at the minute, thank God. Frank is keeping busy at work and I'm busy with the children at home. No great news really, just happy we are all healthy and well.

I was chatting to Frank last night about Connie, and we both wanted to say that she is welcome to come and stay here any time she is free. We heard she is going into student halls of residence which will be handier for her, but if she wants to come out any time we would love to see her.

If she is looking for any weekend work, Frank says he would be able to find her something in the hotel, in the bar or as a chambermaid. We are often looking for a baby-sitter as well, if she wants to earn a few pounds, and I'm sure Bridget would be glad of an extra pair of hands in the boarding house as well.

I'm sure some of the family will be over visiting Connie when she is at university, and it goes without saying that you are all welcome to stay here any time you like! Noel and Leo love company and would be only too delighted to see you all.

I'll finish off now as I've got an appointment in Stockport in an hour, and I want to get this in the post beforehand.

Love to everyone, and again – well done to Connie!

Tara, Frank and the boys xx

Chapter 17

Kate Devine walked briskly along the Arden Road, enjoying the light warmth of the early morning sun on her face. She turned into the main gates of Tullamore Hospital and walked at the same pace down into the grounds towards the main entrance.

She was greeted by two ambulance-men she knew as she went in, and she gave them a cheery wave. Inside, she had a few words with the woman on reception about the nice morning and the weather forecast for the coming week. She then continued on along the long corridor, passing the lift, until she came to the turn for the stairs which she made herself use by habit.

Kate had always been slim, but a few years ago she had put weight on over Christmas and somehow she had gradually kept eating little extras until she found she could not get into any of her usual skirts and slacks. When she went to the chemist's and weighed herself, she was shocked to discover she had put on almost two stone, taking her up to ten stone. The realisation that she was heavier than she had been at her highest pregnancy weight shocked her into dieting and exercise for the first time in her life.

She and a friend who needed to lose weight, another nurse called Delia, decided they would cut out all the cakes and scones in work and stop taking sugar. They also decided they would walk every morning or night during the week, depending on their shifts, for over an hour. If Delia was unavailable, Connie often went with her. Some days they walked out to Charleville Castle and back, and at other times they did a whole circle of the town. The effort had been huge, but Kate had been determined that she would keep at it until she was back down to eight stone.

It took her almost a year of eating carefully and walking to get the excess weight off again, and she decided she would never use the lift again.

At the top of the stairs she walked along the corridor to the Nurses' Station.

The morning was busy enough and she then had to take one of her elderly patients down to the X-ray department in a wheelchair. She pushed the chair along the corridor towards the lift, chatting to the lady as they went along. She found that a lot of the older patients enjoyed a bit of banter as it helped take their minds off whatever was wrong with them. When they reached the ground floor, Kate pushed the wheelchair along the winding corridors, still chatting away, until they reached the X-ray department. She went to the desk and handed in the lady's file and was told to go straight down to the X-ray room where they would be seen to before the Outpatients people started to arrive.

When they got down there, Kate helped the old lady to change into a gown. A few minutes later a radiologist in a blue coat, who Kate did not recognise, came out with a young man on crutches wearing a plaster cast on his leg. The radiologist had a few words with the patient and gave him a file to drop into the radiology reception office on his way past.

The radiologist then turned towards Kate, his eyebrows raised and an expectant look on his face. "And who do we have here?" There was an impatient note in his voice.

"A lady from the Medical Ward," she told him, without smiling, then she handed over the file.

He leafed through it. "That all seems in order," he said. He moved towards the wheelchair. "I'll take over from here." And then he wheeled the old lady into the X-ray room and closed the door behind him.

Kate sat down in a chair outside the door, feeling annoyed at the radiologist's condescending manner. Why did some people have to act as though they were better than others, she wondered? Quite a few of the doctors had that same abrupt manner, and even some of the Ward Sisters. They just gave off an air of disdain towards anyone they thought was lower than them. She took a deep breath to calm herself down, and sat back on the hard, uncomfortable chair with her arms folded. Then, as she saw the figure limping off in the distance, something suddenly dawned on her. The young man on crutches – who was now swinging his way towards the office – was Emmet Ferguson.

Her heart started to race, and before she could stop herself she was up on her feet and walking down the corridor after him. He was leaning in through the glass partition, talking to the lady behind the desk. Kate slowed up, and waited until he had finished speaking and had tucked a folded piece of paper into the top pocket of his jacket. Then, using both crutches, he swung away from the office and headed out towards the main door.

Kate went quickly behind him, her soft shoes hardly making a sound. When she was well away from the office and could see there was no one around to overhear them, she moved into a short trot to catch up with him just as he made to go through the doors.

"Emmet?" she said. "Can I have a word with you, please?"

He swung around to look her, and she could tell by the look on his face that he did not recognise her.

He took in her white nurse's uniform. "Sorry, did I forget something?" he asked.

She had no time to waste. The old lady wouldn't be long. "I'm Kate Devine," she said. "I'm Connie's mother."

Emmet looked at her now, and then a deep flush came on his face. "I'm sorry," he said, "I didn't recognise you." He lifted his leg with the plaster cast from the ground, and then moved his crutches a few inches, as though trying to get into a more comfortable position.

Kate swallowed hard. She knew she had to play this carefully, because she was in work and speaking to a patient. "How are you keeping after the accident?" Her voice was stiff and formal.

He moved again on the crutches. "I'm not too bad, I'm getting there ..."

"I rang your mother the morning I heard about it," she said. "The morning after the party in Moate. I couldn't understand what went on that made you drive off like that." Kate looked at him carefully now, watching his reaction. She knew she could not let him away as though nothing had happened.

There was an awkward silence now, during which she kept her gaze on him, making it clear that she was waiting on some explanation.

"I'm sorry about it all," he said, looking away from her now. "I was stupid ... I drank too much. I suppose in many ways I deserve what happened. I brought it all on myself." He moved one of the crutches now, and looked towards the door.

The gesture told Kate that he thought he had apologised now and that the conversation was over and done with. That he was getting ready to move on about his business and not waste any more time talking to an older woman he hardly knew. She glanced back down the corridor, making sure no one else was around. "You know you could be in very serious trouble for what you tried to do to Connie?" she said in a low voice.

His shoulders slumped. "I was drunk and upset," he said. "I didn't know what I was doing."

"You shouldn't be drinking if it does that to you. It makes you a danger to any young girl. You shouldn't have put your hands on her the way you did."

"It wasn't like that ..." His eyes suddenly filled up now. "I didn't mean it the way it happened. I was ..." he paused, "I was upset about her going to England and I was doing everything, saying everything I could so we could stay in touch, but she didn't seem interested and then ..." he paused again, "and then she disappeared and I got worried and when I went to look for her I found her with him – the English fella."

Kate wanted to ask him where he found them and what they were doing. She took a deep breath. She wanted to believe Connie's version that it was all innocent.

"That was what caused the whole thing," Emmet went on. "That was what made me feel such a total eejit – me talking about going over to visit her in Manchester and her saying we should break things off, and then the next thing I find her canoodling with him upstairs. I didn't know what to do, so I ended up going back to the party and downing a few bottles one after the other, and then I didn't know what I was saying or doing."

Kate felt a sudden jolt at the description of Connie and William Fitzgerald 'canoodling', but she steeled herself. "That still didn't give you the right to do what you did to her."

His face crumpled as though he was going to break down. "I was only trying to talk to her ... honestly. Maybe I was a bit heavy-handed, but I was just trying to make her stay and listen to me. I didn't want her to give up on us. We've got on great these last few months and I really like her. I didn't want her to make a snap decision that we were all finished because she had to go to university in England. I wanted her to see that we might have a future together. There are plenty of couples who have to travel back and forwards to see each other." He shook his head. "I just wanted her to give us a chance ... and then I lost it when I saw her with that other lad. I didn't mean to hurt her in any way."

"It's all very well thinking about what *you* want," Kate said, "but Connie is entitled to her feelings too." Again, she glanced around to check there was no one listening. "Well, from what Connie told me, it sounds like you tried to *rape* her. She said if that other couple hadn't appeared, she didn't know what might have happened."

Emmet moved forward on his crutches now and put a hand on Kate's forearm. "Please believe me, Mrs Devine. I think the world of Connie and I would never have hurt her ... I would never want to hurt any girl. I was just trying to hold her on the bench to listen to me. What I did was stupid and wrong and it came across badly because I was drunk. I am really, really sorry for what I did, and I've learned a big lesson from it."

"I hope you have learned a lesson, because you could have ended up in court after what happened." Kate looked at him now, wishing she could believe all he had said. Wishing she could tell him that it was a stupid incident, and that he should go home and forget all about it. But she could not get the picture of Connie's face, when she described what had happened, out of her mind.

Then, she heard a door opening further along the corridor and saw two porters coming out, wheeling a man on a trolley. She leaned in closer and whispered in an urgent tone. "My advice to you is to stay well away from Connie from now on," she said, "and stay well away from drink. If it makes you behave like that, then it's something you need to forget about from now on." She gestured towards his plastered leg. "And you're lucky you got away with a broken leg – you could have killed yourself."

"I know," he said, "I know."

"And if I happen to hear anything about you doing anything like this with another girl, believe you me, you won't get a second chance. And I'll be listening out for any news."

He lifted his plaster from the floor again and shifted around. "I have a car coming now … It's to pick me up outside."

Kate started to turn away now. She felt drained and light-headed. But she had confronted him and said her piece. She thought she had made her point loud and clear. But she knew that unless they wanted to start a court case or something huge like that, there was nothing more could be said or done. She had to let it rest now.

"Mrs Devine," Emmet said, "will you tell Connie how very, very sorry I am?"

Kate stared coldly at him and said nothing in reply. She was not going to make him feel better in any way. She turned away.

"And I know it's none of my business after what's happened but tell her to be careful with that Fitzgerald lad … I don't know if they are still in touch, but I wouldn't like to see her being made a complete fool of."

Kate wheeled back round, her brows raised. "What do you mean?"

"Jim Fay called out to see me last night," he said, "and when I told him …" He looked embarrassed and awkward now. "When I told him what triggered this whole thing off, about the business between Connie and Fitzgerald, he was more than surprised."

"Why?" Kate asked.

"Because he thought Fitzgerald was a decent, honourable type of fellow. He said he had known the lad for years and couldn't imagine him 'stringing two girls like that along'."

"*Two girls?*" Kate repeated.

"It seems Fitzgerald is engaged to be married to another girl back in England."

Kate looked at him in shock. "*Engaged?*" She said the word very slowly. "Are you *sure?*"

Emmet nodded. "He told Jim that he needed a break from all the wedding plans and work and everything, and that's why he came over to Ireland."

His confident tone now told Kate he was telling the truth.

"But we would have heard," she said. "We hear all the news ... Connie's grandfather is on the phone to them every week. There's been no mention of an engagement." She was sure that Tara would have been on to Shay and Angela, announcing the great news. Anything about the Fitzgeralds would always have to be great.

Emmet shrugged. "Jim said for some reason he wanted to keep it quiet, and he had asked him to say nothing until it was all official. And it looks as though he didn't mention it to Connie. Well, I couldn't imagine that he did or she wouldn't have been acting so starry-eyed with him." He pursed his lips together and moved his head up and down. "I'm not lying about it and I've nothing personal to gain by telling you this. I know Connie would never look at me again ... but, at the same time, I wouldn't want her to be made a fool of by the likes of him."

There was a little silence, and then he made a gesture with his hand.

"Bye now, Mrs Devine."

Kate stood staring after him as he limped off towards the front door.

She walked back down towards the reception desk, where she saw the radiologist talking to one of the women on reception. Beside him was Kate's lady in the wheelchair.

She quickened her step. "Sorry," she said, as she came towards them. "I just had to check something out."

The radiologist had a sour look on his face. "We thought you had gone AWOL," he said. "You should have stayed where you were. We have other patients to see, as I'm sure you know."

Kate gave him a bright, cheery smile. "I'm really very sorry," she repeated.

"It's not even ten o'clock and we're behind schedule now." He gave an exasperated sigh.

Kate looked at her patient. "All okay now?"

"Grand." The old lady smiled up at Kate. "It's nice to get out and about for a bit. I've been in bed for nearly two weeks now, and you begin to forget that there's a bigger world out there." She winked at Kate and then gestured towards the radiologist. "And it's a long time since I got wheeled around by a handsome young man."

The radiologist looked at Kate and then at the woman, who was still smiling. Then, all of a sudden, an embarrassed grin broke out on his face. "It was my pleasure," he said. He looked back at Kate and shrugged. "I'd better move – there's a trolley waiting outside the radiology room."

As she wheeled the chair back down through the corridors and then into the lift and back up to the ward, Kate kept up a light-hearted conversation with her patient.

"I think I gave him a bit of a shock saying he was handsome," the old lady said. "I did it for a bit of devilment, because he was there giving out to the receptionists about all the appointments that had been booked in."

"He's a stand-offish sort. Not used to mixing with ordinary folks like us."

The old lady started to laugh now. "I'd say he doesn't get too many remarks passed on him like that. The look on his face was priceless."

As she settled the old lady back into bed, Kate's mind kept flitting back what Emmet had said about William Fitzgerald. Initially, she had been shocked when she heard about the engagement, but she was now beginning to feel a sense of relief as it would mean the romance would soon be abruptly ended. But the thought of the hurt Connie would feel when she heard the news took the edge off it. She consoled herself by thinking that it was better to know this now than find it out later.

She hoped Connie would see it the same way.

Chapter 18

Connie carried the heavy galvanised watering-can through the front of the shop and then outside. Since it was a fine afternoon, the door of Eileen's Flower Shop was wedged open, and all the shrubs and plants suitable for garden borders or for pots were displayed on stands outside on both sides of the door. To the left of the door, there was also a tall black plastic stand filled with packets of flower and vegetable seeds for the more serious gardeners who were planning ahead.

It was now half past four and had been a long day as they had come in early that morning. Apart from the usual customers buying the usual random bunches of flowers and plants, Eileen and Connie had been working on a big order for a Golden Wedding in one of the local hotels. It was a well-known family in the town, and they had invited a hundred and fifty guests.

"Bigger than many ordinary weddings," Eileen had commented, "but then they have ten children, and I suppose by the time you count in husbands and wives and then God knows how many grandchildren, the numbers would easily go up. They're a very decent family anyway, because the daughter who came in with the order said the ten of them were paying for it all between them."

They had to make up two dozen table arrangements for the guest tables, and then three bigger arrangements for the top table.

Then there were special bouquets to be made to be presented to both the lady celebrating her anniversary and the lady who had been her bridesmaid.

Just after four o'clock, Davey the van driver had come in and then they all carried the flower arrangements carefully out to the van, and he took them off to the hotel to be put out on the tables in plenty of time.

Connie went slowly along the row of potted plants and flowers with the watering-can, giving each a good soaking with the mixture of water and plant food. Eileen was an easy-going boss in most respects, but the one thing that Connie had discovered that annoyed her was healthy plants drying out and dying. It was different with bunches of cut flowers which would only last up to a week, and there was nothing anyone could do when they were past their time – but potted plants were an entirely different matter. There would be a month or two of selling-time in the non-flowering shrubs and if the flowering varieties were well-watered and dead-headed, they could last long enough too.

She went in to fill the can for the second time and came back to continue where she had left off. This time she went more slowly, distributing the water, as she could see that some of water from the first plants was now running down the pavement and into the gutter. She would have to go back and go over them all again in case some of the plants had shrunk from the side of the pots and not absorbed any of the moisture.

As she moved along the rows with the can, she wondered if she would see William before he went back tomorrow. She knew there was a chance he might not manage to squeeze any more time for her in. When he'd dropped her off last night, he had told her that practically all of today was spoken for as he was going over to Kildare with Angela and the children in the afternoon, and in the evening he had been invited by Aiden's family to a meal at their house in Birr. He'd explained that there had been several things planned for him that he had already cancelled so he could go to Dublin, and it would be actually rude of him to back out of anything else when Angela and Aiden were always so kind and good to him. He also wanted to squeeze in half an hour somewhere to visit Shay and Tessie before leaving. He'd seen Shay out at the hotel on two occasions, but hadn't seen Tessie as yet.

Connie had assured him that she understood and had not expected him to spend any more time with her, that he had been more than good taking her to the cinema and then to Dublin and that he needed time to himself.

"But, you know, if it had been possible, I would have liked to see you again before I go," he'd said.

"I know there are other things you need to do and other people you need to see," Connie had said. She kept her voice light as though she was not disappointed. "And, really, you've been very good driving me to Dublin and all of that. I've had the most fantastic time, and it will be lovely to remember these last few days."

"It feels so much longer than a few days."

"It does," she'd agreed, "but that's all it was."

Now she finished watering the plants and then went back inside to see if there was anything else that Eileen wanted her to do.

"Oh, Connie," the shopkeeper said, "would you be good enough to take out those half a dozen pink rose bushes that are at the side of the desk, and give them a good watering too? I did them only this morning, and they are as dry as a bone already."

"No problem," Connie said, going through to fill the can again at the sink. "It's lovely outside and will do them good to let them drain and have an hour in the fresh air before we close."

She lifted the full can out of the sink and carried it back to the door, and then went to lift the rose bushes two at a time out to the front pavement. She was just coming out with the last two when she recognised the figure in the nurse's uniform coming quickly down the street towards the shop. She put the rose bushes down and then stood with her hands on her hips, smiling and waiting for her mother. She occasionally dropped in when Connie was at the shop, but she had never come in straight from work.

"Did you fancy a bit of a walk, since it was a nice day?" Connie asked.

"I did. It's been lovely, hasn't it?" Kate looked down at the wet pavement and the freshly watered flowers. "I can see you've been keeping busy."

Connie told her all about the Golden Wedding order as her mother knew the family from church.

"We're nearly finished in the shop now," she then said. "We don't usually sell much at this time of the day so I've been tidying around and watering things." She indicated the rose bushes. "I'm just on the last ones here. Any news?"

Her mother glanced into the shop to check if the owner was within earshot.

Eileen was just coming out with another rose bush she had remembered for watering. When she saw Kate she smiled.

"You can see what a great worker your daughter is!" she said.

"I'm glad to hear it!" said Kate.

"We've had such a busy day!" Eileen said. "Connie, when you've finished watering there, you can go home with your mother. You were in early so I owe you the time. Davey will help me bring the plants in when he comes back with the van."

"Are you sure?" Connie said.

"Just finish watering and lift the seed stand in, and that will be fine. You never know who'd pinch a handful of the seed packets when they think there's no one around." She rolled her eyes. "Men are more likely to go for the vegetable seeds than a bunch of flowers." She smiled at Kate. "I'll get on now as I've a couple of phone calls to make."

"You're lucky there," Kate said, as Eileen disappeared back into the shop. "There's many a young girl run off her feet in some of the other shops or hotels who never gets a word of thanks."

Connie lifted the can to finish off her job. "I was just wondering," she said, not looking directly at her mother, "if there was a reason you had called down here straight from work. Is there anything wrong?"

"Not wrong as such," her mother said. "I just wanted to chat for a few minutes on our own." She halted. "I didn't want to be talking about it in front of your father and the lads …"

Connie put the can down again. "What is it? You've got me worried now."

Her mother took a deep breath. "I was in the X-ray department this morning, and I bumped into Emmet Ferguson."

"Right," Connie said, nodding her head. Just thinking about him now made her feel anxious. With her thoughts more concentrated on William, she had managed to keep him out of her mind for most of the time recently, but she knew it was bound to happen that someone would eventually meet him.

"I just wanted to reassure you that he won't ever trouble you again. I had a good firm word with him and he was nearly in tears by the time I had finished with him."

"Did he admit it?" Connie asked.

Kate nodded. "Oh, he admits everything."

"Well, thank God he at least had the decency to tell the truth about it."

"He said he was so drunk he didn't realise that he had unintentionally hurt you or frightened you in any way. He says he really didn't mean any harm. Oh, he blames everything on drink, and he regrets it all now." She touched Connie's arm. "I'd say he would do anything he could now, to make it right. I'm sure he would apologise face to face to you if you gave him the chance."

Connie went rigid. "I don't want to see him," she said. "And I'm not going to listen to any excuses from him. I know how he acted and what he tried to do."

"He didn't say anything about seeing you – he probably knows you wouldn't give him the chance." Kate paused. "I came to tell you that he's sorry, so you don't have to worry any more about it. To my mind, it's good news. It puts an end to the matter."

"Well, I am relieved," Connie said. "And I'm glad he didn't deny it."

"We won't talk any more about it just now," her mother said, "not with your boss around. We can chat about it walking home."

Connie finished off the last plants, and then, with the help of her mother, they went to lift the lightweight but awkward seed stand inside the shop. But, just as they did so, a car came along the street and slowed to a halt alongside them. Both stopped what they were doing to see who it was, then Connie felt her stomach flip when she recognised the car and realised it was William.

He rolled the window down and leaned out. "Hello, Connie, hello, Mrs Devine, nice to see you both," he said. "I'm just on my way back from Shay and Tessie's and I thought I'd drop by and have a few words." He looked at Kate. "I'm heading back on the boat in the morning, and I thought I'd take the chance to say goodbye."

Connie watched as her mother nodded her head but did not speak or smile.

"I'm actually just finishing up," Connie said, "and my mother's on her way home from work too." She was trying to sound casual, hoping that William would not notice how unfriendly her mother was being – and she was trying not to let her mother see how pleased she was to see him again, even if it was just for a few minutes.

"I'd be happy to drop you both home if you're going straight there?" he said. He leaned behind to open the back door. "You're welcome to sit in, Mrs Devine."

Kate looked at him for a few moments, her eyes narrowed in thought. Then she said, "I will take the lift, thanks."

Connie was taken aback. She hadn't expected her mother to accept as she always said she needed the walk home to clear her head after work. She thought her mother would have gone on ahead and left them on their own since it was just a quick call. Something about it made her feel uneasy.

She started walking back into the shop, taking her apron off as she went. "I'll just collect my bag."

When she came back out, her mother was sitting in the back seat. Connie slowed down, unsure whether to get into the passenger seat or get in beside her mother in the back.

"You sit in the front, Connie," her mother said.

As she opened the car door, she suddenly thought William looked different. The smile had disappeared and he looked really uncomfortable. Her mother had said something and she dreaded knowing what it was.

When Connie was seated, her mother said quietly. "Connie, I want to have a quiet word with you and William, and I've asked him to drive a bit further up the road there, where Eileen won't see us."

As William started up the car, Connie swung around to her mother.

"What's wrong?" she asked.

"Wait," said Kate.

William drove on then pulled in to the side of the road and turned off the engine.

Connie turned to stare at her mother. "Well?" she asked.

"I heard some news that William has kept from everyone."

Kate's voice was calm. "The news he should have told you when you met up at the party the other night."

Connie turned to look at William. "Do you know what this is all about?"

William was silent.

"I've just told him what I've heard today," Kate said. "And I want him to tell you."

William closed his eyes for a few seconds and gave a deep sigh, and said, "Oh, God!" Then, he turned towards her. "I'm really sorry, Connie ... your mother is right, I should have told you."

"What?" Connie said.

"I'm engaged."

Connie's hand flew to her mouth. "You're engaged to be married?"

He nodded.

"Since when?"

"Just a few weeks ago." He held his hands out. "It was unofficial – we haven't even told all the family or anything." He took another deep breath. "I'm presuming that this news came from Jim Fay? He's the only person I told about it, but I hadn't told him all the facts."

Kate shook her head. "He didn't tell me. I don't even know the boy. It was somebody else who was at the party ..."

Connie looked back at her mother. "Emmet!" she said. "It has to be Emmet. My mother had a big long chat with him this morning."

"I had intended to tell you, but I wanted to get back home first," he said. "I wasn't sure I was doing the right thing, but things just ran ahead. To be honest, that's the reason I came over to Ireland. I knew I needed some space to think things over. But I never imagined I was going to meet up with you again, Connie, and then I thought it was better to go home and see how things were before saying anything."

Connie turned her head away from him, as though she was looking out of the window. The conversation, this sitting in the car with her mother and William Fitzgerald, felt like some bizarre kind of dream.

"And how do you think your fiancée would feel if she knew you had been acting the single lad, and playing around with another girl at a party?" Kate said.

"It wasn't like that," he said. "I would never have approached another girl that night – it was only because I recognised Connie. It was because we'd always got on so well when we were younger."

"Well, how would she feel about you being out at the cinema with Connie, and then spending the next evening up in Dublin with her? Do you honestly think she would be happy to hear about it?"

William rubbed the bridge of his nose with his finger. "With the greatest of respect, it's not as straightforward as it seems, Mrs Devine. And whatever Connie thinks of me for not telling her, she will vouch for the fact that we did nothing wrong. I've not tried to take advantage of her or anything like that."

"I know you were good with her when she had the trouble with Emmet, I know all that. But you had no business getting involved with her at all – even for a few days – when you're a man who is promised to somebody else. I know you're an educated lawyer and all the rest of it – but there's no way you can talk your way out of that."

"I'm not trying to, Mrs Devine. I can see how it looks and it's obviously not reflecting well on me."

"And the other girl aside, you can't deny you led Connie on, because I know from the way she was – the sparkle in her eye – that she had a real notion for you. You must have known it."

Connie suddenly swung around. "Mammy!" she snapped. "That's enough."

Kate reached over for the handle and opened the car door. "Okay, I've said my piece now and I'm going to leave the pair of you to sort it out between you."

The car door slammed and then there was silence.

Connie sat staring ahead with her hands clenched tightly. She was trying to work out the most mature and dignified way by which she could exit this unimaginable situation.

"Connie," William said. "I was going to tell you when –"

"There's no need," she interrupted quietly. "There's no need to tell me anything." She tried to smile, but realised that would not work. She took a deep breath instead. "I've had a lovely time, William, but I fully understand that it was just this week while you were over. And whatever my mother has said about any feelings I have for you, I didn't expect anything more. It was just a nice few days in the summer."

"But what if I have feelings for you?"

"You shouldn't have feelings for anyone else if you are engaged to someone. You should never have spent time with me at the party or kissed me or ...." She closed her eyes for a few moments and when she opened them she stared straight ahead.

"I just want to explain," he said. "I should have done much earlier, but I don't know how things are going to turn out and I didn't want to make things more complicated."

She shook her head. "You don't have to explain. There's no point now." She halted. "But, I would like to know the truth about the phone call when we were in the cinema. Were you ringing the girl back in London?"

"Yes," he said, "I was, but what I told you was true. The call was to do with a meeting her father was organising with a law firm for me. It was, in truth, a business call, as I explained to you."

"Okay," Connie said.

"And all the things I said about it being difficult to find a phone box were all absolutely true. I didn't tell you any lies."

She turned to look squarely at him. "Well, I suppose some people would say there was a lie of omission involved. You didn't mention about a fiancée when we were together at the party." She moved her eyes to the car ceiling. "But when I think back, I didn't ask you anything like that, did I?"

"I'm so sorry this has happened, Connie. In all honesty, I thought I was buying some time to sort things out. If I'd stopped to think, I might have realised that this wasn't a good way to handle it. If I'd known how much it would hurt you – hurt us both – I would have done it all so differently."

Connie felt her eyes beginning to fill with tears. Then, from somewhere, she summoned a little smile. "It's probably for the best. I should have realised after what happened with Emmet that I need a break from boyfriends, and that's what I'm going to do. When I get to Manchester, I need to concentrate all my time and energy on my studies, so it's just as well that we didn't make any plans."

William's shoulders slumped. "Do you honestly mean that?"

"Yes," she said, looking straight at him. "I do mean it." Her eyes were bright and her voice determined.

"Won't you at least let me explain about the engagement thing?

163

Even if we don't see each other ever again, I would like you to understand the situation I found myself in. I think if I tell you how it came about, you might be able to forgive me for what has happened. It's really important to me that we don't part on bad terms."

"I'm not parting on bad terms, William, honestly." Connie lifted her bag from the floor and then hugged it tightly in her arms, to try to stop her body from shaking. To give the impression she was all right. "I'm going now, and I just want to say that I wish you and your girlfriend every happiness in your future life."

She leaned across and kissed him lightly on the cheek.

Then, before he had time to reply, she turned and quickly opened the car door. In seconds she was walking briskly up the street, her head erect and her long dark hair swinging as she went.

Chapter 19

When the car pulled up outside the new residential part of Ballygrace House where the family lived, Aiden turned to Angela. "You and William go on into the house, and I'll walk over and see how things are in reception. Most of the cars are in, and it all looks fairly quiet and settled."

"Grand," Angela said. "I'll make a pot of coffee for us and have it ready for you."

Then, as he opened the door, Aiden suddenly had a thought. "You can send Ella out to me in a few minutes, and I'll drop her home."

Ella Keating was Tara's old housekeeper, and a friend she had known from her schooldays. She had continued to work on in Ballygrace House when Angela and Aiden took it over, converted the house and built an extension to turn it into a small country hotel. Ella was happy to turn her hand to anything as she had been involved in the house and Tara's extended family for years, and tonight was earning a few extra pounds baby-sitting Angela's children.

"Are you sure?" Angela said, smiling appreciatively at him. "That would be great, as I would be worried driving after a few glasses of wine."

"It only takes two minutes and it will let her get home." He took

165

her hand and squeezed it. "When I get back I'll have the coffee and we might have a little nightcap too. What do you say, William? I have a nice bottle of Drambuie that a Scottish friend brought me recently."

William nodded and smiled. "No argument here."

They went inside and Angela told Ella that Aiden was outside and would take her home. After she left, Angela made coffee for herself and William and brought it into the sitting-room.

He was in an armchair by the fire, with one of the local newspapers in his hands.

"Thanks," he said, taking the mug of coffee from her. He leaned across and put the newspaper on the coffee table. "That was a lovely night with Aiden's family. The meal was lovely."

"It was," she said, sitting down in the chair opposite. "It's a while since we've been over to Birr on a night out without the children, so it was lovely being able to relax without worrying about their bedtimes." She took a sip from her mug. "It was great you were able to come with us. I know it's only been a short break and you've been busy trying to see your friends, and it was good of you to fit Aiden's family in."

"It was very kind of them to ask me along, and they are such nice people." He smiled at her.

"I'm glad your break has gone so well, and you seem to have done as much as you could in such a short time."

"I'm really grateful, as always, to you and Aiden for putting me up, and especially this time, at such short notice."

"William, there will always be a room in this house for you."

They chatted generally for a few more minutes and then William put his mug down on the table. He folded his hands together in his lap and looked over at Angela.

"To be honest, things haven't been as straightforward this holiday as they have been at other times."

"What do you mean?"

He shrugged and then shook his head. "I didn't want to mention any of this earlier, because I know everyone has their own problems, but I took this week off to come over to Ireland to try to sort out one difficult situation back in London and, instead, I seem to have got myself into a worse situation. Something unexpected happened that I just never could have envisaged."

"Oh? What was it? Nothing too serious, I hope?" Angela frowned, concerned.

"Oh, how do I explain this to you? It's so complicated I don't even understand it myself!"

She gave a little laugh. "Don't forget we've had a few glasses of wine tonight."

"I wish it was just that ... I'm afraid I've made some very big mistakes and no matter which way I look at it, I've ended up hurting people and letting them down." He lifted his gaze and looked straight at her. "If I tell you what's happened, you won't say anything to Tara, will you? I don't want her worrying about me at this stage in my life, and I'd rather tell her about it face to face."

"I won't say a word, I promise. Just start at the beginning and go slow. And don't worry about what you tell me – I've made plenty of mistakes myself. Probably a lot worse than any you've made. You might have even heard about some of the things I got up to over in Stockport when I was younger?" For a few moments she considered lifting the mood by referring to some of the smaller incidents in a light-hearted way – making herself out to be a naïve young Irish eejit who fell into all the obvious traps when first away from home. But, when he said, "No, I didn't hear of any mistakes you made," and shook his head, she could tell that it was the wrong time to make fun of her misdeeds and Tara's reaction to them. She could tell by his manner that whatever was on his mind was serious.

She held her coffee cup between both hands. "Go on," she said quietly, "I'm listening."

"You know I've been going out with Pamela for a while? Pamela Marshall?"

"I did. She's the smallish girl with the short blonde hair I met the last time we were all at Tara's, isn't she?"

"Yes."

"She's a bit older than you, isn't she? A very nice girl though. Didn't you meet her after you broke off with that other girl from Cork?"

William nodded, his face reddening. He wondered if Connie's mother had remembered about his university girlfriend too. "God, when I hear it listed out like that, it makes me sound like some kind of Lothario!"

Angela pulled a little apologetic face. "Oh, sorry, I didn't mean that the way it sounded. Pay no heed to my ramblings. You know what I'm like – I was just working out who it was."

"We actually met through Pamela's father," William explained. "It was last year when I had newly qualified and I was doing vocational training with his firm." He saw the blank look on Angela's face and added, "It's is a period of training you have to do after your degree – it helps you to develop the necessary skills to work as a solicitor."

"And so her father introduced you?"

"Yes," he said. "There was a garden party at the house and he invited me with some of the other staff."

"A garden party?" Angela said. "That sounds lovely. We don't get the weather here in Ireland to plan things like that."

"I'll just rush through the story if you don't mind, because I know Aiden will be back and he probably won't want to hear all this stuff."

"Sorry – go on."

He then went on to tell about his romance with Pamela which he said had been great at first, as he had just moved back to London after Trinity, and it gave him a new social circle. Pamela, he explained, was working for a well-known Music PR company, promoting bands and all that sort of thing.

"Of course," he said, "it was a little tricky working with her father when I was dating her, but I knew I would only be there a few months, and then I would move on to another legal firm – which I did." He shrugged and moved his hands upwards. "Pamela is a lovely girl in many ways and we had a lot of fun. We went off in a group at the weekend to different places, various parties and concerts and so on. We went up to Manchester for a concert the weekend you met her. She often got free tickets to events because of her work."

Angela nodded. "The sort of things you do in London."

"I really do like her but, in all honesty, I never saw us lasting forever, and I actually thought she felt the same, because underneath it all we're quite different."

"Well, that happens," Angela said, enjoying the story now.

He shrugged. "We never really talked the way I did with ... well, the way I think you should with the person you are closest to. Also, I wasn't that keen on the type of people who were at some of the parties she brought me to." He raised his eyebrows. "Let's just say that some of the bands got up to things that a solicitor shouldn't be involved in – or even a solicitor's daughter."

"Do you mean drugs and all that sort of thing? Like The Rolling Stones?"

William gave a weak smile. "Well, I never really met any of the famous bands, but you know the things you hear about. Anyway, I was waiting for the right time to tell her, but there were a few months when the right time just never seemed to happen. I was working and studying a lot of weekends, and she went off on a family holiday and the time just passed and we were still a couple. And I was still waiting to have the opportunity so we could have a proper talk. I was just going to be straight and say I'd had a great time but that I didn't feel we were on the same wavelength – that I was a bit 'square' for her type of social life, and I really thought she would see it exactly as I did and agree to part as friends."

"And how did it work out?"

"It didn't," he said. "The problem is, somehow, I seem to have got myself engaged to her."

"*Engaged?*" Angela echoed. She put her mug down on the table and then stared at him in shock. "And Tara doesn't know?"

"Nobody knew until tonight." He closed his eyes. "It's all such an absolute mess. Before I got the chance to ring her to meet up, Pamela turned up unexpectedly at the office one lunch-time and told me she thought she might be pregnant. It was stupid of me to be shocked – but I was, because we had actually only slept together a few times."

Angela was in shock too now, realising that William was telling her something very serious. She listened in silence as he continued.

"She said, if it was confirmed she was pregnant, that we would have to get married, and when I thought about it there seemed to be no other option. It was the only decent thing to do, so of course I agreed."

"Oh, William! And you're still so young!"

"That night we met up again, and Pamela said she had been

thinking about it all, about her parents' reaction and how my mother would be. She was quite upset and worried – not as confident as I had thought she might be which made me feel worse. And she said she thought that it might be better if we got engaged beforehand, so that if the pregnancy news came a month or two later, it didn't look as if we were having a shotgun wedding."

"She really had worked it all out," Angela said.

"Not quite," William said. "We agreed to keep it quiet until we had bought the ring the following weekend. But then, the Saturday morning we were due to go shopping for the ring, she discovered that she wasn't pregnant at all."

"You must have been relieved," Angela said. "So, did you not tell her then?"

"I tried to," he said, "but she went almost hysterical. She said she thought I really loved her and wanted to get married. I told her that I did care for her, but that I felt neither of us were mature enough to commit to something so huge when there was no rush. I said maybe if we gave things a few more months to see if we really wanted to go ahead with it then." He gave a huge sigh. "And then she admitted that she had told her parents that we were going for the ring and made them promise to act surprised when we arrived at their house. She said she had wanted me to do everything by the book, you know, formally ask her father for her hand in marriage and everything." William's eyes filled up now. "I feel like an absolute fool just listening to myself. How on earth could I have got myself into such a situation?"

"So you didn't back out?"

He shrugged. "I couldn't. I decided that if we gave it a try, then we could always break up later. You often hear of engagements breaking up later, don't you? So, I ended up going through with the whole charade to appease everyone."

"So you got the ring and you are now engaged?"

He nodded. "I asked Pamela's family to keep it to themselves for the time being. I said my mother wasn't too well, and that I would rather tell her when it was a better time and they understood. It was actually true – as you know, my poor mother is often not well with her nerves."

"I know, I know." Angela's head was bobbing up and down,

picturing Elisha Fitzgerald's reaction if she knew all this. "Does your mother like Pamela?"

"She's actually only met her a couple of times, and I don't think she really registered with her. She thought she was nice, but I think she used the word 'flighty' to describe her."

"So, what's going to happen?"

"The one thing I know for sure is that I can't go through with a wedding to Pamela. I came here to clear my head, and I am now surer than ever that it would be completely the wrong thing to do. But breaking up is not going to be an easy thing. Since I've been here, I've just discovered that Pamela's father has arranged a meeting for me next week with another one of the top law firms in London." He held his hands out. "It's for next year, the next stage in my law training."

"I thought you were qualified when you got your degree from university?"

William smiled now. "I wish it were that easy. There's an awful lot more to it than that. You have to go through various stages and keep sitting exams afterwards." He sat back in his chair. "So, I'm in an awful position. I know the right thing to do is just tell the truth to everyone now but, apart from hurting Pamela and her family, it's really going to affect my future career. Her father is well-known in the London law world, and can you imagine the sort of reputation I'm going to have if I tell them that I didn't really mean it after all when I asked for Pamela's hand in marriage!"

"Oh, God, William," Angela said, "I can see what you mean ..."

"I've spoken to Pamela since I've been here. I rang her from Tullamore the other night. I tried to cancel the meeting for the day after I go back. I said to her that I don't want to use her father's contacts, but she said he will be very put out if I don't go ahead with the meeting at least."

"Is there a chance," Angela said, "that if you give things a little more time that Pamela might mature a bit more? You might then discover you've more in common. I know it might sound a silly thing to say, but that happened to me. I'm sure if Aiden had met me when I was younger, he wouldn't have looked twice at me."

"The thing is," William said, "Pamela is actually five years older than me."

"Oh," Angela said, "I didn't realise ... but that's not a really big gap."

"She doesn't look it, but she is that little bit older. I do know what you're saying about maturing, but I think the problem is our personalities. I think that fundamentally we're quite different people. I can't really explain what I mean, but I think, regardless of age and time passing, we'll always see things from different angles."

"Maybe she doesn't realise. Have you talked seriously to her about the friends and the parties and the things you're not happy about? Maybe if you gave her a chance."

"I have, and again I think she would make an effort to do things differently, but whether that would bring us any closer I don't know ..."

There was a noise outside now and they both looked towards the door as Aiden came in.

"Everything okay?" he asked, seeing their serious faces.

"Grand," Angela said, "We're just having a bit of a chat, catching up on news ..."

He came into the middle of the room. "There's a problem with the lights over the main cooker, two of the bulbs have gone. I said I would get up in the morning to replace them before breakfast starts, so I'll have to be up before seven." He looked over at William. "You don't mind if I skip the coffee and nightcap and go off to bed?"

"Not at all," William said. He got to his feet and went with his hand outstretched to Aiden. "Thanks for everything – your hospitality, and for generally making me so welcome. You always do."

"Any time," Aiden said, giving a firm, warm handshake. "Any time." He smiled over at Angela and then indicated the long mahogany cabinet. "The Drambuie is in the bottom cupboard."

After he left, Angela said, "Would you like a little drink? I'll have one with you."

William smiled at her. "I will, thanks. It might just help. There's a bit more to the story."

"I'm all ears. I'll just get the drinks first." Angela went to the cupboard and came back with two tumblers filled to a third with the liqueur. She handed one to William and then sat down and took a drink from her own. "Oh," she said, pulling a face, "it's a bit

172

strong …" She gave a little cough. "I think I might have to put some lemonade in it."

William bit his lip, trying not to laugh. "I think Aiden might not be too impressed. If you take a smaller sip you might like it better." He took a sip himself, demonstrating. "It's lovely when you get used to it."

Angela took another smaller drink. "You're right," she said, "it's not as bad." She lifted her eyes in thought. "I think I can taste honey in it."

"You probably can," he said, smiling encouragingly.

Angela kicked her shoes off now, sat back in the chair and tucked her feet under her. "Now," she said, "where were we?"

"Basically," William said, "Pamela and I are now unofficially engaged, and when I get back I have to tell my mother and the rest of the family. And then, I think Pamela's parents want to throw a party for us."

"Probably another garden party," Angela said, "since it's the right time of year for it."

"Meanwhile, I'm just digging myself in deeper and deeper, knowing that I'm going to be with a lovely girl – but the wrong girl – for the rest of my life."

"When you put it like that it does sound serious."

"It is, especially now I've recently met another girl, who has made me realise how amazing it feels to be with someone who is much more in tune with me."

"Ah! So now we're getting to the root of it all. You've met someone else." Angela let out a long, low whistle. She took another sip of her Drambuie, and then looked at the glass and took another little sip. "Is it someone in London?"

"No. It's here. And it's a lot more complicated than that." He lifted his glass and took a long swallow. "You're going to be shocked now." His voice had a tremor in it. "It's actually your niece … Connie Devine."

Angela's eyes widened. "*Connie?* Are you *serious?*"

He nodded. "Very serious. I've seen her almost every day since I've been here. I told you I met her at the party, didn't I?"

Angela sat up straight again, amazed at what he was telling her. "Oh, I knew that … and I knew you were out at the cinema with the lads."

"They didn't come out with us. I invited them all here for a meal one evening, but apparently it's not the sort of thing the lads do and they had other plans." He shrugged. "It was just the way it worked out. So, I ended up spending more time with Connie. We even went to Dublin yesterday evening. You were busy over in the hotel yesterday afternoon before I left, and then we were with the children and I didn't get the chance to tell you."

"I understand," she said. "Sure, there are times when I don't get five minutes to tell Aiden things myself."

"I wasn't intentionally keeping it a secret." He rolled the glass between his hands, looking down at the floor. "But, I suppose in many ways I was afraid to say anything. I knew from the minute we met out at Jim Fay's house that there was something between us."

"And how does Connie feel?"

"She did feel the same. We got on so well, we had such a great time together. Every single minute we spent together felt just right. I know she is a few years younger and just starting university, but we love the same music, enjoy reading the same things, and we both just have such a laugh together."

Angela nodded as he spoke, her brows knitted together in thought.

"We always got on well when we were teenagers, and now that she's older we just have so much more in common than I ever had with Pamela."

"What a situation!" she said. She shook her head. "Although, if anything was to come of it, it's probably easier now that Connie is going to university in Manchester." She paused. "Although her mother is not too happy about it. Daddy and Tessie were out at the house, and he said you could have cut the atmosphere with a knife when the subject of Manchester came up."

"Her mother wasn't too happy when she found out about me and Connie either," William said. "Well, actually, it was more to do with the fact that she found out about Pamela and me being engaged." He shook his head. "A chance in a million that she would have heard. I only told one person in Ireland about it – Jim Fay, the chap whose party we were at – and he unfortunately blurted it out to the wrong person. He didn't mean any harm but

174

the news travelled nevertheless. I never imagined for a minute that anyone, especially Connie's mother, would hear about it. I was waiting until I got home and saw how things were with Pamela before telling Connie."

"Oh, no ..." Angela said. "I presume Kate told her?"

William nodded slowly and then he lifted his glass and drained it. "Yes, this afternoon, and that's where we are up to now."

"How did Connie react?"

"I think she was shocked the way she found out. I was shocked too when her mother hit me with it in the car. I'd just offered her and Connie a lift home and it was the last thing I expected."

"It's her daughter and she wants to protect her. My mother would have done the very same."

"I can see that," William said, "but I never got the chance to explain to Connie. She wouldn't listen."

"Was she very angry?"

He thought for a few seconds. "No, not really," he said. "I might have felt better if she had been angry."

"Maybe she's trying to work it out," Angela said. "She's a clever girl, and she might realise that you were obviously not happy with Pamela if you enjoyed spending so much time with her."

William shook his head. "I think she has made up her mind already. We had a few nice days together out of the summer and, as far as she is concerned, that's all we amounted to."

175

Chapter 20

At ten o'clock on a Tuesday morning, Kate Devine was standing at the kitchen sink, having just put her cleaning cloths into a basin of hot water and bleach. She was on a late shift in the ward, starting at two o'clock, so had plenty of time to clean and tidy around the house, while a piece of bacon cooked on the hob for the family to have for dinner that evening.

She looked out into the sun-filled garden, at the tidy rows of lettuces and cabbages and the tall tomato plants which Seán had carefully supported with cane stakes. There was already a full dish of the small, just-ripened tomatoes in the fridge, and every day Seán would add more to the collection. More than they could possibly use. Tomorrow Kate would fill another dish and bring it into the small nurses' staff-room on her ward for the other nurses to help themselves to. She would do the same with any extra lettuces that they had or anything else that Seán brought in from the garden.

Things had been busy over the last few weeks, getting everything sorted for Connie leaving, and her departure was now starting to become real. It had already been established that Connie had far too much stuff to take over in one suitcase. After some discussion about plane fares to Manchester and a ticket which covered the coach and the boat, it had been decided that Seán bringing the car over on the ferry would be the handiest thing of all.

So far, Kate was not sure whether she was going to accompany them or not. She would like to see the university and the halls of residence where Connie would be living. What she did not want was to suddenly feel upset when the time came to say a final goodbye, because she knew they would not see Connie again until the Christmas holidays. The other thing she did not want was to see Tara and all the crowd in Stockport. She did not want them to see how hard she found it to have Connie so far away in England – how hard she found it knowing that Connie was only a bus ride away from them and a whole Irish Sea away from her mother. She did not want to imagine Connie becoming closer and closer to Tara and Bridget Roberts, the way that Seán's sister Angela had done.

She had already been over and over it all in her mind, and had now resigned herself to it. Connie was going to England and whether she waved goodbye to her at home in Tullamore or when they dropped her off in Manchester, she would get through it. She would grit her teeth and get on with life back at home. She had already decided she would join in with any evening winter activities she liked, that would also make the weeks pass quicker until it was December. She had accepted the role of prompter for the local amateur dramatic group which she used to do regularly, but hadn't done these last few years. She would be attending rehearsals two or three times a week from late September and the play would be ready for production late November. That would take her into the run-up to Christmas and she wouldn't feel it then until it was time for Connie to come home. She would have to juggle around with her evening shifts in the hospital, but she didn't mind as it would mean she was busy working or in rehearsals almost every night of the week.

She finished tidying around the kitchen, and then went over to the cleaning cupboard to get the Hoover out to vacuum the hall and the front room. She was just pushing the Hoover into the hall when she heard the letterbox banging on the front door.

She waited a few moments until the postman had gone, then she went to collect the post.

She was surprised to see four envelopes on the mat – two brown printed and two white handwritten ones – one of which felt like a card. She bent down to pick them up and immediately felt a stab of annoyance when she recognised the handwriting on the two white envelopes.

They were from Tara. The card was addressed to Connie and the letter to her and Seán.

She went back into the kitchen and took the boiling kettle off the stove and then got the teapot. In a few minutes she was sitting at the table with a strong cup of tea reading the flower-decorated pages written for her and Seán.

She read Tara's letter through twice, and then she sat back in her chair drinking her tea and thinking it over. What she had dreaded was now starting to happen. She was going to lose Connie completely. She was going to go to Manchester and become part of Tara's family and become embroiled with all her friends. She would become so influenced by them all that she would come home at Christmas and be like a complete stranger.

Kate closed her eyes, trying to remember all the things she had promised herself that afternoon in the church. That she would be grateful for having such a lovely, decent and respectful daughter who would make them all proud when she became a doctor. That she would allow Connie to live her own life and try not to interfere with her life in England. That when she felt down and at her lowest about all this that she would remember and say the words of the Serenity Prayer: *God teach me to ... accept the things I cannot change.*

She then said the 'Memorare' to Our Lady again, asking for her help in finding a solution to her problem. She sat for a while in silence and then she blessed herself and moved away from the table, to go out into the hallway to finish her hoovering.

It was a good hour later when the answer to her request came in the shape of her second cousin, Sheila Doyle. She had been pondering about travelling over to Manchester with Connie and her mind had gone back to the last time the family had been over there. She had recalled the various places they had visited such as Bramhall Hall and Lyme Park and the place with the zoo and all the hurdy-gurdies, the name of which she couldn't remember, when Sheila's face had suddenly flashed into her mind.

She and Sheila had gone to school together in Tullamore, and were in the same class. While Kate was small, slim and blonde, Sheila was tall, dark-haired and wore glasses. They had directly opposite personalities as Kate was quiet and unsure until she got to know someone well, and then when she got to know them better, she gradually became more chatty and open. Sheila on the other hand was very confident and on the school debating team. Outside of school she was never shy in offering her opinion on politics, religion or anything that was currently topical to anyone who would listen.

The girls had never been close friends or even visited each other's houses regularly, but, being second-cousins on their mothers' side, they had always had a connection with each other. They also saw each other at Mass most Sundays and occasionally met up at family weddings and the like. After school, they had both gone on to train as nurses, Kate in Dublin and Sheila over to Harrow in London.

While she was still doing her training in Harrow, Sheila had met a lad from Limerick called Finbar, who was working in the Harrow bank branch that she used. He invited her to a concert and they started going out regularly, and after a while they got engaged. Finbar then got promotion which entailed moving to another branch up in Manchester and, the following year after she qualified, Sheila applied for a nursing position in a hospital near to her fiancé. When she was offered the post, she immediately accepted and moved up to Manchester to live in digs near his and to plan their wedding. Everything was working out fine and they were both due to go home to Tullamore that summer to sort out the church arrangements.

Sheila had only been in Manchester for six weeks when Finbar came around one night to tell her that he was very sorry but that he couldn't marry her. It turned out that in Sheila's absence he had become close to one of his female bank colleagues. When he told the woman in question that Sheila was moving up, they agreed it was only right to go their separate ways, and let him get on with his wedding plans.

Unfortunately, fate had other plans when his colleague fainted behind the bank counter at work while serving, and when he helped her out to the staff room he discovered that she was almost three months pregnant with his child. He would still be getting married, Finbar explained, but unfortunately Sheila would not be the bride.

Given that he was an Irish Catholic, the same as herself, Sheila knew there was no room for manoeuvre. Finbar would have to do the right thing and marry the girl.

Next time she wrote a letter home, she told her family the devastating news – which quickly spread around the town – and everyone expected that she would hand her notice in at the hospital and come back home. Sheila took a few weeks to think things over and then she informed her family that she had no intentions of returning to Tullamore and that she liked her new job and liked living in Manchester more than she had in London. After that, the interest gradually died down in Sheila being jilted and she just seemed to quietly get on with her life.

Time passed and all three Devine children were at Secondary School when Seán and Kate decided they would go over to Stockport for a holiday. Tara had organised two rooms for them in the Cale Green Hotel. The Sunday before they went, Kate was coming out of early morning Mass when she saw Sheila's mother coming out of the side-entrance to the church and waved over to her. Mrs Doyle greeted her warmly and when Kate mentioned their trip to Manchester the following week, she asked her to call in on Sheila as she worried about her living on her own with only a spoiled little poodle for company.

Kate thought quickly. Visiting Sheila could be a handy excuse to get away from Tara and the crowd in Stockport for an afternoon or an evening. It all depended on how near it was to the hotel where they were staying. Mrs Doyle gave her the address and phone number and she wrote it down on an envelope she had in her bag.

"I'll ring her once I'm settled in at the hotel," Kate said. "And hopefully I'll catch her at some point over the first few days and make arrangements to meet up."

"Go out to her house," Mrs Doyle said. "It will be nice for you to see it, so you can picture where she is." She paused. "Did you say you were staying in a hotel? Is it the one that Tara Flynn owns?"

"Yes," Kate said.

"What's the name of it?"

"It's called the Cale Green Hotel."

"Imagine Seán's sister owning a hotel. Hasn't she done well for herself?"

Kate raised her eyebrows and nodded. She could have kicked herself for giving an opening to have praise heaped on Tara yet again.

"And then there's Seán's other sister who has the lovely place out in Ballygrace. Imagine two of them doing so well for themselves! Isn't it a credit to them? When you think they both came from such ordinary circumstances and, between you and me, Shay Flynn wasn't always the best father to them." She gave a little smile. "Oh, he's always been the likeable type and he's the finest fellow you could meet these days, but we all know he wasn't dependable when the family were young. Far from it."

Kate did not need reminding about Shay Flynn's shortcomings. Poor Seán had spent all his life making sure he was the opposite of his outgoing and hail-fellow-well-met father.

She looked at her watch. "I'd better move," she said. "I have to get the lads and Connie out of bed now for the ten o'clock Mass, and then get the breakfast cooked for them coming back."

"Well, have a safe trip over," Mrs Doyle said. "And I'll be looking forward to seeing you when you get back and hearing any news you have about Sheila."

A couple of weeks later after Kate arrived back home, she went up to Mrs Doyle's house one free afternoon to fill her in on the news about her visit to her daughter. She told her how welcome Sheila had made her and Seán in her beautiful house, and all about the lovely salad she had waiting for them on her dining-room table. She also said how glamorous Sheila was looking and how well she had done to be promoted to a ward sister in the big hospital.

"Seán and I both think she's very settled over in Stockport," Kate said. "She has a good job and talked about all the friends she has, and the dances and fancy restaurants she goes to at the weekends. And of course she has Poppy, her little poodle."

"There's no man though?"

"She didn't mention anyone," Kate said, "and I didn't like to ask. She talked about her friends and their busy social life."

"She's still putting a brave face on it, I'd say. She's never got over that Limerick fellow, and I don't think she ever will."

After the visit, Kate and Sheila had kept in touch more, with Christmas cards and the odd letter if Kate had any news about old school friends or nurses they both knew in Ireland and abroad. But on the whole, as she went about her daily life, Sheila Doyle was rarely on Kate's mind.

But now, a thought had occurred to her, and she suddenly felt grateful she had kept up that sporadic contact. If she could get Sheila to keep an eye on Connie, it would not only be reassuring to her and Seán, but it would save Connie from having to depend on Tara if she ran into any problems.

She would ring Sheila and see if she could suggest some sort of Saturday or weekend job for Connie that would give her a few pounds' pocket money and keep her busy.

Kate went back downstairs to the kitchen, feeling happier and more in control than she had felt in weeks. If Sheila could not come up with any ideas for a weekend job now, she might come up with something in the coming weeks or months.

She went over to the stove and put the warm kettle back on to boil, then she went to the table and picked up the letter from Tara. She cast her eyes over it once again and as she did so, she felt a wave of anger rising inside her. Then, before she had time to give any thought to what she was doing, she ripped the flowery pages first in halves then in quarters. She paused for a few moments and then she started ripping at it again until the paper fell like small petals onto the table.

She stared down at the pieces and then she quickly gathered them all up and went over to the stove and opened it and threw them into the burning flames. She went back to stand by the window and then turned back and picked up the card addressed to Connie. She turned it over in her hands several times, wondering what to do. Could Tara have written another letter with all the same details about offering Connie to stay and work at the hotel, and put it inside the card? Could she have written a shorter note about it in the card? Any young girl would jump at the offer, and before anyone knew it would be all organised and Connie's life would take a different turn if she was to spend so much time with the Kennedys.

Kate could not take that chance.

She went over to the boiling kettle now and held the sealed side of the envelope over the steam. She turned it around and around

182

until she saw the edge beginning to lift.

Then, she moved back to the drawer and got a smooth-edged knife out and very gently lifted the flap of the envelope back.

She slid the card out. On the front it had an amusing cartoon picture of a girl wearing a mortar board and gown and holding test-tubes, with the words *To a Real Smart Gal!* Kate took a deep breath and opened the card. A five-pound note fluttered and then fell back into place. She held her breath as she looked at the writing on the card and digested it. Then, she let out a long, low sigh.

Tara had not mentioned anything about the hotel or going to stay with them or anything like that. She had just written:

We are all so, so proud of you and can't wait to see you when you come over to start university in Manchester. Use the little gift enclosed to buy something you might need for starting out on your big adventure as a student!

Lots of Love from Tara, Frank and the little Kennedys xxxx

Relief washed over her. *Thank God,* she thought to herself. She felt bad enough for tearing up the letter, but it would have left her feeling much worse if she'd had to destroy the nice card and then work out what to do with the money. The letter was different. She had no option but to burn it to buy her time to sort something out. No one else had seen it, so she would just act as though it had never arrived.

Her heart lighter now, she carefully slid the card and five-pound note back into the envelope. She held the envelope up to the heat of the stove until it gently dried, then fetched a bottle of glue and applied a very thin layer to the flap. Then she pressed the flap down with a clean tea-towel. A wave of relief washed over her when she examined it closely and could see that it looked as though it had never been opened.

Then, she left the resealed card down on the table for Connie to see when she came in from the flower shop.

Chapter 21

Sheila Doyle pushed her black patent-leather bag high up on her left shoulder, and shifted the small box of groceries to the same arm to allow her to put the key in the Chubb lock and open the front door.

Once inside, she walked a few steps along the hallway and then dropped the box down on top of the pine chest of drawers. Then, with a little sigh of relief, she kicked off her black patent stilettoes and slid her feet into a flat, comfortable pair of tan, suede loafers. She went along the hallway to the kitchen, smiling as she heard the scratching sound on the door. When she went in, Poppy was there jumping around and licking her legs to welcome her.

She ushered the poodle through the utility room to the back door leading out into the garden, which was a reasonable size for a semi-detached house in Hazel Grove.

At times, she still could not believe her luck in finding the house some years back as it was much bigger than she had ever expected to buy for her first house – and it had been an absolute bargain.

She had put down a good deposit and then taken out a small mortgage with enough over to furnish it and do up any rooms that needed decorating. In less than a year, Sheila had the house and garden of her dreams, and a bedroom furnished with white furniture which was like nothing she had ever seen back in

Tullamore. The town she rarely thought of these days, and was never likely to return to.

She led Poppy down the three steps from the kitchen to the outside area. Just outside the back kitchen door there was a small paved area with a white wrought-iron table and four chairs. While Poppy went off to the grassy area at the bottom of the garden to 'do her business' Sheila looked at the flowers, and wondered whether she would need to cut some to bring indoors at the weekend.

She always waited until a Saturday to see if she received a bought bunch as a gift, as she did every few weeks. She smiled to herself, thinking how her family and her old friends at home pitied her for not being married with half a dozen kids running around. They still thought of her as the young, naïve nurse who had been more or less dumped at the altar. How completely wrong they were. The last thing she needed was children making demands on her life. She found herself in a difficult position at times, because people assumed since she was single that they were doing her a favour including her in family events or asking her to baby-sit. In fact, recently she'd had to put her foot down as a couple she knew had asked her on several occasions – at very short notice – if she could help them out with their two small children. They had come up with long, convoluted explanations as to why they were so desperate and she didn't feel she could refuse without offending them, so she had stepped in and helped. But Sheila knew they were the scatty, haphazard kind that would continually use her as a fall-back position when they felt they had used up their time with everyone else.

There was no way she was going to allow that to happen. She was grateful that she had not become a mother herself and tied down with all the constraints that went with it. She was not going to take on another woman's burdens.

In her forties now, Sheila still had a great life. She could go where she wanted to and do what she liked without answering to anyone. And she was not short of company. She had plenty of female friends to go out with at the weekends and to go away with on holiday. That's if she didn't have a better offer. She was entirely independent and didn't have to explain anything to anyone.

Poppy came running back to her now and they both headed back into the house. In the utility room, Sheila took a damp cloth and carefully wiped the poodle's paws. As she did so, she heard the phone ring. She went quickly out into the hall and into the sitting-room.

The phone was on a small side-table by one of the fireside armchairs – a perfect place for her to chat while having a cigarette, or drink her coffee or a gin and tonic.

Just as she went to lift the receiver, she cast a glance at the clock on the white marble mantelpiece, wondering if it was likely to be her mother. She thought for a quick moment – if it was, it was probably just to let her know that the money she had sent last week had arrived safely.

She lifted the receiver. The voice on the other end was uncertain and it was not her mother's.

"Is that Sheila Doyle?"

Sheila's mind raced as she tried to work out who it might be. She thought it was an Irish accent, but the woman had spoken so quickly she couldn't be sure.

"Who is calling?" she asked in a low voice.

"It's Kate Devine ... Kate Devine from Tullamore. Is that Sheila?"

Sheila sank down into the armchair. "Hello, Kate," she said. "What a surprise to hear from you. Is everything okay at home?"

"Absolutely fine," Kate said. "I was just thinking of you the other day, and thought I might give a ring to see how you were getting on. I have a bit of news for you. My daughter, Connie, is coming over at the end of September to study medicine at Manchester University."

"Well, isn't that just wonderful news!" Sheila said, smiling into the phone. "I'm delighted for her and for all the family. You must be very proud of her."

"Oh, we are, we are," Kate said, sounding a bit breathless. "And how are things with you? Are they still keeping you busy at the hospital?"

"Indeed they are," Sheila laughed. "So busy, there are times that I wish I hadn't taken on the ward sister's position. You never get a minute, there's always someone who needs to check things – can't make a decision on their own. I'm sure you know the kind of nurse I'm describing. You have them in every hospital."

"Indeed I do," Kate said. She paused for a few seconds. "And how is little Poppy? Keeping you on your toes as usual?"

"She is, the little madam! She has me wrapped around her little finger and that's the truth – though I suppose dogs have toes not fingers! Although I don't know what I'd do without her."

"Oh, I'm sure you'll have her for a good few years to come."

"I certainly hope so."

There was another pause, which made Sheila think that there was a reason that Kate had rung, and she guessed it was something to do with Connie coming over to Manchester.

"And tell me," she said, "is Connie all excited about starting university or is she feeling nervous about it?"

"A bit of both, I suppose," Kate said. "But I'm sure she'll get on fine. It's just a case of getting stuck into her studying and doing everything she is told to do."

"She'll be grand," Sheila said. "And you want her to have a good time being a student as well and enjoy a bit of freedom."

"I suppose so ..." Kate sounded very uncertain.

"I know I certainly enjoyed my nursing training down in London," Sheila said. "All the great dances we went to and all the parties in the Nurses' Residences. We had the time of our lives. I'm sure you did in Dublin as well?"

"Ah, we had a good enough time, I suppose ..." Kate paused. "We were just thinking that Connie is going to be looking for a weekend job and I was just wondering if you might know of anything that would suit her?"

Sheila smiled to herself. She had known there was a reason for Kate's call.

"She's a sensible girl," said Kate, "and has had great experience working this summer in a local flower shop in Tullamore. She can do wedding bouquets and floral displays and everything."

Sheila raised her eyebrows in interest. "And is it shop work she's looking for?"

"Not necessarily. Anything really. Just something to give her a few pounds and to give her something to do at the weekends."

"Offhand, I don't know of anything myself, but I'll ask around at the hospital," Sheila said. "And there are plenty of nice flower shops around Stockport and Manchester, especially near the cemeteries and hospitals." Then, before Kate got a chance to rope her into phoning places or calling in on Connie's behalf, she quickly added, "She would be best going around the shops herself when she gets over here. They will want to see her in the flesh rather than an older woman like me speaking for her."

"True ..." Kate's voice had a tinge of disappointment. "But if you hear of anything in the meantime."

"Of course," Sheila said.

They chatted for a while longer, Kate passing on some local news, and then when there was no common ground left to discuss, the conversation came to a natural conclusion.

Sheila shook her head and tutted as she put the phone back in the cradle. She had known Kate Devine hadn't phoned for just a friendly chat. Why was it that people always seemed to want something from her?

Chapter 22

In the middle of the afternoon a few days later, when Kate had her day off and was busy tackling the washing of the bedding from the two boys' beds, the phone rang. Her heart lifted when she heard Sheila Doyle's voice, and lifted even further when she heard the news.

"I might have found something for Connie," Sheila said. "I've been speaking to some younger friends of mine – a couple in their thirties called Ian and Vanessa Hamilton. They have an Interior Design business, which has a shop and they go out to people's houses as well. They are a very respectable couple and they have done exceptionally well for themselves."

"What kind of business did you say?" Kate interrupted.

"Interior Design," Sheila repeated. "It's a shop that sells furniture and curtains and cushions and that kind of thing. They also go out to people's houses and advise them on the sort of colours and designs that would work for them."

"Oh, right," Kate said. "It must be a shop for the very well-to-do by the sound of it. And do they want Connie to work in the shop?"

"No," Sheila said. "They need help at home. They have two lovely little children aged four and nearly three, and they need a bit of extra help at the weekend. They already have a woman called Audrey who helps out with the kids during the week, and another who comes in a few days a week to do the cleaning and tidying and sort the children's meals and that kind of thing." She halted. "They have the most beautiful big house in Wilmslow – a very expensive area just outside of Manchester. It's an old house, but you wouldn't think it when you go inside – it has every gadget you can imagine. She would probably stay there the Friday and Saturday nights as they have to do a lot of socialising for their work. She could do her studying while the children are in bed."

Kate bit her lip. The thought of Connie living with complete strangers in a strange place worried her now. "And are the family Catholics?" she asked.

"Are they *Catholics*?" Sheila repeated, her voice high with surprise. "Sure that sort of thing doesn't matter over here. Do you only want her to work for Catholic people? If you do, then you're going to find it hard asking people personal questions about their religion. It's not the done thing over here. Connie will soon find that out at university. It's a case of live and let live."

"I'm sorry, I didn't mean it like that," Kate said. "I was just thinking about her getting to Mass on a Sunday morning."

"Oh, I'm sure she'll be able to arrange something. There are churches of all kinds everywhere. She'll find somewhere to go to Mass easily enough."

Kate's mind was whirling. "And is it very near Stockport?" she asked, wondering if it would it be anywhere near Tara.

Sheila paused. "Well, she'll be travelling from Manchester University, won't she?"

"Yes, she will."

"Well, I think it's easy enough to get a bus there straight from Manchester. In fact, she can probably get a train from Piccadilly Station to Wilmslow."

"So, she wouldn't have to go near Stockport?"

"I don't know if the train passes through Stockport or not. Does it matter which route the train takes?" Sheila sounded exasperated.

"No, no ... I was just wondering." Kate wished she could explain why she didn't want Connie to be too close to Stockport or Bramhall, but she didn't want to talk about Seán's family to anyone

– and she had a feeling that Sheila would be the last one to understand her reasoning.

"Maybe you would prefer her to look for a weekend job in Stockport? You have relatives out there, don't you? The ones that have the hotel. Maybe they might have something more suitable."

Kate closed her eyes. It was clear by the tone of Sheila's voice that she was in danger of talking Connie out of the job. "They are actually relatives of Seán's," she explained, "but we're not very close and we don't see them that often. I wouldn't like to be under any kind of compliment to them to ask for a job." Her heart sank now as she thought of Tara's letter and heard herself telling outright lies. "To be honest I'd prefer if she got something through you, Sheila, since we've known each other all those years. And the family you mentioned sound fine. If you recommend them then there's no problem."

"Well, if you're sure," Sheila said. "Because they'll be able to find another student or au pair easily enough. The house is like something out of a film, you've never seen anything like it."

"Sure, your own house is a palace," Kate said. "It's about the nicest house I've ever been in."

"Ah, go away!" Sheila said, laughing. "It's nice enough, but it's certainly not in the same league as the Hamiltons' out in Wilmslow, that's for sure." She paused now to light a cigarette. "Tell you what, I'll ring Vanessa at the shop now and tell her that Connie will be available in the next few weeks. How does that sound?"

"Oh, that would be great!" Kate said. "She'll be delighted, and it will keep her out of trouble and give her a bit of pocket money."

As she put the phone back in its cradle, it crossed her mind that Connie could refuse the job, but she had a feeling that she would go with it for a while at least, so as not to cause any upset.

Later that evening, when Connie came in from the flower shop, Kate, all smiles, guided her into the front room so they could talk in private.

Connie sat down on the edge of the sofa while her mother sat on one of the armchairs by the fire. She felt slightly on edge as her mother seemed in a particularly good humour.

"Now, Connie," Kate said, "I have some news. My cousin, Sheila, has sorted out a weekend job for you whenever you go over to Manchester. She lives over there, not too far from the university, and she knows a businesswoman who needs help with her children. I was speaking to her on the phone a short while ago and mentioned you going to university and she said she would do her best to find something for you, as most of the students have little jobs to help them out."

"Your cousin Sheila?" Connie's brow wrinkled. "I can't remember her. Do I know her from when I was small?"

"She's lived in England a long time," Kate said, her tone even. "She called out to the house here a few years ago, but you might not have been in, and me and your father went to visit her one of the times we went to Stockport. She is a cousin on my side of the family. Anyway, Sheila has the job all sorted for you. The family live in a big luxury house out in a place called Wilmslow, and the wife was looking for someone to help out at the weekends. They have an older woman there during the week. When she heard you were going to be studying medicine, she said you would be ideal with the children." She clapped her hands together. "Isn't that great? It will give you pocket money and you'll be able to do your studying when the children are in bed."

Connie nodded, trying to take it all in. "Is it every weekend? What if there is something on in the university – a social event or something like that?"

Kate shrugged. "Well, I'm sure they will be able to work something out. They sounded like a very modern couple the way Sheila described them. They have some sort of furniture business, and they do up houses for people."

Connie felt overwhelmed with all this new information. She was still reading her University Prospectus and the medical books she had been advised to buy in advance to prepare for the course. She was still trying to picture herself in the rooms where she would go for her lectures, imagining herself in the Student Halls of Residence and eating in the refectory and walking around the grounds of the University Campus. She found herself going over and over all the information in the prospectus, so that it would all feel familiar to her when the time came to go.

Now, her mother had just given her another totally different world to think about.

Chapter 23

Kate looked out of the sitting-room window and then at the clock, then she looked at her husband who was dozing in the chair opposite her. The whole family were supposed to be watching an American murder film, but it had descended into an unbelievable farce which Ollie had decreed "pure shite". He and Terry were the first to vacate the room, saying they were off for a run out to Rahan, to see a friend who had bought a second-hand van the day before – Terry had said he would have a look at the indicators – so the lads decided it was a better bet than the film.

Connie had given up too, and taken herself off to her room to knit and read.

Kate sat for a while, thinking that soon this would be it. Her and Seán sitting at the fire like 'oul' ones'. Connie would soon be gone and, any day now, Ollie would make an announcement and he would get married and go. Terry, you never knew what he could do. At different times over the last year, Kate had come across newspapers from both America and Australia lying around in his room. Both times, the papers had been folded over at the Situations Vacant section, and on one of the papers he had put a ring around several adverts with a biro.

Nothing had ever come of it, and he had never mentioned any

notions about emigrating to New York or Melbourne, but she had seen the evidence with her own eyes, and had begun to prepare herself mentally for it.

She looked at Seán now with a feeling of growing irritation. He was too easy-going and placid for his own good. He took any bad news with a sharp intake of breath and a shrug of his shoulders and a muttered, 'What can you do?'

If anything should or could be done, it usually fell to Kate.

He was a decent enough man – hardworking and handed his pay packet over unopened every week. All he wanted was a quiet life. The garden, the occasional match, a few drinks at the weekend, the odd week away in the summer. At times Kate felt it didn't amount to much, and it was a lot less than she had hoped for in life.

Seán gave a little snort now, which went straight to her nerves. It was only nine o'clock on a late summer's evening, and far too early for him to fall asleep. She had been on an early shift today, and after coming home she had spent hours washing and ironing and then cooking for everyone after work. She was back on her ward early again in the morning, and she felt she needed some break from working in the hospital or working at home. The film certainly had provided no entertainment, and if she didn't shift Seán now it would be too late to do anything. Another day would have gone by.

"Seán!" she said in a firm voice. When there was no response, she got up and went over to his chair and put her hand on his shoulder. "Seán, c'mon now. Wake up."

He stirred, opened his eyes, and looked around him as though he had woken up in a strange and foreign land.

"C'mon," Kate said, rubbing his shoulder. "It's too early for sleeping. We'll move ourselves and go and have a bit of a walk out in the fresh air."

Seán sat up properly now, smiled at his wife and nodded his head. "I'll just wash my face," he said, "and then I'll be as right as rain."

She was standing at the door waiting on him when he came out.

"You're looking very smart," he said with a smile.

She was wearing black slacks, a cream blouse with a tie-neck detail, and a black cardigan over her shoulders in case it got cold.

They walked down towards the Kilbeggan Bridge which spanned the Grand Canal.

"Will we go along the tow-path?" Seán asked. "Or straight on into the town?"

"Into the town," Kate said. "I thought we might call in on your mother and father, and tell them the news about Connie's weekend job. I thought we might invite them out for their dinner, the Sunday before she leaves."

"That would be a nice idea," Seán said. "Make a little bit of an occasion for her."

"That's what I thought."

It had been at the back of Kate's mind that she needed to let her father-in-law know all about Connie's job. Any day now, a phone call would come from Tara and an enquiry as to how her niece's plans were going for the move to Manchester. And then it would come out about the job offer she had made, and then Kate would have to explain that she never received any letter and that they had already gone ahead and made their own plans.

As they walked down the street and Flynn's terraced house came in sight, they spotted the back of Shay's curly grey head in the tiny front garden, digging around a straggly-looking hydrangea bush. Seán called his name, and his stepfather whirled around as though assailed by a flying object.

"Oh, begod!" Shay said, smiling at them both. He leaned on his spade, waiting. "And what brings the pair of you out on this fine evening?"

"A breath of fresh air," Seán said, opening the creaking gate which badly needed oiling, "and we thought we'd call in on the oul' ones and see if they're still alive and kicking."

"You can't keep an oul' dog down!" Shay did a little two-step dance around the spade, finishing with a kicking motion. "Up ya, boyo!" he said, laughing.

They both stopped to inspect the hydrangea that he had been digging around, pretending not to notice the red-faced Shay, who was now trying to catch his breath after the sudden short burst of activity.

"What's the story with the bush?" Seán asked. "It doesn't look up to much. Are you digging it up?"

Shay shook his head. "Feeding the feckin' thing," he said, his chest still heaving up and down. "Connie brought some stuff from the shop for us at the weekend that we have to dilute in a bucket of water and all the rest." He shook his head. "It's a waste of feckin' time if you ask me. It's the soil, it's no good for that type of plant, but try telling Tessie that. She's had it for two years now, and look at the state of it. It's supposed to be growing, but this year as you can see there are only three or four flowers on the feckin' thing. But, you can't tell that to Tessie, she's determined to keep it alive. As long as there's a leaf or a bud on it, she says there's still life in it."

"Well," Seán said, "you know the oul' saying, where there's life there's hope!"

"Go away, you!" Shay said, lifting the spade and pretending to hit him. They all laughed and then he said. "Well, are ye coming in for a cup of tea?"

Seán looked at Kate. "We will," she said, "and catch up on any news."

"Look what I found outside," Shay said, as he walked into the kitchen. "Two oul' crows peering over the gate at me."

Tessie leaned forward in her chair by the side of the range, and a smile broke out over her face when she saw who it was. She got to her feet, saying, "You'll have a cup of tea? The kettle is only boiled."

Within minutes a plate arrived on the table with slices of home-made tea brack and apple tart, then a biscuit barrel came out with an assortment of wrapped chocolate biscuits.

Cups of tea were handed over and then Shay passed the plate around. Kate took a piece of brack and Seán a slice of the apple tart. Shay put the plate back on the table then dipped into the biscuit barrel and pulled out a Kit Kat and a Penguin.

They chatted about the weather and the score of a recent football match, where Shay reckoned that Offaly were robbed by Tipperary.

They then went on to talk about the latest news on the proposed new factory that was supposed to be coming to Tullamore.

"Any news from the others?" Seán then asked.

"I was out at the hotel this morning," Shay said. "They had a coachload of Yanks staying. I was doing a bit of tidying up around the grounds, and I got chatting to a few of them. Big golfers, by all account. Dressed in their yellow jumpers and wearing Donegal tweed caps, and talking about their Irish ancestors from years ago. You know, the usual – the way they go on at times, but what else can you do but listen to them?"

Tessie shook her head and looked across at Seán and Kate, laughing. "Would you take heed of who is talking now? Isn't that what we do with you all the time? We do nothing else but listen to you."

Shay threw a withering glance over at his wife and continued as though she had never spoken. "They told me they're heading to Kerry tomorrow to play at one of the big golf courses down there." He held his hand out, rubbing the tips of his fingers together. "Plenty of oul' money, and most of them retired I'd say, so they have the time to spend it."

"Well, I expect Angela and Aiden will have made their money out of them," Kate said, a tinge of sourness in her tone. "The hotels are only too happy to have coachloads of tourists. Don't they depend on it?"

"Very true," Shay said. "And they look after them all well. Turf fires and everything in the sitting-room, even in the mild evenings. The Yanks go mad for the smell of the turf."

"Sure they all do," Seán said. "There's a few lads who come home from England every few months, and the first thing they do when they get off the coach in Tullamore is stand for a few minutes to smell the turf burning. They say it's the best smell in the world."

"Talking of England …" Kate said.

Shay reached his hand towards the biscuit barrel again and lifted out another Kit Kat.

"That's three," Tessie said, her eyes wide and her tone reprimanding.

"Who's counting?" Shay wanted to know. He shrugged and tore the wrapper off the biscuit.

Tessie looked over at the others. "You can't keep a chocolate biscuit in this house. You hardly have them bought and this fella has them eaten."

"Isn't that what they're for?" Shay said, winking over at Seán.

"Talking of England," Kate repeated, "Connie has landed herself a lovely little weekend job minding children."

Shay turned, all smiles. "With Tara?"

"No, it has nothing to do with Tara. My cousin, Sheila Doyle, who is over in Manchester arranged it all."

Shay's brow deepened. "Sheila Doyle? Which Doyle is she?"

"I don't think you know her – she's a cousin on my mother's side."

"A second cousin," Seán said. "We went out to visit her when we were over in Stockport a few years ago. She lives in a place called Hazel Grove."

"I would have thought Tara or Bridget or some of them would have found her something," Tessie said. "Just so as to be near family."

"I'm sure Tara said she would have something for her," Shay said. "I thought she was going to ring or write or something."

"Oh, she was in touch," Kate said, smiling. "She sent Connie a lovely card with money in it."

"But no mention of a little job for her?" Shay shook his head.

"Well, we don't need it anyway. Connie got sorted out without Tara or anyone speaking for her." Kate took a sip of her tea. "And anyway, it's best if she's not too close to them after the carry-on with the Fitzgerald lad."

Seán's head jerked in his wife's direction and he tried to catch her eye, but she was not looking near him.

"What carry-on?" Tessie asked.

"Did you not hear?" Kate said, feigning surprise. "I thought Angela or Tara would have told you."

There was a silence.

"What?" Shay said. "Told us what?"

"Well, you know he met up with Connie at the party?"

The elderly couple both nodded without saying anything.

"And he then took her out to the cinema and then up to Dublin for the day?" When they still said nothing, she said, "Well, according to Connie they got on great. He took her to meet his university professor and wined and dined her up in Dublin. And poor old Connie fell for it hook, line and sinker. She thought he really cared about her."

All eyes were on Kate now, Seán's especially, his jaw clenched tight.

"And then, just as he was ready to head off back to England, we discovered the truth about Mr Fitzgerald. He had actually just got engaged to another young girl before he came over to Ireland. The only thing is, he forgot to tell anyone else."

"Well," Tessie said, "that's a fine situation." She looked over at Shay. "I wouldn't have thought he would have done a thing like that. He was out here and he never mentioned a word of it to us. And Tara hasn't mentioned it to her father either, has she, Shay?"

Shay shook his head.

"Well, whether Tara knows and is keeping quiet – or whether she doesn't know anything about it at all – the fact is it's true," Kate said. "I was there with Connie when he admitted it. We were both actually sitting in his car at the time. I heard it from somebody who knows his friend over in Moate. The one whose party they were at. So it was as good as first hand. Anyway, the truth came out and when I confronted him with it, he admitted it all. He's been going out with the girl for a good while." She looked over at Shay. "So you can see why I would rather that Connie kept away from him and Tara and all of them in Stockport. I know well they will only take his side. As far as the Fitzgeralds and any of those uppity lot go, Tara thinks they can do no wrong. Well, she can do what she likes, but Connie is our daughter and we'll make sure she's mixing with the right type of people from now on."

"I suppose you have to do what you think is right," Tessie said. "She's your daughter and you don't want to see her getting hurt or upset. Was she keen on him?"

"Keen enough," Kate said. "But she's better off without him. She can do better than William Fitzgerald." Her voice and her body were trembling now. "Connie will be a fully qualified doctor in a few years, and she doesn't need the likes of him. She will have the pick of the best."

Chapter 24

The following morning Shay was up earlier than usual, just after seven o'clock. He quietly dressed while Tessie was still sleeping and then washed his hands and face, put his jacket and cap on, and crept out of the house. He took his bicycle out of the shed and was soon on the road out to Ballygrace.

It was a fine enough morning, and normally he would go along at an easy pace, looking out for any pheasants or hares or even a fox. He would watch the cars passing him on either side, wondering if it was anyone he knew from Cappincur or Daingean. Occasionally someone who he did know might pull up and have a bit of a chat with him which he usually enjoyed. But this morning, he wasn't in the mood for chat. His mind was on the information that Kate had given them last night.

He could tell there was definitely something wrong. Something missing in the whole story. He didn't doubt what Kate had told them, but the way she had come out with it, and the spiteful way she had spoken about Tara had set him back on his heels.

For a start, he didn't know anything about a romance between Connie and young William. He just thought they were innocent friends, that they had just picked things up the same way they were years ago with Connie mixing in with her brothers and the other lads, all codding and laughing and jeering each other, chatting about sport and music.

Though he knew things had changed. Now if young people even went to dances, they were all thundering around like a herd of elephants on the dance floor with their big clumpy shoes – the lads jumping around like eejits and pretending to play guitars and nonsense like that. And courtships just didn't seem the same any more. Decorum had gone out the window. It wasn't the way it was back in Shay's day. Things were far more straightforward then, when you had to go to a dance and formally ask the girls up on the floor, and if you wanted to see them home then you had to ask them properly. And you had to make arrangements to see them again. He didn't expect to be told everything that the young ones got up to. In fact, he didn't want to be told. The world was a different place to the one he grew up in and, if truth be told, he wasn't interested in hearing about their discos and their Bee Gees and all that kind of nonsense.

But this business with William had left a bad taste in his mouth. It all seemed underhand from start to finish. He had been out at their house drinking tea and acting normally and saying not a word about being engaged. And, whatever the young ones did or didn't do, there was no mistaking the intentions behind getting engaged. It was a serious commitment to make. It was not the way he had ever imagined the young lad to behave.

Shay hoped Angela could shed a bit of light on it all.

"You're a fine one," Shay said, "knowing all this and keeping it to yourself." He took a bite of buttered brown soda bread, and then took a mouthful of his tea.

Angela looked at her father across the table. She was still not fully awake. She was supposed to have had a long lie-in this morning, as Ella Keating had come in early to look after Claire and David, but her father's early arrival had put paid to that. Ella had taken the children on a walk down into Ballygrace village to buy some fresh rolls and to give their legs a stretch.

"Daddy, what do you want me to say? I honestly knew nothing about Connie until the night before William left. That was when he told me. The poor lad was all upset about it, and he asked me not to tell anyone else until he got back home and had time to sort it all out."

"Well, it's too late for that now," Shay said. "It's out. Kate told me and your mother the whole story – and she didn't mince her words. Seemingly, he wasn't going to say a word to anybody until he was found out. And, fair play to Kate, she got him to admit the whole thing about stringing Connie along when he had another girl back in London."

"It's not as straightforward as that, Daddy."

"So, is he engaged to be married, or is he not?"

"It's an informal engagement. The girl jumped the gun a bit, before William was really ready."

"A shotgun wedding?"

"No, no!" Angela said, exasperated now. "I meant she told her family about being engaged before it was really decided. Look, Daddy, it's a complicated situation, and I don't feel it's my place to go telling everyone his business."

"Well, you won't need to, because Kate is hell bent on telling everybody about it. She's gone and sorted out a weekend job for Connie over in Manchester, without checking whether Tara could give her work in the hotel."

Angela sighed in frustration. "That's up to Kate," she said. "But if you ask me, she didn't want help from anyone long before this happened with Connie and William. She doesn't want any help from the family. We could have given Connie work here for the summer, but she's in the flower shop instead."

"In fairness it's handier," Shay said. "She can walk out of the house and be there in a few minutes."

"I know, I know," Angela said. "And I don't mean any harm to Connie, she's a lovely girl and it must be nice working with lovely flowers all day. It's Kate who has the problem – she seems to always be making a point that she and her family don't need favours from any of the rest of us."

"I don't know about that," Shay said.

"Well, I was glad of the start Tara gave me over in the hotel in Stockport. If it hadn't been for her, Aiden and I wouldn't have our own business here. She has been so decent to everyone in the family, helping you and Mammy out and very good to all her nephews and nieces. She would have been only too delighted to help Connie. She looked directly at her father. "And, I bet Kate's only too delighted to have found something on William so she can tell Tara."

Shay held his hands up now. "I think you're being hard on Kate now. All I'll say is I'm disappointed in young William. I've always been fond of him and it vexes me to think he's been messing around with two girls like that."

"Daddy, it wasn't like that. He's not happy about the engagement – that's why he came over to Ireland – to think about it all. Then he met Connie and really liked her. The best thing we can do is to keep out of it. What happened is between Connie and William. She's a grown woman going off to university soon and will be leading her own life, and William will have to sort his situation out too." She paused. "It's a pity what's happened, because if the timing had been different, they would make a nice young couple."

Shay looked at her now and then shifted his cap back and scratched his head.

Angela lifted the teapot. "Another cup?"

"Ah, go on," Shay said, sitting back in his chair. "I might as well."

Angela took a bite of her toast, and then she poured them both another cup of tea. The morning news came on the radio, so they sat in silence for a while listening to it. After it finished, Angela looked at her father. "If Tara rings you, don't say anything about this. I'll phone William this evening when he comes in from work and makes sure he tells her. I wouldn't like her to hear it from Kate or anyone else before he had a chance."

Chapter 25

William came up the busy Friday-evening escalator into the Tube station at Covent Garden, dressed in a dark suit, blue shirt and a striped silk tie. He had come straight from the legal office where he was currently working, to meet Pamela for a meal. Their schedules had been such that they had not seen each other since he arrived back from Ireland the previous week.

He had hoped to meet up with her earlier in the week, but Pamela had not had one evening available as a crisis had arisen in her PR office and she had been asked to fill in for her boss who had been taken ill. She had explained that it gave her a chance to work with one of their bigger bands, the Funky Parrots, and she had been frantically busy finalising all the venues and the accommodation for their upcoming European tour schedule.

"I'm so sorry, darling," she had told him on the phone when he arrived home, "but I just can't get a free minute to myself. Things are absolutely mad here, but the brilliant news is that I am actually in charge of organising the whole tour!" Her voice had been high with excitement. "Can you believe it? Poor Charlotte, our Events Manager, has been taken suddenly ill with some kind of stomach problem, just as she was in the middle of sorting out merchandise for all the venues and checking ticket sales and everything, and

Rupert, who normally would have filled in, has just flown out to New York. I just could not believe it when I was brought into head office and asked if I could take over at the helm until Charlotte returns at the end of the week. I almost dropped down dead with the shock, but of course I didn't let it show. I just kept cool and calm and collected."

"Sounds like an amazing opportunity," William said. "I'm so pleased for you."

"Of course I feel bad about Charlotte being ill and everything, but there is a teeny bit of me pleased, as I would never have got this opportunity otherwise."

"When does the tour start?"

"Next Monday," she said. "So I hope to have everything finalised Wednesday or Thursday and the schedule all typed up and ready for Charlotte coming back, so she just has to get packed to join the boys on the tour."

"It sounds like a wonderful opportunity," he said, "and think of all the experience you've gained."

"Oh, it is, it really is! Such an amazing chance for me to show what I can actually do. Usually I'm the one taking orders and acting as a go-between with messages and always answering to Charlotte, but this time I'm actually making decisions." She then went on to tell him about the Funky Parrots month-long tour of Germany, Holland, France, Spain, Czechoslovakia and all the other places. "I have to organise translators to help with everything, make all the transport links and check that the hotels have everything the boys need. The company are really pushing the boat out here. No expense spared as they think they could be the new Rolling Stones. They say that about lots of bands, but these are really so talented." She suddenly stopped, breathless with it all. "You really don't mind us not seeing each other this week?"

"Obviously I would like to see you," he said, "but your career comes first."

"Everything should be okay by Friday," she told him. "Charlotte will be back and everything will be in place for this tour and they will all go off, and things will quieten down again. And we can then make up for lost time. I do feel bad, because I haven't even had a chance to hear about your trip to Ireland. You'll have to tell me all about it when you come home."

William had not responded to that. What could he say? Instead he congratulated her again and said all the right things, but his heart was heavy at the thought of delaying the inevitable discussion about their engagement. But, this was Pamela's big moment and he knew it would be selfish and cruel to drop such a bombshell on her at this time. He would have to wait until she had finished this particular project, and it was the right time for her.

Since arriving back in London, he had slept little. His thoughts had constantly veered from reliving those precious few days with Connie – to trying to work out how he was going to sort out this mess with Pamela. On the boat over to Wales, and then on the drive down from Holyhead to London, he had gone over and over everything in his mind and he had reached the same conclusion every time. He had to tell Pamela that their engagement was a huge mistake and that it was best for them both to break it off now rather than later.

Of course he knew that this decision would carry consequences. She would naturally be upset and he would look an utter fool for calling it off only weeks after buying her an expensive diamond ring. And he knew there would be ramifications with her father and his practice placements. But, he told himself, life happened. This would not be the first engagement to be broken off.

And then there was Connie. He was under no illusions about her feelings towards him. He had really messed up there too. He could still see the look in her eyes when her mother had cornered him in the car and confronted him with everything.

Why, he wondered now, had he not told her about Pamela at the very beginning? Why, when he met her at Jim Fay's party, had he allowed himself to become so enthralled by her that he just could not stop himself from wanting to be with her, talk with her, laugh with her? Listen to her lovely voice as they reminisced about some of the best times of his life. The times when, as a self-conscious teenager, he was escaping from a house down in London that was dark and echoing, and full of his mother's depression over the loss of her other two children.

And then, after he and Connie had got together upstairs at the party, when he suddenly realised that he saw her as much more than an old childhood friend, when he realised that she was now this beautiful, grown-up, witty, clever girl who was like no other girl he had ever met before or was likely to meet again – why had he not told her about Pamela? And then, after he had shown her around the studio, and this thing had suddenly developed between them, and he had held her and kissed her – why had he not told her? Even before Emmet appeared and interrupted them, he knew he should have tried to explain.

Events had overtaken them. The awful business with Emmet and then the awkward drive home with her two friends. And then the cinema and the evening in Dublin. The drive up and down. It had all gone too far and he was afraid to break the spell between them by telling her.

And then, it had all been too late to explain. But tonight he was going to start the process of sorting everything out.

Pamela had booked them a table in an Italian restaurant they had found a few months ago when wandering around Covent Garden. It was lively, with a good atmosphere and excellent food. But not the right place for a serious discussion. He thought that after the meal he would suggest finding a quiet place where they could talk, and where they could each then get the Tube or a taxi back home. He walked through the streets towards the restaurant, trying to think of how he would broach the subject and then the words he would use.

He turned in the open doorway of the restaurant, and instantly caught the smell of the garlic and the tomato sauce and the Italian herbs, which he usually loved – but tonight it did nothing for him. He could hear the low Italian music and the sound of cutlery and plates, and the relaxed hum of Friday-night conversation and occasional laughter.

He looked around the restaurant and realised that he had arrived before her. As the chap on the desk leaned forward to ask under what name the table was reserved, he felt a hand on his shoulder. He turned around and found himself looking at Pamela's father.

"Hope you don't mind me gate-crashing the party?" Edward Marshall said, his eyebrows raised. "Pamela rang me just before I left the office and asked me if I could join you. Apparently she has some big news for us. Do you know anything about it?"

William shook his head. "Of course I don't mind you joining us ... and no, I didn't hear from her today. I was in a conference all afternoon, and the office staff were gone when we finished, so if a call came through I could easily have missed it."

The waiter gave a little cough and William turned back to him and gave his name. He then escorted them to a table in a corner of the restaurant. William was grateful that they were seated by a window as it was warm in the restaurant, and he didn't want to take his jacket off until Pamela's father had taken his off first.

The waiter gave them both menus.

"I won't stay long," Edward said. "A glass of wine and maybe a salad starter and then I'll head home." He smiled. "At least I will have missed the rush hour on the Tube."

Pamela's father chose a bottle of red wine and then, as they sat sipping from their glasses, waiting on Pamela, he asked William about the office he was currently in and the briefs that the solicitors were working on. William gave a run-down on the cases he knew about and then Edward told him about a case he was working on at the moment. It involved two warring neighbours arguing over a right of way which involved broken glass being laid to puncture tyres and accusations of a barking dog being poisoned.

As he listened, William found himself unconsciously gulping the wine to try to calm the waves of anxiety that were building up in his chest, and then had to switch to drinking a tumbler of water to stop himself from emptying his wineglass too soon.

They discussed Pamela's work with the band and the opportunity which had come her way that week and both said it was a real move forward in her career.

Then, Edward leant his elbows on the table and spoken in a low, serious voice.

"I'm glad we have a few minutes on our own," he said, "because I've been looking for a chance to sound you out on a few things." He smiled. "Now that you are to all intents and purposes going to be part of the family."

William reached for his wineglass and took another drink.

"What do you actually think of this job or career or whatever that Pamela has got herself involved in?" Then, without waiting for a reply he said, "The thing is, I'm not wholly convinced it's a good path for her to go down, and I don't just mean career-wise. I'm not sure it's a world she should be mixing in. All these bands, the way the record companies indulge them, the nonsense they get up to." He gave a low sigh. "One of my colleagues is currently dealing with a case recently involving a TV personality, very well-known and revered by the middle-aged female brigade as a great family man, great charity worker raising money for hospices and children's hospitals. It turns out he was involved with procuring under-age boys for a group which involved other famous people including the frontman of one of these rock bands, and someone from one of the long-running sit-coms." He raised his eyebrows. "I could name names easily, but colleague confidentiality and all that ..."

"And is it going to court?" William asked.

"Not if his lawyers can help it. They're doing their damnedest to keep it out of court, trying to discredit the people making the accusations, offering settlements and that sort of thing. And the TV and record companies are on a big publicity drive to show all the people they represent in the best light possible, pulling favours in from here there and everywhere."

"It must be very difficult for a lawyer acting on behalf of people like that," William said. "How do you stand in court, knowing the truth about these people, and try to convince a jury to find them innocent of the charges? How could you sleep at night knowing that you've let people like that back out on the streets, possibly to do the same again?"

"Money, old chap," Edward said. "And lots of it where these cases are concerned. And you wouldn't believe the number of cases we get involving politicians and the higher echelons of the police service too." He paused now, glancing around at nearby tables to check no one was within earshot, then turned back to William again. "Being members of the kind of society that protects them. You get my drift?"

William nodded.

"Not that I'm damning all these network and societies – used correctly they do have their place. Most of the members are decent family men, and use it to help others like themselves. And of course, they do phenomenal charity work that no one will ever hear about." He sipped his wine, his eyes narrowed now as he looked at William. "Can I ask you something? Do you find your Irish background has been disadvantageous to you in any way?"

Startled, William looked at him for a moment. "In what way?" he asked.

"Of course, I know your family are of the right sort, and your stepfather is held in high regard. I just wondered, in the current political climate – the bomb outside the Old Bailey, the recent station bombings ... Do you find that it affects people's attitude towards you?"

William thought for a moment. "I've only come across prejudice against the Irish on a few occasions, when people didn't realise I actually was Irish."

"Your accent, of course, is hardly noticeable. You were educated here, but then went back to university in Ireland?"

William confirmed with a nod, not sure where the conversation was leading.

"I was just thinking, when you go for the meeting with the law firm I've recommended you to, it might be best not to volunteer too much information on the Irish front. Unless you are really pressed ..."

"Really?" William said, at a loss how to respond.

"I think so. Better to lay it on about your education here, and your link with me and the family ..." He looked at the door and then at his watch. "As I was saying to you earlier about Pamela. Whilst we want to boost her confidence and applaud her work being recognised with this high-profile tour etcetera, I think after this particular project has died down – with the wedding and everything coming up – we should be encouraging her to get out of the music business and into a more conventional PR type of work. I was thinking along the lines of working in an Art Gallery, Literary Agency, Publishing houses – that sort of thing." He held his glass out to William. "Something to keep her busy until the babies start to appear on the scene, what?"

William caught his breath. "The thing is ..." he said, "we're not in any rush ... better to take things slowly. It could be some years before we're ready for a family, and in the meantime I don't want Pamela to feel railroaded into a career she doesn't want." He looked towards the door now, willing Pamela to appear to get this night moving on, to do what he had to do.

"The thing is, William, before we know it, Pamela will be heading towards thirty. You would never know it looking at her of course, and she has always had a young outlook ... Taking all that into account, you may need to consider going down the family route a little quicker than you planned." He smiled. "And, like her mother, I would guess that Pamela will be so besotted when the first one arrives that she will be only too happy to stay at home."

"If we rush things, she might feel she has missed opportunities she might regret later."

"You need to toughen up a little here, old boy," Edward said, smiling and shaking his head. "She is my daughter and, believe me, no one knows her better than I do. Even her mother. Pamela needs guidance and a bit of structure in her life. She can't play the teenager forever." He held his hands out, palms up. "We'll let her have her little bit of glory with this project, and then I'll put the feelers out with a few old chums, see if there is anything more suitable out there."

William suddenly felt he needed to move from the table, get some fresh air. Then he remembered something he had intended to do earlier on, that would serve as the perfect and truthful excuse.

"Excuse me, Edward – if you don't mind, I need to make a quick call home. My mother had an appointment today about getting cataracts removed. I said I would ring later to see how she got on."

"Of course, of course," Edward said. "Decent of you to think of her." As William stood up, he lifted the wine bottle to top his glass up. "Says a lot about a man's character."

"If I remember, there's a pay-phone just by the cloakrooms ..."

And then, as William looked towards the door, there came Pamela rushing towards them, her short blonde hair slicked back in a boyish style and her eyes shining.

William stood and waited to greet her. He could not tell whether this was a better situation or a worse one. For the last twenty minutes, as Edward had grilled him, he had sat there feeling like the absolute fraud that he knew he was.

"So sorry I've kept you both waiting, but you'll know why in a few moments!" She threw her arms around William, kissed him on the cheek and whispered, "I have *so* missed you!" She then moved

211

quickly to hug and kiss her father. "I have the most amazing news!" she said, pulling a chair out. "You will not believe this!"

Her father's face creased in what looked like a mixture of an indulgent smile and an impatient grimace. "Go on, darling," he said. "William and I have been waiting all evening to hear this news. Put us out of suspense, please!"

She joined her hands together. "Well," she said, "it turns out that Charlotte's tummy problem is actually a pregnancy! And the doctors have banned her from work and any travel for the next few weeks. So ..." Pamela's voice rose with excitement, and her eyes were glistening with tears, "you are looking at the official Tour Organiser for the Funky Parrots!"

They both stared at her.

"Which means," she said, "that I am setting off on Monday morning for a month's touring with the band in Europe! Can you believe it?"

"Congratulations, Pamela," William said, moving to hug and kiss her.

"My goodness ... a whole month," her father said. Then, he stood up too and kissed her and congratulated her.

"What a great chance for you," William said. "They must really believe in you to give you all that responsibility."

"I keep pinching myself," she said, "to have finally found someone who believes in me. Believes in what I am capable of when given a chance."

Her father held up the bottle of wine, his eyebrows raised in offer.

She shook her head and made a little face. She looked across at William. "I'm not mad on red, maybe a bottle of something ..." She shrugged. "Something more *celebratory*?"

William got it. "Great idea," he said. He turned around in his chair to look for the waiter, and when he caught sight of one he got up and moved towards him so Edward could not hear him. "A bottle of champagne, please," he said. "Medium range will be fine."

When he got back to the table, Pamela was explaining about Charlotte. "I was so shocked," she said. "Charlotte – of all people – having a baby!"

"She is married, isn't she?" her father said.

"Oh, yes, for several years, but there had not been one hint – not a teeny suggestion that when she was sick it could have been something like that." Pamela put her open hand on her chest. "And when I was sorting everything out this week, in my mind it was all for Charlotte. Never for a minute did I imagine I would be going on a month-long, European tour!"

The waiter appeared with the champagne and Pamela made a little face and mouthed 'Thank you' to William and then they toasted her success and congratulated her once again.

When they gave the waiter their order, Pamela was disappointed when her father said he would just have a starter with them and then go.

"Oh, Daddy, have your main meal too," Pamela said. "I'll travel back with you, as I've loads to do tonight."

Edward shrugged and then smiled. "Well, if you two don't mind me playing gooseberry?"

Both of them reassured him that he was most welcome so he agreed to stay. He took the bottle from the ice-bucket and filled the champagne flutes again.

As he lifted his glass, he said, "Have you told your mother yet?"

"Oh God, no ... I didn't get a chance to ring. I did mean to. Can you tell her, Daddy?" She drained the last of her third glass of champagne, which she told them had helped her relax for the first time in days.

"Of course," he said. "She'll want to get things organised for you going away. You'll have to get packed and sorted over the weekend now, won't you?"

"I've got to go into the office again tomorrow," she said. "Just a last-minute brief with the band's manager, and then I have to pick up my flights out to Germany where the tour is starting."

"Very exciting," her father said.

"It *is* exciting," she said, "but it's also a little scary. I'll be completely and totally responsible if anything goes wrong."

William put his hand over hers. "I'm sure nothing will go wrong," he said. "You will do a brilliant job."

"There are all these company rules I have to check out as well. When Rupert our office manager rang from New York, he reminded me not to wear my engagement ring as the fans and groupies hate to see women with the entourage who they think

213

might secretly be married or engaged to one of the band."

"Or even living with them, heaven forbid!" Edward laughed. "With those sorts, anything goes!"

William's stomach churned as he realised Pamela had told her work colleagues about the engagement, after agreeing to keep it to her immediate family. If the news was out there now it was probably spreading and would soon reach the ears of his mother or stepfather, Harry. But there was not a damn thing he could do about it now. He lifted his flute and took a big mouthful of the champagne. He hoped that and the wine would begin to have some effect on him soon.

Pamela turned to William. "We're not going to have any time together over the weekend, I'm afraid, darling. After my meeting tomorrow, I'm going to have to get to the hairdresser's to have my colour freshened and I'll have to beg the girl in the beauty salon to squeeze me in for a manicure and whatever else they can manage."

"What about Sunday?" Even as he asked, he knew if she were free he could not say anything as she was preparing to leave.

"Don't you remember?" she said. "Sunday is my annual day out with my old school friends. We're in Oxford this year – lunch at one of the girls' houses and then we have dinner booked at a restaurant." She looked at her father and shrugged. "I just can't wait to tell the girls all my news about my European tour!" She leaned over to squeeze William's hand. "And my more exciting news about the engagement. None of them live nearby and I'll ask them to keep it quiet."

The main courses came, steak with a pepper sauce for Edward, spaghetti bolognese for William and lasagne for Pamela. William sat quietly, concentrating on his food as Pamela filled her father in on her old school friends, the children most of them had and the work their husbands did.

When he had eaten as much as he could, he pushed his chair back and said, "If you'll excuse me, I just want to make a quick call home."

"Ah yes," Edward said. "Your mother's cataracts."

The phone was situated under the staircase – and partially covered with a Perspex dome to give the impression of privacy – which led up to a small function room and the ladies' and gents'

214

toilets. He got through quickly and his mother gave him an account of her visit to the London Eye Hospital. Basically, she needed to have both eyes done, but they were going to do them one at a time. She wasn't worried, she told him – it wasn't a major operation and any physical pain afterwards was easily handled with medication.

"If only," Elisha Fitzgerald said, "everything else could be cured as easily."

The unsaid thing was the depression and anxiety which she lived with constantly. The feeling of things being out of control. Something William himself was now beginning to understand.

"Any other news?" he asked.

"Yes," she said. "Angela – Tara's sister – left a message for you. She asked if you could ring her as soon as possible. Tonight preferably."

After he hung up, William thought for a few moments and then put his hand into the inside pocket of his jacket and took out a small brown-leather address book.

He flicked through the pages and then he put it down on top of the shelf which held the phone directories, and pressed his hand down on it to make it stay open. He searched in his pocket for the largest coins he had, and then he dialled Angela's number.

Chapter 26

Angela came straight to the point. "I'm sorry to put pressure on you, William, but if you haven't already told Tara about your engagement and the situation with Connie, I think you need to do it as soon as possible."

She then recounted the visit from Shay and how he'd told her all about Kate calling out to their house and telling them the whole story about William being engaged, and how he had led Connie on.

"Oh, God!" William said. "This whole thing has just spiralled out of control."

"I told no one apart from Aiden, just as I promised," Angela said. "He won't say a word, and I have asked Daddy to say nothing about it to Tara, to give you a chance to ring her first before she hears it from Kate or Connie."

"Okay," he said, "I'll ring Tara tomorrow. I did intend to tell her everything."

"Have you told your mother yet?" Angela asked.

"No, I've told no one."

"What are you going to do, William? Are you going to go ahead with the engagement and announce it properly and everything?"

"No, no, I can't," he said. "I know I can't go ahead with it. I've gone over and over it, and I've realised that we would never have

216

considered any major commitment – it had never been discussed – it was only because Pamela thought she was pregnant, and, thinking that she was, I did what I was thought was the right thing by agreeing to marry her."

"So when are you going to tell her?"

"I had planned to do it tonight, but she's just announced that she's going away on a European tour with work for a month. She's leaving Monday and I'm not going to see her until she gets back."

"So, you're going to have to pretend for a whole month?"

William closed his eyes now and leaned his head against the Perspex shield. "I don't know what I'm going to do. All I know is that I've somehow become engaged to a girl I don't love and who I have nothing in common with – and I've met a girl who I can't stop thinking about ..."

"I think you're going to have to do something right now," Angela said. "You can't keep this pretence up any longer. Something bad is going to happen if you don't."

"I've just realised that," he said. "Look, Angela, I'd better go. Thanks for all the advice, and I'll speak to you again soon."

"Take care, William."

"Bye, Angela."

Then, just as he put the phone back in the cradle, William felt a sharp blow to the side of his head which propelled him back against the side of the booth.

"You lying Irish bastard!" Edward Marshall hissed, grabbing William's collar with both hands and dragging him back onto his feet. "I've heard every word you've just said about my daughter. All the things you said about her being pregnant and then suggesting you've been tricked into becoming engaged to her. How have you let this happen if you didn't want it? Are you completely insane?"

William struggled out of his grasp. "I didn't intend for any of this to happen ... I didn't want to hurt Pamela ... I really tried to make it work."

"*You tried to make it work?*" Edward's voice was high and incredulous, almost mimicking. "You thought that getting engaged to my daughter, who you have decided you no longer love, makes everything all right?"

He grabbed William again, but this time William pushed back

and they stood in the hallway opposite each other, red-faced and breathless.

"You sat opposite me for over an hour pretending that you were going to be my future son-in-law when you had no intention of going through with it. You have pretended to Pamela that you are still engaged – you bought her a bottle of champagne tonight, for Christ's sake! What the hell are you doing?"

"I don't know … it's all such a mess … I honestly don't know. I never intended to hurt her."

"And I will see to it that you don't hurt her," Edward hissed. "You are going to pull yourself together and go back inside and tell her you need to go home immediately on account of your mother. Then, you are going to pay the fucking bill for the meal and the wine – and then you are going to walk out of that door and never see Pamela again."

William held his hands up. "How can I do that? How can I leave things like this?"

"I'll sort it," Edward said. "I don't want you going anywhere near her again after tonight. If she writes or phones just make sure you say all the right things to keep her happy. Then, when she gets back from her tour I'll tell her what you've done. I'll tell her the sort of man that you are and she'll realise that she's lucky to be rid of you."

A waiter came out and went towards the staircase, and they both straightened up and remained silent until he had reached the top of the stairs.

"She will get over this. She's got over much worse. You were only a second-best to her, maybe even third choice. She saw you as safety and security – she told me that herself. You won't break her heart. She might look light and sound like a fluffy little thing, but she's made of tougher stuff than you are."

"I'm glad," William said. "She's a lovely girl and she deserves to be with the right person."

"You were never going to be that for her. She was strong enough to walk away from the real love of her life weeks before her wedding, when she realised he didn't deserve her. When she realises what you really are, she'll see she's had a narrow escape."

William took in the information that Pamela had been engaged before, almost married, and hadn't trusted him enough to tell him. But then, he wondered, how many times had they spoken – *really* spoken? They were intimate enough to have had sex ... and yet, they had never talked properly. The way he could talk to Tara and even Angela. The way he had spoken to Connie.

"What happened before I met Pamela is her business," he said quietly. "And as far as her future goes, I wish her nothing but the best."

Edward closed his eyes and then made a snorting, dismissive noise. Then he suddenly moved towards William again – and put his face so close to his that their noses were almost touching. "And you can forget your meeting with the law firm in the city on Monday. In fact, if I have anything to do with it, you can forget your law career in London. Believe me when I say that I will use every and any contact I have, to make sure no firm ever takes you on." Then, he stood back and looked him up and down as though seeing him for the first time. "Now fuck off back to Ireland where you and your kind belong."

Chapter 27

Sometime later, William came across a plain, old-fashioned bar on the other side of Covent Garden – a dozen streets away from where he had left Pamela and her father drinking their coffee, Pamela still excited about her tour and her father pretending all was still well. The guitar music coming through the open window drew him inside. That, and the knowledge that he could not go home yet. Not until he knew his mother and Harry would be in bed.

It was early yet. There was a solo singer on a small make-shift stage. The place was already three-quarters full of people like William who had wandered in, and groups who had come for the music. William went to the bar, still carrying his briefcase. But, it was Friday night, it was London and no one noticed these things. He looked at the gantry, no idea what he wanted to drink, and then he spotted the Drambuie and remembered the night he sat up drinking it with Angela. He ordered a double with ice, paid for it, and then he waited until the song was finished and found a small table for two at the other end of the bar.

He sat on the hard wooden chair, and put his case on the floor and then he loosened his tie a bit further. He took a sip from the glass, deliberately going slow, conscious of the wine he had already drunk. Then he sat back and listened to the singer who was playing a mix of folky and popular, easy-listening songs.

People came and went, passing him by as they headed to the bar or outside to move on elsewhere. Someone asked if they could take the spare chair from his table and he smiled and helped them move it out.

The singer stopped at one point and asked for requests and William recognised a Dublin accent. People gave him slips of paper and then he moved on to play Bob Dylan and Leonard Cohen numbers, James Taylor, Donovan and Al Stewart, which suited William's tastes more.

Somewhere between leaving the restaurant and stumbling upon the pub, he had discovered a different feeling. One he hadn't felt for weeks, months. A feeling of relief and a calmness, where before he had been riddled with anxiety. The worst had actually happened. No more sword of Damocles hanging over his head. The apocalypse he had imagined when the truth came out had not completely obliterated him. The earth had not cracked and broken and the skies had not fallen down. He had survived. The burden of worry had been lifted off his shoulders by that well-deserved punch from Pamela's father.

And whilst he would carry the guilt for hurting Pamela and the feeling of utter stupidity about himself for some time to come, at least he now knew that the time would eventually come when he could look to a future that was built on openness and honesty.

Not a future with Pamela, and not the future career he had recently imagined with a law firm in London. Whether Edward's threat about ruining his career would come to pass, he didn't know. He would have to think about all this over the coming weeks.

He would have to think about a lot of things – he would have to examine himself and the streak of weakness that lay within that had almost ruined his life and hurt other people. He would have to work out why he had let Pamela drift into his life, and then, by the very act of having slept with her on just a few occasions – had allowed it to push him into a direction he had neither planned nor even considered. A direction which could have altered his future for years to come.

And had he not met Connie Devine that night, and discovered that a deeper more fulfilling relationship was possible, he knew he would have ended up living a shallow and unfulfilled life with someone he was not suited to. And if her father was being truthful, Pamela had been prepared to do the exact same thing.

As the bar began to fill around him, William retreated further into a corner where he sat sipping his drink, letting the music and the pleasant atmosphere wash over him. When it was quiet the barman came to the end of the bar and chatted to him about football, the weather and the slump in the housing market. He remarked on William's accent, trying to place it. William told him he was Irish but had spent time going between there and London, and the barman told him that the singer was called Ruairi and he was over from Dublin for the summer.

"He'll be stopping for a break soon," the barman said, "so you should have a chat with him."

William ordered a second drink and a short while afterwards the singer left his guitar and microphone down and came towards the bar. The barman pulled him a pint of lager and chatted to him for a few minutes then he nodded over in William's direction. The musician slid his drink along the bar until he was alongside his table.

He stretched his hand out. "I hear you're another Paddy? I'm Ruairi, a Dub, from out Rathmines way."

William shook his hand and introduced himself. "My family are from near Tullamore in Offaly, but we've been over in London a long time."

"Well, this is my second summer in London," Ruairi said. "I'm actually a music teacher in a secondary school and we get a good long summer holiday – which we most definitely need." He rolled his eyes. "As the joke goes, there are only three good things about secondary teaching – June, July and August!"

William laughed. "Good one!" Then he said earnestly, "Your voice is fantastic. You do a great range of songs, and it's just really relaxing, listening to you."

"Thanks – what do you do yourself?"

William told him about his law degree and the firms he was working for. They chatted for a few more minutes and then Ruairi headed back to the small stage to his guitar and microphone, while William leaned back in his corner, listening and trying not to replay any of the night's events in his mind.

The singer started off with 'House of the Rising Sun', then he moved on to 'Imagine' and a string of other popular songs. Then, as the night drew to an end and people started to leave he gestured down towards William.

"This is for my Irish friend in the corner. It's a song by John McGlynn and it's called 'In Your Eyes'."

As William sat listening, the words and lines began to resonate with him.

"Just call me, you'll find me ... By night and by day ... Your sweetness still haunts me ... And won't go away.' Connie and all the memories came back to him through the beautiful, haunting song. *"I've searched through the wind and the rain ... Just to be where you are ... But you couldn't be further away ... If I'd reached for a star."* And suddenly, he felt the tears stinging at the back of his eyes. *"I'd wanted the world ... When all that I needed was you ... And too late then I wished for you back ... But it didn't come true."*

What a mess he had made of things! He would call Tara tomorrow and tell her the whole story as he had told Angela. He would leave nothing out. He would admit to all the mistakes he had made, and hopefully she would not think too badly of him. There was no point in saying anything to his mother now. She had enough things to make her anxious and he would not add to them. In a few weeks, he hoped, it would all be water under the bridge.

The work situation worried him the least. Somehow, he would sort it out. London was a big place and there was bound to be law firms that Edward Marshall could not influence. He would give himself a few days to clear his mind and sort it all out.

He checked with the barman where the nearest Tube station was, and then he straightened his tie and buttoned his suit jacket.

"Your briefcase," the barman said. "Don't forget it."

He shook hands with both the singer and the barman, then he headed out into the street. As he walked along, the words of the song echoed in his head. *"Just call me, you'll find me ... By night and by day ... Your sweetness still haunts me ... And won't go away ..."*

As he came towards the Tube station, he saw an old down-and-out guy with a long grey beard, sitting back against the wall, and holding an empty plastic cup. As he came towards him, he paused for a moment, put his briefcase on the ground and then started to feel around in his trouser pocket, and came out with a fifty-pence coin.

"God bless you," the man said in a Scottish accent.

"You're welcome," William said. He bent to lift his briefcase and, as he did so, he swayed and almost lost his footing. He leaned against the wall to steady himself up.

"Are you okay, son?" the man asked.

"I'm fine," William said. He lifted the case and then straightened up.

"Good night, son, and safe journey home."

"Thanks," William said, feeling suddenly touched by the man's gentleness.

He walked on into the Tube station, bought his ticket and then headed for the escalator. As he went downwards, he thought of Pamela and her father, then he thought of Connie and her mother in the car. Then his thoughts moved to Ruairi and his songs. Tears started to trickle down his face, but he did not care.

He was in London where nobody noticed anything.

Chapter 28

Manchester

October

Connie checked everything was reasonably tidy before the cleaners did their twice-weekly visit to her room in the university halls of residence. Then, she gave her hair a quick brush, picked up her books and pens and put them into her Indian-style woven bag with the beads and little mirrors. The leather satchel her grandparents had bought her for starting university was stowed in the luggage compartment above her wardrobe. She felt guilty for not using it because she knew it had cost them a lot but, as soon as she had arrived in Manchester almost three weeks ago, she had quickly discovered that only the lecturers or mature students used leather briefcases or satchels. All the other first-year students who had gathered for their introductory talk had a variation on the ethnic kind or a military-style, canvas Che Guevara-style slung over their shoulders or worn sideways.

That first afternoon — accompanied by her new friend Christine, a girl with curly red hair from Devon, who had moved into the room next door to hers – Connie had walked down into Chelsea Girl in the city centre and bought herself a more suitable, modern bag, a bag that immediately made her feel she fitted in with the other students. She had also learned, in a matter of an hour, how easy it was to buy almost anything she needed within walking distance of her new accommodation. And not just the basic things that she could have bought back home in the shops in Tullamore – but the items she had to travel to Dublin two or three times a year to buy. All the modern tops and trousers she went shopping for on special occasions, she could now buy every day if she had the money. And the best thing was – there was a far bigger range here and everything was cheaper. She hadn't really realised this when she was younger, because her mother paid for everything, but now she was in charge of what she bought with her own money, she knew the difference. She thought it wonderful that everything was fairly cheap in Manchester and that all her basic needs like accommodation and meals were provided for her.

Connie could not have imagined how quickly she would become absorbed into her new life. The first afternoon she had arrived weary, on the coach into Manchester, after an early sailing from Dublin to Holyhead. She had felt self-conscious travelling as she lugged a heavy case, a bag slung over her other shoulder and a rucksack on her back. When she arrived at the university to register, she realised she was only one of hundreds of other students laden with an assortment of luggage. Some were worse than her, struggling not only with bags, but with guitars, violins and heavy sports gear.

Within days, she had settled into her study-bedroom, which, although a basic single room, had everything she needed. Her mother, she thought, would approve of her room when she came to visit. Everything was clean and fresh, with walls and woodwork which had recently been painted in cream and white. The blue curtains with a cream border and plain blue bed cover had been matched to the blue-and-grey-and-cream-striped rug which lay at the side of her bed. The storage spaces were well-planned with fitted teak wardrobes, a good-sized desk with shelving, a high bookcase and even a vanity unit with a sink and mirror.

As well as the living accommodation, the halls of residence also had small study libraries and common rooms with long leather sofas and pouffes, and a kitchen area with kettles and small electric ovens, where the students could make hot drinks or warm up snacks.

It was mainly the new students who lived in the accommodation, she discovered, as the second and third year students often preferred to be more independent and lived in lodging accommodation or 'digs' as they were more commonly known.

After enrolment, a committee of third-years showed the students to their accommodation and then waited to take a group of the new students on a tour of the university recreational facilities. That first evening she was shown around the large refectory where all her main meals would be served as part of her board, then she was taken to the other cafés which were open all day to drop into for drinks and snacks. These extras were not part of her board, and if she decided to go there she would have to pay for anything she bought herself.

They were also taken around the Student Union Bar which Connie thought was huge and a great barn of a place with red plastic benches and stools and a large stage. This, they were told, was where most of the students socialised. It was open every evening and also served snacks like hot meat-and-potato pies, sausage rolls and baps filled with ham or cheese.

They were also shown the small shop next to the bar which sold all the basic necessities such as soap and toothpaste and deodorants. All the things, their third-year guide told them with a grin, that older people thought scruffy, unwashed students never used.

After the evening meal she attended a meeting in the communal area of her hall of residence, which gave her the chance to meet more of the people she would be living with. The house tutors who had responsibility for the block gave each student a folder which contained a list of rules to make communal living easier and practical information about things such as using the public phone on the ground floor, where the fire hydrants were kept, when their rooms would be cleaned and bed linen changed, and what everyone should do in the event of a fire safety procedure or a real fire.

Nothing had been left out, Connie thought, and the pack was well-planned and relevant. The most enjoyable part of the evening came later when all the new students met up in the Student Union Bar.

The following morning – her first official day as a student – along with two hundred other new medical students, Connie had found her way around the six huge lecture theatres and the Medical

Faculty Library, and had also been introduced to all the lecturers she would be studying under. Everyone she met seemed to give her sheets of papers or small booklets, and she quickly amassed folders full of details. She also collected more papers which gave information about the classes she would attend that term, and all the different medical subjects she would study. She and the other students she had become friendly with spent a lot of their first days drinking coffee, and discussing their time-tables and syllabuses.

Although she had studied chemistry and biology for her Leaving Certificate, seeing the list of medical subjects she was going to study every day made her catch her breath. Anatomy, Biology, Biochemistry and Physiology. Something about the words made her realise that she was now in a very serious field of study, and she now saw that some of the subjects at school she had regarded as being challenging enough – English, Geography, History and French – seemed like easy reading in comparison.

When she had first applied, she had been told that Manchester Medical School would be expanding and that, if accepted, she would be one of the very first batch of students to study in the newly opened Stopford Building. At the time, it had meant nothing to her, because she knew nothing about how any university functioned. But when she arrived, she began to realise the huge change that had taken place in the university, and how proud she should feel to be one of the first medical students to benefit from it. Apart from the students studying medicine, she discovered there were also sixty dental students and twenty studying nursing.

The first two weeks flew in, and Connie now felt she had been in Manchester for a much longer time. After initially feeling overwhelmed by the large numbers of people, and feeling that she would prefer to be walking around the quieter streets of Tullamore, she no longer thought about it.

She was firm friends with Christine, and now knew most of the young women in her hall of residence by sight, and she had a group of around half a dozen other female students on her floor who she could walk over to breakfast with, and then afterwards walk with to the lecture halls. She had also got to know some of the male students and some of the mature students who attended her classes. She no longer worried about getting lost, where to sit or who to sit beside. She began to take things in her stride.

The first few days she constantly felt anxious about being in plenty of time for lectures, and was careful to listen at all times and make sure to take the appropriate notes. She felt she was on the alert, and if she did not pay attention she might suddenly be asked a question and find herself looking foolish. But as the days went past and she did not once see the lecturers or professors pounce on anyone, she eventually began to feel herself relax more and more. She discovered that if she did not understand anything, someone else's hand was bound to shoot up to ask the lecturer to go back and explain the point again. If she still wasn't sure, she knew she could easily ask Christine or one of the other girls to explain it to her, or she could hover around after the lecture to catch the tutor at a quiet moment and ask him to go over it with her.

The social life was beyond her expectations and even beyond what the University brochures had described. By her second week she knew enough people well enough to find someone to sit with any time she went into the refectory or the cafés, and in the evenings people from her floor knocked on her bedroom door to check if she was going out with them. The Student Union Bar had something on in it practically every night, even if it was only the juke-box playing which Connie loved. Every other night they had some sort of live music on the stage, which ranged from solo singers with guitars playing folk music or popular music to full-blown rock bands who filled the big hall with a huge air of excitement as they did their best to blow everyone's ears off with screaming, high-pitched electric guitars and thumping drums.

On those evenings, a small charge was made on the door to cover the cost, but everyone knew that if they waited until after the halfway mark of the night, the students on the door had either wandered off or become too drunk to care when people walked past the table without paying

Some evenings, a group of the university's own students entertained them for free with a range of musical instruments and an even greater range of musical ability.

The biggest event came the third weekend, on a Friday night, when the Freshers' Ball was held in the large university sports hall. Connie and her friends couldn't believe it when they heard that Hot

Chocolate was booked to play. It was a formal night, and she and Christine and two other girls from her floor, Babs and Vicky, went into Manchester looking for something that was dressier than their usual jeans or loon pants and casual tops, or Indian-style kaftans and long beads. They checked out the shops around Piccadilly and all agreed that John Lewis was too expensive and old-fashioned for them, and the usual boutiques had nothing special enough.

Babs told them that one of the third-years had suggested a second-hand shop near Victoria Station that had fabulous good-as-new clothes, which were brought up from London from shops like Biba and Mary Quant and other places on the fashionable King's Road.

"Second-hand?" Connie had questioned, wrinkling her nose. "I've never been in a second-hand clothes shop before. I don't know if I could wear other people's dresses."

"But they're brilliant," Christine said. "We have quite a few in Exeter. Don't you have them in Ireland?"

"No, and I can't imagine anyone going into them in Tullamore." Connie shook her head. "My mother won't go near Jumble Sales or anything like that when they are held in the church halls. She always says you never know who could see you walking around the town wearing their clothes, and laughing at you. Or, worse still, you could be walking around in the clothes of someone who died, and you would never know."

The girls dissolved into fits of giggles.

"You are priceless, Connie!" Babs said. "All the things we hear about this little town of Tullamore in Ireland. We must all come home with you for a weekend some time and find out what it's really like."

Connie giggled along with them, knowing that it was unlikely that she would ever take them home with her. Her mother would not be in the slightest bit impressed with Babs and her outspoken, confident manner or with Christine, whose parents were divorced. Vicky, she knew, her mother would find too uppity and posh for them.

They walked down Market Street and after asking several people for directions, found Victoria Station and the second-hand shop. As soon as they walked inside and heard the music playing and smelled the joss-sticks, and looked at the amazing dresses and tops hanging on the wall, Connie conceded that this type of second-hand was very different to what she had imagined.

They all separated around the big shop to search through the rails for something spectacular for the Freshers' Ball. Then, armed with a selection of outfits, they went into the communal changing room to try the dresses and long skirts on, while the others gave their opinions.

An hour later they all came out carrying bags with a variety of outfits and sparkly evening bags. Connie was delighted with her fashionable, flattering bargain, which defied all notions of second-hand garments she had previously held. After much trying on and laughter, she had picked out a full-length, olive-green halter-neck dress. It had a high neck, studded with diamanté which gave a choker-style effect, which then tied at the back, leaving long flowing pieces of material which emphasised her bare back. The girls all loved it on her and said she should wear her long dark hair piled up on her head to show off her rear view.

If she had had any doubts about how well she looked in the dress, they were quickly dispelled on the night by all the male students who asked her to dance and complimented her on how gorgeous she looked. At the break, several boys she knew offered to buy her a drink, and one asked her to go out for a walk with him around the gardens to get a breath of fresh air.

She accepted drinks from two boys in her class, but later bought them drinks back. And she refused the offer of a walk in the gardens. The incident at Jim Fay's party with Emmet was too ingrained in her memory, and she would not take any chances with boys who she had only recently met.

At the end of the night Christine and the popular, busty Babs went off with lads while Vicky and Connie, tipsy from glasses of lager and wine, walked back to their hall of residence together, and sat over mugs of coffee giggling and laughing.

Most evenings, Connie wandered down to the bar around ten o'clock with some of the other girls and each night she felt she had really enjoyed herself. If it was a performer or a band they liked the sound of, they went early and paid their money to make sure they got a seat inside before it got too crowded.

Over the days and weeks, a pattern began to gradually emerge where Connie now knew where she had to be at all times of the day and could anticipate what she might like to do at night, whether it was socialise or stay in her room listening to quiet music while she studied her medical books.

It was early in the year and people were getting to know each other, but already she could see couples forming and beginning to see each other exclusively. Although she had become friendly with most of the boys on her course, and was happy to sit with them at lunch and have a dance with them in the student bar, she had stuck to her decision about not getting romantically involved with anyone.

She had a ready-made excuse for anyone who asked her out which she now used automatically. "I'm really sorry, but I'm already promised. I have a serious boyfriend back home and we've agreed not to see anyone else."

So far, it had worked fine, and she had even roped in her closest friends to make sure they backed up her story. "If anyone comes asking about me, tell them I'm already spoken for. And if it's at the weekend and I'm not around, you can even say I've gone to meet up with him."

"But what if Mr Right turns up?" Christine wanted to know. "You could be turning down the love of your life."

"If there is a Mr Right," Connie laughed, "he will know to turn up at the right time."

Her studies were the main thing on her mind, and she was determined to keep up to date with everything on her course. So far, nothing had challenged her to the point where she was in any way worried. But, in the midst of her busyness, every so often when a quiet moment came, William Fitzgerald would creep into her thoughts.

At first she fought them back, got up and did something like knock on her friend's door to chat or made herself concentrate on a list of medical terms, a magazine or a piece of music. She did what she had done back in Tullamore, in the weeks after he had gone back. She did anything she could to banish thoughts of him from her head. To banish the memories of the four days they had spent together.

But still the thoughts came back when she least expected it.

Trying to forget him was the hardest thing she had ever done.

She rang home when she first arrived to assure everyone she had got there safely and afterwards she rang every weekend from one of the two call boxes in the hallway at the entrance to her block. In her last chat with her mother, Kate had told her everyone at home was well and then asked Connie how her studies were doing and checked that she was going to Mass on Sundays as she had promised. Connie reassured her on all counts, saying that she had received the results of her first biology class assignment back and had got over ninety per cent. She then told her about an elderly woman who she had met outside the church and discovered was originally from Mullingar, as she knew this would be a piece of information that would console her mother and make her feel that she had not been overtaken by the heathen, English way of life so far.

Then she had taken a deep breath and told her mother that she had forgotten to say that she had rung Tara when she had arrived as she had promised, and that the previous Sunday afternoon she and Frank and the children had come out to her hall of residence. She had shown them around and then they had taken her to a lovely restaurant in the city centre. As she expected, her mother had gone quiet.

"It would have been very bad-mannered not to get in touch with Tara when I arrived here since I'm only living half an hour away from her," she said, before her mother could interrupt. "And I promised her I would be in touch when I rang her to thank her for the card and the money. They were so good to me, Mammy, and the children are lovely ..."

"As long as you don't start running back and forward to visit them when you should be studying," Kate said. "It would be easy to get caught up in them all out there in Stockport, that Bridget and all the crowd at that boarding house. You don't need to get mixed up with them." And, then, before Connie could get a word in, she said, "And don't forget you have to contact Sheila Doyle about your weekend job. She was good enough to sort that out for you, and I don't want her to think we didn't appreciate it. It will give you an extra bit of pocket-money."

"That's another thing," Connie said. "Tara kept apologising

again about the letter that she sent to you that went missing. She said she should have written on my card about me working in the Cale Green Hotel ..."

"Well, I don't know anything about any letter, and there is nothing that can be done about that now," her mother interrupted. "And it's best if you don't get too involved with Tara after that trouble with William Fitzgerald. Best to give it a bit of time. She's bound to feel very awkward about it all."

She did not tell her mother that Tara had mentioned William to her on the quiet, when Frank had taken the children for an ice cream, and said he had sent his best wishes to her for starting university. Tara said he felt dreadful about what had happened between them, and Connie had said that it was okay and that she was over it. And she repeated what she had told William: "I really didn't expect anything more from him. It was just a nice few days in the summer."

"It will do you good to spread your wings," her mother had gone on to say, "and those nice people are depending on you to help them out. You told Sheila that once you were settled you would ring her. You have her number there, don't you?"

Connie assured her she had, and promised she would ring soon.

"Ring her straight away," Kate said. "If you don't, Sheila will be offended with me, and the chances are that someone else will get the job, and you'll be sorry you missed it."

Connie wanted to say that she would be happy to miss the job as she would prefer to have worked for Tara, but she knew that would cause ructions at home between her parents. She would even have preferred to find something handier around the university area, something like in a café or even a bar, but she knew it would cause trouble.

It took her three attempts to catch her mother's cousin but, when she did, she was relieved to hear a confident, worldly woman on the other end.

"And how are things going?" Sheila had asked. "Is your university accommodation working out fine?"

"I love it," Connie said. "The room is great and I've met some lovely people."

"Well done!" Sheila exclaimed. "I was worried that you might be homesick or struggling with the big city life. I half-expected a call from you last week to come and rescue you."

"No, I'm not homesick at all," Connie laughed. "I'm really enjoying every single minute of it so far."

"That's what I like to hear!" Sheila said. "You're getting a wonderful opportunity to get out into the bigger and brighter world to better yourself and you need to grab it with both hands. Forget all the small-town, Holy God attitudes and the begrudgers who think life begins and ends in the bogs of Offaly."

Connie was relieved. She had dreaded making the phone call to this unknown cousin, as she had imagined from the way her mother had talked that Sheila Doyle was going to be an old-fashioned, spinster nurse who didn't drink or socialise much, and who probably spent half her life in church. She liked the sound of this strident, confident woman on the other end with the half-English, half-Irish accent.

"I ring home every week and that keeps me going," Connie said. "Everything is going absolutely great at university. The course lecturers are all really helpful and, so far, the work is easy enough as long as you do the reading and studying and everything. Everyone does everything they can to help you."

"Well, I must say I'm very impressed," Sheila said. "You sound like you've taken to living in England like a duck to water. I'm so delighted to hear you're all settled in." They chatted for a few minutes longer about her course work, and then Sheila said, "Sorry to cut across you, but I'm going out soon, and I just want to check when you thought you might be available to start a bit of weekend work out at the Hamiltons' house?"

"Well, any time really," Connie said. "We're usually free from Friday afternoon on. A few of my friends go home at the weekend, so it's fairly quiet."

"Great," Sheila said quickly. "So does this coming Friday suit?" Connie confirmed that it did.

"I'll ring Vanessa now and, if you give me your number there, I'll ring you back with the arrangements."

"Sorry, Sheila," Connie said quickly, "is this just an interview to see whether I'll suit?"

"No interview necessary," Sheila said. "I've already spoken to them and they said if I vouch for you then that's good enough. But I think they are most impressed with having a medical student as a childminder. I told them you were considering going into Paediatrics, and that nailed it for you."

"I'm not too sure about that," Connie said. "I haven't decided what I'll specialise in yet. It's a long way off."

"Well, they're not going to know that, are they?"

Connie hung up, and then went to sit on the bench in the hallway, which was quiet for a change.

Less than five minutes later Sheila rang and arranged to pick her up outside Piccadilly Station at four o'clock the following Friday. Connie had to go to the bank in the city, and the station, Sheila said, would be the easiest central place to pick her up.

"Vanessa is over the moon you can come this weekend," she said. "They have do's on Friday and Saturday night, so bring your overnight things and clothes."

"And my medical books," Connie said, laughing. "No rest for the wicked. I'll have my weekend studying to do when the children go to bed."

"It will keep you on the straight and narrow – and out of the dances and the bars." Sheila laughed. "Although I wouldn't be too sure when it comes to the Hamiltons, as they are very big into parties and social nights. You never know what could happen in the big house on Silver Street."

It was only after Sheila had hung up that it dawned on Connie she hadn't asked her what colour her car was. It didn't matter, her mother's cousin did not sound like the sort of person who would be reticent about introducing herself.

Chapter 29

Connie was standing against the wall at the entrance to Piccadilly Station, her rucksack and bag lying beside her when the sleek, black car passed her and pulled up a few yards ahead. She moved away from the wall, checking as discreetly as she could whether the driver was a thin, plain woman with short dark hair as her mother had described. She went towards the kerb, her head bent to get a proper look. The woman in the car had expensively cut dark hair with reddish highlights, distinctive silver earrings and a large pair of sunglasses. When Connie realised it was not Sheila Doyle, she quickly moved back, feeling embarrassed

Connie moved further along the pavement, trying to look casual, while scanning the constant stream of cars coming towards the station on either side of the road. She did the top toggle up on her mulberry-coloured duffle coat and then glanced at the darkened sky, hoping that she would be picked up before the rain started.

A siren sounded and the busy Friday-afternoon traffic slowed down to let an ambulance go past. Connie automatically blessed herself, thinking of the poor person inside who was the cause of the emergency.

As she felt the first drop of rain, she turned back to her bags to kick them closer to the wall so they would not get too wet.

Then the door of the black car opened and a voice called, "Connie?"

Connie stared as the driver stepped out.

The tall, elegant woman took her dark glasses off.

"Sheila Doyle?" Connie said. "I'm sorry – I didn't realise it was you."

This was definitely not the picture she had built up in her head of her mother's cousin. She was tall certainly, but she was not the gawky sort of woman Kate Devine had described. With her long smooth black bobbed hair, her fitted black polo-neck sweater and her short hounds-tooth patterned skirt accessorised with several long, looped gold chains, she looked like one of the glamorous university lecturers Connie had recently admired.

"I never thought about you not recognising me," Sheila said. "I should have suggested that we both wear a red carnation!" She laughed and then motioned with her head. "In you get, we don't want you getting soaked. I'll open the boot so you can stick your bags in it." She then climbed back inside the car and the boot sprang open.

Connie hoisted her rucksack up on one shoulder and lifted the bag with the other. She went over to the boot and dropped them both inside and, as she closed the top back down, she noticed the BMW badge on the back, and closed it very carefully.

Terry, she thought, would love a drive in a car like this. He wouldn't believe that an older woman from Tullamore was driving such a fancy car, especially their mother's cousin. She would enjoy telling him all about it when she rang home Sunday night.

She went around to the passenger side of the car and slid onto the soft, green-leather seat.

Sheila turned sideways in her seat, to look straight at her. "Lovely to meet you at long last, Connie."

"And lovely to meet you too," Connie said, smiling.

There was a few moments silence during which Connie felt Sheila Doyle's eyes taking in everything about her – her hair, her dangly earrings, even her new Chelsea Girl duffle coat.

Sheila smiled and nodded her head up and down approvingly. "Your mother didn't tell me what a good-looking girl you are. I was picturing some little country mouse from Tullamore, and here you are looking like the modern, confident Miss Manchester University student."

Connie started to laugh. "I wouldn't be too sure about being modern and confident."

Sheila turned the key in the ignition and the car started to purr over. "Well, I would never have picked you out for a country girl. That's the reason I sat here like a lemon for the last five minutes – I was sure you were a second or third year student."

"I didn't think I looked that old." Connie paused, then smiled, feeling immediately comfortable with this straight-talking woman. "It's funny, because you're not a bit like my mother described to me. I was expecting someone very serious-looking with short dark hair and glasses. Reading glasses – not sunglasses."

"Is that how your mother still sees me?" There was a note of amusement in Sheila's voice. "In fairness to Kate, I think that's because that's exactly how I looked for a long time. I always had a pair of bloody reading glasses on a chain around my neck because I was always losing them. When I was younger I didn't care what I looked like. A case of take me as you find me." She looked at Connie and raised her eyebrows. "But you learn as you get older. Now I keep the reading glasses in my handbag and use them more discreetly."

"I don't think my mother imagined you wearing sunglasses somehow." Then she quickly added, "I think they are lovely, really glamorous."

Sheila laughed. "That's the idea. I like the Jackie Kennedy mysterious look." She indicated towards the sky. "Not that I need sunglasses now. When I left the house the sun was beaming down, now we're heading into a bloody miserable night. But the weather is not going to bother you one little bit tonight. The minute you step into Hamiltons' house you won't be thinking of the rain outside."

"You said it was lovely – is it very modern?"

"Yes and no, you'll see it when we get there." She reached into the pocket in the door and took out a packet of cigarettes. She opened it and held it out to Connie. "Smoke?"

Connie shook her head. Her mother used to smoke, but stopped a few years ago. She could never imagine her mother offering any young girl a cigarette.

"Good girl, it's a filthy habit but it keeps me going and stops me eating so much." She put a cigarette in her mouth and then reached down into the pocket again to search for her lighter. She found it, lit her cigarette and took a deep drag on it.

As Connie watched her hold the cigarette, her eyes were drawn to Sheila's deep-red, perfectly manicured nails. She was surprised at a nurse having such well-kept nails as her mother constantly complained that she had to keep hers short for working in the hospital.

"Now, I'm going to be quiet for a while as I need to pull out here, and it's very busy being Friday."

She manoeuvred the nose of the car out and then after a few moments put her foot down on the accelerator to smoothly glide out into a gap in the stream of traffic. "Thank God for a big engine," she said. "All the years I was overtaken on the motorway by men and I didn't understand the difference a powerful engine makes. I was always afraid of them, thinking that I had more control with a smaller engine. Then, when I was changing my car before this one, a young guy in the garage convinced me to try out a 2-litre engine and that was it. I've never looked back." She winked at Connie. "Or, I should say – I'm always looking back, because it's me who now leaves all the other cars behind." She laughed and took another puff of her cigarette, then flicked the end of the ash into the tray between the seats.

"Do you mind me asking how long you've been in England, Sheila?" Connie asked. Then she quickly added. "Do you mind me calling you Sheila or would you prefer Miss –"

"You're not going to suggest calling me Miss Doyle, I hope?"

"I wasn't sure."

"I may technically be a Miss, but it's the one title I cannot abide. It's like something out of Jane Austin. Miss Doyle – spinster of this parish and all that. At work I'm called Sister Doyle, which suits me grand, but I'm not going to ask you to call me that. Sheila will be just fine."

"Okay, Sheila," Connie said.

"I've been in England a long time, since I came over to train as a nurse in London. Around the same time as your mother did her training at home. We're the same age – we were in the same class in school."

It was on the tip of Connie's tongue to say to Sheila that she seemed younger in both her looks and certainly in her manner, but thought it would be disloyal to her mother. It wasn't that her mother wasn't an attractive woman – she undoubtedly was, and she took care with dressing up for occasions – it was more to do with her mother's ways and old-fashioned attitude.

"So, what can you tell me about the family we're going out to?" Connie asked.

"They're mad busy," Sheila said. "That's their biggest problem. They are always running to catch up on themselves. They have Audrey to help during the week, but their weekends are always busy with the shop and everything, and they often need someone around then as well. Not every weekend, Vanessa said, but she would like you to be available most weekends. They are such a lovely couple and the two children are lovely too."

"How old are they – the children?"

Sheila thought for a few moments. "Toby is four and Belinda is coming up to three."

"And how do you know the family?" Connie asked. Then, something about the quick way that Sheila looked at her made her think she might be coming across as nosey or even pushy. "I didn't mean that to sound nosey or anything, I'm just keen to know a little bit about them."

"I did a little private nursing work for the family," Sheila said. "I helped them out with Vanessa's father when he was ill. Of course, it's not the sort of thing you go talking about to everyone."

Connie nodded her head slowly, feeling she had crossed a line she should not have crossed. There was then a gap in the conversation, but she kept silent now, unsure about asking anything else. Sheila switched the radio on to a channel which was playing the Top Twenty, so Connie felt on safer ground when Rod Stewart came on singing 'Oh No Not My Baby'.

"Do you like this sort of music?" she asked.

"Oh, I love Rod Stewart," Sheila said. She turned towards Connie, laughter in her eyes. "Sure, he's mad the way he carries on on-stage, but he's brilliant. I loved 'Maggie May'. I think it's still my favourite."

"Oh, I really like him too," Connie said. "I'd love to see him in concert." She was relieved to have found a safe subject. Her mother could not stand Rod Stewart, saying he was a 'show-off and a bad example kicking a football on the stage when he was singing'. But then, her mother could not really see beyond Irish singer, Joe Dolan, and some of the other showband types, so Rod Stewart was hardly likely to be her cup of tea.

Sheila turned to her, all smiles now. "We must remember that the next time he comes to Mancheste and, do you know, we'll go together."

"That would be great," Connie said. She could not tell so far whether it would actually be great to spend an evening with Sheila, or whether it was best to keep things at a safe distance. Something told her she would not like to get on the wrong side of her mother's cousin.

They talked about music and continued talking about each hit that came on in turn, as Sheila drove them down one town road after another until she turned down one road and they suddenly seemed to be out in the country. They drove along for a while and then more houses started to appear until they were in a busier, built-up area with shops and lots more houses.

The news came on the radio, and Sheila stretched her arm to turn it off. "We're nearly there now. They live on one of the streets just outside the town. You won't have heard of Wilmslow, I suppose?" She gestured to a signpost with the name of the town.

No," Connie said, sitting up straight now. "I don't think I have." She became aware of a little fluttery feeling in her stomach now, which she knew was due to being anxious about what was to come, about meeting all these new people.

She was not sure why she should feel worried, because she was usually good at mixing with people she didn't know well. From what she had been told, she knew she would not only get on fine working for the Hamilton family – but that she would love it. But still, the fluttering continued. She did not have the same exciting, confident feeling about meeting people that she had starting university. She wondered if it was because Sheila was the only person she knew in this part of Manchester, and that soon Sheila would be gone leaving her in a strange town in a strange house with people she did not know.

She turned her face towards her passenger window now as they drove through the main street of Wilmslow town, trying to distract her anxious thoughts by looking at the different types of shops there were in the small town.

At one point, as she glanced at Sheila, she realised she did not feel any connection with this woman who was a blood relation of her mother. In reality, she was with a total stranger, someone she had never even heard of until her mother had organised that they meet up. And, although Sheila had been kind enough to organise this job for her and come to Manchester and pick her up, Connie was beginning to feel that somehow her mother had been presumptuous in expecting her to do that. She thought of Malcolm and the comments he had made about Irish people getting sucked into an exclusively Irish community in England, depending on their own kind.

As those thoughts went through her mind, and in case she was correct, Connie decided that she would make it explicit to Sheila that she very much appreciated the effort that she had made, but that she expected nothing more from her. Why should she? And then, another thought crept into her mind. If her mother thought she should get a weekend job so quickly, why hadn't it occurred to her to ask Tara? Tara was her aunt, and a much closer connection in every way. When she thought back, even her grandad had said that Tara would sort her out with work. Surely there had been no need to contact someone her mother had only seen a handful of times over the years? It did not make sense.

As the car turned down what looked like a narrow laneway, Connie caught sight of the plaque on a wall which said Silver Street, and she knew they had arrived.

Chapter 30

The car went down Silver Street, which gradually broadened until it was a good-sized street with large detached houses on either side.

"Ah, now I get it," Connie said, smiling at Sheila. "Why they've called it Silver Street. The silver birches on the pavements on either side of the road."

"Clever girl," Sheila said. "That didn't dawn on me."

"We did a project in school years ago about trees, and the teacher took our class for a walk around the local bog and we had to find the various trees from the description. I loved the silvery white bark on these birches, and I've never forgotten it."

"You must tell Vanessa and the children that interesting little detail, because they might not know either. I suppose when you move in somewhere you just take the name for granted without asking questions."

"It's a lovely street," Connie said, as she looked out at the large detached houses, separated from their neighbours by high walls or fences. Some were hard to see as they were set way back in grounds and hidden away behind more tall trees and bushes.

"Vanessa and Dave live at the very bottom, in a sort of cul-de-sac," Sheila said. "They have the whole corner. They were lucky to get that particular house, and especially in such a nice setting as this. Most couples their age are starting out in two-up two-downs. But then, they have worked hard for everything they have."

Connie thought that Sheila sounded very fond of the couple – or even proud of them and their achievements. They drove to the bottom of the street and she could then see what Sheila had meant about the Hamiltons being lucky to have such a house. Even though it had high greyish-white stone walls obscuring most of it, she could see exactly how big and grand the house was.

Sheila slowed down to go through the high, black gates and then up the curving gravelled driveway, landscaped with shrubberies and rose beds on either side, towards the imposing, double-fronted white house with what seemed like a multitude of black-edged windows. As they passed Connie noticed the row of tall grey, decorative lampposts and could imagine what the driveway would look like at night with them all lit up.

From her scant knowledge of buildings and from what she could see, it seemed to be an old house, but she wasn't quite sure as there was also something modern-looking about it. The rooms on both sides of the doorway had tall bay windows with leaded glass, as did the rooms above. To the right-hand side she could see a circular-shaped conservatory with stained-glass details of creeping vines with purple grapes going across the windows.

Sheila circled a stone fountain with cherubs and came to a halt at the front door. "Well," she said, "what do you think?"

"It's fantastic," Connie said. "It's absolutely gorgeous. And I bet it's absolutely beautiful inside as well."

"Did you see all those big bushes coming in?" Sheila said. "Well, they are rhododendrons, and you should see this garden when the blooms are out in early summer. They are in every colour, red, purple, pink, white. The garden is a blaze of colour."

"I can just imagine how beautiful it would look," Connie said, looking around.

"Now, before we go in," Sheila's voice suddenly sounded urgent, "I want to give you a quick piece of advice. Just to say that it's best to keep certain things private, not to volunteer too much information if you don't have to."

"About what?" Connie asked, suddenly feeling anxious again. "What sort of information should I not give?"

"Well, personal things about back home. It's perfectly fine to tell them all about you training to be a doctor. In fact, I'd mention that every opportunity you get because that's the kind of information that speaks well of you. But, I'd keep other things to yourself."

"What sort of things?"

"Things like what your family does, and where they live and that sort of thing. Be vague about the details, and the kind of house your family lives in, because it's nobody's business but your own."

Connie caught her breath, suddenly reminded of the questions that she had been asked about her family when she was interviewed for a place to study medicine in Dublin. It was plain that Sheila was suggesting that her background was something to hide. Something to be ashamed about. But if that was the case, then Sheila must think the same of her own background because, according to what her mother had told her, it was very similar to their own. Apart from Sheila's family having what her mother described as a 'small bit of a farm', they sounded very alike.

"I don't worry about things like that." Connie's voice was quiet and even and respectful. "All the people I've met at university have asked me questions like that, and there hasn't been any problem. It's one of the first questions that students ask each other. And they've all been fine when I told them I was Irish and from a small country town in the Midlands."

"I'm not saying there is anything wrong with Tullamore and the kind of houses we grew up in," Sheila said, "and I'm not talking about students who are too busy running mad, enjoying their freedom, to give a damn about things like that. It'll all be different when they are qualified and earning a good wage and have to think of mortgages and the like. Then what the other person does and earns will matter." She waved a dismissive hand. "We haven't time to go into a big discussion now. I'm not saying anything about Vanessa and Dave, they are the finest, but I'm just explaining that they mix with all kinds of people because of their business, and some of them are all about old money and backgrounds. And there are others who are not too keen on Irish people, and use any excuse to look down on us. We don't want to give those types any ammunition to be prejudiced about us. That's all I'm saying."

"Why would they be prejudiced towards us?" Connie asked.

"Well, they have a certain image of the Irish, about them being low-class, heavy drinkers and not being too fussy about cleanliness. And while some people have let their country down over the years by having all those awful traits, it is certainly not true for the likes of us. But nevertheless, it doesn't stop ignorant people from thinking it."

Connie felt like asking Sheila why she was friends with people who would think badly of her for being Irish, but apart from the fact they did not have time to talk now, she had the feeling that Sheila might lose patience with her.

They got out of the car and, as she looked at the black-painted door with the shiny knocker and letterbox, Connie could feel her heart pumping in her chest.

"Don't forget to get your bags out of the boot," Sheila told her. "The catch is just down below the badge. If you put your hand underneath you'll feel it."

As Connie went around to the boot, Sheila came to the other side of her.

"And it goes without saying," she said, "that you don't answer any questions about me or my family back home either. Give no information to anyone who asks."

"Well, if I say I don't know anything, it's the truth," Connie said, "because I don't really know anything about you or your family."

"Well, don't say that," Sheila said, "or they'll think we're complete strangers. Just say that your mother and I are related and you were too little to remember when I went off to England."

It struck Connie that although her mother and Sheila were worlds apart in many ways, there was a similarity between them in that they were both very cautious about people and suspicious of their motives.

Then, before any more could be said, the black door opened and a young man just below average height, who she thought looked to be in his twenties, came out. He had whitish-blond hair and was holding a little girl in his arms. Then she heard some childish laughs and screams and a boy came running out past his father to meet them, brandishing a gun. He stopped dead, aimed the gun at each one and made a shooting noise, and then turned and ran back into the house.

The little girl seemed shy, as she had her head buried in her father's neck. She had little or no hair on her head, while the boy had surprisingly long blond hair for a boy. Connie felt herself begin to relax now that she had met the two children she would be looking after. They might be from a wealthy family, but they struck her as being just ordinary little children doing the ordinary things that all children do. She was also warmed by the friendly smile on the man's face.

"Thank heavens the cavalry has arrived!" he said, laughing and holding his free arm out. He stood back, making a bowing and then a sweeping gesture. "Welcome, ladies, please come in."

"Oh, I'm only the delivery lady, Dave," Sheila said, her voice light and easy now. "This is the clever medical student – and your new right-hand woman, Connie."

"Well, a very special welcome to Connie," he said, beaming at her. "We're all at sixes and sevens here so you couldn't have come at a better time. Vanessa has been held up with a house consultation, and Audrey is at a funeral, so it fell to me to pick the kids up from the crèche." He looked at Sheila and rolled his eyes. "I don't need to tell you what it's like here at times."

"You certainly have busy lives," Sheila said. "But I'm sure neither of you would like it any other way."

He made a face now, which reminded Connie of a schoolboy caught out doing something wrong. "You could be right there, Sheila," he said, laughing.

Connie could feel Sheila's hand on her back, guiding her along towards the door.

Dave Hamilton had his hand outstretched to Connie now, and when she took it he gave her a very firm handshake. The sort of handshake, she imagined, that he used with other businessmen. Close up, he wasn't as young as she'd originally thought – more like his late thirties as opposed to twenties – and she noticed that his blond hair was dyed, the roots a light brown with little tips of blonde on the ends.

Dave looked at the little girl. "Now, Belinda, this lovely young lady is going to be looking after you and Toby. Say hello to Connie."

Connie leaned over to put her face closer to the child's. "Hello,

Belinda, are you and me going to be nice friends? Are we going to play some lovely games?"

The child studied her for a few moments, and then gave a quick smile before burying her head back into her father's neck.

"She'll come round," Sheila said. "Don't you worry about Belinda. She's as lively as the other lad when she gets to know you."

"Worse at times," Dave said, laughing. "How was the traffic? The usual Friday afternoon?"

Sheila told him how the traffic had been hellish in Manchester but fine after that.

He held the door open for them to go into a hallway with the black-and-white tiled floor. Sheila went first and Connie came behind, carrying the rucksack and bag. In the brief moments they waited for the door to close, Connie's gaze wandered to the wide staircase to the right with the polished wooden handrail and the white wrought-iron railings. As her eyes moved upwards, she was not surprised to see a huge chandelier.

As she walked along she recognised the scent of roses and she passed a huge golden urn filled with at least two dozen deep-red roses and gypsophila. It was sitting on top of a long antique walnut table with a marble top and a gold French-style mirror above it. As she thought how lovely it all looked, the dusky, sweet smell took her back to the flower shop in Tullamore and she felt a little pang, feeling the loss of familiarity and the safe routine in the shop and in her old life.

"And how are you settling in at university, Connie?" Dave looked over his shoulder at her. "A big change from Ireland, I would think."

"It's going well, thanks," Connie said. "Lots of studying now, but I'm enjoying it all, and so far managing to keep up."

"Good girl," he said.

She wondered if Sheila had noticed that she had been careful and had not been drawn into talking about home, even though Dave had mentioned Ireland.

"And how is the social life?" he asked now. "Mad, I would imagine?"

Connie thought now that it would not sound good to mention the discos and the Freshers' Ball to a prospective employer.

"I've not seen anything too bad at all," she said. "All very well behaved so far." And then, thinking that what she had said might sound a bit old-fashioned – the sort of thing she might say to her mother, she added, "But I suppose the term is only a few weeks in."

"I saw a thing on the news about Rag Week a few months ago, and I couldn't believe the things they get up to in the name of raising money for charity. Crazy buggers!" He shook his head and laughed. "One group of them kidnapped a businessman I knew last year, and wouldn't release him until he organised a cheque for a hundred pounds to be handed over."

"If they held that fella in some of the student digs I've heard of," Sheila said, "he'd be glad to hand over a thousand pounds to get out of it!"

"True, true," Dave said laughing. "And in fairness, the money raised from their antics is all for a good cause." He hoisted Belinda up on his shoulder now, and started walking quickly ahead, as though he was in a rush. "I wonder where that Toby has gone?" he muttered as he turned into a room. "Now, Connie, I think it might be best to show you the kitchen first, because it's the busiest room in the house, where everything happens, and the kids have their playroom just off it."

They walked along the hallway past doors to other rooms and paintings and modern sculptures on stands, and then they came to double doors at the bottom.

They followed him inside to a large, open-plan kitchen which Connie thought was beautiful and had that same feeling of a mix of old and new. The walls were the grey-green colour, the floor had big old flagstone tiles – the sort you would see in an old cottage – a yellow Aga, the biggest fridge she had ever seen with two doors, a variety of cupboards painted in a buttermilk colour and a matching dresser. The dresser was similar to the old pine one they had at home only bigger, but this was not like her mother's which was filled with a random cups and mugs hanging from little gold hooks, and a conglomeration of ornaments and plates inscribed *A Gift from Ballybunion, Blackpool* or *Donegal*. Neither did it have a collection of miniature dolls wearing the national dress of various countries or a *Mrs Beeton's Cookery Book*, whose pages her mother had plumped out with cut-out recipes from magazines and handwritten ones on backs of envelopes.

The dresser in the Hamilton family's house was elegantly stacked with a matching range of cream and white hand-made pottery. A jug from the same collection stood on one of the shelves, filled with yellow roses. As she noted all the extra little details, Connie could tell why Vanessa was in the interior-design business, as her own home showcased her extremely good eye for detail.

There was a breakfast bar with six high, pale-green leather-backed chairs which swivelled around. At the far end of the room there was a round white table with six more chairs around it, and to the side of it was a new-style, leather corner sofa and a matching chair, a coffee table and a television. Connie could imagine that this was where the children would curl up to watch cartoons while their mother was cooking.

She was not sure whether it was appropriate to comment on the kitchen. She had always felt giving a genuine compliment was the right thing to do, as staying silent, she thought, often gave the impression of coldness or even jealousy.

"This is a really lovely house," she said.

"I'm glad you like it," Dave said, nodding his head and smiling. "We put a lot of work into it."

"And money," Sheila said, moving over to sit on one of the high chairs. "But it is beautiful, and it will all add to the value."

Connie kept standing, not sure if it would be presumptuous to sit down too.

Dave stooped down now to drop Belinda to her feet. "Go and find Toby," he told her, patting her on the bottom. "Find where the little rascal went. He's probably upstairs in his bedroom."

"He has a gun – he's a bad boy!" Belinda said, her face puckered in mock-anger. Then she ran off out of the kitchen and down the hallway.

It occurred to Connie that Belinda was a bit young to be running around such a big house unsupervised. Anything, she thought, could happen to her. Her instincts were to go after her, but she wasn't sure it was the right thing to do. She had not been shown upstairs yet, and it might look as though she was being critical of Dave for allowing her to run off, so she decided to stay quiet.

Dave shook his head and laughed at his daughter, and then he turned back to them. "Now, what can I offer you? Tea, coffee or a nice glass of chilled wine?"

Sheila looked at her watch. "At this time? It's not even five o'clock yet."

Her words sounded disapproving, but Connie noticed her tone was high and almost playful. She herself did not answer, because there was a tiny part of her unsure as to whether she was included. Although she had made the big step of moving from school to university, she wasn't at all sure if she would be included if alcoholic drinks were offered even at home.

"It's a Friday evening," Dave said, going towards the fridge, "and I don't know about anyone else but, with the week I've had, I'm ready for it." He came out with a bottle of wine and then went to a drawer and took out a corkscrew. He then went to one of the higher-up cupboards and lifted down three large gold-rimmed goblets.

"Go on," Sheila said, crossing her legs now. "You've twisted my arm." She turned to look at Connie and gave her a conspiratorial wink.

Connie smiled back at her, unsure what the wink was about. Something made her think that Sheila was referring to them being offered wine, as though it was an indication of the good position she had procured for her.

Sheila then bent down to lift her handbag and retrieve her cigarettes. As she did so, Connie noticed that her skirt had risen high up on her thighs, revealing the darker shade of her stocking tops. And it struck Connie that there was something odd about Sheila compared to the women of her mother's age back home. Sheila had to be in her mid-to-late forties, of a similar age, but none of her mother's nursing colleagues or friends would wear a skirt that short, nor would they be sitting on a high chair swinging their legs and drinking wine. Connie wondered if it was something to do with the way women in England were, but then she thought of Tara and Bridget, and she knew that it was more to do with Sheila herself.

Sheila held the packet of cigarettes out to Dave.

"Thanks," he said, taking a cigarette and putting it down on the worktop. He uncorked the wine and filled the three glasses and handed them around.

"Cheers!" he said, holding his glass up and then taking a good gulp of the cold wine. "And let's hope that Connie, with all her youthful, student energy, is going to sort out our little pair of hooligans!"

Sheila held her glass out. "I'll drink to that," she said laughing. "Because there are times when they've run me ragged."

"Aw, they seem really lovely," Connie said, smiling and holding her glass out too. She took a sip of the lovely cold wine and then another one.

Then, Dave went to the cupboard and came back out with a bowl filled with nuts and another one with fancy crisps in it. "A few nibbles to keep us going."

He passed the bowls along the breakfast bar, and Sheila and Connie both took a handful of the nuts. Dave lit his cigarette and he then sat down opposite Sheila and asked how her BMW was running and as they chatted Connie sipped more of her wine and looked around the lovely kitchen again, taking in all the details and looking at how things had been arranged, and then her gaze moved out into the garden. What a place, she thought. She couldn't wait to get back to university on Sunday to tell the girls on her floor. Most of them had gone home for the weekend, so they would all be together in the Student Union Bar at night, each giving a run-down on their weekend. She would also ring her mother as usual, who she knew would love to hear about the great place Sheila had organised for her. She would tell her about the house and the children, the sort of domestic details her mother would love. She would say nothing about Sheila and her odd ways or the fact they were all sitting in the kitchen on a Friday evening drinking glasses of wine, as though it was the most normal thing in the world.

Connie was halfway down her glass when she heard a screech from one of the children – it came from out somewhere beyond the hallway, perhaps upstairs. She looked at Dave.

"Will I go and see if they are all right?" she asked.

He nodded. "Yeah, that would be great. They are probably upstairs in their bedrooms." He rolled his eyes. "You'll find your way – just follow the noise."

Connie went quickly out of the kitchen and down along the corridor. She glanced at the reception rooms downstairs as she went by – all seemed quiet, their doors closed, and no sign of two lively children through the shadowy glass panels.

She went up the stairs and, as she reached the halfway mark, she heard Toby's voice from somewhere in the distance shouting, "What do you say? What's the word?"

As she got to the top step she could hear Belinda's wails. She halted for a few moments listening, and then she called the little girl's name, not sure which room they were in. When she got to the first bedroom, the door was slightly ajar. She called 'Belinda?' again, but there was no answer. After listening for a few moments for any noise, Connie carefully pushed the door open wider to check if they were there.

As soon she stepped inside the room, Connie realised she was in the master bedroom. A dark wood, four-poster bed stood opposite the door beside an open window and the fluttering lace panels caught back with bows on each of the four posts drew her eye. She had seen beds like this in magazines or in pictures of old stately houses, but she had never seen one in a real house. The mahogany wood looked polished and flawless and she wondered if it was an antique or if it was an expensive reproduction. Her gaze swept around the large room, past what looked like matching dark wood furniture, to where she could see another half-open door revealing an attached bathroom. From what she could glimpse in the distance, it looked as though there was a sunken bath.

The child was obviously not there and Connie knew she should not be there either.

Resisting the urge to stay for a few more moments, she turned to leave but, as she did so, her eye caught a painting on the wall to the side of the bed. It was an oil painting she thought, of shadowy, smudgy, slightly abstract figures in inky blues, purples, greens and brown. A couple, their arms around each other and faces tilted upwards. It had something of a Picasso-type touch about it, she thought – it reminded her of one of his blue paintings of a group of depressed-looking people. Her eyes narrowed as she stared at it, working it out. Then, as she suddenly realised what she was actually looking at, she felt a red flush creeping over her face and her neck. Unless she was mistaken, it was an almost life-size nude painting of Dave and she presumed, Vanessa, in a pose simulating Adam and Eve.

She turned and moved out of the room as quickly as she could. How on earth could they possibly have a painting like that in the house, she thought, when there were two young children who would see it?

She hurried along past two more bedrooms whose doors were open and showing double beds that were obviously for guests, then she opened a door to find a huge, luxurious bathroom.

Before she had time to look around it, she heard the children's raised voices echoing along the bottom of the corridor. When she got to the end, she saw steps going downwards to another small corridor where there were three more rooms. She ran down the steps calling "*Belinda?*" and then she eventually heard a little voice through sobs, calling, "*I'm here ... I'm here!*"

When she reached the first room she opened the door and stepped into what was plainly Toby's room as it had a Scalextric racing-track set up over by the window.

Toby was standing on top of a red-painted chair which was decorated with stickers of Paddington Bear. He had his gun high up in his arms and was aiming it. "She's here," he said. "I captured her."

When Connie looked, there was the little girl sitting on the edge of the bed, her arms and feet tied up with a skipping rope.

"God almighty!" Connie whispered to herself. She turned to Toby. "Get down now, before you hurt yourself. You'll be in trouble when your daddy hears what you've done."

Toby pointed a finger at his sister. "She's not allowed in my room – she broke the rules and I captured her." He now aimed the gun at Connie, then closed one eye. "*Bang! Bang!*" he said. "And I'll shoot Daddy too!" He jumped down off the chair and ran out of the room.

Connie turned to look at the white-faced little girl. She smiled at her and shook her head. "You're okay, darling, I'm going to look after you." She moved quickly to the bed to unravel the skipping rope. "Your brother is a very naughty boy."

Belinda nodded her head, tears in her eyes. "He's very bad ... Mummy says he's a bad, bad boy."

Connie freed her from the last of the rope and then instinctively gathered the little girl into her arms. "You're okay now," she said, kissing her on top of the head. "You're safe now, I'll look after you. You're a good girl."

Belinda buried her head into Connie's chest, the same way she had done with her father earlier. "I'm a good girl," she repeated.

A lump came into Connie's throat now as she felt the child's fear and vulnerability. And she felt guilty she had not been brave enough to follow her earlier on and save her from the boyish exuberance of her brother. But she knew that the child's father should have checked. Surely, she thought, he must know that his son gets carried away with his vivid imagination with the gun.

She lifted Belinda in her arms and took her back downstairs.

Sheila and Dave were sitting there, chatting away and smoking.

"Here she is," Dave said, beaming at his daughter. "And looking like she's made a new friend."

"Oh, she has," Connie said, cuddling her closer. "You have a new friend now? Haven't you?"

Belinda hugged Connie tighter. "Toby's a bad boy," she told her father.

"He's a brat," he said. "But hopefully, Connie, you might be able to teach him a few manners."

He pointed his finger in the direction of the window, and when Connie looked she could see Toby high up on a climbing-frame. The fear he had instilled in his little sister just a few minutes earlier had obviously not concerned him one jot.

"Well, he is a bit ..." Connie hesitated, she wanted to say that the boy was badly behaved and had bullied and terrified his little sister. That she thought he needed a much firmer hand, and at least a strong telling-off for what he had done to his sister but, as she glanced at Sheila's serious face, she thought better of it. She compromised. "He's a bit of a livewire. I hate to tell you, but he actually had his poor little sister tied up with a skipping rope ... poor little mite was terrified."

"What?" Dave said. "The little bugger!" He grinned and shook his head. "What can I say? He's an out and out bucko – a real lad. He needs to get out there and burn off all that energy, keep him busy. There are times when he can drive us to distraction, when he gets overexcited, but then I suppose we'd have more to worry about if he was the other way – a bit of a sissy. Then, we'd have a real problem."

"Lads are better being lads," Sheila said. "And soon he'll have football and rugby and all those things to focus his energy on."

"Exactly," Dave said. He looked at his watch. "I'm just thinking I should show you where your bedroom is, Connie. If you want to bring your bags, I'll show you. Sheila won't mind keeping her eye on the kids for a few minutes."

Putting Belinda down to play with some toys, Connie lifted her rucksack and bag and followed Dave out into the hall and up the blue, thickly carpeted stairs.

"You're just along the hall from the kiddies," he told her as they reached the top, "so if you're in bed you should still be able to hear them no problem."

"That's great," she said. "I know where I am then, because I've already been in Toby's room."

As they walked down the hall past the master bedroom, Connie felt her face flush at the memory of the nude painting. It also crossed her mind as she went down the steps to where the children's bedrooms were, that most parents would have their children sleeping in rooms closer to them.

Dave quickly showed Connie Toby's room and then he opened a door across the corridor which was festooned in pink, which he told her was Belinda's.

They walked to the room at the very end. "And this," Dave said, opening the door wide, "is your room and private bathroom."

As Connie stepped into the room she felt her feet sink into the thick, beige-and-cream shag-pile carpet. The double-size bed had a high brown-leather headboard and a matching bedspread and pillows with brown and cream squares. Two fancily shaped brass reading lamps stood on either side of the bed on mock-crocodile covered cabinets, each with three drawers. The room was fitted with cream and brown wardrobes and a matching, square, modern dressing-table. A leather-topped stool stood in the big bay window.

"This is absolutely beautiful," she said. "It's like something out of a magazine." She had not imagined having a bedroom as big as this, and certainly not one with its own bathroom.

"Good, good, I'm glad you like it," Dave said. He laughed. "Believe it or not, it has actually been featured in a magazine. We used it in one of the newspaper adverts for our interior business." He pointed to a door. "You'll find the bathroom in there." He checked his watch again. "I'll head back downstairs and I'll leave you to sort your things out."

When he closed the door Connie stood for a few moments, looking around the room. She noticed that the main light was brass and had five shades all shaped the same as the lamps. She walked around, opening doors and drawers, thinking that it was more like a hotel room than a home. She then went to the bathroom and opened it to find she had both a bath and a shower cubicle all to herself.

When she came back downstairs, Sheila met her with a knowing smile. "Well," she said, "isn't the bedroom something else? That's the one I've used when I've stayed overnight here when I was baby-sitting. I absolutely love it."

"We'll just have to find you another room if you and Connie are here at the weekends in future," Dave said, winking at her. He lifted his wineglass and drained it. "Now, Connie, it looks like Vanessa is going to be another while and I've got to go. There's a guy I've got to catch before he heads home for the weekend."

He went over to the freezer, opened the door and peered inside, then he lifted out a box of fish fingers and a pack of potato waffles. "The old standbys," he said, putting them out on the breakfast bar. He went to one of the cupboards and brought out a tin of beans. "Ten minutes and it's all done. There's ice cream in the freezer for afters." He paused then he opened the fridge and looked inside again. "You just have a rummage around here and I'm sure you'll find something nice for yourself. There's some nice Chicken Kievs and some salmon. Or if you fancy a salad, there's cold meats and coleslaw and curried rice in different containers. Or I can leave you the number for the local Chinese – they do a takeaway delivery service. The food is top-notch."

"Not at all, I'm happy to have the fish fingers too," Connie said, "It will be nice for us all to have the same thing."

Dave looked at her, his eyes filled with amusement. "Are you sure?"

She smiled at him. "Yes, it's ages since I've had them." The idea of the Chinese takeaway sounded great to her, but she did not want to seem grabbing, especially with Sheila here. She would save it for another time.

He glanced out into the garden now, where Toby was climbing the steps up to the slide.

Sheila took a last drag on her cigarette then stubbed it out in the ashtray. She stood up and lifted her glass to finish her wine off. "I need to be going too."

"Anything nice planned for the weekend?" Dave asked.

She moved her head sideways and back, as though considering it. "Maybe," she said.

"The dark horse again," Dave said, laughing. "You never like to give too much away, Sheila, do you?"

She lifted her bag. "Tell Vanessa I'll ring her," she said. Then she turned to Connie. "You have my number if there's anything."

Connie nodded. "Thanks," she said. "And thanks for the lift over – it was very good of you."

"No problem, you'll be able to find your own way over on the bus next time." Sheila winked at her then checked Dave was out of earshot. "Don't take any nonsense from that Toby. He will probably try it on because you're new, but let him know who's boss. And get a bit of studying done when the children are in bed. We don't want you falling behind."

"I will," Connie said. "That's exactly what I plan to do."

She followed Sheila to the door, Belinda in her arms, and just as the cars pulled out of the drive, Toby came charging out through the kitchen, past Connie and Belinda and down the front steps.

"Where has he gone?" he said, throwing his hands up in the air.

"Daddy will be back soon," Connie said, putting her hand out to take his.

He brushed it away then folded his arms up high. "He always says that and then he's gone a long, long time."

Connie put her hand behind his head and guided him back inside. "We're going to put some cartoons on the telly for you now," she said, as they walked back into the kitchen, "and then we're going to have some lovely fish fingers and beans and waffles."

Toby looked up at her uncertainly, his brows down, pouting.

"And if you are both very good," she said, "we're going to have ice cream afterwards."

"*Yayyy!*" he said, punching the air. "Ice cream!"

"*Yay!*" Belinda shouted, copying him.

She walked over to the sofa and put Belinda down and then she turned to Toby and pointed to the opposite corner. "You sit here," she told him, "and we'll see what's on." She went over to switch the television on and, after fiddling with the knobs for a few moments and checking channels, she smiled when Bugs Bunny appeared on the screen. "Now, you both sit there and Connie will make you a lovely dinner."

Half an hour later all three of them were sitting at the kitchen table, eating together. Connie had Belinda beside her, and encouraged her not to pick the cut-up pieces of food with her fingers, but instead to spear them with her child-sized fork. Toby, after some initial guidance from Connie, was making a good attempt at feeding himself.

They were just at the end of the meal when the front door opened and high heels tapped their way down the hallway, and then a small, slim woman with long blonde hair, wearing a black trouser suit with a large silver pendant, came into the kitchen. She dropped her black business case at the door and came striding across the tiled floor.

"Connie?" she said. "I'm Vanessa." She shook Connie's hand, and then she turned to quickly cuddle both children and kiss them on the head. "So sorry I wasn't here for you arriving, but I had a very fussy client to deal with. How are things here?"

"Oh, we're all great," Connie said, smiling and nodding her head. "We're just finishing dinner now."

"Look, Mummy!" Belinda said, carefully spearing two beans with her fork. "Connie showed me."

"Clever girl!" Vanessa said, clapping her hands together. She turned to face Connie again. "Looks like you've been thrown in at the deep end with the cooking."

For a fleeting moment, Connie could feel Vanessa's eyes on her, taking in her hair, her clothes, generally weighing her up. It didn't worry her – in fact she took it as a good sign. A mother, she thought, should be checking on the sort of person who was in her house looking after her children.

"Audrey usually picks the children up from crèche and sorts dinner for us, but she had a funeral today, so Dave had to come home to sort it out." She closed her eyes and shook her head. "It's been a complete nightmare, last thing you need on a Friday evening. The curtains and the bedding that we had made to measure and then supplied to the client are a different shade of blue, and she wants them identical."

Connie wanted to ask why Vanessa was using the word 'client' instead of customer, but then it occurred to her that not many shops went out to people's houses to advise them on how to decorate their rooms

"They must have sent us a different batch of material, or something," Vanessa went on. "But I couldn't argue as the curtains looked more grey than blue compared to the bed linen. I couldn't let any of the staff deal with it or we would have lost their business." She held her hands up. "Anyway, I've agreed to have the curtains re-made for them and do a blind for the en-suite in the same material free. It's all I could do. They want us to do their sitting-room for Christmas, so I couldn't lose the business for that because of a pair of bloody curtains." She stopped and pressed two fingers to her lips. "*Language!*" she whispered to Connie. "I keep forgetting little ears are always listening."

Connie smiled, thinking of the language she had heard from her grandfather at times. "Well, your client must be happy with that, and it's all sorted out now."

"Let's hope so," Vanessa said, nodding and looking off out into the garden. "I'm shattered now. Now I know the kids are fed and okay with you, I'm going to go upstairs and run myself a lovely bath." She lifted a strand of her blonde hair. "I had to cancel my usual hairdresser's appointment as well. It will just have to do now for the weekend." She sighed. "I suppose I can always stick a few rollers in it if it looks too flat."

"Your hair looks lovely. It's sitting absolutely perfectly." Connie also thought that her employer looked like one of the little fashion dolls that older children played with. Sindy or Barbie dolls. The kind that came with different outfits for different occasions. One was blonde and the other was brunette, but she couldn't remember which was which.

Vanessa's face lit up. "Oh, you're an absolute sweetie. Good, I'll just backcomb it then or do something to give it a bit of a lift." She looked towards the door now. "Where's Dave?"

"He said he had to go and meet some man," Connie said. "He went about an hour ago."

"Oh, bloody hell!" Her shoulders sagged and she gave an impatient sigh. "Tonight of all nights. He's always doing that. Did he say when he'd be back?"

"He just said he wouldn't be very long."

Vanessa pursed her lips together and took a deep breath as though to steady herself. "Okay ... I just hope he remembers we have to be back out the door again for seven o'clock. Did he mention it?"

"I think he did," Connie said. "Do you want me to make you anything to eat or a cup of coffee or anything?"

"Oh, that's kind of you, but no thanks. I had a roll at lunchtime and that will keep me going until tonight." She went over to the fridge now and lifted out a bottle of tonic water. "It's an art exhibition opening," she continued, going to a cupboard now to lift down a bottle of Gordon's Gin and then reach for a tall tumbler, "and they always put cheese and sausages and things on little cocktail sticks, so I don't want to eat anything now or I'll feel all bloated."

As Connie watched her employer pour a hefty measure of gin into the glass and then top it up with tonic, she thought it was no wonder she was so slim, not eating anything all day, and she guessed that determination and constantly being on the go kept her that way. Vanessa went over to the door and picked up her briefcase, brought it back to the table and opened it up. Connie expected her to lift out a sheaf of papers or a brochure or something work-related like that, but instead she lifted out a copy of *Vogue* magazine.

"So, when Dave comes in, tell him to come upstairs and get ready, and if anyone rings," Vanessa said, lifting her glass and the magazine, "you can tell them I'm in the bath and will ring back later." She let out a long weary sigh. "I need half an hour to myself, just to clear my head."

"No problem," Connie said. "I'll clear up here now and then I might take the children into the garden and let them burn some energy off."

"Thank you." Vanessa gave a weary smile. "You don't know

how grateful I am to have you here with the kids, and to see them looking so calm and contented. It's not everyone they take to."

Connie glanced over at the two children now and smiled. "I think we're getting along just fine."

Dave arrived back half an hour later and when Connie told him Vanessa was getting ready he rushed upstairs. A short while later Connie could hear Vanessa's raised voice and she could tell that there was a row about him being late.

She sat and watched cartoons with the children and then the couple appeared downstairs all dressed and ready. Vanessa, Connie thought, was like something from a fashion magazine in a black trouser suit which had diamanté lapels and a black lace vest showing underneath. Dave was dressed more casually with an open-necked black shirt and jeans and a striped blazer.

Vanessa showed Connie where the bread was to make toast for the children's supper and where crisps, nuts, crackers and biscuits were kept. "Help yourself to Coke or Fanta or a glass of wine," she told her, opening the fridge. "And there's cold meats and cheeses and pâté and stuff here as well. Just rummage around and take anything you fancy."

Then, both Dave and Vanessa went over to tell the children to be good for Connie, and to go to bed when she told them. Belinda started to cry and held on to her mother, so Vanessa said she would walk to the door with her, and then she handed her over to Connie saying, "She's just tired. After her supper, give her a bottle of milk to take to bed and she'll settle easily."

It was nine o'clock before Toby settled. Belinda was asleep in minutes, sucking her bottle and cuddling a toy, but Connie had to keep going up and down the stairs to check on her brother. He kept moving out of bed, playing with toys and talking to himself. Connie found she felt too far away from the children downstairs to hear properly if they were settled, so she went into her bedroom and read a magazine she had brought. After about fifteen minutes she went back to check on Toby and found he was fast asleep too.

After another glance in at Belinda, she went back downstairs and made herself a coffee with boiled milk and a cheese sandwich and then she curled up on the sofa in the kitchen, studying one of her anatomy books.

Around ten o'clock Vanessa rang to check everything was okay and was delighted to hear the children were both settled.

"Now that I'm reassured everything is okay," she said, "we might go on for a few drinks to a club. Is that okay with you?"

"Of course," Connie said. "We're all perfectly fine. I'm just writing up some notes and then I'll probably head off to bed, and I'll hear the children if they wake up."

She studied for another hour or so, and then watched a bit of a film on television. It was just before midnight when she decided to go on up to bed. She checked everything was tidy downstairs and then she headed up to check on the children. Belinda was lying peacefully, her covers more or less in the same place as when Connie had put her into the cot. Toby was lying face down, his blankets kicked to the bottom of the bed.

She very carefully moved him onto his side, feeling that he could breathe easier in that position, and then gently covered him up. She went quietly down to her own room, put the lamp on and then started to get ready for bed.

She had just come out of the bathroom when she heard a noise downstairs. She went quickly to the door and listened. She could hear loud talking and laughing, voices she did not recognise, and she realised that Vanessa and Dave had brought some friends back. She went back over to her bed, wondering if she should go downstairs and let them know how the children had been, or stay put, presuming they would guess all was well and she had gone to bed.

She was just searching around in her rucksack for her nightdress when she heard footsteps coming along the corridor and then she heard a light tap on her door and Vanessa's voice saying, "Are you still awake, Connie?"

Connie went towards the door and opened it quietly, thinking of the children. "Yes," she said. "I just came upstairs five minutes ago. Belinda and Toby are both fast asleep."

"Did they settle okay?"

"Yes, Belinda went down fine and Toby was asleep for around nine."

"Great, great," Vanessa said. "We just wondered if you would come downstairs for a few minutes so we can introduce you to some of our friends. We told them how good you were tonight, and they really want to meet you."

"They want to meet *me*?" Connie said "Now? I was just going to get into bed ..."

"Just for two minutes," Vanessa said. She joined her hands together as though pleading. "*Please*? We've been telling them all about you and I know they would love to meet you."

Connie realised that it would look rude to refuse. "Okay, if you're sure ..."

As they went downstairs Vanessa told her about the art exhibition which she said had been really terrific. "A bit like Lowry only bigger, rounder figures – and set in and around Manchester. It was not," she said, "like the dreadful modern pieces that you get and have to pretend you like and even understand."

When they got downstairs and into the kitchen, Dave came rushing over to put his arm around Connie and guide her towards the four guests, who were all sitting around the table. They were all, she saw, like the Hamiltons, dressed in fashionable, expensive clothes.

"This is Connie, everyone!" he said. "Our clever medical student who is doing a great job of looking after Toby and Belinda." He then introduced the two couples as Alan and Sue, and Colin and Shirley.

Connie went around them all, shaking hands and feeling self-conscious and not at all sure why she was there. Vanessa offered her a drink but she thought if she accepted she would have to stay long enough to drink it, so she said thanks, but no.

Sue told her that they had a little girl called Karen, who was around the same age as Toby.

"Only much quieter," Vanessa said laughing. "And Colin and Shirley are the lucky ones – they just got married a few months ago, so they have the quietest life of all with no children yet."

"We've heard how good you are with the children," Alan said, "and we wondered have you ever been to London?"

Connie shook her head. "No, not yet. I'm hoping to go soon."

"Well," he said, "early in November we're all planning a trip to London, staying in a lovely central hotel. We were chatting earlier, and we wondered if you would like to join us to help us with the children? It's really for night-time, when they will be in bed and we might go out to see a show or go to a concert. We'll make sure you have a nice room in the hotel, and plenty of time to see all the sights during the day and maybe wander down into Carnaby Street or to the markets in Portobello Road. It's full of students so you will love it."

"What do you think?" Vanessa asked. "We would pay you as usual, and so would Alan and Sue, so you would have a lovely weekend and get well paid for going."

It was now clear to Connie that this had all been discussed before she came downstairs, and that they were now seeking confirmation that she would go, so they could make further plans. They all seemed nice and she could see no reason to refuse them. She was free that weekend, and when would she ever get the chance of an all-expenses-paid trip to London again? All her friends would jump at the opportunity.

"It sounds great," she said, smiling at them. "I would love to go."

"If it's okay with you," Sue said, "I could bring Karen over here next weekend so she can get to know you in advance, and won't act strange with you when we all go to London."

"That's great," Vanessa said. "We can go ahead and book the hotel rooms in the morning." She looked at Connie. "I know it sounds a lot, but there will be no problem for you having certain weekends off when you have things on at university. We can always get Audrey and Sheila anytime we are stuck."

"And just to remind you, I'm going home at Christmas," Connie said.

"Have we a boyfriend back in the Emerald Isle?" Alan asked.

Connie shook her head and smiled. "No, nothing like that. It's to see my family."

"What about at university? I'm sure a lovely-looking girl like you will have them flocking around you."

Connie shook her head again, beginning to feel embarrassed. "I'm not interested. I'm concentrating on my studies."

"Good girl!" Vanessa said. "Your career is more important – you can meet fellas any time."

"You're only saying that so Connie keeps her weekends free," Dave laughed.

Connie looked at the clock now. "It was lovely meeting you all, but if you don't mind I'm tired so I'm going to head to bed now." She looked at Vanessa. "I'll check on the children as I go by."

"Have a long lie-in the morning," Dave said. "Vanessa is in the shop for nine o'clock, and I take the kids swimming on a Saturday morning, so there's no rush."

Chapter 31

Tara fastened a long gold chain around her neck and then stood back to check her reflection in the wardrobe mirror. She had on a navy jersey dress with long batwing sleeves which emphasised her still slim figure. The colour, she thought, looked well with her Titian curls, which she had caught back with a large tortoiseshell clip. She turned backwards and forwards again, checking that the dress wasn't too short or too clinging and that her high gold-and-silver strappy sandals worked with it. Satisfied she looked okay, she went back to sit at the dressing-table to finish off her make-up.

As she was brushing on her mascara, she heard the doorbell go and hoped Frank would get it before her baby-sitter, June, rang it again and woke Leo. He was teething and had been harder to settle than usual, and she didn't want to go out for the evening thinking he was awake and upset.

She went out into the hallway, listening, and heard the door open and then she could hear the murmur of voices downstairs. She tip-toed across to her youngest son's room and listened for a few moments until she was satisfied that he was still fast asleep. Noel was still downstairs with his father, and Frank would lift him upstairs soon and settle him before they went out.

She went back into the room to put on her lipstick and spray

268

some *Shalimar* perfume on her neck. As she did so, her hand automatically went to the top of her left breast to feel if the tiny lump she had noticed the other day was still there. Her brow creased as she detected it again. Another blocked milk duct. She'd had trouble with this on two previous occasions since having Leo and she knew she would have to go back to the doctor again. She sighed as she lifted the perfume again and gave a light spray to her wrists, and then she picked up her handbag and headed downstairs.

They did not go out on their own as often as they used to, and it had been she who had suggested that they needed a Saturday night out on their own. Lately, Frank had been coming in from work more tired than usual, and working in his office after dinner until late most evenings. The new housing estate he was involved with, one of his biggest building ventures, Tara knew, was proving more problematic and costly than had been predicted. But Frank was an astute businessman, and always planned for these things happening, had good credit with his suppliers, and always had a contingency fund which had been bolstered by the sale of the house in Alderley Edge and a dance hall he had sold out in Levenshulme.

He looked surprised and pleased when Tara told him that morning that she had booked a table for two at the Grosvenor for them.

"We can kill two birds with one stone," she said. "A nice meal and a few drinks, and we can see how things are doing at the hotel at the same time." She had rolled her eyes and smiled. "We need to keep an eye on our investment."

Tara sat and chatted to June while Frank was upstairs reading Noel his bedtime story. June worked in Bridget's boarding house in Maple Terrace, and was always happy to help out baby-sitting. She was a rough-and-ready sort, her language not always the best, but Tara liked her and knew she was trustworthy and good with the boys.

When the taxi arrived in the driveway, June shooed them both out, saying to go off and enjoy themselves and not to worry, as the boys would be fine and she knew where everything was.

"It's good to see the restaurant so busy," Tara said, as they followed the waiter to their seats.

"It's Saturday," Frank said, glancing around at the tables. "We would really be in trouble if it wasn't busy."

The menus arrived and they both decided on a light melon starter then Tara chose rack of lamb while Frank went for rainbow trout.

After they ordered, he picked up the wine list. "Are you okay with white wine?" he checked. "It goes better with the fish, and I just feel it's a bit lighter on the old stomach."

"Are you okay?" Tara asked. "I just wondered when you ordered the fish – you usually have the steak or something richer."

He shrugged. "I just fancied the trout for a change." He turned now to indicate to the waiter that they had chosen the wine.

When the bottle was brought to the table and the glasses poured, Frank held his up to Tara. "To the most beautiful woman in the restaurant!"

Tara laughed and touched her glass to his. "It's great to get a night out together, isn't it?"

"Absolutely," he said.

"I nearly thought of asking Bridget and Fred," she said, "but then I thought it might be nice to have the time to chat on our own. The last few weeks we've been like ships passing in the night, with you up early in the morning going to work, and we seem to be going to bed at different times as well." She smiled and rolled her eyes. "Leo is at that mad, lively stage and I'm running after him all day. I remember it all with Noel, so I know it's a passing phase and he'll settle down in a year or so." She suddenly laughed. "A *year* ... my God ... there are days when I just look at them and still can't believe we have them both. One was a dream come true. I never imagined, at our age, being lucky enough to have two."

"Well, I'm never surprised when people take me for their grandfather, since I am one twice over. But you still look like a young mother, and it really suits you. Although, a few years ago, I could never have imagined the cool, collected businesswoman changing nappies and down on the floor playing with building bricks."

"I don't know about that," Tara laughed. "When I'm at the mother and toddler group and see mothers as young as Connie with children, I really feel like the *elderly prima gravida* as the doctors described me when I had Noel."

"Talking of Connie, what's the news there? Everything going okay at university?"

"Great," Tara said. "She's passed every exam so far. She's a great student, constantly studying. No interest in going out at weekends or anything, and certainly no interest in boys or anything like that. She has her mind fully focussed on her career."

"I thought we might have seen more of her."

"I did too, but she's at university all week and then she's out with the couple in Wilmslow at the weekends. According to Angela, who heard from Kate, they are very good to her and pay her extremely well. Apparently they are taking her to London with them sometime soon."

"She'll do well," Frank said. "Although it's such a pity the way things happened with her and William. I'd say they would have made a nice young couple. A solicitor and a doctor. A nice young professional couple."

Tara sipped her wine. "That whole thing with Connie and the other girl took a lot out of him. And Pamela's father has caused him a fair bit of trouble. He said the last placement he had, the reference he was given was very bland, and yet he was under the impression he had done very well with them. In fact, he was told that before all the trouble happened. He is still looking for a set of chambers to do the first six months of his pupillage, then he has to find another one after that." She gave a little sigh. "I don't really understand it all, but it sounds as though he's struggling to get the pupillage which gives him the day-to-day practical experience working with solicitors and clients. Apparently, if he doesn't get it, he won't qualify for a full-time working position. It will really hold him back."

"He needs to get away from that area of London," Frank said. "He should move out to somewhere like Oxford or Cambridge or even go back to Dublin."

"I might suggest that to him when I'm chatting to him next. He has a good friend over in Dublin, an old lecturer who might be able to find him something in Ireland. I do worry about him stuck down there with Elisha, especially when he feels so down in himself."

Their meal came and as they ate they moved on to talk about Bridget and Fred and how things were going better in their boarding house than ever. They had help in the mornings and for a few days a week with laundry and cleaning, which gave Bridget time to herself. Fred was still running the bar in Tara's Cale Green hotel, so all in all life was good for the Roberts family.

"Did I tell you that Bridget and Fred are going to Malta with Fred's parents in early November?"

"No," Frank said. "That's great. They're surely branching out. I thought they did well going to Spain with the kids last year, but now Malta ..." He shook his head, smiling. "Fred's dad wants to go because he was stationed out there when he was in the army," Tara explained, "and I think the old couple were nervous going on their own, so Fred suggested it."

"Good old Fred!" Frank chuckled. "I haven't seen him for a few weeks now. I always mean to drop down to the Cale Green to have a drink with him, but ..." he gestured with his hands, "with the way things are at the minute, the days just disappear."

As they sat chatting over coffee, various people either leaving or coming in for the later seating greeted them, and then afterwards in the hotel bar they ran into Eric Simmons and John Burns, two of the men who, like Frank and Tara, each had a fifth share of the Grosvenor Hotel. The men were delighted to see them and both immediately asked after the children.

"Such a coincidence we met up tonight," John said. "We were talking earlier and said how much we miss seeing Tara around the hotel in her managerial capacity. The chap in charge is doing a good job of course, but to us it's not the same."

"That's kind of you," Tara said, smiling warmly at them both.

Frank put his arm around her shoulders and drew her close to him. "She's doing even better now managing the Kennedy household and the two livewires who rule the roost!"

They all laughed, then Tara gestured around the bar. "Thankfully, the hotel seems to be as busy tonight as ever. And it seems to be holding well, considering how businesses and people throughout the country are struggling with strikes and four-day weeks."

"Very much so," John said. He looked at Frank. "I have those figures for you when you get time to call into my office. And we've spoken to Gerry McShane about it too."

Tara turned to Frank, her eyebrows raised in question. What, she wondered, had he and the other shareholders of the hotel been discussing that she had not been part of?

"We won't talk business tonight," Frank said. "I'll call you on Monday."

"Of course," John said. "I'll look forward to hearing from you."

The four of them had one drink together and then, as soon as the men left, Frank turned to Tara. "I'm sorry about that, Tara," he said. "I didn't want to spoil tonight by telling you about this. In fact, I was hoping to wait until Monday until I had more news."

"What is it, Frank?" she asked. "What's going on?"

He took a deep breath. "I've asked the others to check out what my share in the Grosvenor would be worth."

"Why?" Her tone was low and concerned.

"It's nothing definite, and it's nothing for you to worry about." He reached over now and squeezed her hand. "I just wanted to have the information to hand, should I need to release money for the housing estate."

"But I thought that was all sorted … I thought the money from the sale of the house in Alderley Edge gave you a good contingency fund until the new investor from Birmingham came on board?"

"It did," he said, "but, unfortunately, that has now fallen through. He rang on Thursday morning to say that the bank has pulled the plug on him, and won't advance him the money for another venture until he has settled his current business overdraft." He shrugged. "They gave him no warning – apparently they've had a number of businesses go to the wall recently – and last week was the start of a clamp-down on business loans. The guy was really upset about it all, and he has tried everything to raise the money – but he is not going to be able to meet the time schedule for paying the building contractors and suppliers. It means that I'm going to have to meet all the bills myself. Everything is in my name."

Tara's felt her stomach tip sideways. She put her other hand over his now and held it tightly. "Oh, Frank!"

"I didn't want to worry you … and I am so sorry if it looked as though I was keeping information or secrets from you. You know I would not do that without good reason. I was hoping it would work out somehow. It was my last big venture, my chance to make enough money so that we could relax more, enjoy our lovely home and not have to think of the day-to-day finances."

"You don't have to apologise," she told him. "I know you, Frank, and I know what a good man – what a good husband and father you are … I know that everything you are doing will be with my and the children's best interests at heart."

He looked at her now, and he smiled and said, "Thank you. You don't know how much that means to me." He pressed a finger to his lips. "If only I'd known how things would suddenly turn in this downward way, I would never have bought the land and started building the damned houses. And, I certainly would not have gone for such big houses with such a grandiose design." He joined his hands together. "What's that they say … *the higher you climb …?*"

"Don't, Frank," Tara whispered. "You're being too hard on yourself. It will all work out. I'm sure it will."

As he sat back in his chair now, she noticed the weariness in his eyes due to all the early mornings and late nights in the office, and she realised how much this had taken out of him. And it wasn't just this latest, ambitious building project – it went back further to the stress he had been through with the sale of the house in Alderley Edge, and then losing the first investor for the housing project.

Now, as she watched him take a drink of his whiskey and observed the sag of his shoulders and the crinkling at the corners of his eyes, it struck her with force that Frank had suddenly aged. The thought sent an icy shiver through her veins.

She had always been aware that he was a good ten years older than her, but he had never, at any point before, looked his age. Handsome and fit, his energy and enthusiasm had always been that of a man twenty years his junior. Even as his hair had started to show more grey than black, he had only grown more attractive and distinguished. And in all the years they had been together – and even when they were apart – he had looked out for her and protected her interests.

She thought back to when they both invested in the Grosvenor, and how he had told her that he had kept enough money in a personal fund to make sure that, if things had not worked out, she would never be forced to sell Ballygrace House. He knew how much it meant to her as it was the home she had shared with her first husband. How many men, she wondered, would do that?

She reached her hand over to touch his knee. "We'll get through this, Frank," she told him. "Together we will get through this. I also have a share of the hotel, which we can sell, and we can sell the Cale Green Hotel too."

He closed his eyes and shook his head. "I couldn't do that, Tara. You worked so hard for everything, and you also used the money you inherited from Gabriel. I couldn't do it, darling."

"We'll think of something," she said. "And whatever happens, you, me and the boys, we will all be fine."

Chapter 32

At three o'clock on a cold Friday early-November afternoon, Connie settled into the middle of the back seat of Dave Hamilton's Mercedes Benz, Belinda on her left-hand side and Toby on her right. There was a bag on the floor, below the little girl's dangling feet, which Connie had filled with books, small toys and a container of bubbles to keep them entertained on the journey down to London. She had packed another bag which was under Toby's feet, which held sandwiches and fruit and drinks, and a few little sweet treats for them.

"Are we all set?" Dave asked, turning around to smile at the three of them.

"Yes," Connie said, smiling back at him. "All fine here." She looked at the two quiet children who, Vanessa told her, were due their afternoon nap. They usually slept around two o'clock, but their mother had asked Connie to take them for a walk down Silver Street to keep them awake, so they would sleep for a few hours in the car.

"The motorway will be busy," Dave said, as they pulled out of the drive and onto the birch-lined street, "but at least we'll beat the Manchester rush hour by getting off that bit earlier. And we should miss the rush hour at the other end. I'm guessing we should get into London for eightish. Alan and Sue were setting off around lunchtime, so they will be ahead of us, and the others were leaving around the same time as us."

"Well, if nobody minds, I'm going to catch up on my sleep," Vanessa said. "Otherwise, I won't be fit to enjoy the weekend." She held up a black eye-mask, so that Connie could see it. "I came prepared. I have this and I've taken half a sleeping tablet which hopefully should knock me out for the journey. I hardly slept last night, thinking of everything I had to do, and then I was rushing around putting out new stock this morning." She paused, sorting the mask over her eyes. "You'll be okay there in the back with the kids, won't you, Connie?"

"Yes," Connie said. "We should be fine." She settled back into the soft beige leather, looking forward to her first trip to London.

Within a short time, Vanessa was fast asleep in the front, and the two children were curled up in the back, Belinda's head in Connie's lap. Dave put the radio on low, and apart from odd comments he made to Connie about the motorway signposts or about a song that was playing, they sat in silence so as not to wake the others.

Connie had brought a couple of medical books with her, so she alternated between reading and watching the scenery as they went along.

Around five o'clock the children woke and she gave them their sandwiches and drinks. Half an hour later they stopped at a service station and, since Vanessa was in a deep sleep, Connie said she would take the children to the toilet and give them a little walk in the fresh air to stretch their legs. Belinda had stopped using the potty some time ago, but Connie kept a close eye on her because she still had the occasional little accident.

Dave jokingly said he wouldn't go to the Gents' until they came back, just in case anyone ran away with Vanessa. Toby and Belinda both took her hand as she walked across the car park, chatting to her about the sausage-dog that a man was walking over on the grass verge, and she thought how good they were since the first night she had arrived. Toby in particular had quietened down, and was mainly well-behaved as long as he was kept entertained and busy. Connie had worked on his manners and attitude to his little sister, who was a much gentler child altogether. She was delighted with the hugs and kisses she got from them each weekend she turned up at the house. Audrey was ready and waiting for her, and was gone as soon as Connie arrived. She always looked exhausted and it made Connie wonder how the poor woman managed them all week on her own.

After they had been to the toilet, she took them into the shop for another a little walk around while she bought a magazine for herself. While she settled the children back in the car, Dave made a quick dash to the toilet and was back within minutes, and then they were on the journey again.

The second part of the journey Connie found harder, as she had to keep the children occupied for a lot of the time. While it was still light, she read them stories and pointed out things to them as they went along, and then got Toby to count all the red cars he could see.

As it got dark, she changed to saying nursery rhymes with them and telling them stories she knew off by heart. Belinda dozed off again just after seven, and she kept Toby occupied by watching the lights of the cars that passed them.

"We're heading into the North Circular now," Dave said, just after quarter to eight, "so I reckon we should be at the hotel in the next half an hour."

Since they were in a lit-up area, Toby was happy to watch the other cars again, and point out the shops and houses as they went along. As they got nearer the centre of the city, Dave tried to rouse Vanessa. He started off talking to her gently at first, but when he got no reaction he resorted to gently shaking her arm and prodding her.

As she listened to Dave trying to waken his wife, Connie suddenly felt like an intruder. She felt that what was happening was too close and personal for her presence. It was the sort of exchange between a couple which she thought should take place in the privacy of a bedroom or somewhere like that, and not in view of children or the person who was minding them. She wondered if Sheila had witnessed anything like this and, if she had, how she had reacted.

When they stopped at a set of traffic lights, Dave took Vanessa by the shoulders and shook her, saying, "You need to wake up, Van, we're almost there. You can't let the others see you looking like this."

Eventually she responded with a series of startled grunts, saying, "What's happening? What's happening?"

"Take the mask off," he told her in a patient voice, "and you need to sort yourself out before we arrive."

Vanessa pulled the mask off. She sat in silence for a few minutes then she looked at her husband. "I think I slept, didn't I?"

"You certainly did," he said in a grim tone. "And I hope it's bloody well done you good."

Connie felt a little hand slipping through hers and, as she looked down, Toby was smiling up at her.

"There's another red car," he whispered. "It's just across the road."

Then, as Vanessa pulled down the sunscreen to look at herself in the mirror, Connie wondered would have happened if she had not been in the car to entertain and comfort the children? Vanessa, she had begun to realise, spent very little time with her son and daughter on her own. She was either working or someone else was helping her to look after them. Could she, Connie thought, actually cope with them if she was there on her own?

As they passed a sign for the Tower of London, Connie suddenly felt a sense of foreboding about the weekend ahead.

Chapter 33

Tara pulled up outside the boarding house in Maple Terrace on Saturday morning. She went up the stairs and rang the bell then waited. There was no answer, so she rang it again. Then, just as she was ready to turn and go back down to the car, a red-faced Bridget opened the door.

"Oh, sorry, Tara," she said, ushering her in, "I've been watching for you at the window for the last hour, and I suddenly needed to spend a penny!"

"You can't help it when nature calls," Tara said, smiling at her. "No kids?"

"Frank is at home with them," she said. "Thankfully, he didn't have to go into work."

"God, I need to get fit," Bridget said, as they walked along the hallway to the kitchen. "I am totally out of breath, rushing down those stairs. That's not good for someone just turned forty, is it?"

"Go away with you," Tara said. "I would be the same if I came running down the stairs. You look great, you're the slimmest I've seen you in a long time and your hair looks lovely. It has a nice chestnut tone to it."

"I got it done yesterday," Bridget said, delighted with the compliment. "Just a couple of inches off it, to keep it in the bob shape. It's the best style I've ever had, and it's easy to keep."

"Where are the kids?"

"Gone swimming with Gary, our youngest lodger. Michael and Helen love him. He's a fitness fanatic, running in the mornings and swimming at the weekends. Fred is down at the hotel and everyone else is out, so we have the place to ourselves."

They went into the kitchen and Tara pulled a chair out at the long table that all Bridget's lodgers sat at every evening.

"I've got the kettle boiled," Bridget said, "so I'll make us a cup of tea."

As she sorted the teacups and cut up an apple tart, they chatted about the children and about how busy Fred was with weddings in the Cale Green on both the Friday and Saturday.

Then, when they were both seated, Bridget looked at Tara.

"How did you get on? Is it just the milk duct again?"

Tara bit her lip. "The doctor got the report back from the specialist. He says he isn't sure about the lump – he says he needs to take a biopsy before he can go any further."

Bridget's hand flew to her mouth. "Oh, God ... when?" She suddenly felt sick. The thought of anything happening to Tara. She hadn't for one minute thought it was going to be anything serious.

"Next week."

"Do you want to phone Frank now and tell him?" Bridget always felt better when Frank was around if anything went wrong. He always seemed to sort things.

Tara shook her head. "I haven't told him about it, and even if I wanted to ring, our phone is on the blink since yesterday. I told him I needed a couple of hours this morning without the boys, so you and I could catch up. It's the truth in a way."

"So he doesn't know anything about the lump?"

When Tara nodded, Bridget's shoulders dropped.

"But I thought you were going to tell him about your hospital appointment last week?"

"I decided not to. There was no point in worrying him if it was the same harmless thing as before. He has enough on his plate at the minute with the housing estate business. I've never seen him so worried and I don't want to add to it."

"What about the Grosvenor shares?" Bridget asked. "I thought you told me he was thinking of selling them."

"He thinks it's going to take too long," Tara said. She lifted her cup to her lips and took a little drink from it. "He's hoping to sort something out." She paused. "I've offered to sell the Cale Green Hotel if it would help, but he's adamant he doesn't want that to happen. And again, how long would it take to find a buyer, the way things are at the minute? And if we did find one, it would probably take ages for all the legal paperwork to go through."

Bridget gave a long, low sigh. "I can't believe this is happening to you," she said. "It seems to have just all come out of the blue ..." She lifted her apple tart and took a bite for something to distract her, as she was afraid to say any more in case she started to cry.

"It has," Tara said. "But we've had four or five years where everything has gone well. Nobody had died and nobody has been seriously ill. We've had the boys and we've lived in two lovely houses – and they are all the important things in life." She took a deep breath. "We're lucky in that we've never had to worry about money before – neither me nor Frank. I shouldn't really be complaining, compared to other poor people we are very well off and I know it."

"But you have been good to other people, Tara. You're not one of these selfish people who look out for themselves. I know how you've helped your family and friends financially and giving them work and everything." Bridget shook her head. "And Frank Kennedy is the most decent man. You know if he gives you his word about something, he will always follow it through."

"At the end of the day we will be fine," Tara said. "If we can just get through all this now."

"I suppose the housing estate was a huge thing to take on," Bridget said.

"Not if the other investors had worked out as planned," Tara said. "But nobody could have foreseen the big slump in the economy, and the way the banks have pulled back in. Frank says he's never seen anything like it before. Everybody he talks to in the building trade is saying the same thing."

"I wish I had the money to help you out myself," Bridget said. "But our bits of savings would only be a drop in the ocean in this situation." She leaned across the table and patted Tara's hand. "If anyone can work it out, it will be Frank Kennedy. I've always had absolute faith in him."

"I know you have," Tara said, tears coming into her eyes now. "You had faith in Frank all those years when I wouldn't even speak to him."

"That's all water under the bridge now …" Bridget paused, not knowing what to do or say. It was usually the other way around, her asking Tara for help and advice. "What can I do to help, Tara? Can I at least come to the hospital with you next week?"

Tara lifted her handbag and took a hanky out. "I haven't thought about it yet. I haven't decided whether to tell Frank or not. I might wait until he has this next meeting with the bank and tell him afterwards."

Bridget suddenly thought. "Maybe a night out would do Frank good. Fred was talking about a big wrestling match that's on in Salford tomorrow night. He said to me that he'd like to go. Do you remember how they both used to travel all over for wrestling matches? Wouldn't that be something to take Frank's mind off everything?"

Tara thought for a few moments. "I think you're right. He's only going to be sitting at home, thinking about the meeting the next day. A night out with Fred would do him good. He was just saying recently that he'd been meaning to drop down to the hotel to catch up with Fred." She smiled at Bridget. "I'll tell him when I get home and get him to ring to make arrangements." She rolled her eyes and smiled. "If the phone hasn't been fixed, the walk out to the phone box at the bottom of the hill will do him good!"

Frank was standing at the door with Leo in his arms when Tara arrived back. "Everything okay with Bridget and Fred?"

"Great," Tara said, as they walked inside. "Bridget had her hair done, so it was all women's chat about fashions and that kind of thing."

"Are you ready for a surprise?"

"Oh, what have they done now?" Tara said, expecting to see some sort of model Noel had made from his Lego or discover that something had been broken. Anything was possible.

But, when she walked into the kitchen, there, sitting at the table was William with Noel on his knee.

"I don't believe it!" Tara exclaimed, rushing over to hug her brother-in-law. "What an absolute surprise!"

"It's lovely to see you, Tara," he said. "You look wonderful as usual."

"Ah, you're very kind," she said, beaming at him. "When did you arrive?"

"Just ten minutes ago," Frank said. "He got the early train up from London."

"I'm so sorry for arriving unannounced," William said, "but I did try ringing yesterday to check with you, and I couldn't get through. I thought I'd chance coming over to Bramhall anyway, and if by some chance you had gone away I would have gone down to Bridget's and slept on the spare bunk in Michael's room."

Noel got down onto the floor to play with his cars, then Leo came toddling over and William lifted him up onto his knee.

"We've had problems with the phone," Tara said, taking her coat off and slinging it over the back of a chair. "I rang the company from a neighbour's yesterday, and they said they would try to get out today." She sat down beside him. "Well, what brings you up to Stockport at such short notice?"

"Well," he said, "I have an appointment with a solicitor's office in Manchester on Monday morning. I've just been telling Frank all about it."

"Good lad," Frank said. "You're doing the right thing getting out of London for a while. Let things die down a bit."

"What do you mean?" Tara asked, looking from one to the other.

"You know the difficulties I've been having finding a pupillage placement for the New Year? Well, I was considering going back to Dublin and I rang a good friend of mine – Malcolm McKenzie, he was a law lecturer at Trinity – and he advised me to finish off my training in the UK, as it would complicate things to go back and forth between the two countries. He said to give him a few days and he would ring around. Anyway ... he's somehow managed to get me an interview with a law practice out in Altrincham."

"Really?" Tara said, her eyes lighting up. "And if you get it, does that mean you will be up here for a while?"

"Six months at least," he said. "And if that doesn't work out, he says he can arrange another one for me out in Liverpool, which isn't too far away either."

"Oh, William," Tara said, going over to hug him, "we would be so delighted to have you near!"

"I've already told him that there's a room here for him for as long as he wants," Frank said.

"Well, if things work out," he said, "I might well take you up on your kind offer." He ruffled Leo's hair. "It will give me a chance to spend some time with the little fellas."

They chatted for a while and then Tara looked at the clock and realised it was lunchtime, so she went over to the fridge and began lifting out cold meats, a selection of cheeses, tomatoes and a tub of coleslaw. These she placed on the table then added oven-bottom rolls and a long French stick which she had bought when she stopped off at Pilkington the Baker's in Davenport on her way back from Bridget's.

As Frank brought a pot of coffee to the table, Tara suddenly remembered. "Oh – Bridget asked if you would like to go to a wrestling match out in Salford with Fred tomorrow night. You could go too, William."

"That sounds fun," William said, "Fred used to take me when I was young and I always enjoyed them. I haven't been to anything like that for years."

Frank looked at him. "I've been meaning to catch up with him for weeks and it might be a change. What do you think? Shall we go?"

"I'm game for it," William said, grinning at him. "Fred knows all the wrestlers and it will be a bit of a laugh."

"Well, if you are going," Tara said. "I'm afraid you're going to have to walk down to the phone box to ring him at the Cale Green and let him know so he can book the tickets."

"We can do better than that," Frank said, winking at William. "We might take a drive down to the hotel this afternoon and catch him then."

"And no doubt catch a pint of beer while you're doing it?" Tara said, raising her eyebrows. Then she laughed. "You've already done your stint with the boys this morning, so go on, the pair of you."

When they had finished eating, Frank went to change out of his casual shirt into a more formal one and William helped Tara lift the dishes over to the dishwasher. Tara asked him about his mother and he said she was doing okay, and that Harry had taken her to a nice hotel in Warwick the previous weekend.

"She has her good days and her bad days," William said, "but I'm used to it – she has always been that way." Then, as he wrapped the cheeses up to put them back in the fridge, he quietly asked. "Any news about Connie?"

Tara then told him that she had seen very little of her since she arrived, but they had rung each other almost every week. She told him that Connie was doing well on her course, had made nice friends, and then explained about her working for the family in Wilmslow at weekends.

"Okay," William said. "So she doesn't come to Stockport very often?"

"No," Tara said, "which is a pity, as I would have loved her helping here with the boys and just having her company generally. She is a lovely girl."

"Does she work on Sundays?"

"I don't think so," Tara said. "I think she usually stays overnight Saturday and goes back to her hall of residence after breakfast on Sunday." She looked at him. "You're not thinking of going to see her ... are you?"

"I thought I might," he said. "Just as a friend. How do you think she would react if she saw me again?"

Tara considered it for a few moments. "I really don't know. But I wouldn't get your hopes up."

"Did she say anything about me to you?"

"She just said something along the lines of you having had a nice time together ..."

He gave a sigh. "That it was just a few nice days in summer?"

Tara nodded. "Something like that."

Chapter 34

Connie stopped to look at a trestle-table laden with a variety of bric-a-brac and old jewellery. She picked up a hair-clasp decorated with grey, white and black pearls.

"How much?" she asked.

The women had been at Portobello Market for an hour, and she already had a bag filled with a colourful cheesecloth skirt, a green velvet jacket with a hood, books, various strings of Indian beads and bangles.

The woman behind the table took a puff on her cigarette and thought for a moment. "Seventy-five pence, love." She had on a fur coat and her blonde hair done up in a beehive style, which Connie thought looked as though it had been almost sealed in place with several cans of strong lacquer.

Connie put the hair-clasp back down and then lifted a small, nicely shaped, amber glass decanter, which had a hunting scene with horses and dogs painted in cream all around the bottom. It had six little matching glasses.

"It's a brandy decanter. They used to use those in the posh houses in Victorian times," the woman told her. "The stable lads would bring out a tray with them on for the people in the hunt." She made a sweeping gesture over her fur coat. "You know, the ones that chase after the foxes – they wear the red and black jackets and the hard hats?"

"They're lovely," Connie said, turning the bottle around to look at the little scene depicted on it. She thought it was beautiful, a work of art. She wondered if her mother would like it, and almost as soon as she thought it, she dismissed it. Her mother would think it odd and probably old-fashioned – she preferred shiny and new, preferably cut-glass crystal.

"One pound fifty pence," the woman said. "And it's a bargain. That's a real heirloom."

Vanessa suddenly appeared behind Connie. She leaned across the table with money in her hand. "I'll give you one pound fifty for the clasp and the glasses." She put her hand on Connie's arm. "She's with me."

The woman's eyes flitted from one to the other.

"Take it or leave it," Vanessa said. "There are plenty of other stalls with similar stuff, and this is the dearest I've seen. She's only a student."

The woman sighed and threw her eyes upwards. "Go on," she said, holding her hand out for the money.

Connie went into her tapestry bag for her purse.

"My treat," Vanessa told her, giving the woman the money. "A little thank-you for looking after the children on the journey down last night."

"There's no need," Connie said. "Honestly, I have my own money."

"I insist."

The woman put the cigarette in the side of her mouth and then lifted the decanter and quickly wrapped it in crumpled tissue paper and stuck it into a used carrier bag. She then did the same with the six glasses and the clasp.

"Thanks," Connie said, taking the bag off her. She wasn't quite sure what she would do with the decanter and glasses long-term, but for the time being she thought they might sit nicely on her window ledge in her room.

"You're welcome, love," the woman said, smiling at her. Then, when Vanessa turned away, the woman winked at Connie, pulled a face and then gave Vanessa a rude two-finger gesture behind her back.

They walked back to meet the other women, past the book stalls, the tables filled with LPs and single records, stalls selling greeting cards and postcards, old linens and lace, and Connie's favourite – the flower stalls, which had metal containers filled with every kind of bloom, some of which she had never seen before. And while she always felt a little pang when she remembered her old flower shop and Tullamore itself, when she thought it through she was not ready to return to it yet. She had far too many things to do and places to see yet. Her adventure in England was only starting.

And so far, Connie loved everything about London. Manchester was great, but this was in a whole different league. Hotel Rubens, where they were staying, she thought, was beautiful, and grander than any hotel she had seen or imagined. She had been taken to the Grosvenor in Stockport and shown around and, whilst it was undoubtedly lovely, it did not have the feel of this old and beautiful place. And of course Hotel Rubens was very close to Buckingham Palace which made the world of difference, and within walking distance or short taxi rides of lots of exciting places.

The night before, after changing into smarter clothes, they all had a meal in the hotel restaurant. Connie had worn a white shirt with ruffles down the front and ruffled sleeves, along with her black velvet trousers, which she thought would be suitable. The only other formal outfit she had brought was the olive-green dress that she had bought for the Freshers' Ball. When she got down to dinner, Dave told her that the hotel had given them a table in a small area which was sectioned just off the main dining-room, as it was late to have children in the restaurant. Connie thought it was a good idea, as she felt a lot of the people were older than their group and she could imagine the disapproving looks if the children were noisy or cried. When she joined them at the table, she discovered she was the only one wearing trousers, as Vanessa and Sue and Shirley were all dressed in sparkling, glamorous evening dresses. She felt slightly awkward at first, but after two glasses of sparkling wine, she felt much more relaxed about it.

The couples were all nice to her and made sure to include her in their conversations, but she could tell they were being careful with their language and topics of conversation because she was there. She sat beside the three children and helped to feed them, and volunteered to take them to the toilet any time they needed to go.

After dinner – going on for ten o'clock – she offered to take the three children to bed. It was well after their usual bedtime and Belinda had fallen asleep in her arms. Karen had dozed off in her buggy and Toby was beginning to get fractious and had started climbing on chairs and rolling around on the floor beside them. The children were in a room adjoining hers, which Vanessa had said would be really convenient, as she could keep the partition door open all night and listen for them if they woke up. Vanessa made a weak offer about taking them up to bed, but Connie insisted she was happy to do it. Vanessa looked exhausted and besides, Connie wanted to relax in the quietness of her room in her pyjamas and read in her lovely big bed.

The following morning, when Connie woke around half-past eight, she noticed that the adjoining door was closed over and, when she opened it, she saw Vanessa drying both children after giving them a bath.

"Good morning!" she said in a chirpy voice. "I feel great after my night's sleep and I'm all rearing to go on our sightseeing tour today."

Connie could immediately tell that Vanessa was back to her old lively self again, having been teased by all her friends at dinner for being slow and groggy. The difference was obvious. Vanessa's eyes were shining and she seemed brimming with energy as she talked about the places they were planning to visit.

"We'll squeeze as much as we can into our two days," she said. "We don't need to leave until late Sunday afternoon, so if we get moving early tomorrow, we'll get more done. Dave says around five would be the best time to leave and then the kids will sleep most of the way back home."

They were all seated for breakfast in the dining-room for nine o'clock, and were dressed in coats and scarves and walking and pushing buggies down to Buckingham Palace around half past ten. Although Connie thought that Dave had seemed annoyed at his wife last night, she was relieved to see that today they were both laughing and joking with each other. Toby was enjoying the attention from his parents and their friends, and Belinda was quiet as usual as she was pushed through the crowds in her buggy.

After Portobello Market they caught taxis across to Covent Garden for lunches of burgers and salads and chips in a big airy bar which Sue and Alan had been to before, and then the men stayed on drinking for the afternoon while the women went shopping. At one point, when they stopped at a nice place for coffee and cakes, Vanessa told Connie to go off and have a couple of hours to herself. She pressed ten pounds into her hand and a little card with the address of the hotel and said, "You deserve a few hours off. Treat yourself to a nice dress and shoes for dinner tonight, and get a taxi back to the hotel when you're ready."

Although she was thrilled with the idea of the extra money and having the time to shop, Connie wondered if Vanessa thought she had got the dress code completely wrong the night before with her trousers and top.

As she went in and out of the boutiques and wandered around the beautiful flower shops, her mind drifted back to last summer and to William. He lived in London, although she did not have a clue whereabouts. They had talked about so many other things, but it was a subject that had not come up. She wondered if there was the remotest chance she might bump into him here in London, but as she looked at the crowded shops and streets, at the different colours and races, she knew that this was not like bumping into people in Tullamore or even Manchester. Bumping into someone you knew in London would be like finding a needle in a haystack.

She thought back to their evening in Dublin – and found herself smiling when she remembered their visit to Malcolm's house, and then she felt sad when she recalled their beautiful walk around Stephen's Green. She had told him that the days she had spent with him had been the best days of summer. She would always remember them, because deep down she knew they were the best days of her life.

Why, she wondered for the hundredth time, had he led her on? Why had he not told her the truth?

Chapter 35

William looked across the table at Frank. "So, now you know the whole story, what do you think I should do?"

They were sitting in a corner of the small bar in the Cale Green Hotel. There were a few locals sitting at the bar and there were other tables occupied by residents enjoying a quiet afternoon drink. Fred was busy with the wedding in the function room, checking that the waiters had put the wine on the tables, and the right amount of sherry and whiskies were poured and waiting on trays for the toast when the speeches were made. He told Frank that as soon as the first course of the meal was underway, he could relax and come and join them.

Frank took a deep breath. In some ways, he was in a difficult position, being married to William's brother's widow, but on the other hand, they had always got on very well. He did not expect William to have the same deep affection for him as he had for Tara, and he was grateful that he had never shown any resentment towards him. William treated him with the same friendliness and respect that he showed to Fred and Bridget – who he had known much longer – and as far as Frank was concerned that was good enough.

This was the first time that William had come to him for advice in preference to Tara, and he wanted to get it right.

"If I were you," he said, "I would go and see her."

"Really? You don't think I'll get a bad reaction?"

"I didn't say that. I don't know what kind of reaction you'll get. I just said I think you should go and see her. If you don't, she'll never know what you were thinking. She will never know you have feelings for her."

"But what if she closes the door in my face – or even slaps it?"

"She might well close the door, but I think if she was going to slap you she would have done it back in Ireland, when she first found out."

"What if she doesn't want to talk to me?"

"Then you will just have to respect her wishes and walk away."

"And what then?"

"You'll just have to hope that she might think about it and *maybe* ..." Frank paused to emphasise it, "and *maybe* she might, given time, give you a second chance."

William gave a huge sigh. "It all sounds very negative and disappointing."

"What you did to her was also very negative and disappointing. You deceived her and she was humiliated. Some people never get over something like that. Especially if she had real feelings for you." Frank lifted his glass of beer and took a drink from it. "Do you know what her feelings are – or were?"

"I think we got on really, really well," he said. "When I think back to the party where we met, how we could talk so easily, how we laughed at the same things ... She told me she thought we were really similar, and she hoped we would keep in touch when she went to university. We had agreed I would come up to visit her as soon as she was settled in." His eyes suddenly filled up. "I've never met a girl like her before, and I know I'll never meet anyone like her again. I really did not set out to deceive her, I just wanted to sort things out with Pamela before getting involved with Connie. I thought it would only complicate matters. I thought if I told her I was engaged she would not have wanted to see me."

Frank gave a wry little smile. "Well, that sounds like deception to me."

"None of it was planned," William said. "It was as if fate just took over and I was swept along. I just wanted to be with her, no matter what. I didn't think about the circumstances or the consequences."

"There's a word for that."

"What?" William asked.

"Love," Frank said. "It makes us all act stupid." Then before William started asking him questions he did not want to answer he said, "Go and see her, William. Try to talk to her and, if she listens, make sure you say all the right things. Tell her how sorry you are, and how your desperation to be with her made you take a foolish risk, which did not work out."

"Okay," William said. "I'll go tomorrow afternoon, before we go to the wrestling. I'll take the train into Manchester and go to her hall of residence. Tara has already told me where her block is."

"Are you going to tell Tara that you're going to see her?"

"Yes, I think I should."

"Good," Frank said, "because if you didn't I would tell her. When she and I got together, we both said we would always tell the truth, no matter how difficult it was. I wouldn't keep anything like that from her."

"Right," William said, "that's the decision made. Tomorrow afternoon I'll go out to Manchester and I'll just take things as they come. Nothing ventured, nothing gained."

"Good man!"

"My turn to get the drinks, is it the same again?"

Frank looked at his glass. He didn't feel like drinking any more. "Just a coffee," he said, "and ask the girl to make it with milk, please."

As he watched William striding over to the bar he thought of all the things he could have told him, but did not. He didn't want to frighten him off or disillusion him. How could he have said that if William was serious about winning Connie back he would have to be prepared to wait for as long as it would take. It might take months, or it might take years. Five years or even ten years. It might take all the years that Frank had to wait for Tara. He had never been brave enough to work out how long exactly that amounted to, but it had been a long time.

All the years of feeling alone – feeling he was only living half the life he should have been. All the times he had pretended with other women that there might be a future with them, knowing that the relationship would never measure up to what he had with Tara.

He hoped that William would learn from this painful experience that keeping secrets never worked. The truth always came out. Frank had faced all that himself when he hadn't told Tara he had still technically been married. And she had held it against him for many years. William's situation was similar, but he and Connie were not Tara and Frank. They were younger people living different lives.

He hoped with all his heart that William would not go through the hell that he had.

Chapter 36

Connie found a dress she loved in a small boutique in Covent Garden. It was long and black, sleeveless with a high neck decorated with black and silver beading. Simple, she thought, but the sort of thing that could not go wrong. It was one she would happily wear for the fancier university events, and she hoped it would be suitable for dinner that night. Instead of shoes, she bought a pair of suede, high black boots, which laced up to her knees. They were more suitable for the winter coming in, Connie thought, and would work under skirts and dresses and she could wear them over tight jeans as well.

She arrived back at the hotel before anyone else, so she made a coffee with the small kettle in her room, and then relaxed for ten minutes with a magazine. She then went and had a quick bath and afterwards she put on one of the new T-shirts she had bought in Portobello Road and her jeans. She then laid her two dresses on the bed too. When she heard Vanessa coming into the children's room, she knocked and went in to join them. They told her all about their afternoon, and she then helped get them washed and dressed for dinner which was at half past six as the three couples were going on to a show later while Connie stayed in the hotel with the children.

When the children were all ready, Connie asked Vanessa to come and look at the dresses and give her opinion on which one she thought was best for dinner.

"They are both gorgeous," Vanessa said, and when she added, "I would wear both myself," Connie knew she had got it right.

Vanessa also loved the boots and tried them on, but they were a couple of sizes too big for her tiny slim feet.

Connie again thanked her for the money and the other things she had bought her that afternoon.

"You're worth it," Vanessa said, giving her a little hug. "I could never have done this trip without your help. Dave doesn't have a clue how hard it is trying to hold down a career and bringing up two kids at that age. Audrey is brilliant during the week, taking them to nursery and play group and collecting them, but she doesn't have the energy to look after them all day. And she doesn't do all the reading with them or the games and things that you do."

"I'm glad you're happy," Connie said.

"Honestly, Connie, if it wasn't for your help with them, I feel I would have no life outside of work or home at all. You've given me my weekends back." She gave a little giggle. "I was beginning to feel tired and older lately, but having you around makes me feel younger again."

"But you are young!" Connie said. "You're like a model with your lovely clothes and slim figure. I don't know how you do it. You must be about a size eight. No matter what I do, how much I walk, I can't get into anything less than a twelve."

Vanessa suddenly looked serious. "Believe it or not, I was the same until a few years ago. I was bigger than you by a mile, and then the doctor gave me these slimming tables. I lost three stones." She closed her eyes. "They are absolutely brilliant – they take away your appetite and give you more energy."

"Do you mean amphetamines?" Connie said.

Vanessa's brow wrinkled. "I don't actually know what they're called. As far as I know they only have caffeine and harmless ingredients in them. I only take them now and again, when I've a big show on, or if I think I've put on a few pounds."

"And does the doctor still prescribe them for you, even though you're so skinny?" Connie asked.

Vanessa shook her head. "No, he said I had lost enough weight. But I have a business contact who needed to lose weight," she rolled her eyes, "a *lot* of weight! I mean she was over a size twenty, and I recommended the tablets to her. She gets them from her doctor and she gives me some any time I need them."

"You know you're not supposed to do that," Connie said. "You're not supposed to take medication prescribed for someone else."

"I know, but I've already been prescribed them before so I know they are not doing me any harm. Dave doesn't like me using them – he says they make me too wired if I'm on them for more than a few days. But, to be honest, I love the extra energy they give me. I can get loads done without feeling a bit tired." She shrugged. "It's fine for Dave to criticise, but he's only delivering the furniture or going out measuring up and hanging curtains – it's me who has to go out to houses and be all sparkly and creative and enthusiastic." She gave a fake, bright smile to emphasise the point. "And it's me who has to deal with all the complaints."

"I hope you don't think I'm talking out of turn," Connie said, "but you need to be careful with those sorts of pills. We've been learning about drugs in our medical class and there have been studies about the use of amphetamines and they can cause problems."

"You don't need to worry," Vanessa assured her. "I'm not stupid and, as a matter of fact, I'm very anti-drugs. I saw what heroin and LSD and all that stuff can do when I was at Art College. The slimming tablets I take are harmless and just give me the energy to keep me moving. They're just like a big boost of caffeine."

Connie shrugged. "As long as you know what you're doing ..."

"You're really going to make a great doctor, Connie. Students get a bad name for drinking and drugs, and here you are, studying every chance you get and the complete opposite."

When Connie appeared downstairs later with the black dress and her hair tied up in a loose bun, all the women complimented her and asked where she had bought the dress. But when Vanessa told Connie to lift up her dress and show off her new boots, she suddenly felt self-conscious when all the men's eyes focussed on her legs. Although none of the men commented, she felt that the boots had made them see her in a different light, and she remained quiet for the rest of the evening so as not to draw any more attention to herself.

Sunday passed in a flurry of visits with a morning walk down Carnaby Street, a visit to the Tower of London and to Madame Tussauds. And then they had a late lunch back at the hotel before they all set off in their various cars. Sue had given her ten pounds for her help with Karen, which Connie had tried to refuse to take, and she knew that Vanessa or Dave would pay her even more in the morning before she left. She also had a bag full of lovely new clothes and jewellery and her little glass decanter and glasses.

As they drove along the motorway in the luxurious car, with the sun setting and the radio playing, Connie thought how wonderful she had found London and what a lot she had learned about the buildings and the history. She would enjoy telling the girls back in her halls all about the luxurious Hotel Rubens, and the shops and the markets and generally what a brilliant weekend she'd had, and she knew her mother would want to know every little detail when she next rang home.

She would go back again some time on her own, when she would be able to concentrate on what the tour guides were saying without worrying about Toby running away or having to take Belinda to the toilet. She would go with a friend who appreciated the old buildings and the parks – someone who did not want to spend the whole time in pubs or trying to pick up a new boyfriend.

She knew who her ideal companion would be. The one person who would love the same things that she loved, who would enjoy the same music – and who would laugh along with her.

She looked out at the darkened sky as the car moved along, Vanessa and the children asleep, the radio on low, Dave concentrating on the road. Every mile took her nearer to her student life in Manchester and further away from where William Fitzgerald was living his life with his new fiancée.

Chapter 37

Tara came into the sitting room carrying a box of mixed crackers and biscuits, and a plate with several different types of cheese and a square of duck-and-orange pâté. She put them down on the polished mahogany coffee table. "If you pour the wine, I'll bring us a plate each and the crisps and nuts."

There was a time when she would have dreaded sharing a drink with Bridget, when her friend had come to depend much too heavily on it. But, thankfully, she had got it under control and rarely drank these days. When she did, she only drank on special occasions like tonight, and was careful not to exceed her limit of more than a couple of glasses. She now made it a policy never to touch drink when she was upset as it had caused serious problems in the past.

"Oh, lovely," Bridget said, uncurling from her position in the corner of the sofa. She went over to the coffee table and poured the red wine she had brought into one tall glass and then the other.

Tara came back in with the two bowls and put them down and then gave Bridget a plate and a cheese knife. "I have a nice pineapple cheesecake I made earlier, so we can have it when we've finished with all this."

"Pineapple! You know that's my favourite. This is a real Sunday-night treat for me, being up in your lovely big house in front of a roaring fire." Bridget gave a contented sigh. "And it's even better knowing that when I go home later, June will have the school uniforms ironed and pressed for me!" She looked at her watch. "And she will probably have the two girls all bathed and in bed by now. Michael should be home from his lacrosse match anytime soon, so she'll give him his supper and then they'll all be safely tucked up when I get home tonight!" She closed her fist and made a little punching gesture. "*Wee-hee!* We can't let the men have all the fun, can we?"

She then lifted her wineglass and clinked it against her friend's.

Tara laughed at her. "You are a devil, Bridge – you never change. But, seriously, you don't have a bad life at all. You are your own boss in the boarding house and you have a man who would do anything for you."

"True," Bridget said, picking three crackers and a digestive from the box. "And you're the same. We're lucky with the two that we found." She cut a few slices of cheddar and put them on her plate. "I'm delighted that it worked out for them going to the wrestling match, and even better young William was here and able to go with them. It's just like old times, isn't it? He used to love going with Fred and Shay years ago."

"Was Michael disappointed he couldn't go?"

"Yes, he was, but he knows he can't miss lacrosse. He's one of the best under-sixteen players they have, and it was an important match tonight. They were playing Altrincham and there's always a bit of rivalry between those two teams."

"I hope William enjoys it," Tara said. "He was a bit flat when he came back from Manchester. He went out to the university campus to see if he could talk to Connie."

"What happened?"

"Nothing. She wasn't there. He saw one of her friends and the girl told him that Connie had a boyfriend and they had gone off somewhere for the weekend."

"What?" Bridget gasped.

"I don't think it's actually true," Tara said. "I reckon Connie was either there and just didn't want to see him – or else she was out with her friends or over with that family she works for in Wilmslow. In fact, come to think of it, I'm sure she said she was going to London with them one of these weekends. That's probably where she was."

"But the girl might have been telling the truth, she might have a new boyfriend just as easily."

Tara shook her head. "She doesn't strike me as a girl that would go off for a weekend with a new boyfriend. She's never mentioned a boyfriend to me, and I just don't believe she's the sort to do that."

"You never know," Bridget said. "People can get carried away. Physical attraction can sometimes just strike when two people meet and they can't resist each other." She went silent then, and after a few moments took a bite out of a cracker.

Tara picked up her glass and took a slow sip from it. In her younger days, Bridget was the one person who knew about being swept along by physical attraction, but unfortunately it had often carried her in the wrong direction.

"I suppose you could be right," she said, "but, whatever the truth is, William came back home with his tail between his legs, having not seen her."

"Do you think there's any hope there? Do you think when she knows his engagement is off that there might be a chance?"

"I really don't know," Tara said, "but it's not going to happen this time. He has to head off back to London in the morning. He still has a lot of studying to do to for the next part of his qualification, and he has an exam coming up before Christmas."

Bridget took a drink. "If Connie doesn't really have a new boyfriend now, I'll bet she'll have one by Christmas with all the end-of-term parties and dances. She's bound to meet someone nice at university; all those lovely long-haired young fellas that will turn out to be doctors will be looking for a gorgeous girl like her."

"Did I tell you that Angela got her hair cut?" Tara said. "She was telling me that she got it cut up to her shoulders. It sounded lovely the way she described it."

"She has beautiful blonde hair – she could wear it in any style."

Then both women gave a sudden start as the doorbell rang.

"Jesus!" Bridget said. "That nearly put the heart out of me."

Tara glanced at the clock and then put her glass down on the table. "It surely can't be the men back yet, it's much too early ..." She got up and went quickly across the room and out into the hallway. A few minutes she later she came rushing back in. "Bridget, it was Mr Jackson, our next-door neighbour. With our phone still not working, somebody has phoned there for me and asked if they can talk to me. Apparently it's urgent. I'm just going to Jacksons' now, to see what it's about, and I'll be back in a few minutes."

As she ran down the driveway from their house, then out onto the pathway and up the Jacksons' drive, Tara felt a sense of fear and foreboding.

Was it her father, she wondered – as Shay still had occasional funny turns – or Tessie? Or maybe, she thought, it was her Uncle Mick or his wife Kitty. She felt her chest tighten as she ran along. Too many times she had heard bad news. At least, she thought, Noel and Leo were safe and sleeping in their beds. She could not imagine how she would cope if anything ever happened to them.

Bridget took another cracker from the box and spread it thickly with paté. Then she lifted a magazine from the shelf underneath the coffee table and tucked her feet under her and started to read.

Five minutes later she heard the front door opening and Tara's heels on the hallway. Then Tara opened the sitting-room door and just stood there, her face ashen. "Something terrible has happened." Her voice was shaking and her whole body trembling. "The men ... they've been in a car crash on the A6 ... they ran off the road and hit a tree ... and they've all been taken to Stepping Hill Hospital. They've been there for the last two hours."

Bridget stared at her as though not comprehending what she was hearing.

"Fred and William are in Accident and Emergency. They said something about a broken arm and cracked ribs, concussion ... things like that ... but they're okay, they're talking and everything, so hopefully it's not too serious ..."

"Oh, my God!" Bridget said. "That all sounds serious enough." She put her hands up to her mouth.

Tara started to sway. "It's Frank ..." she said. Her legs suddenly gave way and she crashed down onto the floor.

"What is it?" Bridget rushed to help her back onto her feet. "What is it?"

Tara took a huge gulp of air to steady herself. "It's Frank," she said. "He's in intensive care. He had a heart attack at the wheel."

Chapter 38

Before she left for Hamiltons' on Friday afternoon, Connie went downstairs in her student block to the phone box, to ring home to wish her father happy birthday. He was delighted to hear from her, and told her that he and her mother were going for a meal that night to the Hayes Hotel with the money she had sent, and Kate had used the rest to buy him a new shirt.

"It was far too much," he said. "Sure, we should be giving you the money, not the other way around."

"I'm fine, Daddy," Connie reassured him. "I'm paid really well for baby-sitting at the weekends. I've even bought all my Christmas presents already. Now, make sure you have a good night and enjoy yourself."

"Ah, we will. I'm not much good for meals in restaurants, but once we're there I'll enjoy it, and Ollie and the girl and Terry are coming to meet us after for a few drinks."

"That all sounds lovely," Connie said, delighted to hear they were going out to celebrate.

"And tell me," her father said, "how is the studying coming on?"

"It's actually going great," she told him. "I'm well up to date with all my essays and question sheets. The anatomy and chemistry can be heavy going, but so far I'm managing it all. I had a meeting with my personal tutor and all the reports from my classes have been fine. I just need to get my head down and study for my Christmas exams. I'm baby-sitting over in Wilmslow this weekend, so I have my chemistry and anatomy books with me, to take notes when the children are in bed."

"How are they all out in Stockport?" he said. "Have you heard how Frank is doing?"

"Frank? No, I haven't heard anything," Connie said. "I rang at the beginning of the week and their phone was out of order."

There was a silence.

Then: "Did you not hear about the car crash?"

"What car crash?"

"Frank had a heart attack at the wheel."

"Oh, no! Is he all right?"

"He's very ill by all accounts," her father said. "He's in intensive care still."

"Oh, God! Poor Tara! And I didn't even know anything about it. I feel terrible. Was anyone else hurt? Did he crash into another car?"

"No – they ran off the road and hit a tree." There was a pause on the line. "But Fred was in the car with him ... and so was young Fitzgerald."

Connie felt as though her stomach had suddenly been wrenched. "William? And was he hurt?"

"I think both he and Fred were knocked about a bit, all right. They were in hospital for a few days. Your grandad told us all about it – he's in an awful state, going on about going over to visit them and everything."

"Daddy," Connie said, "how badly hurt are they?"

"I really don't know. They mentioned broken ribs and a broken ankle."

"Have you or Mammy not phoned Tara yet to find out?"

"Your grandad is keeping us up to date with everything, and I went out to Ballygrace to see Angela when I heard." His voice dropped. "Your mother said the last thing they need is different people phoning and annoying them all the time."

"But that's not annoying them!" Connie said, her voice rising. "It's showing that you care. Tara is your sister, Daddy! Maybe not your full sister, but she's been good to us all over the years."

"I know, I know … but your mother can be awkward about them at times. You know what she's like. She hates to be beholden to people, and she says that Tara always makes her feel like that. Sometimes you just have to agree for an easier life."

Connie took a deep breath. It was her father's birthday and he wasn't to blame for any of this. "Okay," she said, keeping her voice even. "And is Frank improving at all?"

"From what Angela said, he's still in intensive care while they're doing various tests on him."

"Look, Daddy, I'm going to go," Connie said.

"Your mother is here – do you not want to speak to her?"

"I haven't time. I'm going to go and ring Tara right now. I just wanted to wish you a happy birthday and say I hope you have a nice night out." And then, before he could say any more, she put the phone back down into the cradle.

She went over to the bench at the side of the wall and sat there for a few minutes, thinking and trying to take in everything her father had told her. Then, she got to her feet again and went to dial Tara's number.

Tara was just going out the door when the phone rang. She rushed back in and when she picked it up and heard the voice, she gave a little smile of relief.

"Connie, how are you?"

"How is Frank? I'm so sorry for not being in touch, Tara, but I've only heard this very minute when I rang my dad at home."

"Don't worry about it," Tara said. "It's good of you to ring." She paused. "He's coming on, he's slowly improving. They have moved him from Intensive Care to Coronary Care, so that's a good sign."

"I couldn't believe it when I heard the news!"

"It was a terrible shock for everyone, but they are all improving. Fred and William got out of hospital a few days ago."

"How badly injured were they?"

"Fred broke his arm and William cracked some ribs and he has a lot of bruising. He also had concussion as he banged his head, so the doctors kept him in hospital for observation for a few days until they were sure everything was okay."

"Oh, my God ..."

Tara lowered her voice. "William is actually here at the house now. He's upstairs having a rest. Would you like to speak to him?"

Connie halted, not knowing what to say or do. "I don't want to disturb him," she eventually said.

"Maybe another time?" Tara said.

"Would you pass on my best wishes to him, and would you thank him for the book he left for me last Sunday? It was nice of him to drop it out to me." She felt it was the wrong time to mention that he had also given Christine a small bunch of flowers and a card in a sealed envelope which said, '*I hope you are well and that everything is going great at university. This is the book about Stephen's Green I told you about, and the flowers are because I wanted you to know that I think of you every time I pass a flower shop!*' He had drawn a face with a smile on it.

"Of course I will," Tara said.

"I was in London at the time," she explained, "with the Hamiltons, the family whose children I look after." She waited, wondering if Tara would say anything about what Jane had told William about her being away with a boyfriend. Her friend had no idea who William was, and had automatically trotted out the excuse used to put off any boys who seemed keen on Connie.

"Did you enjoy London?"

"Yes, it was great, thanks." From the way Tara spoke, Connie thought, William must not have said anything to her. And now, with all they were going through after the accident, it was probably the last thing on his mind. "I was wondering if it would be okay to visit Frank next week? I could get the bus out to the hospital for the evening visit."

"Oh, that's nice of you. For the time being it's just immediate family until he is well enough to decide what they're going to do. Hopefully, he will be all sorted and home soon." Tara paused. "But you know you can always come out here any time, Connie. We would love to see you. I know you're very busy with the family you help, but it would be nice for you to get to know your little cousins properly."

"I will, I'll really try to make the time to get out to see you all," she said. "I did actually ring last week, but the operator said the phone line was down."

"Oh, it was," Tara said, "and it caused us all sorts of problems at the time. Thank goodness they got it fixed."

"I'll be in touch again soon," Connie said, "and tell Frank I'm praying for him and I'm thinking of you all."

"If you don't mind I'll ring you when we can have more visitors," Tara said. "It's just that we have lots of calls and I'm afraid Noel might overhear me talking about Frank. I'll ring you at your student block number, and if you're not there, I'll give one of the other girls a message for you."

"That would be great – just ask them to write a little note and leave it under the door."

They said goodbye and then Connie hung up the phone. She felt a real pang of guilt that Tara had mentioned about her not spending any time with the children. And as she ran upstairs to collect her bags and books for another weekend with the Hamiltons, it suddenly struck her how well her mother had engineered her time off from university, so that she did not have any spare time to keep up with her relatives.

Chapter 39

The following Wednesday Tara was in her bedroom, just getting ready to drive back into the hospital for the evening visit when the phone rang yet again. It rang morning, noon and night with people checking how Frank was. If Tara had been in any doubt as to how well thought of he was, she now knew. She went over to Frank's bedside table where the upstairs phone was.

It was John Burns from the Grosvenor group.

"Hello, Tara," he said, "I just wanted to check how Frank is doing?"

Tara gave him a quick update and told him that she would let him know when he was allowed more visitors.

"I wonder if you could give him a message from myself, Simon and Gerry? He had asked about selling his share to fund the building of the estate in Bramhall, but when we looked into it, apparently it was going to take too long to sort out the paperwork. Well, we've given it some thought and –"

"Oh, I'm sorry, John," Tara interrupted, "but I don't want Frank thinking about things like this while he is in hospital. I don't want him having anything else to worry about. The doctors are concerned that stress at work might have contributed to his heart attack."

"Oh, Tara, I do beg your pardon. I think I may have worded this all wrongly. I am well aware of Frank's serious health situation and I was actually ringing because we may have come up with something to help things along."

Tara moved to sit on the side of the bed. John Burns was a nice and a kind man, but she really did not want to have to think about Frank's business at the moment. She was exhausted with all the worry and, during the last week, she had feared she was going to lose the father of her two young boys – she feared she was going to lose the love of her life.

But she knew that this last building project meant a lot to Frank, and if the group had found a way to release money that would lift the pressure off him then she would have to be involved on his behalf.

"Okay, John," she said "I'm listening."

An hour later she walked into main entrance of Stepping Hill Hospital. As she walked along, as always heads turned at her striking Titian hair and lovely face, her classic camel coat and her confident stride. Oblivious to the looks, in her head she was busy going over all the things she needed to organise over the coming days.

William had been a saviour. He was at home with the boys which had helped enormously as it kept them in a routine with the same person there every night while Tara went into the hospital. William had told her he was staying on until there was definite news about Frank being allowed home. In the evenings, she made sure Leo was already in bed, so William did not have to lift him and risk hurting his ribs. Noel was able to walk upstairs and get into bed himself. When she went in to visit Frank during the day, Noel was at nursery school and she dropped Leo down with Bridget or else June came out to the house to look after him there and help with the housework or cooking.

William's ribs were still strapped up and his face and shoulder were all bruised from the impact in the car. "It will all mend," he had told Tara. "Accidents happen all the time. But if you don't mind, I'm not going to mention the crash to my mother. She couldn't handle it and she would only come rushing up here, worried sick about everything and everyone. I'm just going to tell her that Frank had a heart attack and I am staying with you until he recovers."

When Tara reached the Coronary Care ward she rang the bell and waited until she was admitted. Then the nurse took her over to the curtained-off corner bed, where the pale Frank was sleeping. She crept over to the chair, and then she sat quietly just watching him. After about ten minutes he stirred and then gradually opened his eyes.

"How are you, darling?" Tara reached forward to take his hand.

"All the better for seeing you," he whispered, smiling at her.

She bent to kiss him on the lips, and then she froze when she felt his arms move to hug her. "No, you need to stay still, Frank," she told him. "We don't want you straining yourself in any way."

"I have good news," he told her. "The doctor was around this evening and they're happy with my recovery. The heart attack was mild, and with medication and bed rest, everything seems to be settling down." He smiled. "There's a chance I could be out next week."

Tara felt a huge wave of relief wash over her. "Oh, thank God," she said. "That's what I've been praying for." She took his face between her hands and kissed him again. "You will never know the fright you gave me. The thought of losing you – of the boys losing you –"

"I'm going to be fine, Tara," he said. "Honestly. I just know from the way I feel that it will be okay."

"You're going to have to take things easier. You're going to have to ease off at work and all that sort of thing. You've been putting yourself under too much strain with the housing estate."

He closed his eyes for a few moments and then he nodded as though agreeing.

As she watched him, she saw for the first time a look of defeat on his face, and it went straight to her heart. Nothing that important had ever defeated Frank. In all the years she had known him, he had found solutions to almost everything. There was the odd occasion when he knew it was wiser to walk away from something, but he did so as a positive decision not to lose more money or waste his time. But, when he dedicated himself to a project that he knew was worthwhile, he would find ways to make it work, and he would always see it through.

But this time, she hoped, he didn't have to take the whole burden on.

"I have news too, Frank," she told him. And as his blue eyes fixed on hers, she smiled and said, "Good news." And then she told him about the call from John Burns and the offer he had made.

"Are you serious?" he said.

"Yes, all three of them in the group want to invest in the Bramhall housing project. They have checked it out and feel it's a really sound investment. They said working with you on the Grosvenor has proved all of you together are a good team and they think that it's a great opportunity for them. If you agree they will get all the legal paperwork drawn up quickly so the building work can go straight ahead."

Frank took a deep breath. "I don't know what to say ... it's just unbelievable. I would never have thought of approaching them. I had it fixed in my mind that it would be someone else involved in the construction work."

Tara's face became serious. "There is one stipulation, Frank. They want to hire a new project manager, and they don't want you near the building site for at least six months. They want you to take a total break from all work, until you've had the all-clear from the hospital."

He was silent for a while and then he looked at her. "I'm not going to argue ..."

"Really? You'll take six months away from everything?"

"Yes." His voice was low and quiet. "I've had time to really think this week, Tara. While I've been lying here, I've had time to think about everything the doctors have told me." He closed his eyes for a few moments. "I'm not going to pretend. I have had a real scare and I know that if I don't do what I am told I might not get a second chance."

For a moment Tara felt she could not breathe. The thought of Frank not being around terrified her. The thought of Noel and Leo losing their father was unthinkable. Two such little, vulnerable boys who needed both of them for the next twenty years at least. The feeling eased a little and she reached for his hand. "You're going to be fine, Frank," she whispered. "We're going to make sure you do all the right things – having a break from work, slowing down, living life at an easier pace." She squeezed his hand. "You'll have time with me and the boys, and you can get back to doing things like reading, and going for walks in the park and all the lovely things you haven't had time to do for the last few years."

He slowly nodded.

"I never imagined how much I would enjoy being at home with the boys. How much the simple things in life mean. It's taught me how things can change. Work is not our priority at this point in our lives, Frank."

"I understand everything you're saying," he said, "but I need to be honest with you, Tara. Even with the investment for the housing project, I am concerned about money in the meantime."

"We'll manage," she told him. "We have an income from the two hotels and that will cover all we need until the houses are built and sold. And if need be, the Cale Green can be sold." She shrugged. "I let Ballygrace House go when the time was right, and that was far more important to me. The hotel will eventually go at some point in the future – five years, ten years. It might go in one year. These are not the important things."

He gave a little sigh and then he smiled. "Okay," he said, "you're the boss. I am not going to argue."

Tara started to laugh. "Can I have that in writing?"

They chatted for another while and then she asked him about letting his grown-up family in Ireland know.

He shook his head. "I'm not going to worry them. If it had been really serious, then that would be different. I'd much rather we keep it to ourselves and the ones close to us here."

"Are you sure?"

"Absolutely. I would be more anxious if I knew they were travelling over at this time of the year, maybe bringing a young child." He shook his head. "I'm going to be fine, so there's no need."

After a while the nurse came and asked Tara if she wouldn't mind going in the next five minutes as Frank needed to rest. She assured the nurse she was just going and then she asked her if he could have a visit from a close friend – Fred – the following day. The nurse said that since Frank was improving it would be fine.

"I have to take Leo to the clinic tomorrow afternoon," she told him, "so I won't make it in. Both Fred and William have been waiting to see you, so if you don't mind I'll let Fred come in during the afternoon, and William can visit in the evening?"

Frank immediately agreed. "You've been here every day," he said. "Now that we know things are going to be okay, you take some time for yourself and the children."

As Tara walked out of the ward, through the corridors and then back out to the car, she told herself that things were infinitely better than they had been a few days ago. She was reassured by both his appearance and by the nurse saying that Frank was improving. The conversation she had dreaded about him making the immediate changes had proved much easier than she could have hoped for, and the biggest and most immediate worry about money had been lifted from them. John Burns was now busy sorting the moving of funds into the housing-project accounts. He had also said that they would look into finding a new manager for the building work, and would have him in place as soon as possible. The building work would resume soon, and things would be back on an even keel in the next month or so.

Everything she could think of had been sorted and Frank had been reassured that they would manage. The only thing she had to deal with now was herself. Tomorrow morning, Bridget would accompany her to the hospital and she would have the biopsy done on the lump in her breast. All being well, she would be recovered later in the afternoon, by which time Fred would be visiting Frank. Hopefully, she would feel well enough to visit him the following day.

She had thought long and hard about telling William about her biopsy and then discussed it with Bridget.

"I don't want to worry him," Tara said. "Especially after the accident and all the trouble with Pamela."

"He's a grown man," Bridget said, "and I think he will be upset when he finds out, and knows you didn't tell him. And, I'm sure you'll be grand, but you don't know exactly how you're going to feel when you come home from hospital. If you feel you need to go to bed or anything, he might guess there's something wrong and you'll have to tell him then."

Tara took her friend's advice. William was both shocked and concerned for her, and even offered to come to the hospital with her.

"I'm grateful, William, but Bridget is coming with me, and I'll feel better knowing you are here with the boys. The less people who know about this the better, because I don't want Frank finding out. I'm sure it's nothing serious."

"If there is anything at all I can do," he said. "I am here to help." And then he had come over and put his arms around her. "You are the one person I could always rely on Tara, and I want to be the same to you."

Whatever happened, she would not let Frank know about this for the time being. Worrying over her would only set back his recovery. By the time he came out of hospital it would be over and done with. All the other immediate problems had been solved – and this would be solved too. It had to be.

She opened the car door and slid into the driver's seat. She sat for a moment, thinking about what lay ahead the following day. She was not afraid of the operation itself. The specialist had explained that it would involve an incision of about an inch and a half to remove part or the entire lump, depending on the size. He said they would then probably put in six stitches. It was not, she thought, a big operation. She'd had stitches in a gash on her cheek after a collision in her car some years back, and it was of a similar size. It had faded and she hardly thought of it any more.

None of this worried her at all. She just wanted it over and done with. What did worry her was their two little boys. At such a young age, they had no awareness of Frank being in the hospital or the fact that he was now recovering from a heart attack.

And they would have no understanding of what she was going to go through for the next week as she waited on the results of the biopsy. It would go one way or the other. It would either be huge relief or it would be the unthinkable – cancer.

Tara suddenly felt as though a terrible weight had descended upon her. Visions of her two boys growing up without a mother – as she herself had done – engulfed her, and she felt that same suffocating feeling that she had felt earlier on.

She closed her eyes and laid her head on the steering-wheel and wept.

Chapter 40

By the following weekend, Connie had not heard anything from Tara about visiting Frank. She had thought about ringing again, but was aware of what Tara had said about the constant phone calls and not wanting Noel to overhear anything. Another reason she was reluctant to ring was in case William was still at Tara's house and might answer the phone. She guessed he might have gone back to London by now, but she had no way of knowing.

She went as usual to Hamiltons', and unusually they had nothing big planned for the Friday night, so Dave got them all a takeaway meal and they had a quiet night in watching television. Connie went to bed early with *Grey's Anatomy*, trying to get to grips with a section for an exam the following week.

On the Saturday morning she woke early and came downstairs as Vanessa was sitting the children at the table for breakfast. Both little heads were turned in the direction of the television, watching cartoons.

"I'll sort their cereals if you want to go and get ready for work," she offered.

"Are you sure?" Vanessa checked. "I would be grateful though, as both Dave and I need to get in a bit earlier – we're redoing the window displays for winter. We are really busy at the moment and the girls we have on today aren't up to doing displays, so we'll both be working on it."

"I'm fine," Connie said, lifting the packets of Rice Krispies which Belinda liked, and Frosties which were Toby's favourite. "Have you any plans for tonight?"

Vanessa made a little face and sighed. "Drinks and nibbles at a client's house for six thirty – they're friends as well – and then we're meeting up with the usual crowd and all going on to a fund-raising dinner with an auction at the Grosvenor in Stockport. I think that's around eight thirty."

Connie's eyes lit up. "I've been to the Grosvenor a few times," she said. "My dad's sister is one of the owners."

"Really? Your aunt is involved in the Grosvenor?" Vanessa sounded impressed. "It's a lovely hotel, but I can't say I know any of the owners. This is a big annual 'do' for a children's charity and we can't miss it. It's the last thing I need as I'm shattered. I didn't sleep well, I was up half the night, but what can you do? When you own the business, you can't just ring in and leave someone else to sort it all out."

"I'll deal with the children," Connie said. "If you just tell me what you want them to wear."

"I'll leave their outfits out on the bed. Oh, would you mind bathing Belinda? She had a little accident this morning."

"No problem."

Half an hour later, Connie lifted Belinda out of the bath and wrapped her in a big striped towel, then carried her into her bedroom to dry and dress her. She was just putting on the grey-and-pink wool dress laid out on the bed for the little girl, when she heard Vanessa's quick steps approaching. She came into the bedroom, dressed in a striped navy and white tunic over navy jeans.

"Ah, I thought that dress would be lovely on her," Vanessa said. "It was a present from Dave's sister and it's been too big up until now. The grey tights will look lovely on her and keep her warm."

"The weather forecast says it's to be dry and mild today," Connie said, "so I was thinking of taking Toby and Belinda into Wilmslow this afternoon. I'll take the buggy for Belinda – Toby will be fine walking."

"Oh yes, they'll love that," Vanessa said. "I never get time to take them."

"We're going to the library first. It's in the middle of the town, isn't it? Dave pointed it out to me when we were in the car."

"Yes, walk from Silver Street down to Alderley Road, then turn down South Drive. You'll see the signs for it, you can't really miss it."

"That's great," Connie said. "I want to look something up in a medical reference book, and I thought we might spend a little while in the children's section looking at the picture books."

"You're very brave taking them into the library! I took Toby in there last year when I was with a friend with older children, and he ran riot, shouting and throwing the books about. I was mortified, the librarians were all tutting at us and I had to take him out. I've been too terrified to take him back in again."

"He's older and much better behaved now," Connie said. "I am sure he'll be fine. If he's not, I'll just take him out."

"Well, good luck with that. I've left a cottage pie I bought from Marks and Spencer in the fridge," Vanessa told her. "There should be plenty for the three of you for dinner, so you can have it any time you want. We'll just be rushing in and out again, so you work to your own timetable."

As she turned to go out the door, Connie noticed how disturbingly thin she looked, even thinner than when she had first met her.

Vanessa suddenly turned back. "Just thinking, why don't you drop into the shop when you're in town? You've not been in yet. We're not far from the library. Just come back out onto Alderley Road, and walk on past Finnigans' Department Store. We're on the same side of the road, so if you just keep on walking past you'll find Hamiltons' Interiors."

The walk down into the town took almost half an hour as they went fairly slowly, counting all the trees on Silver Street and then talking about the colour of the doors on the houses. They sang songs and then stopped to talk to an old lady with a small friendly dog.

Connie thought the library was surprisingly modern and bigger than she had imagined. It was quite busy with people queuing to have books checked in or stamped out, and she had to wait until one of the librarians was free to take her into the reference section which was empty.

"We're not supposed to let children in here," the librarian said.

"I'll be really quick," Connie said, bending down to get her bag from the undercarriage of Belinda's buggy. "I just need to check something out from the medical section and write down a few quick notes."

"How about if I take the little boy down to pick a book?" the librarian said, smiling at Toby.

"Will you go with the nice lady to see the books?" Connie asked him. "You'll have to be very good."

Toby nodded. "I'll be very good."

When the woman left, Connie heaved a sigh of relief and searched in her bag for her notebook and a small biscuit for Belinda to keep her occupied.

A short while later a smiling Toby came back carrying a *Noddy* picture book.

"I'm just finished my notes," Connie said.

She thanked the librarian and then she took Toby and Belinda down into the children's section. She let the little girl out of the buggy for a while and walked around with her, picking up books and looking at the pictures, whilst Toby ran back and forth to the bookstands, showing Connie all the interesting books he had found about dinosaurs and tractors and dogs.

Later, as they walked along the main road towards the shop, Connie praised Toby and told him how good he had been in the library, and he nodded and beamed up at her.

"You really are a very good boy," she told him and Belinda repeated in a loud voice, "Good boy, Toby, good boy, Toby," until Connie had to gently tell her to stop.

As they approached the shop, Connie heard knocking on one of the windows and then saw a smiling Dave waving at them. By the time they reached the door, he was there to open it and usher them inside. He told Connie that Vanessa was busy in the office sorting an order, and then he led them over to a quiet spot away from any customers where the children told him all about the books they had seen and generally chattered away.

"I'll take them upstairs to our staff room and give them a drink and a biscuit," Dave told Connie, "if you want to have a little break and a look around the displays."

Delighted to have a few minutes to herself, Connie wandered around looking at the lovely sofas and chairs and beds, all covered in tiny floral prints, and the bookshelves stacked with velvet cushions, and rolled-up matching bedspreads. There was another area which had shelves filled with wallpaper in varying patterns and curtains and cushions and bedding which all matched. There was a special children's section with dreamy, lace-decorated Moses baskets and cots, and piles of pink and blue and lemon blankets. And small blankets and pillows covered with pictures of Beatrix Potter animals.

There was also a giftware section which Connie loved with white-framed, French-style prints of girls in straw hats and billowing dresses running in meadows, and picture frames in all sizes which were covered in floral-sprigged material. She stopped at one point to sink down into a cane sofa, which had feather-filled cushions covered in cheery yellow dandelions, and a coffee table which had a matching dandelion tablecloth. She considered buying her mother a floral picture-frame but stopped herself because she thought Dave or Vanessa would insist on her having it without paying, and because her mother might think it odd.

She followed a winding painted wrought-iron staircase up into a gallery which had whitewashed walls hung with Mexican-style rugs and blankets, and pale pine beams from which hung swathes of materials in all different patterns. There were more squashy sofas and armchairs covered in a variety of tapestries patterned with flowers, trees, butterflies and dragonflies.

When she went over to a stand which had hundreds of samples of material for covering sofas or making curtains, she could immediately see how the business took up so much of Dave and Vanessa's time. She moved on then to study a large pine-framed print of a field filled with lavender with an old rambling house in the distance, and it struck her that there was a similarity between a shop like this and a flower shop where you were surrounded with beautiful things which gave people a great feeling to look at or to own.

As she moved from display to display, she found herself

imagining what it would be like to be married and have her own house. What it would be like to go into shops like Hamiltons' Interiors and pick out furniture for all the various rooms, or to ask for advice on matching things up. It was so unlike any of the furniture shops she had been in at home, which were mainly filled with modern teak or veneered wood, and where sofas and chairs and beds tended to be practical and sturdy as opposed to fun or beautiful.

It would be a long way off in the future before she would need to think of buying and furnishing a home – if she ever met the right person to share it with. Then, her mind flitted to William Fitzgerald, and for a few minutes she allowed herself to imagine the fun they would have together, choosing and arguing over things.

It was, she knew, a complete fantasy and something she was doing more often again. Since he had called out at her hall of residence and left the book and the flowers for her, she was now back in the same position she was in when they parted back in Ireland. Knowing that he was still thinking of her had stirred up all the memories and feelings she had buried with her new life and studies. The book about the beautiful park they had wandered around in Dublin and the flowers with the little message had broken through the shield she had built around her. She was now drifting back into dangerous waters again, imagining that they somehow might sort things out. That he would appear and tell her how sorry he was and that he was finished with Pamela and they could now start all over again.

But she knew she was only deluding herself. Any future with him would be tainted by the fact that he had deceived her and led her on.

"There you are! Well, what do you think?" Vanessa had suddenly appeared in front of her, bright-eyed and all smiles. She waved her hands around and gave a little bow. "Hamiltons' Interiors. Our business empire – our second home!"

Vanessa seemed so lively, almost theatrical, Connie thought. She wondered if this was the way she had to be every day with the customers – energetic and upbeat. "It's beautiful," Connie said. "I love it. I love everything in the shop."

"Good, good!" Vanessa put her arm around her. "You are

exactly the sort of customer we're aiming at – well, when you are qualified of course. The young professionals with disposable income to buy good quality and very individual home products." She looked straight into Connie's eyes. "All you have to do now is find the right man to set up home with."

Connie looked back at her employer and smiled.

I found him, she thought, I found the right man – but I lost him just as quick.

Chapter 41

By the time Connie and the children had lunch with Vanessa and Dave in the restaurant in Finnigans' Department Store, then had a walk around the shops and later walked all the way back home again, it was time to start sorting the evening meal.

It had been a lovely day, Connie thought, as she filled a spouted mug with orange juice for Belinda and a tumbler with lemonade for Toby as they quietly sat at the table with the colouring books and crayons that she had bought for them. Toby smiled at her and said "Thank you" and then Belinda copied him.

When she went back to put the cottage pie into the oven, she paused for a moment and looked at the two little heads, bent over the books in total concentration. I like them, she suddenly thought. I really do like them. They are lovely children.

All the weekends of working hard on Toby's behaviour, she could now see, had paid off. And because he had quietened down and had stopped all the shouting and crashing around the house, he was now able to do things at a normal pitch instead of driving everyone mad and frightening his little sister. Belinda, Connie had also noticed, seemed chattier and more confident.

It was later, as she put the cottage pie and the carrots and broccoli she had cooked on the plates, that it struck her that she knew these children far better than she did her own little cousins in Bramhall. This was something she was going to have to sort out. She decided that as soon as things settled down and Frank was back home, she would tell Vanessa she needed a weekend off to spend some time with her family. She didn't care how her mother reacted – it was the right thing to do, and she was going to do it.

Just after six, Vanessa came rushing in again with Dave following.

"Thank goodness we had that lovely lunch together," she said, putting down her huge handbag. "Because we've hardly time to get changed now before heading out again. It's a quiet night with the children then bed I need, not running out the door again."

Dave came up behind her, and placed his hands on his wife's shoulders. "Don't pay any attention to her, Connie. She loves it. Vanessa would be bored if she didn't have this busy lifestyle. She was even busier before the children came along. A few quiet weekends in and she'll be complaining that she has no life."

"Would you listen to him?" Vanessa said, her voice incredulous. "This is the man who has two-hour lunches if he can get away with it."

They both started to laugh and then Vanessa went over to kiss the children and admire their colouring-in and ask them about the pictures.

After five minutes she looked at her watch and threw her hands up. "Must go and get ready or we'll be late."

A short while later, Belinda was reaching for a crayon and knocked the remains of her orange juice over her dress.

"Come on, darling, and we'll clean you up," Connie said, taking her over to the sink. She unbuttoned the child's dress, then took it off her and put it on the worktop. Then she checked the vest she was wearing underneath and saw there was a small damp patch on it. "I think it might be a good idea if we get you changed into your pyjamas now. You go back to your colouring book like a good girl, and I'll run upstairs and get them for you."

She went upstairs and hurried along the corridor. The door of Dave and Vanessa's room was ajar and she could hear raised voices. She went quickly past and down the steps to Belinda's bedroom to get the fresh pyjamas.

She was coming back along the hallway when she heard Dave shouting.

"*Enough is enough, Vanessa!*" he yelled. "*You're going to have to fucking well sort this out!*"

"*You're no help!*" Vanessa screamed back at him. "*How am I supposed to keep going day after day? How am I supposed to juggle everything? I got three hours sleep last night!*"

"*I'm surprised you got any sleep at all!*" he shouted. There was a pause and when he spoke again his voice was lower but still full of anger. "Don't think I don't know what's going on, Vanessa. You might fool everyone else, but you don't fool me."

"Maybe if you did more work and less time doing business lunches every other day, I wouldn't have to push myself beyond the limits! Maybe if you did more around the house and with the kids!"

Connie had stopped in her tracks, not sure whether to keep going or whether to go back down to the bedroom and wait until things quietened down. She stood still, her heart hammering.

Dave's voice suddenly rose again. "Listen to who's talking – mother of the year! When was the last time you made dinner for the kids or put them to bed? You have Audrey during the week, and now you have Connie running about doing your job at the weekends. The kids do more for her and are better behaved for her than they are for you!"

"*You're going to drive me to a nervous breakdown!*" Vanessa screamed. "*Is that what you really want?*"

There was silence for a few moments, so Connie decided to take a chance. She had just passed the room when she heard Dave shouting again and then she heard a small crashing sound, like a small plastic ball or toy hitting the door.

"Oh, that's really mature of you, Dave!" she heard Vanessa say in a scathing tone. "You're acting more like Toby than a mature man. Throwing things like a spoiled kid. Well, you can bloody well pick them up!"

Connie went down the stairs as quickly and as quietly as she could.

She was back at the table, reading the children a story when the couple came back down the stairs ten minutes later. They were holding hands as they walked into the kitchen which Connie took as a sign that they had made things up.

"Now, you two," Dave said, "be very good for Connie."

They went over to cuddle and kiss the children.

"Oh, I almost forgot," said Vanessa. "I got you some Smarties today for being so good at the library. They're upstairs in my big handbag. You know my big blue handbag, Toby? It's just inside the bedroom door."

"Smarties! I'll get them!" Toby got down off his chair and scooted out into the hall.

Belinda got down off her chair. "Me get them!" she said, following her brother.

Dave looked up at the kitchen clock. "We need to get moving."

"Two minutes," Vanessa told him. "I'll just wait to see their little faces when they come back with the sweets."

Connie lifted the children's colouring books and flicked through the pages, as she found it hard to look at either of them after hearing the vicious argument just a short while ago.

Toby came back down first, waving the tube of sweets in the air. Then, a few minutes later Belinda arrived.

"I found the sweeties!" she said, holding her tube up. "And I put some of them in my pocket."

"Clever girl," Vanessa said, lifting her back up to sit at the table. "Now, eat your sweets nicely and don't make a mess." She turned to Connie. "Don't wait up for us. These things can go on fairly late at the Grosvenor, so you go off to bed."

"I will do," Connie said, nodding and stroking Belinda's hair.

She heaved a sigh of relief when the door closed behind them. She decided there and then that she would ask for the following weekend off to go to Tara's, and if that didn't work out, she would have the weekend in her hall of residence. After that, she would decide whether she actually wanted to continue working for the Hamiltons. She was very fond of the children, but she had an uneasy feeling that Dave was right. By being available every weekend, she was doing the job that their parents should be doing.

The more she thought about it, the more uncomfortable she felt, because she knew she was playing a part in the situation. In a way she had accepted the fact that Vanessa and Dave were not around from the very beginning, because she had been almost dazzled by the fabulous house, the glamorous lifestyle and by the unbelievably generous money they were giving her every week.

Just after eight o'clock, when they were all sitting on the sofa watching television, Connie noticed Belinda nodding off.

"Okay," she said, clapping her hands, "time for brushing teeth and then into bed!" She looked at Toby. "You be a good boy and run up to the bedroom and put your pyjamas on."

Toby ran on ahead, singing to himself and pretending he was riding a horse. Connie lifted Belinda down onto the floor and then, as she noticed the child swaying, she moved quickly and caught her.

"You're a very tired little girl tonight," Connie said. "Up to bed now."

"Carry me," Belinda said. "My head is tired."

"Come on then, Miss Lazybones," Connie laughed. She lifted her up into her arms and carried her upstairs.

Toby was already in the bathroom and in his pyjamas, waiting for Connie to put the toothpaste on his Yogi Bear brush. She put Belinda standing on the floor, and once again the little girl started swaying and then staggered backwards into her brother.

"Are you okay, Belinda?" Connie said, catching her two hands. As she did so, something small and white fell from her hand. Connie's gaze moved to the floor, and suddenly her heart lurched. She bent down and picked up the small white pill.

"Belinda," she said, "where did you get this?"

"It's the sweeties."

Connie opened both her hands to check. There was nothing there. "Did you eat any of the sweeties?" she asked.

Belinda nodded her head. As she did so, Connie noticed her eyelids fluttering and then closing. Then, she remembered what Belinda had been saying earlier when she came down with the Smarties. With one hand around the little girl's waist to hold her steady, she put her hand inside the little pocket in her pink pyjama jacket. She felt a wave of relief when she found it empty. Then, holding her breath, she put two fingers into the other pocket and when she felt two more little tablets, her heart almost stopped. She took them out and looked at them in the palm of her hand. She had no idea what they were – they didn't look like aspirin or any ordinary medication she knew. But as she stared down at the pills, she knew without a doubt that they were something to do with Vanessa.

"Belinda!" she said, gently shaking the child. "Belinda ...did you eat the tablets?"

"She's asleep, Connie," Toby said. "Belinda is a tired little girl and she needs to go to bed."

Connie's hand flew to her mouth as she tried to work out what was happening and what she needed to do. She lifted Belinda and went over to lie her down on the bed, then she turned to Toby.

"Be a good boy and stay with your sister. I'll be back in a minute."

She ran out of the room and up the steps to the main corridor then down to the master bedroom. The door was still ajar so she pushed it open and switched on the light. There on the bed was a small brown plastic bottle with the lid off and there were both white tablets and pale yellow ones scattered on the bed. And then it came back to her. The row she had overheard – the small object that Dave had thrown at Vanessa. It was the pill bottle, and they had been rowing about her taking the pills.

With trembling hands Connie scooped the tablets back into the bottle, and then put them into her jeans pocket. She didn't want to take a chance on Toby taking any, and she also needed to show the doctors exactly what Belinda had taken. Knowing what Vanessa had told her in London, they could be anything from sleeping tablets to amphetamines. And, whatever they did to an adult, she knew they could kill a child.

The thought of the worst happening brought beads of sweat out on her forehead now as she tried to think. Should she phone an ambulance first, or should she phone Vanessa and Dave? She tried to remember where Vanessa said they were going before the Grosvenor – a client's house she remembered, but she didn't know the name or where they lived or anything. She could look up the Grosvenor's number in the telephone directory. She looked at her watch. It was only quarter to eight, and she was sure it had been mentioned that dinner was at half past eight. She couldn't wait until then to get Belinda seen to.

Salty water, she suddenly thought. That was what you were supposed to give people when they took medicine they weren't supposed to. She ran back down to the bedroom. Toby was there, sitting silently on the edge of the bed, watching his sister.

"Good boy, Toby," Connie said, giving him a hug and a kiss. "Now, we're going to take Belinda back downstairs to give her a little drink. You can be a very good boy and get her teddy and bring it down for her." Then she thought of what might lie ahead for them and said, "And put your Paddington Bear dressing-gown on too."

She lifted Belinda in her arms, shaking her and talking to her as she walked quickly out into the corridor and downstairs. She laid the child down on the sofa in the kitchen and went to the sink to get a glass of water. She half-filled the glass, and then with trembling hands lifted out the salt container and poured what she thought was a couple of spoonfuls into the water.

Then she went over to Belinda and sat her up, and talked to her, telling her to take a big drink. The child opened her eyes and made a few little sounds as though trying to talk, and then she leaned against Connie's chest and closed her eyes again.

"Come on, darling," Connie said, "take a big, big drink. It will make you feel better." She pressed the glass against Belinda's lips and she almost cried with relief when the child opened her mouth and took a drink. Then, just as quickly, she started to cough and the salty mixture trickled back out of her mouth. Connie tried again and again, but the same thing happened each time.

Toby, who had followed them downstairs, was asking what she was doing and why Belinda wouldn't talk to him.

"She's fine, darling," she told him. "You go to the table and colour in more of your book."

Unusually quiet and watchful now, Toby went and did as he was told.

Connie looked at the time again. Could only ten minutes have passed since this nightmare began? And yet, it was another ten minutes for the medication to do more damage. She laid Belinda down on the sofa and hurried over to the phone.

There was nothing more she could do. She had to get an ambulance here as quickly as possible. She rang 999 and spoke to the operator as calmly and clearly as she could, giving her all the details of the medication and directions to the house. They told her it would take another ten minutes and in the meantime to try to keep Belinda awake.

When she hung up, she turned to Toby again. "Would you be a very good boy and show Belinda your book and all the nice pictures you've coloured in, while I make another phone call?"

She went across to her bag which was lying on the floor and took out her small notebook. She leafed through it and then stopped when she came to Sheila Doyle's number. She had not seen her since she started working at Hamiltons' weeks ago, and had only spoken a couple of times on the phone to her. But, Sheila was a sister in the hospital and the only person she knew who would be able to advise her about contacting Vanessa and Dave.

The phone rang and rang, and just as she was about to hang up, Sheila came on the line. Connie took a deep breath and briefly explained the situation to her just as she had done with the operator.

"Jesus Christ!" Sheila said. "The child could die if she's taken too many!"

"I've phoned 999 and the ambulance is on its way," Connie told her.

"Good girl, that's exactly the right thing to do."

Connie then told her about the salty water and how she was trying to keep Belinda awake but that it was getting more difficult to get any response from her.

"You've done everything right. You go to her now and try the salty water again, and do your best to keep her conscious. I'll be in A&E waiting for you when the ambulance arrives. I'll also phone the Grosvenor and leave a message at the reception to tell Vanessa and Dave to go straight down to the hospital. It's only two minutes from the hotel. And thank God you phoned me too – I was just ready to leave as I was supposed to be going to the same charity dinner tonight as well."

Reassured that Sheila was now taking care of letting Vanessa and Dave know, Connie hung up and went back to trying the salt and water again, and trying to keep the very groggy Belinda conscious.

The ten minutes passed and Belinda was now in a deep sleep and Connie was starting to panic again when suddenly she heard the sirens and saw the whirling lights, as the ambulance came flying down Silver Street and into the Hamiltons' driveway and up to the door.

And then, after feeling each single minute dragging by, everything started to move at an amazing speed. Belinda was taken out of Connie's arms and she and Toby were ushered into the back of the ambulance by two nice but serious ambulance men who introduced themselves as Graham and Tom.

As they sped back down the driveway and out into the street again, Connie held tightly on to Toby, and tried to keep herself calm and reassure him that Belinda was only asleep and would soon wake up. As they got out onto the main road and the ambulance gained speed, she looked over at the grim-faced Tom who was feeling for Belinda's pulse and then she looked at the child's white face and prone little body.

Tom got to his feet and went to the small window separating them from the driver. He slid it open and said, "As quick as you can, Graham. We haven't a moment to lose."

Chapter 42

As soon as the ambulance pulled in at the A&E, the doors were opened by staff who were waiting and Belinda was carried off.

Connie followed behind, holding Toby by the hand. She was shown into a small side-room and then a middle-aged, serious-looking doctor and a young Welsh nurse came to talk to her.

"Who are you?" the doctor asked. "And what is your relation to the child?"

She explained that she was a student and looked after the Hamilton children most weekends.

"And what are you studying?" he asked.

"Medicine," she said, and when she saw the surprised look on his face she quickly added, "but I'm just in my first year. This is my first term."

His eyes narrowed in thought. "Well, you will know enough to realise that this is a very serious situation."

He then went on to ask for all the details about Belinda and the medication. Toby sat quietly on her knee as she told them all she knew. He was asking her to describe the tables when she remembered the bottle in her jeans pocket. She set Toby on the chair next to her and then stood up and took the small bottle out of her pocket and handed it to the doctor.

He opened it and spilled a few of the pale yellow pills onto his hand then studied them for a few moments. "Valium," he said, with a sigh. Then he tipped the whole bottle out into his hand and picked up one of the small white ones. "These are something else but I don't know what." He examined the bottle and then he looked at Connie.

"There's no pharmacy label or name on the bottle. Who do they belong to?"

"They were in the parents' bedroom," she said. "I found them lying on the bed, and I saw they were the same ones that were in Belinda's pocket – the white ones – and she told me she had eaten some." She shrugged. "I have no idea how many she's taken and whether she ate both kinds."

"Hopefully, we'll soon find that out." He nodded his head. "Have you any idea where the tablets have come from?"

Connie looked blankly at him.

He held the bottle up, shaking it back and forward so that it made a rattling noise. "These drugs are prescription only. If they have not been legally prescribed, then they must have come from someone else who was prescribed them."

Connie thought back to London and what Vanessa had told her about getting slimming tablets from a friend. She bit her lip now. If she said anything that she was not sure about, it could have serious consequences for Vanessa and Dave.

"I don't know anything about the tablets," she said truthfully, "and I have no idea where they came from."

"But you say you found them on the bed in the parents' bedroom?"

Connie nodded. "Yes."

"How can any sensible parents leave medication lying around when they have young children?" He waved a dismissive hand. "What kind of people are they?"

Connie looked at him but said nothing. His words echoed the thoughts which had been in her head during these last few weeks.

As he walked out of the room a feeling of foreboding came over her. She was suddenly afraid of saying the wrong thing and she wished she had someone beside her who could advise her on what she should say or do. A picture of Tara flew into her mind, but she knew she hadn't the time to phone anyone just to comfort her and make her feel better. Belinda was the important one – the sick child came before anything else.

She hoped and prayed that she had done all the right things.

Another younger doctor came in at one point to ask Connie where Belinda's parents were. She told him they should be here soon, and then he explained that they couldn't wait any longer and they were going to have to go ahead now and pump the child's stomach.

After he left the room, Connie gathered Toby closer to her as she went over the events of the night again, wondering if there was anything else she could have done differently.

Shortly afterwards she heard footsteps and when the door opened, a tight-faced Sheila Doyle came in, looking strangely glamorous in the stark hospital setting. Her hair was newly styled, her face carefully made up. She was wearing a fitted black dress, a large gold necklace and she was carrying a purple satin stole and a sparkly black evening bag.

Connie felt weak with relief at seeing someone familiar.

"Vanessa and Dave should be here anytime now," Sheila told her. "The Grosvenor has a member of staff waiting on them at the door, and there's a car ready to bring them straight here." She sat down beside Connie and Toby. "This is terrible. I can't believe what has happened. How is she?"

"They're pumping her stomach …" Connie closed her eyes and pictured Belinda on the operating table. As she took a deep breath tears slid down her cheeks. "I'm terrified that it's going to be too late, that I didn't get her here in time. But I had no idea that she had taken anything until she started swaying on her feet."

"Do they know yet what she took?"

"Valium they think, but there were other tablets in the bottle. The doctor didn't say what they were. Thank God I thought to bring it with me. The doctor said it saved time trying to work out what she had taken."

"How on earth did the child find a bottle of tablets? Did you leave her on her own? Did she climb up to a cupboard or something when you weren't looking?"

Connie shook her head, realising that she hadn't yet given Sheila the details of what had happened. "No, it was nothing like that.

This all happened before Vanessa and Dave left the house. Vanessa told the children to go up to her room. She had bought them chocolate, and her bag was in the bedroom. The bottle that Belinda found must have been lying on the bed when she went in."

"Very strange," Sheila said. "I can't imagine them being so stupid as to leave pills lying around like that."

"It's probably because they are rushing around all the time. They are often just in the door, getting changed and then rushing back out." She paused. "And there are times when they seem under a lot of pressure with work and everything."

"What do you mean?"

"Well, earlier tonight before they went out, I heard Dave and Vanessa arguing." She bit her lip. "When I think back on it, I think they were arguing about her taking tablets. I don't know about the Valium, but she told me when we were down in London how a friend gets her these slimming tablets."

Sheila's eyes widened. "What? She actually told you that?"

"She said they gave her the energy to keep going when she was tired, and that they help keep her slim."

Sheila looked towards the closed door then she bent her head closer to Connie's. "And have you told the doctors any of this?"

"I just told them I found the tablets."

Sheila prodded Connie's arm with her finger. "You need to be very careful what you say to these doctors." Her voice was low and serious. "Saying things about arguments and what Vanessa told you about taking tablets could cause very serious problems."

"But it's the truth," Connie said.

Sheila looked at her for a few moments without saying anything. Then, she lifted her bag and stole and stood up. "I'm going to wait outside for Vanessa and Dave. I'll be back as soon as they arrive." She halted. "Now remember what I said. Give as little information as possible. The doctors will know what to do with Belinda."

The next ten minutes passed very slowly. At one point Connie thought she heard Dave's voice outside and waited for them to come into the room, but when they didn't, she realised she was mistaken.

Eventually the door opened and the doctor came in followed by Dave, then Vanessa and Sheila.

"We have finished the procedure with Belinda," he said, "and we are confident that we've cleared everything in her system. She is coming round now, so hopefully all will be well."

"Oh, thank God!" Connie said. She could hardly breathe now, and felt that she could almost get sick. And then, tears of relief poured down her cheeks. "Oh, thank God she's all right!"

Vanessa suddenly pushed past the others to stand in front of her. "No thanks to you!" she said. "You were supposed to be looking after our children and instead you've nearly killed one of them!" She snatched Toby from Connie, and handed him back to Dave.

"What are you talking about?" Connie gasped. "I did my best – I brought her straight here when I realised that she'd taken something."

"Taken what?" Sheila said.

Connie looked at her, not understanding.

The doctor turned to Connie. "We have just heard a very different account of what happened earlier tonight. These people are claiming to know nothing about the medication and are suggesting that anything found in the house was brought in by you." He looked back now to Sheila, Dave and Vanessa. "This has very serious implications for this girl's medical career – you know that, don't you?"

"I have never taken drugs of any kind," Connie said. "Anything Belinda took, she got from home."

"We know we had no tablets of that kind in our house," Vanessa stated. "You can check with our doctor. Neither Dave nor I have been recently prescribed any of those pills. How could we have got them without a prescription?"

Connie's eyes suddenly flamed. "You know where you got them from, Vanessa! You told me about the slimming tablets when we were in London, and you took pills that made you sleep all the way down there." She looked at Dave. "You know that too. I heard you arguing about them last night, when you threw the bottle with the tablets against the door in the bedroom."

Dave shifted his gaze from Connie to Vanessa, then he looked down at the floor. "I have absolutely no idea what you are talking about."

The doctor shrugged and walked towards the door. "The child

has been treated, so this is no longer a matter for the hospital. I should let you know that since I spoke to you earlier, the police have been informed and will be here shortly to interview everyone involved."

Chapter 43

Hours later, Connie found herself standing alone outside the police station in Stockport.

She had been briefly interviewed in the hospital, and then taken in a police car down to the station where she was interviewed again and asked to make a statement. She once again went over the events of the evening, and told the two officers everything that had happened. She did not waver in any detail from what she had already said, as she was telling the absolute truth.

She had not seen Vanessa or Dave since the hospital, but she had glimpsed Sheila out in the corridor of the police station, but she either did not see her or she deliberately ignored her.

It was only when the police officers asked her where they could find her the following day that she realised that her ordeal was far from over.

"Why do you need to see me again?"

The officers had looked at each other, then one said, "The parents are still giving statements. Later, we will be examining all the statements and doing any follow-up investigations necessary. We have officers out at the house on Silver Street at the moment."

"So we need a phone number or address where we can contact you tomorrow," the other said.

Connie didn't know what to tell them. She could not possibly have the police phoning her or coming out to her hall of residence. It would cause a huge drama and she might be asked to explain what was going on to the university authorities. She then thought of Sheila. That door, she realised, was firmly closed to her. From the way her mother's cousin had acted tonight, she believed the Hamiltons.

The police officer tapped his biro on the table. "Your contact details?"

Connie thought frantically. Then, as she came on the answer, she let out a little sigh of relief and an unexpected feeling of calm descended on her. The one place where she knew she would be safe, and more importantly, where she would be believed – was at Tara's.

As she walked towards Stockport Town Hall, she looked up at the clock. It was a quarter to twelve. It was late and Tara would probably be in bed. But, she knew that it didn't matter. She would understand. Tara was the sort of person who seemed to understand everything.

She walked farther along, and then she crossed the road to the phone box just outside the college on the A6. She needed to ring first to ask for the address of Tara's new house in Bramhall. She felt embarrassed having to do this, because it underlined the fact that she had been in Manchester all this time and had not been out to see the new house. She had not been out to visit her aunt or her little nephews. Once again, she realised how selfish and disinterested in her aunt and her family she must seem – and yet, how far from the truth that was.

As she opened the door of the phone box it gave a loud groaning creak, and when she stepped inside, her nose wrinkled at the awful smell. The ash-tray was overflowing and the floor was littered with more cigarette ends, chip wrappers and empty sweet packets. There was also a suspicious damp patch in the corner.

She dug into her bag, and then as she checked her notebook for Tara's number, a wave of anger suddenly hit her. She was in this awful, embarrassing situation with Tara due her mother's interference. Had she done as she wanted herself, she would have been in much more contact, and could have been out at Tara's house at weekends helping with her two lovely boys. She thought about the Hamiltons and Sheila Doyle and the nightmare she was now involved in – she would never have known them if it had not been for her mother's interference and her completely wrong judgement.

Her mother knew nothing about the Hamiltons and the life they lived. And, even worse, her mother knew nothing about Sheila Doyle – the person she had entrusted her daughter to. Sheila, most certainly, was not the person her mother thought her to be.

She found the number and then checked in her purse for the necessary coins, put them in the slot and started dialling. It rang and rang with no answer. Eventually it stopped and the line cut out. Connie pressed the button to have her unused money returned, and was grateful when the coins came back out again. She inserted the coins again and the phone gave one ring and then it was immediately answered.

"Hello, Tara? It's Connie … I'm so sorry ringing you this late at night. I would never do it normally, but I'm in the middle of a real emergency."

"It's me, Connie," the voice said. "It's William. Tara is in bed."

Connie went to speak, but a tight feeling had wound its way up from her chest to her throat and the words would not come out.

"Connie? Are you still there?"

She opened her hand and then hit it against her breastbone several times.

"Connie?" His voice was full of concern now. "Are you okay?"

She eventually found her voice. "No, William … I'm not okay. I'm in very serious trouble."

"Oh God," he said. "Can I do anything? Anything at all."

"I'm in Stockport now. Do you think it would be okay if I got a taxi out to Tara's?"

"Of course it would," he said. "I'll be waiting here for you."

Connie paid the taxi-driver and then went in the gate and up to the front door.

It was ajar and as soon as she opened it, William came out of a room and into the hallway.

"I was watching at the window for you," he said in a quiet tone.

Then he came towards her and put his arms around her. "Whatever is wrong," he said, "we'll do everything we can to help."

Connie found herself collapsing against him. She laid her head on his chest and for a few moments closed her eyes. Then, she felt him straighten up and move slightly away from her and she suddenly realised what she was doing.

"I'm so sorry," she said, her face burning now. "I'm just in a state and I'm not thinking right."

"No, *I'm* sorry!" He made a little face. "It's my ribs," he said. "They're still very tender."

She touched her hand to her head. "I'm so stupid," she said. "I hope I didn't hurt you?"

"I'm absolutely fine – I was only explaining why I moved away from you." He guided her into the front room.

In the midst of her misery Connie took a few seconds to register her surroundings. She recognised the leather sofa and the Italian mirror and other things that had been in Tara's previous house in Stockport and she found that their familiarity comforted her.

"Can I get you tea or coffee or anything?" he asked.

Before Connie could answer, the door opened and Tara came in wearing a dressing-gown. Her face was paler than normal and her red hair was tousled. When she saw Connie her eyebrows shot up.

"Connie! I didn't realise you were here … have you just arrived?"

"Oh Tara," Connie said, "I'm so sorry for wakening you – and for turning up at this hour of night, but I didn't know where else to go."

"What's wrong?"

Connie sank down into the chair. She joined her hands together as though praying. "I don't know where to start …"

It was an hour later when William came into the sitting-room with three mugs of tea and a plate of toast.

When they were seated around the fire Tara looked over at William. "Surely they can't get away with this?"

"Hopefully, the police will have spotted something that doesn't add up in the statements."

"From what Connie has told you, can you see any flaws in their story? Anything at all that could force the truth out of them?"

"Without seeing their statements it's hard to tell, but I'm sure at some point the truth has to come out."

"When I think about it all, I feel sick," Connie said. "I keep seeing poor little Belinda's face … imagining what would have happened if I hadn't called the ambulance. Imagining if I had just thought she was tired and put her to bed."

"That could have happened any time when you weren't there," Tara said. "And by the sounds of it, those parents would not even have noticed." Then she saw the look on Connie's face. "Thank God you did spot that there was something wrong. You might well have saved the child's life."

"I don't know if anyone else but you will look at it that way."

"Connie," Tara said, "I think you need to let your parents know."

"I can't think about that now." She shook her head. "I couldn't deal with my mother's reaction at the moment."

"Well, we'll leave it for tonight." Tara looked at Connie's weary face. "I think you need to go to bed soon," she said, her voice gentle. "You will have to be as fresh as possible in the morning." She stood up now. "I'm going to head upstairs now, because Leo will be up early. I'll leave you a spare nightie and a dressing-gown on the bed. You're in the second room on the right at the top of the stairs."

"Thank you," Connie said.

"I'll get up with Leo," William said.

"No, you've been up the last few mornings. I'm fine now. Hopefully, he might sleep on until eight or nine." She went over to Connie and embraced her. "I'm glad you came out to us, Connie, and we'll do everything we can to help you. Everyone will know you're innocent, so try not to worry."

Connie's eyes filled up. "Thank you," she said, kissing Tara on the cheek. "You and William have been so understanding – and knowing you believe me means everything. I'm just so sorry about the timing, when you have all the worry about Frank."

"That's life," Tara said, moving towards the door. "Thankfully, he's doing well. Last week we didn't know if he would even pull through."

When Tara went upstairs, William looked over at Connie. "I will do everything and anything to help you with this."

"That's really good of you."

"I owe you that and more."

"You don't owe me anything. We sorted it at the time."

"We didn't really sort it," he said. "But, if you will give me just a few minutes, I want to explain it to you now. I don't want this left between us like some kind of elephant in the room."

Connie lowered her eyes. She really didn't want to hear about the terrible mistake William had made with her, and how sorry he was for leading her on.

"I just wanted you to know that it's all sorted out between Pamela and me." His voice was now low and more serious. "There never really was a proper engagement."

He then went on to explain the situation about the pregnancy scare and him feeling he had to do the honourable thing by marrying Pamela, even though he didn't think they were well-matched, nor did he have the proper feelings for her. He described then about the pregnancy being a mistake, and how things suddenly escalated when Pamela assumed they would continue with their vague wedding plans.

"I am aware I do not come out well in this story," he said, shrugging. "I should never have slept with her. It was only on a few occasions and it didn't mean anything. But it was wrong, and there were consequences. Very serious consequences." He directed his gaze at her. "All I can say is that I have learned the biggest lesson in my life. I will never again be in a physical relationship with someone I don't love."

Connie stared at him, not knowing what to say. She knew from being at university less than a term that casual sex went on all the time. It always had with some people, she supposed, but now it was much more open. Babs, her university friend whom she liked and respected, had slept with three or four boys so far this term. She had been quite open about being on the pill and saying it was okay to have sex with someone if you fancied each other and were both free. She felt uncomfortable hearing William talking about it and didn't want to imagine him sleeping with another girl, but she knew it was normal enough to happen.

"Thankfully," he continued, "after stumbling through a series of calamities and disasters, the relationship is all over. It's finished."

"And how is Pamela?" she asked. "Is she very upset about it all?"

"I think she's got over it." He gave a wry smile. "According a friend from London she was in a London paper a few days ago, pictured passionately kissing the lead singer of the band she represents. They're on a European tour, and apparently they were a big hit in Paris where they were photographed." He shrugged. "I suppose that sort of thing goes on all the time on tours."

Connie moved her head up and down slowly, trying to take it all in.

"I've told Angela and Tara the full story," he said. "And I wanted you to know because it's something I should have told you in Ireland, but I just could not work out what was happening between us. It was so sudden and so unexpected. When I realised, I wanted to go straight back to London and sort it all out with Pamela, and then come to you with a clean slate. I planned to explain it all later."

"I wish you had told me at the time," she said. "I would have understood."

"But we might not have had those days together ... you might not have wanted to be with me." He sighed then threw his hands up. "You're perfectly right. It was not just my decision to make and I should have told you."

"I don't know what I would have thought ... or how I would have felt about it."

"I know exactly how I feel now. I haven't stopped thinking of you since I last saw you. Not for one hour in my waking day have I not had you in my mind, wishing I could undo all the damage that I did."

Connie's hand moved to her throat.

"I don't know if it's too late, or if all I have told you has given you an even worse view of me. But – for what it's worth – my feelings are deeper for you than I ever imagined possible. I'm pretty sure I love you, Connie."

Whether it was the warm, soft tone in his voice or the words he said, or whether it was the culmination of the night's events, but Connie suddenly started to cry. And not just tears – her shoulders started to gently shake and then it grew until her whole body was shuddering.

William rushed over to kneel beside her. He took his handkerchief from his pocket and pressed it into her hand. "It will all be okay," he said. "You did nothing wrong and you have nothing to be afraid of."

"What if the police don't believe me?" Connie's words were almost unintelligible. "What if I end up going to prison? My medical career ... my whole life will be ruined."

"It's not going to happen, Connie," he said. "I promise you, I won't let it happen."

Connie took a few deep breaths, trying to control herself, but again she dissolved into sobs. Eventually, she gave up trying – she leaned her tired and aching head on William's shoulder and cried until his shirt was saturated with her tears.

Chapter 44

The following morning, when Connie came downstairs quietly around eight o'clock, William was sitting at the kitchen table in jeans and a T-shirt, with sheets of paper spread around him.

When he saw her come in, he put his pen down and tidied the sheets into a pile. "Did you sleep okay?"

"Eventually," she said. "I was awake for a good while, but I did eventually fall asleep." She looked around. "Is Tara not down yet?"

"No," he said. "The boys must still be asleep." He moved from the table over to the kettle and switched it back on again. "I was just going to make a fresh pot of coffee, would you like some?"

"That would be great." She stood with her hands leaning on the back of one of the chairs.

"Toast?" he said. "There's a loaf of lovely brown soda bread that Bridget made." He moved down towards the toaster.

"No, I'll do it," Connie said. She turned around and they collided. "Oh, I'm sorry; I hope I didn't hurt your ribs again?"

"Not at all," he said, smiling at her. He stepped back. "You go on then, if you don't mind doing it."

She cut two thick slices and slid them in the toaster while William made the coffee. They sat down with their toast and coffee.

"You look busy," she said, gesturing to the pile of papers. "Is it for your law studies?" She lifted her mug and took a drink from her coffee.

"Sort of," he said. "I'm just working out some questions that we might need to ask if you're called back in today."

Connie looked alarmed. She had been trying her best not to think too deeply about it this morning. "Do you think they will? It's Sunday so I thought they might not work today."

"It depends, but I thought it would do no harm to start preparing." Then he leaned towards her, looking towards the door that led to the hall. "There's something I think I should tell you. Tara might not want you to know, but I'm terrified of keeping things from people any more. I'd rather be in trouble for saying the wrong thing than have it look as though I've lied, especially to you. I don't want any other misunderstandings between us – whatever happens."

Connie put down her coffee cup and reached out to fleetingly touch the back of his hand. "William, I don't care about anything like that at the moment, so you don't need to worry. I can't think about anything else apart from what has happened. I'm just hoping Belinda is back to her old self this morning."

"She is in the best place, and if the doctors thought she was recovering last night, then she should be much better today." He paused. "Look, what I was trying to tell you ... Tara has been in hospital this week and had a biopsy on a lump in her breast. She won't get the results for another few days."

"Oh, no!" Connie said. "I don't believe it. Not something else. This is just too much." She shook her head. "Poor Tara! She's really going through the mill with Frank and everything."

"It's awful," William said. "Thank goodness I was here when it all happened, and I've been able to help out a little."

"It's not been a lucky time for you either, has it? You're still recovering from the crash." She paused. "At least you were here to help. All I have done is turn up unannounced and land a huge problem on Tara. I should have been here at the weekends helping with the boys and being part of the family." She closed her eyes and sighed.

Then they heard noise and laughter and Noel and Leo came in, Tara following behind.

"I need to feed these two," she said, "but first, I need to tell you both something important that I've just discovered. I've been on the phone to Frank – I phone him first thing every morning – they have these mobile units that they bring to the bed. I told him all about Connie and the Hamiltons, and you're not going to believe it, but he knows them."

"How?" Connie asked.

"They did some work for him in the dance hall he used to own. Apparently they did curtains for the stage and organised chairs to be re-covered and that kind of thing. He was delighted with their work. Anyway, he had men working on a show house around June this year, for one of the big homebuilders, and they were asked to find an interior designer and Frank gave them the card for Hamiltons' Interiors. Apparently, a few things went wrong with measurements and the wife –"

"Vanessa," Connie interjected. "Vanessa and Dave."

"Apparently Vanessa threw a complete tantrum in front of the builders. She was shouting and screaming at her husband and, when she saw the men watching, she shouted and swore at them."

"I can just imagine it," Connie said. "That's the way they were carrying on that night."

"That's not all," Tara said. "Frank said there was a bit of a do for all the main people involved, when the show house was finished – cheese and wine, that sort of thing. He was there with the other contractors, and apparently Vanessa got drunk and ended up arguing with someone, and Dave had to take her home." Tara stopped to catch Leo as he toddled across the floor wanting to be lifted up. "The following day Dave rang the chap who had organised the party to apologise, and he said that Vanessa had a problem sleeping and had taken pills to give her a boost and they had clashed with the alcohol. He said he was worried about her as she was taking stuff to make her sleep then the next day taking different medication to keep her awake."

"That's exactly what she told me," Connie said. "The weekend we went to London, she took medication on the way down, and was in a sort of drunken state when we arrived and all her friends were teasing her about it. The way they were all talking, it's common knowledge that she has been taking it for a while."

William lifted his pen. "Do you know the names of the other friends?"

Connie told him.

"They might come in useful," he said. "Any witnesses we can get hold of that can state she has been using medication will help enormously."

"They will be like Sheila Doyle," Connie said. "They won't want to get involved." She paused. "But the main problem is the fact she's denying they were her pills. She is saying that she is not on any prescribed medications, that her doctor will verify that."

"Well, she must be getting the tablets from somewhere," said William.

Connie shrugged. "But how are we going to find where?"

"The information that Frank has given us is hopeful," William said. "We have something to go on now. We have something to tell the police that they can check up on."

"They won't admit anything," Connie said. "I had hoped Dave might tell the truth about their argument, but he just acted as though I was completely insane. And Sheila Doyle was the same. I can't believe that a relation of my mother – the person who organised the job for me – would refuse to believe me."

"Connie," Tara said, "I have a confession to make. I rang Angela and she is going out to let your parents know about this."

Connie felt her stomach lurch.

"I had to," Tara said. "It's the right thing to do. Angela has already rung the airport and there is a flight with spare seats on it over to Manchester at three o'clock this afternoon." When she saw the look on Connie's face, she said again, "It's the right thing to do."

Chapter 45

After breakfast, Tara put Leo in his playpen and William took Noel upstairs to supervise him showering, and to have a shower himself.

When they were on their own, Connie turned to Tara. "William told me about your hospital visit, and I just wanted you to know that I'm really sorry to hear you've had something more to worry about."

Tara looked at her solemnly. "It's the last thing I needed, but hopefully it will all be okay."

"Is it still painful ... where you had the biopsy?"

"No, not really. I just have to be careful when I'm in the bath or shower, or lifting the boys."

"I'm really sorry I've not seen much of you, or been of any help to you since I arrived. I wanted to spend time here – and being near you was one of the things that attracted me to university in Manchester – but this weekend job just took up every minute of my spare time."

"Don't even think about it," Tara said. "Student life is very busy, I know that. I didn't see much of William when he was studying."

"None of this would have happened if I'd been coming to you instead of going to the Hamiltons ..."

"Everything is great in hindsight, Connie. Stop blaming yourself, we all get into situations we didn't imagine." She paused for a few moments then she smiled. "You seem to be getting on well with William. Have you sorted out your differences?"

"I think so. He's been very kind and helpful."

"He is kind. I know he got things wrong over the summer, but I can tell you that he is one of the most decent young men I've ever met. He just handled that situation badly – very badly – but none of it was deliberate. He was so upset about it when he told me that he actually shed tears."

"I'm sorry to hear that," Connie said. "Last night he explained what happened. And I can see now how one thing going wrong led to another."

"We all make mistakes," Tara sighed. "Believe me, I've made my share of them. But the main thing is to learn from them, and William certainly has learned a lot from this." She looked at the clock. "Are you up to going to Mass this morning? There's one on at ten o'clock in Our Lady's in Shaw Heath if you want to drive down with me and the boys. We usually meet Bridget there with her crowd and then we go back to their house at Maple Terrace for a cup of tea."

"I'd love to," Connie said. "I'd like to see Bridget again – she's a lovely person. I don't get to Mass every weekend with working at Hamiltons'. They're not Catholics, so it's not always easy to drop things and go." Then she suddenly thought. "The only thing is, I don't actually have any clean clothes. My jeans are okay – they were fresh on yesterday – but I've worn all my tops and underwear."

"I'm sure I have something that will fit you."

"What about William?" Connie asked. "Will he go to Mass too?"

"I'm sure he will – he's always easy-going about anything we do. It might help to take our minds off everything for a short while. And anyway, I think we all have plenty to pray about today."

They all set off in Tara's car, William in the front passenger seat, smartly dressed in a dark suit and striped tie, and Connie, wearing a pale blue cashmere sweater, in the back seat alongside Noel and with Leo on her knee. Tara was dressed in a long beige suede coat with a charcoal-coloured sweater and smart grey trousers.

Connie felt a little better after being at Mass, and she enjoyed seeing Bridget and Fred and the children. Fred still had his arm in a sling, and since it was a mild day for the time of year, he and William went out into the garden with the younger children and the dog. Tara had told Connie and William that she wasn't going to tell Bridget about the problems with the Hamiltons just yet.

"You need a break from talking about it and explaining things," she said to Connie, "and it's difficult to talk at Bridget's because Michael and Helen are older and at Secondary School now, and you can't always shoo them away to talk about adult things."

Bridget had fussed about Connie, telling her how grown up she looked and admiring her lovely long hair. Then she had asked about her parents and Angela and Shay and Tessie, and they had a good laugh talking about Shay and his antics.

"Any idea when they're coming next?" Bridget asked. "Shay used to come regularly, but with one thing and another he's not made it over recently."

"They're actually thinking of coming over for Christmas," Tara said.

"That's great news," Bridget said.

Connie looked at Tara. "Oh, we'll miss them at home in Ireland."

"Yes, and they might stay on another few weeks after that until you're back at university, so you can show them all around it and where you are living."

"And I hear you're working in a very luxurious big house out in Wilmslow," Bridget said and winked over at Tara. "I can't believe it's even bigger than Kennedys' house in Bramhall!"

"I'm sure it is," Tara laughed.

Connie swallowed hard. "It's a beautiful house," she said. "Absolutely gorgeous."

Tara looked at the clock. "Oh, we'd better get a move on. I have things to do before going in to the hospital later."

"Give Frank our love," Bridget said, "and let me know when I can visit him."

"I will," Tara said. "We're hoping he can have more visitors from this week on."

When they arrived back at the house, Angela rang to confirm that Seán and Kate were on their way up to the airport. When Tara told her, Connie was very quiet about the news.

"I've offered them to stay here, or stay in a room in the Cale Green Hotel," Tara said.

"If you don't mind, I really would prefer them to be in the hotel," Connie said. "I don't think I could cope with my mother at the moment. When she finds out that William is here, God knows how she'll react. She will probably want me to go into the hotel too."

"We'll do whatever suits them," Tara said. "And the hotel might be the easiest option at a time like this."

William asked Tara if he could use the phone upstairs to make a quick call to Dublin.

Sitting by the phone, he took his notebook from his pocket, checked Malcolm's number and then dialled it. Over the last few months he had spoken with him on a number of occasions, mainly looking for a sympathetic ear and advice about the situation with Connie. He had a number of friends his own age he could have confided in, but he found himself turning to his old law lecturer. Even though Malcolm was a heavy drinker and had made mistakes in his own love life, William trusted his judgement.

Malcolm was the most intelligent person he knew, and he felt now that Connie desperately needed his impeccable legal knowledge and experience. Plus, if Malcolm didn't know a particular point of the law, he always knew someone else who did.

When Malcolm answered the phone, William was relieved to hear he was sober. He told him what had happened and gave him all the information that he had, then he answered any questions that Malcom asked.

Half an hour later, he came back downstairs and asked Tara if he could have a word with her in the front room.

When they came back out, Tara checked if Connie could look after the children for an hour or so, and she immediately agreed.

"We just need one thing," William said. "The directions to the Hamiltons' house."

Connie looked from one to the other. "But why are you going there?"

"I've spoken to Malcolm," he said, "and I explained everything as best as I could to him. He's advised me to go out to see them now, and give them a few pieces of information that might help to put you in the clear."

"I'm going to go with William," Tara said, "because I think it will add a bit of weight if there are two of us."

"And you certainly can't go, Connie," William said. "You can't be in contact with them or seen near them or anything like that for all sorts of legal reasons."

"Do you think it will make any difference?" Connie asked.

William shrugged. "I have no idea, but I'm certainly going to give it my best shot."

Connie looked at them. "Thank you," she said. "From the bottom of my heart. I am so grateful to have you both on my side."

Chapter 46

As they drove along Silver Street, Tara said, "Are you sure you know what you're doing, William? It's not too late to back out if you aren't sure."

"We have nothing to lose," he said.

"They might not even let us in."

"We'll never know unless we try. And we have no other option. This is already very serious for Connie – and there's every chance it might get worse." He paused. "Her whole career depends on this. Her whole future depends on it. I owe it to her to do the best I can."

They halted just outside the gates, double-checking they had the right house.

"This is it," Tara confirmed. She put her foot on the accelerator again and said, "Okay, Perry Mason, let's go!"

There were three cars in the driveway. Tara went around the fountain, and parked the car facing back towards the gate. They both got out and walked to the front door.

They rang the bell, and then they both stood waiting.

The door opened and Dave Hamilton came out. He looked at them with unsure eyes – the smart, professional young man and the striking, elegantly dressed woman. "Yes?" he said. "What can I do for you?"

"We would like to have a word with you regarding the incident at your home last night. We're representing Connie Devine."

Dave went to close the door, but William moved fast and stuck his foot in.

"We have information which you really need to hear." William's voice was loud and clear. "Your children's future could be at stake if you don't listen."

The door opened again. "What is it?" Dave asked.

"Can we come in, please? We can't discuss this on the doorstep."

Dave led them into the formal front room which was rarely used.

"I'm William Fitzgerald and this is Tara Kennedy."

Dave nodded. He did not sit down, nor did he ask them to sit.

"Is your wife around?" William asked. His voice was polite but firm. "It would be best if we saw you both together."

"I'm not sure she wants to talk to anyone about this."

"It would be in her best interests to listen to what we have to say."

Dave went out and closed the door after him.

"What do you think?" Tara whispered.

"It's good," William said. "He actually let us in."

A few minutes later the door opened and Dave came back in followed by Vanessa and a very wary-looking Sheila Doyle.

"Thank you for coming in," William said. He looked each of them in the eye. "Now, we can remain standing, or we can be civilised and sit down to talk this situation out."

"We know nothing about you," Vanessa said. "Why should we sit and listen to you?"

"Well," William said, "I'll give you a few good reasons. First of all, I'm a qualified lawyer so I know exactly what I'm talking about, and secondly I am going to advise you what to do if you don't want to lose your children to Social Services."

"*What!*" Vanessa shrieked. "How dare you say something like that in our own home!" She pointed to the door. "Right, you can get out now!"

"If you don't listen," William said in a calm voice, "I am taking the file I have with me straight to Stockport Police Station."

"And what's in the file?" Sheila asked.

William realised he had a slight edge. "I am going to sit down now," he said, moving backwards to sit in one of the armchairs. He motioned to Tara to sit on the sofa, which she immediately did. The other three remained standing.

"I believe that both of you are denying any knowledge of the medication that was found in your daughter's system."

"Absolutely," Vanessa said. "Those tablets were not in this house. They were brought in by someone else. And the only person that could possibly be is Connie Devine."

Tara sat up straight. "I've known Connie a long time," she said, "and she would never do such a thing." She looked at Vanessa and then Dave. "Why would she put her medical career at risk over something like this?"

"Why would these people put their business at risk?" Sheila asked. "Why would they put their children at risk? They have a lot more to lose than a student, who has easy access to drugs and pills of every kind. Everyone knows what they get up to."

"Not Connie," Tara said. "And if you know her family, you must know the kind of girl she is."

"Sure, I hardly know them at all," Sheila said. "Her mother just got in touch with me out of the blue, looking for work for Connie and I knew Vanessa needed some help."

Tara looked at her in amazement. "So you recommended a girl you didn't know to look after young children?" She looked over at Dave and Vanessa. "It doesn't sound like a good recommendation to me. Surely she told you that Connie was a good worker and from a decent family? You wouldn't leave your children with her otherwise."

"She did," Dave said, glaring at Sheila. "And up until this happened, we were very happy with Connie. The children loved her."

Sheila's mouth opened and then closed.

"And she loved your children," Tara said. "She is absolutely heart-broken about what happened to Belinda."

"Well, no thanks to her," Vanessa said. "Belinda has recovered. We brought her home this morning, and we have a lovely, sensible girl from one of the houses on Silver Street looking after her and Toby. They're out in the kitchen now, happily watching television with her."

"I'm really glad to hear she is fine," Tara said. "But I disagree with you. I think that it was all down to Connie's observation and quick thinking that she is well again."

William opened his file. "I have information here from a person who was present at the opening of a show house in Altrincham in June of this year. A person who witnessed Vanessa Hamilton in a very inebriated state. That person also states that he was told that Vanessa used both sedative medications and amphetamines."

"Rubbish!" Vanessa shouted. "Pure rubbish!"

"We also know that you were seen by a number of people in a similar state only a week ago in a hotel in London, and the following day you told Connie Devine that you used amphetamines to boost your energy and control your weight."

Tara sat in silent amazement at William's confident and professional manner. She had never seen this side of him before, and had imagined that she would have to bolster him up.

Vanessa shook her head. "More lies," she said. "It was the other way around. She told me that she had friends who could get her slimming tablets or any other sort of medication. She said the medical students could easily get them from the hospitals."

Sheila Doyle's head suddenly jerked, and again, for a moment she looked as though she was going to say something.

"That little bitch is making all this up to save her own neck and to ruin us," Vanessa said. "It won't work. She is the guilty one and any jury will see that."

"Do you really want this to go to court?" William said. "Do you really want to commit perjury in front of a judge?" He pointed his finger at Dave, then Vanessa then Sheila. "Believe me," he said, "you won't know what hit you if you have to face all the witnesses and evidence I will drag up against you." He held the file out to Dave. "This is just the start. I've only had a couple of hours talking with Connie this morning, and already I have a list of names and addresses. When I really start digging around I can assure you that I will come up with a lot more."

There was a silence now.

"You work in a hospital, Sheila, don't you?" Tara said. "I think Connie said you were a ward sister."

Sheila stared at her with cold eyes, but said nothing.

"And I believe we are both from Offaly," Tara said. "I'm originally from very near Tullamore."

Sheila sighed and rolled her eyes. "I'm not here to make small talk," she said. "I'm here to help these innocent people."

William swung back to Dave. "But you're not innocent, are you? None of you are innocent and you're prepared to see a young girl's life ruined to cover up the mistake you made." He shook his head. "It's a pity you won't see sense and just tell the truth. That you left medication about by mistake, and that you lied because you were afraid." He held his hands up. "Judges are people too, and they are very understanding of people who admit their mistakes." He paused. "But what they really don't like is people who commit perjury or people who try to implicate and blame others for their mistakes." He shook his head. "Perjury is a very, very serious crime." William left a silence grow now, letting the implications sink in.

Tara looked over at Sheila. "And taking medication from the drug cabinets at work is also a serious crime," she said quietly. "It might be something that the police haven't thought of."

"That's it!" Sheila said, turning towards the door. "I'm out of here. I'm not listening to any more of this nonsense. I only came to the hospital because Connie rang me and I was worried about the poor child, and now I'm being slandered and accused of things!"

"When the truth of this situation finally comes out," William said, "and make no mistake, it most certainly will, you will all be facing charges of slander. I will be advising Connie Devine to sue for defamation of character and anything else I can think of."

Dave's hand suddenly flew up in the air. "For God's sake!" he said. "Where is all this leading?"

"It all depends on how truthful and sensible you are."

"Think of your children," Tara said. "I have two little ones around the same age as yours. Nothing would part me from them. Are you going to put yourselves and your children through that nightmare?"

Dave's hands came to cover his face now. "No," he said. "That is not going to happen." He looked over at William. "What did you say would happen if we say we own up to making a mistake about the tablets? If we say we were afraid?"

"It's a far less serious crime – it's more domestic."

"Right, I'm going back down to the police station."

"*Dave!*" Vanessa shrieked. "*What the fuck are you saying?*"

"*Shut up!*" he told her. "*Shut up!* You've got us into this bloody mess."

"Dave," Sheila said. "Be very careful here …"

"No!" Dave said. "It's you two who need to be careful. I've had enough of your nonsense. All the uppers and downers – taking one to cancel the other out! It's madness. We nearly lost our lovely little daughter because of those fucking pills! The next time we might actually lose her or Toby. I'm not taking the risk. I'm going down to the police station to make a new statement."

Vanessa's hands flew to her mouth. "If you do this," she said, her voice shrill and almost hysterical, "if you blame me for all this, we're finished!"

"We can't go on like this," Dave said. "Lurching from one disaster to another. And we can't do this to Connie, we can't ruin her life. She genuinely cares for Toby and Belinda and you know it."

Tara felt a mixture of contempt for the couple and a surge of hope now for Connie's situation.

Vanessa stood, her body trembling. "I'm not taking all the blame for this."

"You need help, Vanessa," Dave said, "and this guy is right. The deeper we dig ourselves in, the more we'll have to answer for – and I am not prepared to lose my kids because of you and those fucking tablets you rely on."

"Thanks, Dave," Vanessa said. "If they didn't have enough ammunition already, you've given them it now."

"*Stop it!*" Sheila said, looking from one to the other, but neither seemed to hear her.

Dave prodded his finger to the side of his head. "You don't get this, do you, Vanessa? It's not sinking in. This is not just about you – it's the kids. Why couldn't you just be a normal working mother instead of trying to be Superwoman, and looking for false energy from bloody pills?"

"And would we have got this far without me having all this energy? We certainly wouldn't have everything we've got if we were depending on you."

"Stop it," Sheila said. "You've said far too much." She looked at Dave. "This is between you and Vanessa. Please don't implicate me any further." She halted, thinking for a few moments, and then she opened the door. "Dave, I need to talk to you privately."

Vanessa turned to grab Sheila's sleeve to pull her back in. "No, you don't! You're not getting into a huddle with him over me. Don't even think about it. You have things to lose as well if all this comes out."

"For God's sake," Sheila said, "this is insane." She stabbed a finger in William's direction. "Don't listen to that young fellow. He's hardly out of nappies himself. We know Connie brought the tablets into the house and that's an end to it. You two just need to fight your corner and stick by it."

William stood up now and gestured to Tara to do the same. "This is becoming a circular conversation," he said. "We are going to go and leave you to think about this. But don't take too long. I will just remind you of the seriousness of perjury and the risk of losing your children." He handed Dave a slip of paper. "Ring me on this number when you have seen sense. If I don't hear from you by five o'clock I will be making my way down to the police station with Connie to hand over all this information."

Chapter 47

Connie opened the door as William and Tara came up the steps. She looked at both their faces, trying to read what had happened.

"Well?" she said. "I'm frightened to ask."

William shrugged, then he gave a terse smile and held up his crossed fingers. "We'll know soon, one way or another. They're going to contact me."

"How was little Belinda?"

"We didn't see her, but they said she's fine," Tara said.

They went into the kitchen where the boys were playing, filling a truck with wooden blocks with alphabet letters on.

"Can I get you a tea or a coffee?" Connie said.

"A quick tea," Tara said. "Then we're going to the hospital to visit Frank. I'll drop the boys down to Bridget on the way there."

"I'll mind them," Connie said, going over to switch the recently boiled kettle back on. "It's the least I can do."

"Your parents will be here in under an hour," Tara said. "And you need time on your own to speak to them." She checked her watch. "Angela said they're getting a taxi out here from the airport."

Connie nodded. No doubt her mother said she didn't want anyone picking them up. She could almost hear her saying, 'We don't want to be beholden to anyone.'

Tara took her suede coat off and sat down at the table. "William was absolutely brilliant," she said. "He threw everything at them that he possibly could, while sitting there cool, calm and collected." She looked over at him and smiled. "Perry Mason couldn't have done any better."

"Thanks for the vote of confidence, Tara," he said, "I did my best, and I must admit at times there was a fair bit of acting involved. I chanced my arm on a number of things."

"Oh, God!" Connie caught her breath, imagining how Vanessa would react. "Are you allowed to do that? I hope you don't get into trouble."

William shrugged. "Legally, I probably shouldn't have gone anywhere near them, and I don't know if anything they admitted today would stand in court, but I shouldn't think any of them would know that."

Tara rolled her eyes. "I wouldn't be too sure about the older woman, Sheila."

"She was a hard case, wasn't she? I was pleased when you picked up on her having access to medication in work. I intended to bring that up myself."

Connie put the three mugs she was holding down on the worktop. "You don't think Sheila got the pills for Vanessa?"

"Nothing about her would surprise me," Tara said. "She was too quiet and watchful. My guess is she's more involved than she's letting on. And if anyone is going to hang onto their original story, it's going to be her."

There was a silence and they both stopped and looked over at Connie, who was now leaning on the worktop, silent tears streaming down her face.

"I liked her and I trusted her," she said, her voice breaking. "And at times I really liked Vanessa and Dave. I thought they were really kind and generous to me. I never imagined for a minute they would do something so horrendous to me. I am so stupid and naïve ... I trusted them all."

William went to move towards her, but Tara gestured to him and she went over instead. She put her arms around Connie and hugged her close. "You did all the right things, Connie, and you have to believe that what they did wasn't aimed personally at you. You just happened to be the person there. I'm sure in their own way they all liked you, but people like that will do and say anything to save their own necks. They would have accused anyone to save themselves."

"It's true," William said. "This is not about you – it's all about self-preservation."

Connie shook head. "But it's me who has been accused," she said. "It's my life and my career that they're trying to ruin."

Connie sat in Tara's front room on an armchair, with both her parents on the sofa opposite. She had told them the whole story and answered all their questions as best as she could. Unusually, it had been her father who had asked more questions, trying to understand the situation and all the implications it might have. Her mother had asked one or two questions, but on the whole had remained quiet. Since they had arrived, she had sat tight-faced and anxious, and had refused the offer of tea or anything to eat.

"I'm really sorry you've been dragged over here," Connie said. "I didn't want to worry you. I was going to wait until I knew what was happening, but Tara went ahead and contacted Angela. She said it was the right thing to do."

"Tara was right," Seán said. "And I'm glad she did get in touch. We couldn't let you go through all this on your own."

"I thought Tara might have had the decency to phone us herself," Kate said, "instead of dragging Angela into it. Letting everyone know all our business."

"Mam," Connie said, "she only asked Angela because she thought it was the kindest way to do it rather than you hearing it on the phone. And she probably knows you wouldn't want to talk to her anyway. When was the last time you phoned her? I don't think you even phoned when the boys were born. Have you bothered to phone to check how Frank is doing after his heart attack?"

Seán held his hands up. "I've told her time and time again, but you know she has a bee in her bonnet about them."

Her mother made a small clucking noise with her tongue and then gave a long, low sigh. "I dreaded the thoughts of you coming over here to Manchester ... I just knew something like this would happen if you got in with this crowd here. And I might have guessed that William Fitzgerald would make an appearance." She shook her head. "Have you no pride after what he did to you?"

Connie stood up, her eyes wide with rage now. "*Have you no idea at all?*" she almost shouted. "This nightmare I've been accused of has nothing to do with Tara and William. It was me who came to them for help. And, for your information, I haven't seen or heard anything from him since the summer!"

Kate looked down at the carpet now, her face white and rigid.

"I had nobody to turn to when this happened. I was literally outside the police station at midnight, on my own, being accused of almost killing a child. And the one person I knew who would help was Tara. And in the midst of worrying about her very sick husband, she dropped everything she could to help me."

"Oh, she would be delighted to help you out," Kate said. "No doubt she was waiting on the phone call from you, thinking that the Devines couldn't make a go of anything as well as she would." She shook her head. "Tara always has to be the big 'I am', she had to be the top dog in everything, the one that helps everyone else. She would just be waiting for you to fall flat on your face."

"What are you talking about?" Seán gasped. "Do you hear yourself?"

"No, Daddy," Connie said. "She doesn't hear herself. She doesn't hear what anyone else says either. She never has."

Kate looked at Connie then her husband. "Are you going to let her talk to me like this?"

Seán turned his head away. "You need to listen to her, Kate."

"Daddy's right," Connie said. "The last thing any of us need now is to fall out, but you really need to listen to me. Tara and William have nothing whatsoever to do with this. They are the ones who have done everything to help me."

Connie saw her mother's face tighten at the mention of their names, but she was determined to continue. "This whole situation started when you introduced me to Sheila Doyle, and then she introduced me to the Hamiltons. It's those people you need to direct your anger and vicious tongue at. From what I've been told today, it looks like your cousin had been supplying drugs to Vanessa Hamilton. And when I rang Sheila for help last night with the poor child, as soon as she realised the situation, she went straight to them to warn them, and completely turned her back on me. Sheila Doyle is a liar and a nasty piece of work – she is not the woman you thought she was."

"And how was I to know that? I was only told she had a great job, and was well thought of." Her mother's voice had an uncertain note in it now. "I thought I was doing good, getting you a well-paid weekend job in a lovely house."

"I could have had it here with Tara, Mam! I could have been staying here and feeling looked after with this lovely family. Tara wrote to you offering me a job."

Kate's face flushed. "Well, I never got it, and I thought I was doing the best I could. I thought it would be better for you to be independent – not to be beholden to anyone."

"But it wasn't just anyone – it was Tara. It was Daddy's sister."

Her mother's hands flew up. "Tara, Tara, Tara! That's all we've ever hear. Tara, bloody Tara!"

Seán whirled around. "Kate, for God's sake! Will you calm down?"

If Kate heard him, she did not register it. "Can nobody else do anything without Tara being involved?" Her eyes were now wide and bulging and the little veins in her neck were pulsing. "Could you not have gone to university in Dublin and become a doctor without her bloody help? Do she and her rich husband always have to be the ones to dole out favours and money to everyone? And Angela is becoming just as bad since she got the hotel. Do me and your father and people like us not count? Can we not do things too?"

Connie shrank back, as though physically retreating from her mother's onslaught. All the years of pent-up anger had just shot out of her – like bullets in a random attack.

Her father got to his feet and went to the door. "That's it," he said. "I'm going. We've had enough. I can't believe all the terrible things you've just said about Tara and the family. You sound like a demented woman. This is all in your head, and I should have told you that years ago!"

There was an awful silence and then Kate Devine's shoulders suddenly slumped and she fell over onto the empty part of the sofa where her husband had been sitting. Her hands came up to her eyes, and then there came a low moaning sound which grew into racking sobs.

Connie went to move towards her, but Seán held up a warning hand, shook his head and mouthed, 'Leave her be'. After what seemed like an age later, the sobbing subsided and Seán went across the floor to her with a hanky.

Connie moved silently out of the room to make tea. Kate lay for a while longer, and then she eventually sat up.

Seán sat down beside her. "Are you all right?" he asked, putting his arm around her.

She moved her head up and down without speaking. There was silence for a few minutes then Kate straightened up and turned to look at her husband.

"No, Seán, I'm not all right."

Seán met her eyes.

"I need to tell you something that has bothered me for years – something I've never really told anyone. It's going to sound childish and stupid, but I think it might be the root of all this business with Tara."

"Did she do or say something wrong to you?"

"No," Kate sighed. "She never did anything wrong. It's the fact that from the very first day I met her at Shay and Tessie's I realised that she could do anything she liked and no one would question her. She came from a family that was poorer than mine, and yet no one would ever say she wasn't good enough – whether it was marrying into one of the top families in the area or buying her own hotel. Even when she was widowed, she went on to be one of the owners of an even bigger hotel, and then married another wealthy man. But not even once did anyone tell Tara she wasn't good enough for any of these things to happen to her."

Seán's frown deepened. "I don't understand ..."

"I wanted to be a doctor," Kate said. "And I was clever enough. I had good enough marks in my exams to probably get a university scholarship."

There was a small silence.

"You never told me that ..."

"I never told anyone apart from a teacher I trusted in school. A teacher who had always encouraged me. Do you know what she said to me? She told me that I was aiming far too high for someone from my background. She said if I went for an interview for medical school the first thing they would ask would be who in my family before me was a doctor. Was my father a doctor or even my grandfather? She asked me if I wanted to put myself through all that, just to be rejected at the end. She told me it was better to know your place in life and you would never be disappointed. She then got me forms to fill in to be a nurse." She shrugged. "So that's what I became – a nurse instead of a doctor."

Sean nodded his head slowly. "I suppose that's how they were back then. If it wasn't the teachers it was the priests."

Kate wiped away a tear at the corner of her eyes. "But it was never like that for Tara – was it? She went straight ahead and did everything she wanted, and everyone in the family – yourself included – just smiled and said, 'That's Tara for you. She does anything she wants.' She was always the most beautiful, well-dressed girl in the town. She was always the best. And no matter how hard I, or any other girl tried, none of us could ever hold a candle to her." She looked up at him now. "Have you any idea what it feels like to never be good enough?"

"But that's not true, Kate," Seán said, his voice softer now. "You've always been the best girl for me. Surely you know that?"

Kate shrugged and shook her head. "I've never felt the best at anything. The only thing I felt proud of was that I was able to give Connie the chance that I never had. That I was able to use the money from my Uncle Arthur's farm to pay for her, without having to rely on help from Tara or anyone else."

"You've done a lot of things that have made me proud," Seán said. "You've been a good nurse and been well-recognised in the town for it. The number of people that have said it to me. How often have I told you that?"

She attempted a weak smile.

Seán paused for a few moments. "I've never given it any thought before, but I think it might have been easier to get into Tara's line of work – commerce and the like – than it would be to get into the medical or law professions. I think you've been hard on yourself. Tara wouldn't have found an easy way into that either. I don't think we're comparing the same things here."

Kate bit her lip, thinking. "Maybe not … but that's how it seemed to me. Tara always seemed to get everything easy."

"Well, if you asked her," Seán said, "you might be surprised about how she thinks life has treated her. Other peoples' lives often look rosier from the outside."

A few minutes later Connie came back in with the tray with cups of tea and a jar of mixed biscuits. She handed them around and then she looked over at her mother.

"I'm sorry you feel so bad about everything," she said, "and I'm sorry you feel so let down about me not going to university in Dublin, but I did my very best."

"We know all that, Connie," her father said. "You've always done your best."

"I need my mother to hear this," she said. "The thing is, I'm nineteen years old – I'm a grown woman now – and I can't keep feeling that I've disappointed you. I can't carry it any more. I know in my heart and soul I've done well compared to a lot of people. I'm proud and grateful that I've got the chance to study medicine – to become a doctor. I know it's a real achievement."

"Of course it is …" Her mother's voice was low and trembling.

"And I'm grateful for the chance you and Daddy are giving me, for the money it's costing you to send me there. I know all that. But, if it's going to cause all this upset, I'll walk away from it now."

Kate's head jerked up. "What do you mean?"

"I'd rather work and earn my own money and be completely independent, than take anything more from you. I'd rather work in a flower shop or a restaurant or anything, rather than have this feeling hanging over my head. It wouldn't be the same as doing the job I've dreamed of, but at least I would have peace of mind. I wouldn't feel I owed you anything."

"You're our daughter," Kate said. "We want to do it for you."

"Yes," Connie said, "but on your terms. You always make me feel that anything I do is never good enough. That *I've* never been good enough."

Kate closed her eyes. "That's the last thing I want you to feel, Connie. Surely I've never made you think that?"

"At times I do feel like that."

"Well, I'm heartily sorry for it if I did. I never meant to."

"I need to live my own life and make my own decisions," Connie went on. "And I'm sorry, Mam, but after the decisions you made about Sheila Doyle, and the way you refused to listen to anyone else, I think I'd rather go by my own instincts in future. How you could have chosen someone like Sheila Doyle over a good and kind and decent person like Tara, I will never understand."

"We all make mistakes ..."

"Well, you have made a huge mistake about Tara," Connie said. "I think she guessed you didn't want me to have anything to do with her, and yet she has not said one wrong word about you or asked me to explain anything. She came with Frank and the boys to see me when I arrived, and told me if I ever needed anything to ring her at any time and they would be there. Since then, she has never once interfered, she has let me get on with my life without feeling slighted or ignored or anything like that."

"She's always been decent," Seán said. "And so is Frank."

"I want you to think about all I've said, Mam," Connie said now, "because what happens when she comes back is going to determine how you and I get on in the future. Tara is not the overbearing, selfish, vain person you just described. She is kind, caring and only wants the best for everyone. She has never said a wrong word about you or any of the family." Her chest felt tight now and she paused to catch her breath. "In the midst of everything, she has done her best to help me with this situation. If I end up going to jail or anything like that because of Sheila Doyle's lies, the one person I know I can depend on will be Tara. She went out to see those people with William this afternoon even though she has all the worry with Frank, and she's waiting to find out if she has breast cancer. She had an operation on her breast just a few days ago to remove a lump."

"Oh, my God," Seán said, "the poor woman! And her landed with all this trouble now too!"

"I'm sorry to hear that," Kate said. "I genuinely am."

"Tara is just an ordinary person, Mam. She has the same ups and downs as the rest of us. Things don't fall in her lap the way you think they do. She has worked hard for everything she has. She told me this morning that they've gone through a tough time recently with Frank's business, and now he's had a heart attack I'd say that will affect his work too. But she's not all bitter and angry about it."

Seán nodded. "She'll just quietly get on with things, the way she always did," he said. "And she's had a lot of sorrows over the years, losing that lovely chap Gabriel – and then her brother Joe through that awful accident." He shook his head. "He was the finest man and the finest priest you ever met. She's never really got over all of that."

Connie looked at her mother. "Have you ever thought of how she must feel at times, Mam? Do you really think that all she wants to do is lord it over everyone? Do you not think that she might just have wanted to be nice to all the family she has left? That she just wanted to help if she could?" She sighed. "Just watch her when she comes in, Mam, and listen to what she says. You won't find any of those things that you've imagined about her. She really is just a nice, kind ordinary person."

Kate sat in silence, her cup between her hands. Eventually, she said, "I've never thought of it that way. She just seemed so confident ... as though she needed nobody."

"I think she needed me here this week," Connie said, "but I was so wrapped up with my own life I didn't realise it either until I needed her." She thought for a moment, and then she decided to take a chance. "While we're talking about needing people, I'm just making it plain once and for all: I've had no contact at all with William until now – he was here helping Tara. He was actually in the car with Frank when the accident happened as you probably heard. Well, he's been absolutely fantastic with all of this – I couldn't have asked for a better friend. As I said, he and Tara have been out to the Hamiltons' house earlier on – they're doing everything they can to help."

"Thank God for them," her father said. "And William is a solicitor, so he'll know what he's doing. What we're up against."

"He was on the phone this morning to the law lecturer from Trinity for advice." She looked over at her mother. "And all that engagement business – it wasn't what it seemed. It should never have happened and he was planning to go straight to London to sort it all out."

Kate looked over at her. "That's his own business – we don't need to know anything about it."

"Well, I think you do after what happened back in Tullamore.

He has explained it all to me, and I'm satisfied that he wasn't trying to deceive me or lead me on. He just handled it all wrongly. He knew even before we met up again that he and the other girl weren't right for each other. And after meeting me, he knew he had to end it." She paused. "I know you're not going to be happy, but after all this time I still have feelings for him."

Her father looked at her. "And what about him?"

"He's already told me he loves me, and I believe him."

"Well, you won't get any interference from me," her father said. "I've always thought he was a decent young chap."

"I don't know what's going to happen to us with all this police business and everything," Connie said. "If the Hamiltons keep lying I could end up with no career and I might even be put into prison ..." She stopped now, tears beginning to choke her. She closed her eyes and wiped the back of her hand over her face. She was exhausted, completely drained.

There was a few moment's silence and then, unbelievably, she felt her mother's hand come to touch her cheek and then move around her to hold her tightly.

"I'm sorry, Connie," she whispered. "I'm sorry for everything that has happened to you ... and I'm sorry for anything I've done to hurt you ... all that business with Sheila Doyle." She kissed Connie on the neck and on the side of her damp face, tears streaming down her own face now. "I'm not very good with words ... but I've listened to what you've said. I know you and your father are right, and I've done things all wrong. I'll do anything and everything to make it up to you, and I'll make it right with Tara. One day, when we've time, I'll try and explain how I came to feel like that. It was all wrong, and silly of me. All I can say is that you won't need to worry about anything like that ever again."

Connie cried in her mother's arms – something she hadn't done for years – sorry for herself and sorry that she had to be so hard on her mother. But she knew it had to be done. She had to hold the mirror up to her mother's hurtful tongue and behaviour before someone else was forced to. Kate wasn't a bad person, but she had got into a wrong, almost warped way of thinking. Hopefully, if she could now see people in a better light it would be one less thing to worry about in the uncertain hours and days that lay ahead.

Chapter 48

Connie had just made a fresh pot of tea and her mother was rinsing the cups out in the sink when Tara and William and the children arrived back from the hospital.

"Just in time," Tara said, smiling. She went over to Kate and gave her a hug. "It's lovely to see you, but I'm so sorry about the circumstances."

"Thank you," Kate said, her eyes suddenly filling with tears.

Tara then went to give her stepbrother a kiss on the cheek and a hug.

William shook Seán's hand and then moved in Kate's direction, suddenly unsure.

Kate put her hand out and he shook it and they both sort of nodded and acknowledged each other without actually speaking.

"Any news?" William asked. "Any phone calls?"

Connie shook her head. "Nothing ..."

Seán asked about Frank and Tara then recounted the story of the crash and his subsequent heart attack. They talked about how he was recovering and all the changes that would have to be made.

"I don't want him going back to work until he is one hundred per cent recovered," Tara said. "And I don't care if we have to sell up the hotel, the house or anything we have, or if I have to go back to work myself. Whatever happens, Frank's health comes first, and he won't be working unless he's able for it." She attempted to smile. "We have two little boys who need their daddy around for a good number of years, so he's got to put them before work."

"You're right, Tara," Kate said. "But please God he'll be fit and able."

They all sat down at the table with tea and a pot of coffee that William had made.

There was a small awkward silence and then, as if she had just noticed it, Tara started. "You probably know everything by now?" she said. "It's a terrible situation for poor Connie, but nobody in their right mind could believe that she would be capable of doing anything like that. Nobody at all."

"I can't believe that Sheila Doyle has got involved with people like that," Kate said. "She sounds like she's turned out to be a strange one. Her family would be mortified at all this. They're highly thought of in Tullamore."

"She's been away from them a long time," Connie said, trying to divert her mother away from the small-town angle. "Unless they keep in close touch they won't know what her life is really like."

"I wonder if that business with the boyfriend jilting her all those years ago had a bad effect on her?" Kate said. "It can happen to some people."

Connie took a deep breath and was just about to cut her mother off again, when Tara suddenly reached across the table and grabbed her arm.

"I was just going to tell you," she said. "I thought I recognised her, but I just wasn't sure. Anyway, I mentioned her to Frank." She smiled and rolled her eyes. "He must know all the Irish people in Stockport and Manchester. You're not going to believe it but it seems that Sheila Doyle goes into the Grosvenor fairly regularly, and she is always with the same man."

"Sheila Doyle has a man?" Kate said, surprised.

"Yes," Tara said. "And it's the man that Frank actually knows, because he works in one of the local banks. And Frank also knows that he's married. Frank got chatting to him one night, and he was quite open about it all." She shook her head. "They say that women are gossips, but I wouldn't be too sure of that – the men can be quite open with each other at times. Of course, in normal circumstances Frank wouldn't bother repeating any of these bar chats to me as he forgets them as soon as he's heard them. But he remembered it all when I said her name and described her. Apparently this bank manager and Sheila have known each other for years. They were actually engaged when they were both living in London, and she moved up here to be with him, and then he met someone else."

Kate clicked her fingers and smiled. "That's all true," she confirmed. "Her own mother told me."

"Well, whether it's true or not, it seems that he and his wife have some sort of weird arrangement. They live together and everything, but at the weekends they go their separate ways. Apparently she has a fellow out in Buxton, and he sees Sheila."

Kate looked appalled. "The dirty things! They should be ashamed of themselves. Her poor old mother would die if she knew."

"Well, we know now that she's done worse things than that," Seán said. "What she does in her private life is up to herself, but what she's trying to do to Connie is very serious."

The phone rang and Connie froze. Tara and William got up and went out into the hallway. They were gone for a few minutes and then they came back in.

William looked over at Connie, his face serious. Then suddenly a beaming smile broke out.

"It's over," he said. "They've caved in! They're going down to make a new statement which will completely remove any question of you being involved."

"What are they going to say?" Connie asked breathlessly.

William shrugged. "It's not your problem anymore. It's between them and the police. After seeing them earlier on, I wouldn't be surprised if they land themselves in more trouble by arguing and blaming each other. I spoke to the husband and he's already trying to blame Sheila Doyle for getting the tablets from the hospital. It sounds as though they're turning on her now."

"Good enough for her," Kate said. "She deserves all she gets."

"I don't know how you've done it," Connie said. "Last night it looked as though the police were sure it was me. It looked as though their stories were all watertight, and that I was the obvious suspect. How did you manage to turn it around so quickly? What did you say or do that made them admit it all?"

"I took Malcolm's advice," he said, smiling. "I rang him this morning and he gave me advice on anything I was unsure of, and told me to get out to the Hamiltons with any evidence I could scrape up against them. Then he gave me the most important piece of advice that he knew."

Everyone looked at him.

"Well?" Tara said. "What was it?"

He paused for a few moments for effect. "Bluff it!"

Connie wrinkled her brow. "What?"

"Bluff it," he repeated. "He said it's like playing a hand at cards. If you have an idea of what the other person has and you hold your nerve and just bluff your way – they will often give in." He wiped his hand across his brow and said, "*Whew!* Thank God for dear old Malcolm and his unorthodox advice."

Connie rose from her chair and went over to Tara and hugged her. "Thank you for everything – you have literally saved me."

Tara hugged her back. "Aren't we family?" she said. "We're supposed to look out for each other and help each other, and that's all I did."

Then Connie moved over to William, conscious that everyone's eyes would be on them. She put her arms around his neck.

"I don't know where to begin to thank you ..."

He laughed and rolled his eyes. "I suppose a kiss would do," he said. And then, to lighten things, he added, "You can buy me a new car after that."

Connie stood on tip-toe and gave him a light kiss on the lips. But, as she drew back, her eyes looked deep into his and then she smiled and nodded. She didn't have to speak: he knew exactly what she meant.

Chapter 49

On Wednesday afternoon, Tara drove along Shaw Heath and then turned down Maple Terrace. She got out of the car, straightened her brown suit jacket and adjusted her hair. Then, as she had done hundreds of times over the last twenty-odd years, she walked up the steps to her old friend's house.

Bridget opened the door, then turned back inside quickly, avoiding Tara's eyes. "How was Frank?" she asked over her shoulder as she walked down the hallway to the kitchen. "Was he as good as last night? Me and Frank thought he looked great."

"He is," Tara said, "and it's all good news – he's getting out on Friday."

Bridget whirled back and wrapped her arms around Tara. "Thank God," she said. "Thank God. All our prayers have been answered."

Tara hugged her and then they walked down the hallway and into the kitchen.

Bridget went into the fridge for milk and then reached for a small saucepan. "I'm making us a nice coffee with boiled milk."

"Lovely." Tara pulled one of the chairs out at the table and sat down. She looked up and saw Bridget staring at her with anxious eyes.

"It's okay," she said. "It's not cancer."

Bridget continued to look at her as though she hadn't spoken. Eventually she said, "Are you sure?"

Tara nodded. "I'm sure. It's some sort of growth that can be caused by hormones. I don't really understand it, but all I know is that it is not cancerous. They are going to keep an eye on me for a while. A check-up every six months, and if everything is okay, then hopefully there won't be anything further."

Bridget leaned back against the cooker. "I didn't sleep a wink last night worrying ... I kept thinking of –"

Tara interrupted. "Ruby?"

Bridget nodded, her eyes brimming with tears. Ruby had been their old landlady – the original owner of Maple Terrace. When Tara and Bridget first arrived in Stockport she had taken them in and looked after them. Tara had gone on to be more independent, while Bridget had remained under Ruby's wing. Ruby was like a mother-figure. Then, just as life was going well for her, Bridget had to watch her old friend go downhill and eventually die of breast cancer. The thought of it happening to Tara – her dearest and oldest friend – had filled her with the utmost dread.

"I knew you would think of her," Tara said, "and I'm so sorry that it brought it all back to you."

"I'm just so grateful," Bridget said. She gave a watery smile. "With all the bad luck we've had recently, Frank and the crash and everything – I was terrified this was going to just top it all."

Tara gave a huge sigh. "No, Bridget," she said. "Not this time. Thank God it all seems to be settling down again. We have yet another reprieve."

"How are things with Connie and William and everyone?"

"Connie went back to university yesterday, and thankfully no one will be any the wiser about the near-disaster. She only missed two days, so it's not a problem. Her father and mother went with her to see her room and to look around the university, and they took her into Manchester for a meal last night. They booked into a hotel in the airport last night as they were flying out on the eleven o'clock flight this morning."

"I bet they're relieved. What a thing for them all to go through. Does Connie wish she had never told them? It was such a huge thing when it happened, and then it was all over nearly as quick."

"I think it was the right thing for them to come over," Tara said. "Connie and her mother hadn't been getting on too well. I'm not exactly sure what it was all about, but it gave them a chance to sort things out. And Kate and Seán seemed okay with William. In fact, they came up to the house again on Monday and we all had dinner together and everyone seemed to be getting on well."

Bridget clapped her hands together. "Go on – the best bit! What's happening with them? Connie and William?"

Tara started to laugh. "I think you need to check your milk before I say any more – it's beginning to boil over!"

"Oh, bugger!" Bridget said, rushing to move it off the flame. She came back to stand at the table, waiting.

"He's staying until Frank gets out of hospital, just to help with Noel and Leo. He will probably go back to London at the weekend."

Bridget held her hands up in exasperation. "And is that it? He's gone to London and she's back in Manchester?"

"He's coming back again the following weekend," Tara said. "He has a new interview with the same law firm, the one he missed with the accident. He spoke to them on the phone and everything seems fine – the interview's probably only a formality."

"So what does it mean?"

"It means that after Christmas he's going to be here full-time for a year. He'll stay with us for a while and then see how he gets on."

Bridget shrugged. "And what about him and Connie?"

"Oh, I'll put you out of your misery," Tara said, rolling her eyes. "They're back together again, and everything is going fine for them. You can just see looking at them that they're mad about each other. They're really suited."

"I knew it!" Bridget said, turning to attend to the coffees. "That will be another wedding for us."

"Not for a while," Tara said. "I think they're happy to be back together again, and I'm sure the time will fly in with Connie's studies and them travelling backwards and forwards to London and Ireland."

Bridget lifted her tea-towel and made a little flicking movement with her hand. "They'll have a high old time, the lucky devils. Oh, to be young and carefree again! Wouldn't it be great?"

Tara looked at her. "Were we ever really that? I'm not sure I would like to go back to when we were younger. When you look back and think of all we've been through ..."

Bridget looked thoughtful. "We've had lots of good times over the years, but I suppose we have had plenty of bad ones as well."

Tara looked thoughtful. "But look at us now – we started out as young girls with no mothers – and not a lot of hope for the future. We both have good men, and we've both been blessed with wonderful children. It's something I never thought would happen."

"You're right," Bridget said. "And there are plenty of women like Ruby who weren't as lucky." She turned now to pour the hot milk into the two mugs and stir in the coffee, and then she brought them back to the table. "Do you know what I think?"

Tara looked at her.

"I think that we've made the best of everything that life has thrown at us. I think we've gone with the ups and downs and we've somehow survived. We've achieved a lot – and the most important thing: we've had a lot of good laughs along the way."

Tara looked at her and smiled. "We have, haven't we?"

Bridget held her mug up in a toast. "To the survivors – and to all the laughs that are still to come!"

Epilogue

Tullamore, County Offaly

December

"Last one!" Connie said, lifting the display of white roses and gypsophila onto the counter.

"Thank God," Eileen said. "We were busy enough with the wedding tomorrow and then to get orders in for a big funeral as well! It was the last thing I expected, but I suppose people can't help when they die!" She smiled over at Connie. "I'm just delighted you were free to come in and help me and Frances yesterday and again this morning. We'd never have managed it so easily without you. It was good of you. I know you only have a week left at home. Who would believe Christmas has been and gone for another year?"

"I'm happy I was here to help," Connie said, taking her green apron off over her head. "I love doing the flowers. I've learned a lot working here."

"You'll be doing an even better job when you become a doctor," Eileen said.

"Well, I've a long way to go," Connie laughed. "I could still be back here looking for a full-time job if I don't keep up with all the studying."

Eileen's face became serious. "Make sure you do keep up. There are not too many girls able for studying medicine. I hope you're not letting the new romance get in the way of things?"

"Not at all," Connie said. "William makes sure I keep my nose stuck in the books. Besides, he's still studying himself."

"You make a great couple," Eileen said. She took her own apron off now. "Right, it's after one o'clock and I'm driving you out to the hotel in Ballygrace now. Frances will keep an eye on the shop, and I'll be back in plenty of time to help her put the flowers in the van."

"That's good of you," Connie said. She untied the green-velvet ribbon in her hair, and let the dark curls tumble down her back. Then she went to the back of the shop to get her coat and the bag with her fresh outfit.

Connie had just settled into the front seat of the car when Eileen passed an envelope to her. "That's for the work you did for the last few days and a bit extra to treat yourself in the January sales. They're supposed to be very good over in England."

"Oh, there's no need!" Connie protested.

"It's good to give and it's good to get," Eileen said. "Never forget that. And another little piece of advice – keep both legs in the same stocking until you have a ring on your finger. Or if you can't do that, make sure you get on the pill. It's easily available now in England, and it's my opinion it should be available here as well."

Connie's mouth opened wide in astonishment. Eileen had never said such a personal thing to her before.

Eileen raised her eyebrows and then started to laugh. "Lawyer or not, he's flesh and blood like the rest of them. Isn't he?"

Connie looked out the window of Angela's sitting-room at the falling snow, then she checked her watch once again.

"Relax," Angela told her, taking a sip from her coffee. "They'll be here soon enough."

Connie nodded and tucked one side of her long dark hair behind her ear. "He said they would probably leave Dublin around twelve o'clock to make it here for lunch. It's almost two now. I was just thinking of that winding road down – it's bound to be bad with ice and snow."

"William is a good driver – he'll be absolutely fine. The roads are probably busier in Dublin, as a lot of people take the week off between Christmas and New Year to go visiting family and friends."

"True," Connie said. She held her cup between her hands, trying not to look as anxious as she felt. "I'm just hoping that everything is okay with Malcolm." She made a little face. "I've told you what he's like. He's the loveliest man, but he's not very dependable. I hope he's not been up drinking half the night with his lodgers or anything like that. He could even have had a drink before he left, and William might have found it hard to get him moving."

"When William rang me yesterday," Angela said, "he told me that they were going out for a meal and a few quiet drinks last night. He said they were going to be looking at the work he'll be doing with the new law firm in Manchester in January. He will have kept an eye on Malcolm, and made sure he didn't go mad last night when he knew they were coming down here for a few days."

Connie gave a wry smile. "Well, let's hope so. Malcolm can be a law unto himself, although he is very kind and entertaining company. It was really good of you to suggest that William bring him down with him for a couple of days."

"When you've grown up with father like Shay Flynn," Angela said, "nobody else seems too daunting. Besides, when I heard the poor man had been on his own in Dublin for Christmas, what else would I do? Nobody should be on their own over Christmas, and it's nice for him to spend a bit of time with William. It's no bother for us as we have the two spare rooms, and they can go over to the hotel for breakfast and their meals."

"You're very kind." Connie looked at her watch again. "I don't want to keep you and Aiden waiting much longer for lunch ..."

"Nobody is in a rush – it's only an ordinary Saturday afternoon lunch. The staff who are on in the kitchen know that there are five of us going in for lunch. Most of the guests have gone to a wedding in Athlone, so it's fairly quiet, and Aiden is only too delighted to have an excuse to be over in the bar having a drink while he's waiting."

"It's great that I could come out here for William arriving," Connie said. "I felt it would be a bit awkward if they turned up at our house first. At least I'll have seen him this afternoon and tonight and I'll be more relaxed by tomorrow afternoon."

"Your mother is fine about him now," Angela said. "Believe me, mammies don't ask people to come for Sunday dinner unless they are sure about them."

Footsteps sounded in the hall and then Clare and four-year-old David came running in.

"There's enough snow now, so can we go outside and build a snowman and throw snowballs?" Clare asked.

Angela raised her eyebrows. "Did you both finish your lunches?"

"Yes," David said. "We ate all our sandwiches up." He tugged Clare's hand. "Didn't we?" He looked back at his mother. "Ella said she would tell you how good we were."

Clare nodded, her eyes dancing with excitement. "Can we go outside now, Mam?"

Angela smiled at them. "Coats and boots and gloves on, then you can go."

They squealed in delight and then ran back out into the hallway to get their outdoor clothing. Angela and Connie turned to watch them out of the bay window, as they ran out into the drive and then over to the lawn which was now a carpet of white.

"You are so lucky," Connie said. "They are two really lovely children."

"Thanks, that's nice of you to say." Angela smiled. She paused, her face serious now. "How are you about the children over in Stockport? Are you getting over what happened?"

Connie took a deep breath. "I do miss Belinda and Toby, and I still think about what happened ..." She closed her eyes and shook her head. "It was a nightmare, and when I think of what could have happened if they hadn't admitted everything, I feel physically sick. I think the investigations are still going on, but thank God it's nothing to do with me any more."

"It's all in the past now," Angela said, "and there's nothing like a New Year to make a fresh start."

Over the next fifteen minutes, they moved to chat about various things and then they both suddenly stopped as a car sounded on the gravelled driveway.

"They're here safe and sound!" Angela said. "Didn't I tell you there was nothing to worry about?"

As they both got to their feet and moved towards the hall, Connie felt her heart starting to race. It had been a few weeks since she last saw William, and she suddenly felt shy and not as confident as when they spoke on the phone the other day. They had parted before the Christmas holidays with a sureness as to their feelings and where their relationship was going. But today it suddenly seemed as though the time she had spent back at home in Tullamore with her family and friends had somehow got between them. She now felt as self-conscious as she had when she first met up with him at the party, and that night in Stockport when she turned up at Tara's unexpectedly. She wondered now if he would feel the same.

The front door banged open.

"William is here!" Clare called. "He's got a man with funny red hair and a red beard with him!"

Angela got up and went quickly out to the hall. "What have I told you about passing remarks about people?"

"Sorry, Mam."

"He's a friend of William's and a lovely man, so make sure you're nice to him."

"Yes, Mam," Clare said, sounding very chastened.

Angela looked back at Connie and rolled her eyes. Then they both started to laugh as they walked outside.

William had introduced a smartly dressed Malcolm to the children, and Connie noticed any concerns they had about him had vanished, as they were busy thanking him for the two large selection boxes he had just given them. She also noticed that he'd had his hair cut and his beard trimmed.

Connie slowed to a halt and watched as William guided Malcolm towards Angela. The lecturer shook her hand and thanked her profusely for having him. He then produced a bag with a bottle of champagne and a fancy box of chocolates.

Then, they all turned and came towards her.

"Connie, my dear," Malcolm said, his arms outstretched. He gave her a great hug. "Delighted to see you again, and in such happy circumstances. We'll have a long chat later and you can fill me in on how your medical studies are going."

"It's great to see you, too," Connie told him, feeling a rush of warmth towards this man who had been so generous with his time and advice when she desperately needed it.

"Lunch first," Angela said. "We're going straight to the restaurant, as my husband is in the bar waiting, and I don't want to give him the excuse of having yet another drink before we arrive!"

"A man after my own heart," Malcolm laughed.

Angela told the children to take their selection boxes into the house and to stay there with Ella until they all came back. Then she and Malcolm fell into step together, chatting away, while Connie and William followed.

"Hello, Miss Devine," William whispered, taking her hand in his.

"Hello, Mr Fitzgerald," she said, looking up at him. For the first time since he arrived his eye caught hers and she felt the immediate bond between them. All the uncertainty about meeting up again suddenly disappeared.

They stared at each other for a few moments then William drew her towards him and stopped.

"I can't tell you how much I've missed you and how happy I am to see you again. I feel as though half of me has been missing."

Without a moment's hesitation she said, "I feel exactly the same."

His hands came to cup her face and then he kissed her lightly on the lips. She closed her eyes, and when he kissed her again it felt so natural and familiar that she knew she would never feel awkward with him again.

"Come on, you two!" Angela suddenly called back to them.

When they pulled apart and looked over, there were Angela and Malcolm grinning at them.

"We'll be with you in a few minutes!" William replied. "You go on ahead." He turned towards Connie again. "I have some presents for you, but I have one in particular I want to give you now."

Connie looked at him, hoping he hadn't bought anything too expensive. She had bought him a Jimi Hendrix album she knew he didn't have and a small L.S. Lowry print. He had mentioned liking the Manchester artist during one of their chats.

He dug into his pocket and brought out a ring box.

"Before you say anything," he said, handing it to her, "it's not an engagement ring. All my grandmother's jewellery was left to me, and I picked this one out as I thought it would suit you."

Connie took a deep breath before opening the black box with the jeweller's initials on it. There, nestling in the red velvet inside was a rich, purple amethyst set in gold claws.

"Oh, William!" she said. "It's absolutely beautiful, but it's too much."

"It's not," he told her. "And I want you to have it. No matter what happens to us in the future, the ring is yours."

She looked up at him, uncertain as to what he meant.

"When I said it wasn't an engagement ring," he said, "it wasn't because I don't want to be engaged or that I'm not ready. It's because I want to give you time to make sure of your own feelings, and to let you settle at university without any pressure." He gave a little sigh. "And if I'm honest, it's also to put a bit of a distance between me and that awful previous fiasco, which I don't even want to think about."

Pamela, Connie thought to herself. She knew he had learned from the situation, but he was letting her know he had not forgotten.

"But," he said, "if you feel the same as I do, I'd like you to wear the ring and know that sometime next year – if and when you feel ready – we will go together and you can choose the best diamond engagement ring I can afford. And we can wait as long as you wish before we set any dates."

There was a silence and then a concerned look came on his face. "Oh God! Have I said the absolutely wrong thing?"

Connie took the ring out of the box and slipped it on the ring finger of her right hand. "Not at all, I love it," she whispered. She looked up at him. "And I also love you, William Fitzgerald, with all my heart."

Also available from Poolbeg

A Letter from America
Geraldine O'Neill

It is the late 60's in Tullamore, County Offaly, and life is full of exciting possibilities for Fiona Tracey, as she prepares to leave Ireland to work for a wealthy family in New York.

Fiona's parents have the local shop and bar, and her younger sisters are already leading independent lives. Bridget is at a convent school preparing to be a nun and Angela has led a life of her own since she was hospitalised up in Dublin for years with childhood polio.

Then, sudden tragedy forces Fiona to postpone her departure for New York. As her mother sinks into illness and depression, her responsibilities mount. When help is offered by her aunt and cousin, Fiona is mystified by her mother's animosity towards them.

As summer approaches, an American architect, Michael O'Sullivan, takes a room above the bar. Within a short time Fiona finds herself involved in an unexpected and passionate affair.

Then, as a surprising incident threatens Bridget's vocation, Angela uncovers information which explodes old family secrets.

Before Fiona can embark on an independent life again, perhaps in New York, she must find a new understanding of her family – and of herself.

Waterford City & County Libraries
WITHDRAWN

ISBN 978-178199-947-9